The

Panids'

Children

Lee M Eason

https://panids-of-koa-books.co.uk

To my editors, with thanks.

Table of Contents

The field,

the constant light, the endless sea, the flowing wind.

A mystery to most

who feel its touch.

A tool for some

who flutter on its breeze.

And above them all,

a few

who soar on the higher currents.

Such is their glory, their majesty,

the Panids,

the Golden Ones.

Attrius of Amar

The Panids-a brief history.

(An extract from The Koan Narrative 2nd Edition by Drassique of New Kallian)

For hundreds of years, the Panids cast their benign influence across the Continent of Koa seated at the great Lantriums of Gillern in Hallorn and Lu-Esh in Urukish. Built by Mennem and the original Panids, the Lantriums were wonders to behold, centres of learning and the beating hearts of the Western and Eastern Panids. Places where any Talent of true ability could hope to earn the title of Panid. With the energy of the field at their command, the Panids' knowledge and powers brought prosperity and peace. Such were their achievements and abilities that nothing seemed beyond them. It was truly a golden age.

When Mennem and the original Panids left, some feared for the future. Fear that was well-founded. Without his guiding hand wisdom became judgement, service became command and humility became conceit. In the decades that followed, the age of wonders reached new heights and the Panids were elevated to a position of awe no King or Queen could hope to match. They were named the Golden Ones, praised above all and worshipped by some as faultless beings who could do no wrong. However, the Golden Ones failed to consider the consequences of their arrogance or acknowledge the darkness in their ranks. The Four, Pheneel, Medard, Ikemba and Ellusian, of the Lu-Esh Lantrium, desired recognition and elevation above their kind. They saw only one path and on it the fall and rebirth of the Lu-Esh Lantrium under their rule.

Feeding the ego and expansionist desires of the Amarian Emperor Karna III, the Four aided his invasion of Nebessa. His forces paused long enough to rename it Firrica before moving on to invade Kiashu, Ciad and Akar. The first step towards Empire for him and a war the Four intended to weaken all of the royal houses in the East and more importantly distract the Lu-Esh Panids. As expected, the Panids of the Lu-Esh Lantrium, irritated by this 'petty' squabble, sought to end the hostilities and ordered the ambitious Queen VaCenet of Urukish to intercede. She sent her daughter, Princess DuLek, to Amaria to demand peace. DuLek was her mother's daughter, a queen in waiting and saw herself as Emperor Karna's equal.

Undaunted, Emperor Karna of Amaria kept the young upstart waiting for days, cancelling audience after audience. Princess DuLek stormed and raged, accused and openly insulted. Slights that reached Karna's ears. The situation had reached a tipping point and sensing the time was right the Four took their next step. DuLek's murderers left enough evidence to point the finger of blame firmly at Karna.

Inconsolable over the death of her beloved daughter the Urukish Queen demanded retribution. The Panids of the Lu-Esh Lantrium were forced to support her as she declared war on Amaria and brought the full might of her armies to bear. The conflict between the two powers quickly escalated, forcing other countries to join the fighting. The Panids of the Lu-Esh Lantrium themselves were compelled to take direct action and bend their powers to destruction and death. At last, the moment was at hand. The Four now made use of the war to remove all opposition within the Lu-Esh Lantrium. Unthinkably, several of its Panids died in isolation or the unclear circumstances of war as the Four consolidated their control.

Far to the west, the Panids of the Gillern Lantrium watched, considering their obligations and the threat Lu-Esh now posed. Their intercession was of a magnitude unexpected by the Four and so the Lantriums were set in opposition. Gillern and Lu-Esh began to tear at each other and caught between them, the peoples and lands of Koa were devastated.

As the war became one of attrition and Urukish and Amaria wastelands, the Four and those loyal to them were forced to fight in the dirt alongside mortal men and women. Fearing defeat, they sought a way to gain the upper hand. They created the Meta. The Gillern Panids hurriedly retaliated with the creation of the Grip. But these creatures only escalated the ferocity of the war as it spread across Koa. As the two Lantriums struggled for dominance, the Panids' Children were created, monsters of even greater power. In due course the Elementals were born, the Gale, the Havoc, the Blaze and ultimately the Fury. The war became an endless cycle of terror and death, each side inflicting yet greater atrocities on the other. Growing voices amongst the Gillern Panids called for the Children to be dissipated and the war ended. It was only after the creation of the Guardians and the destruction of the Lu-Esh Lantrium that the remaining Panids listened, finally accepting their arrogance and taking responsibility for their actions. Pheneel, Medard, Ikemba and Ellusian, the four Panids whose scheming had set events in motion, fled to the coast, intent on escaping to the empty seas of the West and the myths of hidden lands beyond. They were pursued and captured after a final confrontation that cost the Panids the last of the Lantriums.

Only then did the remaining Panids pause to gaze about them and take stock of the desolation. The Lantriums were no more, their ranks decimated, the land scorched, and the people of Koa brought to their knees. In the empty days that followed the Panids turned their gaze inwards and saw only the inevitability of the war's reoccurrence. From this bleak certainty, The Field's Cap was conceived and created to limit the use of the field by all Panids and lesser Talents, preventing the possibility of another war on this scale.

The Panids chose four from their ranks: Kellim of Naddier, Tebeb of Tek, Ethre of Rorn and Etefu also of Tek, individuals embodying the attributes of compassion, foresight and moderation and who had spoken out against the creation of the Children and the wider consequences of the war. Who better to remain, watch over and guide the lesser Talents who would follow. In doing so the Panids hoped to bring a balance to the actions of Pheneel, Medard, Ikemba and Ellusian. Their legacy set, the Panids turned away from the world and with a final glorious act of sacrifice, set The Field's Cap in place.

In the years that followed, the countries of Koa became wary and suspicious of the lesser Talents, who had survived the war, and forced them into Orders to better police and control them. Urukish became a wilderness, the remnants of its people finding refuge in its few remaining city-states, while the Urukish royal family sought to perpetuate itself through the Ildran royal bloodline. Amaria closed its borders and went into self-imposed isolation. Ciad, apparently humiliated and still furious at its invasion, began building the Ciad Enclosure, a great wall that would completely cut it off from the rest of Koa. Pidone struggled to recover and fell into civil war. Firrica declared itself once again independent of Amaria and took back its name, Nebessa. Akar and Kiashu began the long process of recovery and re-instated their monarchies. Akar rebuilt its ruined capital, Kallian, and named it New Kallian so that the losses of the past would never be forgotten. Selarsh seized the opportunity and reclaimed land, long since occupied by Ildra, once again reuniting its bisected nation. Hallorn and the rest of Koa buried their dead and faced the reality of rebuilding their countries and the limitations of The Field's Cap.

Nearly one hundred years later the Great War is history. Royalty and politics exert their influence across the countries of Koa. Only Ildra struggles with the increasing obsession of its UruIldran Emperor, Segat. The Orders of Talents are no longer controlled and have become a source of counsel and support to those who rule. The people of Koa live out their lives with no use for lessons from the Great War or the mistakes of the Panids. Of the four remaining Panids, only Kellim of Naddier continues the role originally set them. Ethre of Rorn, long ago retired to the far North, is a faint memory. Etefu of Tek travels the continent resentful of the past and Tebeb of Tek has not been seen for decades.

As the past is forgotten, Amaria seeks to end its self-imposed isolation, feeling it has finally atoned for the actions of its Emperor, Karna III, and his role in the Great War. Empress Essedra's more enlightened rule has gradually changed the mindset of the Amarian people. Her goal, while being mindful of the past, is to build a secure and prosperous future for Amaria.

Under her direction, the Amar Order of Talents has begun the difficult task of re-establishing links with the other Orders.

The countries of Koa watch with cautious optimism as Amaria opens its doors to the world. Indeed, it worries me that all eyes are turned to Amaria when perhaps it would be wiser for them to watch events in Ildra and be wary of its UruIldran Emperor, Segat.

Drassique of New Kallian

Chapter 1

Kellim looked out of the small window that offered a teasing view of escape. About him, the walls of the ancient fortress pressed inwards. Beyond them, the vast Ugasi desert stretched to every horizon. A cold place where dustleaf and stoneplant struggled to survive, a place where he now wished he'd stayed. He was indeed a long way from help.

The ancient fortress was a relic of a time long passed. It had been utilised during the Great War, but remained unoccupied since then, spending the last ten decades slowly crumbling into the ground. Time was the thing Kellim now stalled for, that and its erosive effects on the patience of others. He placed his hands on a crumbling sill and lifted his face to the last of the sun. It was a challenge to appear relaxed. He'd made a mistake, an error of judgement that should have been beyond him. So many sunsets, so many decisions and so many mistakes. He dared to linger a little longer before finally turning back to the small room.

Candles cast trembling shadows; a marked contrast to the figure sat watching him. Varin had avoided eye contact, perhaps wary of what Kellim might see, but now, as irritation over rode caution, Kellim caught his eyes. The same intensity but a hint of something else. The same thing Kellim had failed to recognise in Ellusian. He had indeed made a mistake. His curiosity had put him and more importantly, Jai and Lewan in danger.

"I'm still waiting for an answer." Varin was becoming irritated by the Panid's apparent indifference. He spoke to break the old man's dithering, but more to push aside the whispering that plagued the edges of his senses. The stillness and now his agitation seemed to attract it. Could the old man hear it too? "Kellim!" This time there was an edge to his voice.

Kellim was listening. He was also aware of the faint whispering focused on Varin. The sounds hinted at another change, the Amarian's link to the field was abnormal. Kellim forced himself to wait a little longer before answering. "Did you say something?"

Even the old man's accent was beginning to wear on him. Varin had tried to place it and then realised the mistake, time, not location made it unfamiliar. This man, this Panid, was from an era long since passed. He was as much a relic as the fortress that contained them. "I ask for the last time," Varin said impatiently. "Were you sent here?"

"Sent?" Kellim stroked his beard. "Was I sent?"

"Answer the question," Varin snapped.

Kellim's hand slipped into his pocket and checked its contents. He braced himself for the unpleasantness to follow. "No, not sent, just my own curiosity." He attempted to keep his voice amiable. "I suppose I should be on my way."

"I think not," Varin rose sharply to his feet. He rubbed at his forehead and pushed the whispering back. The old man was a fool. A confused, befuddled fool! The reality of this legend was pathetic, unshaven, unkempt and wasting his time. This vagabond's unsolicited visit now presented him with a problem. Should he let the old man go and risk having his whereabouts revealed, or should he confront a Panid?

Kellim had turned back to the window, he could feel Varin's focus slipping, his attention distracted. The sun was sinking fast, red and brooding. "It will be dark soon," he muttered.

"You will..." Varin's demand was cut dead as the Panid suddenly flickered out of existence without the faintest trace of focus or field use! There was a palpable dullness to the room, a static click, and for an instant, Varin was at a loss. The old man had played him!

"Guard. Guard!" he shouted. The woman almost fell into the room. "Find him!" She was momentarily bewildered. "The Panid, the old man! Search everywhere!" Just how much had he underestimated Kellim? "And get people out on mounts. Sweep the area!"

The guard left and began barking orders, people obeyed and commands echoed through the fortress. Varin forced himself to pause, uncertainty nagging him. Think, he had to think. A few more nudges and the Amar Order would, at last, be forced to act. Would the old man report his location to the Order? Would they listen? He wasn't ready to take on its Corumn yet. To act too early would mean failure, to act too late... He needed time and so the Panid would have to be stopped.

He sat and closed his eyes, slowed his breathing and drew on the field. The whispering voices were there, reaching out. Again, Varin pushed them away. Precious seconds passed as he regained control. He focused and spread his consciousness across the room and out through the door. He moved through the fortress, past running guards, sliding through walls. Sensing, touching, and searching. Where was the old man?

Kellim flickered out of the air, lost his footing and would have crashed to the floor if Jai hadn't caught him. The younger man let go as Kellim fought to pull his senses together.

The room was spinning. Everything was muffled, blurred. Jai was gripping his shoulders, saying something, trying to make him focus. Suddenly there was icy water! The shock brought the room into sharp focus and the world came flooding in.

"I ... I'm fine," Kellim gasped, water dripping off his beard.

Jai's eyes impatiently strayed to the door.

"The cellar... are we in the cellar?" Kellim asked, dragging a hand across his face.

"Yes."

"Undiscovered?"

"So far."

"Then...Then... we must go. We are in real danger." Kellim steadied himself.

Jai headed for the door and was about to speak when Kellim suddenly stiffened.

"He's searching!" Kellim drew himself in and subdued their presence.

Jai looked to the door and then took a few steps back. "What now? Should we wait?"

Kellim shook his head and then looked at the floor, a puzzled expression on his face. "Odd."

"Odd?" Jai's eyes darted back to the door; his sword half drawn.

"Something. Down there." Kellim paused a little longer his expression distant. "Faint traces of something… something familiar."

"Some-thing. What sort of thing?" Jai hovered uneasily, now looking at the floor as well as the door "Something to do with Varin?"

"No. It's a long way down… undisturbed." Distant noises broke his concentration.

"Then leave it be. We need to go," Jai urged.

"Of course. I was distracted." Kellim checked for movement on the other side of the door. The two hurried out of the cellar, Kellim taking one last troubled look, before following Jai up the steps.

"Which way out?" Jai asked.

"The courtyard. Then the main gate," Kellim replied.

"The main gate! That's the escape route!" Jai almost stopped, but Kellim shooed him on. "You can't be serious, are you sure that last transport hasn't done something… you know?" Jai made some vague gesture of confusion.

"The fortress… is warded," Kellim panted. "Any transport… across the outer walls is impossible… I must be outside of them… to make good our escape."

The stilted conversation continued as the two barrelled up the steps and burst into a corridor. Jai's drawn sword went ungreeted.

"No guards," Kellim attempted to catch his breath. "Varin thinks we're elsewhere."

Jai looked at him, at first baffled. "Oh," he cottoned on. "Those little copper balls of yours."

"Spheres," Kellim corrected. "This way. He'll not be fooled for long."

The old Panid ran off down the corridor. Jai was left standing for a moment and then pounded after him. They paused at a corner just short of the door to the courtyard. They'd expected Lewan to be there. Instead, two guards came in through the door. Jai fell upon them and caught the first by surprise. He dispatched her in two efficient moves. Placed himself ready for the second. Blocked that man's sword, pushed him back and used his knife. The body slumped to the floor.

"We're going through that door then?" Jai gave it a nod, sheathed his sword and retrieved his knife.

Not for the first time, Kellim noted the difference. Jai's actions were driven by anger or guilt. It was an emotional change and a dangerous one. Once again, Kellim pushed aside his concerns. "The courtyard sounds busier than I'd hoped."

Jai shrugged. "It's only going to get worse."

"After three then?" Kellim began and then paused, considering the door and their proximity. "Perhaps a little further back."

They moved away. "One," Kellim spread his consciousness through the fortress. "Two," he found his copper spheres and nudged them. The door and others erupted as confusing echoes of his will reverberated throughout the fortress. "Three!" Kellim shouted as he rushed into the smoke and debris.

They ran through the panic and confusion of the vast courtyard. The night and flickering torch light offered some cover. "The gates!" Jai shouted in alarm. "The gates are still closed!"

Over to his right, a group of soldiers rushed to block their escape. There was a startled scream from their midst. One fell and the others stumbled over him. Another broke from the group and proceeded to attack the rest.

"Lewan," Jai muttered and ran to help him.

Kellim skidded to a halt. All the doorways were blocked, their guards recovering from the initial confusion. The gate had to be opened or they were lost. The Panid focused his will and drew deeply on the field. He unleashed the potential. The gates ruptured in a mess of splinters and metal. The confusion was rekindled.

Kellim gathered himself, struck a dazed guard and ran. The last of the group of soldiers had fallen. But Jai was advancing on another. Calls from the battlements marked the appearance of archers. More soldiers were heading for the gate. Their chance of escape was narrowing. Jai had reached the group with Lewan closing behind. Kellim glanced their way. Focused his will and drew on the field. He felt for the two men. They reappeared ahead of him. Kellim pushed both forward, cleared the gates' debris and located his marker. In a blink of light, all three men were gone. Two more exhausting transports took them miles clear of the fortress and to the last of Kellim's markers.

Mounted soldiers streamed out of the fortress in a fruitless bid to follow. Stood in the remains of a doorway, Varin had noticed something amongst the debris, a glint of metal. He nudged the remnants of a small copper sphere with his boot and, bending to pick it up, examined it. The torch light revealed a surprise. Perhaps time wouldn't be a limiting factor.

"Call back your men!" Varin shouted across to his Captain and looked to the gates. "Not such an old fool after all."

Chapter 2

Merren looked down at the uneven spread of flat roofs. Brilliant white cubes that jostled and crowded their way down to the distant harbour and the ultra-blue of the Ashra Sea. Even from this distance, she could make out the ships that brought the city of Loholt its wealth. By far the biggest port on the south coast of Selarsh; it had been that country's capital and greatest trading centre for centuries. This key fact allowed some of its less than savoury dealings to continue, something she had never been able to accept. The breeze tugged at her, a brief distraction from her thoughts and the heat. She turned to look at her brother.

"He's here," she said and combed a hand through long, dark hair. "The ship's anchoring now." Carrick seemed distracted, thinking through their next move no doubt. She placed a hand on his shoulder. "Carrick?"

"Sorry, my head was in the clouds," he apologised. "Is Aran okay?"

"At this distance, I can't be sure but he's definitely here. I won't be happy until we have him and we're on our way." Merren frowned slightly. "What's wrong?"

Carrick considered his words for a while, he was not one for impulsive answers, but then there was no real point hiding his unease from his sister. "Tired, concerned, perplexed, but mainly tired. We've had a steep learning curve lately." He turned to face her. "Collecting Aran and Cali should have been a walk in the country. But we've been dogged by complications at every turn. Every plan we've made has been turned inside out by political unrest." He paused again. "This is the first place we've been to that seems unaffected by Segat's threats."

Merren nodded. "Well, we did leave things a bit late. If we'd set out to collect them a year ago, they'd both be safe at Naddier by now. But that's hindsight for you. And as for Loholt, as long as the money comes in all is well."

"Where is a Seer when you need one?" Carrick joked half-heartedly.

Merren offered him a wry smile and linked his arm. "No one thought things would go on for this long. Segat makes a lot of noise, upsets the balance and continues to make threats about extending his borders, but doesn't act. While his neighbours re-direct their forces to the borders, slavers, pirates and mercenaries continue to take advantage of the lack of patrols. It's created turmoil and we just happen to be in the middle of it. Not even you can plan for everything."

A hundred years of peace had caught most countries off guard. The period of stability Koa had enjoyed was being threatened by an Emperor with an appetite his country's vast wealth couldn't sate. Royal houses and governments across the board were scrambling to catch up with his re-armament. Carrick and Merren's Order, like many others across Koa, was used to advising and settling petty disputes, not fighting mercenaries and chasing after slavers. The Orders were having to re-think their roles and Talents to up their game as they were forced to fill the gap left by the re-directed military. Carrick and Merren had coped better than most and as a result, been given more to do. But the strain was beginning to tell and now this chase, to get ahead of the slavers, had placed yet more demands on their field skills. They were a long way from Naddier and any further support. The country of Selarsh was central to Koa's economy, its oligarchy of merchants knew that, and so approached anything seen as interference with a heavy hand, a heavy hand Carrick and Merren wanted to avoid.

"You're right," Carrick agreed. "But it would make a change, if for once, things went vaguely to plan. I'd be happier if Segat announced what his plans really are, it might make ours easier to manage. At least cut down on all the troop shifting, leaving them to keep the roads safe and us to get on with what we're here for."

"If nothing else it would speed our progress."

"The Amaria thing, for instance, Segat's long-time obsession," he added when Merren looked puzzled. "What's that about? Using the death of an almost forgotten princess to stir up feeling against Amaria. That is pushing it a bit. There's definitely something else going on there, something hidden under all of Segat's threats."

Merren reflected on her brother's words. "Segat's a direct descendant of that self-same princess, he's the first of the Urukish bloodline to take the Ildran throne. Everyone was unnerved when he seemingly achieved the impossible and then started wondering what else was to come. That mixture of Urukish injustice and Ildran wealth isn't a good combination. UruIldrans haven't forgotten their beloved Princess DuLek, even though it's more than a hundred years since her death. Sooner or later, in this case much later, someone had to get powerful enough and then bored enough to think hey, no Amarian was ever brought to justice or even made to offer an apology for her murder. I suppo...what *are* you doing?" Merren asked, somewhat bemused, as her brother stepped onto the low wall that edged the flat roof.

"Sitting," he said glibly. "You know I don't like history, too many names and dates. I need a rest and Bryn needs time to buy a cart. Sitting seems like a good solution to both problems. This could be our last chance to just sit! Come on," he patted the whitewashed surface.

With more caution, she joined him. They sat for a while in silence, feet dangling, looking out across the hot, noisy city. Carrick leant slightly, nudging her with his shoulder. "Do you remember the last time we were here?"

Merren narrowed her eyes for a moment. "Of course, I'd almost forgotten Drassique! Do you think he still remembers? It must be nine, no, ten years."

"At least."

"Have you still got it?" Merren asked recalling the incident.

"Somewhere," Carrick said evasively. They both laughed at the shared joke.

"It's been a while since I've laughed like that," Merren said eventually. "We could do with more of it."

"We all used to make each other laugh, I miss that. I miss the others," Carrick admitted.

Merren rested her head on his shoulder. "I wonder if Kellim and the boys have reached Harun's yet and how Jai is?"

"Hmm, better I hope," Carrick closed his eyes, letting the heat of the sun keep his thoughts away from the tragedy. "Kara would love this."

"The heat?" Merren asked.

"Hmm," Carrick answered absently.

"Kara would sit in a bread oven and ask for a cloak," Merren smiled, realising how much she'd missed her. "She'll be somewhere hot I've no doubt."

A lone seabird called out as if signalling its intention to turn a lazy curve towards the harbour. It glided down over the rooftops, across narrow bustling streets and then out over the harbour.

Sea-weathered men and women jumped from the ship onto the quayside. Heavy ropes, apparently leaping after them, were efficiently handled onto the moorings. The ragged ship, creaking and groaning in disagreement, soon became tethered to the jetty. An apparent jumble of activity had the vessel unloaded in an hour, ready for the last of its cargo to leave. Chained at the ankle, exhausted, dirty and drugged, the slaves shuffled off the ship five at a time. Harsh words and blunt rods directed them towards the auction rooms.

The first of these lines were herded into small cells at the back of the auction house. Its ground floor consisted of an open space that functioned as the sales area, which in turn opened directly onto the quayside. The place stank of sweat and of the smoking oil lamps that lit it. A number of people were already gathering in the dingy space. Nebessans, tinkling with jewellery of intricate designs, Cians in short-sleeved tunics and loose trousers, Hons in long white garments belted with vivid sashes, even Amarians in rich patterned soodrey that floated on the breeze. Their diverse features and skin colour affirmed Loholt's position in the trading world and their wealth guided its moral code.

Talking with two men from Nebessa, the auction house's owner, a large, black-skinned man dressed in the favoured styles of Selarsh, kept a discrete mental contact with his associate, a tall indistinct figure watching unnoticed in the smoke and shadows.

Outside, Carrick signalled to Bryn as he parked a cart and its team close to the building's open front.

Bryn nodded in return as they approached. "Did you notice the ships in the harbour?" he asked.

"My mind's on getting this done," Merren looked back to see what she'd missed.

"You can see them there," Bryn pointed. "Ildran warships."

"Ildra doesn't have sea ships, Ildra doesn't have a coast," Carrick squinted.

"A fact they've overlooked. There are three of them. Big, well-armed," Bryn added.

"Let's hope that's the Ildran fleet and not a part of it." Merren craned to get a better look.

"Who's allowed Segat to build those?" Carrick puzzled.

"Selarsh," Bryn answered. "Offer enough money and they'll pretty much agree to anything. Segat's been dragging up more than DuLek's death. He's talked about the old Ildran land bridge through Selarsh. He wants a coastline again."

"That hasn't existed since the Great War," Carrick said.

"Seemingly nothing's too old and forgotten for the Emperor of Ildra."

"Maybe they've been trying to appease him by allowing this ship building," Carrick shrugged. "They'd not be happy about invasion. All of this wealth going into the bulging pockets of the Emperor of Ildra."

Merren turned back. "We should go in." She shook her head. "This business stinks. When is King Perin going to speak out about it, or better still force them to outlaw slavery?"

"It's not his country," Carrick replied bluntly. "Selarsh doesn't like interference, money guides what's acceptable here. We'll try and free as many as we can. But remember, Aran's the priority and we're greatly outnumbered." He glanced meaningfully at the large number of guards present. "We've chased Aran a long way to rethink things again."

"I know," Merren said. "I'm trying to ease my sense of guilt. Let's get this done."

"Will you take care of the owner's associate?" Carrick asked. Merren's insight and subtlety were second to none. She understood people, she always had. Her insight had kept them out of trouble time and time again. Now he needed her subtlety.

"Yes. I felt the Talent's touch while we've been standing here. He's hardly subtle."

"Be careful with this Merren. There are a lot of swords here, and even if they wait long enough to ask questions, we're a long way from home; not even Perin's arm reaches this far."

"When am I ever anything less?"

Carrick didn't need to answer and walked into the auction house, his eyes moving over the cells, trying to spot Aran. The Talent in the shadows watched his approach and was about to touch the owner's shoulder, but Merren was a step ahead. His hand faltered and then slowly returned to his side as he sank back into the shadows. It was customary in Loholt for successful traders to retain the services of lesser Talents to monitor the minds of those they did business with. Merren hovered in the entrance way, hoping this house only retained the services of one. She couldn't sense any others but found herself looking about, nerves making her second-guess herself. This time the distraction proved useful, she spotted Aran shuffling in with another group of slaves.

"Carrick," she called; her brother hadn't seen him. "They will do," she tried to sound casual.

Carrick nodded in response.

Their business finished with the owner, the two Nebessans took their leave and went to inspect several lines of slaves.

Carrick caught the owner's eye. "The people entering now," he said switching to Koan, the common language used across the continent for centuries. He gestured at the group in front of him. "I'm in a hurry to be away and they'll suit my purposes exactly. How much do you want?"

The line was abruptly halted to allow Carrick a better view of the 'stock'. They were from various countries; the Selarsh slave trade wasn't fussy. Once they were drugged and their memories wiped it wouldn't matter where they'd come from. Handlers pushed and shoved them into position, grabbing them by their hair to lift their heads. Carrick winced.

A sudden movement outside made some of the guards look quickly in the direction of the cart parked there. Bryn was a tall man, lean and muscular; he was imposing at the best of times, he'd jumped down from the cart and the expression on his face made them uneasy.

"No," Carrick called out as much to stop Bryn as the handlers. "That will be quite alright," he attempted to appear nonchalant. "I've seen all I need to. Let them be."

The owner smiled, there was more profit in a buyer pushed for time, especially one fool enough to show it. The muscular one on the cart needed watching though; he posed more of a threat, a mercenary of some kind, but with a military edge in his bearing. With a subtle gesture, he directed a few of his men to better positions; trouble was never far away in this business. He began sizing up the one called Carrick. Like the mercenary outside, he appeared to be in his late thirties, good clothes, confident, definitely travel-weary and not used to dealings of this sort. All three were probably from northern Hallorn or at least had been born there; the brown hair and brown skin stood out amongst the darker-skinned people of Selarsh; it was unusual to find Hallorns here. This trio's story was becoming interesting even in these unsettled times. The muscular man in the cart would fetch a good price, the woman, again of a similar age, was quite attractive and he mused about her value … The owner's thoughts trailed off as something, a voice in the back of his head, began speaking to him. It was a subtle voice, very calm even reassuring. He looked back at the Hallorn called Carrick. Hmm, what had he been thinking before? His thoughts had drifted away, the voice was very close now. The owner listened. What was the voice telling him? Perhaps this man was not so well off.

Perhaps the Hallorn was a man of limited means. No, he wouldn't be able to push the price up as much as he'd thought and then he looked at the slaves the Hallorn wanted, they were a sorry bunch. In fact, the more the owner looked at them the more he felt he would be well rid of them at the earliest opportunity. He went to check with his associate in the shadows, but the voice quickly interrupted him and he thought better of it.

All of the slaves had lowered their heads apart from one, a look of recognition stirring on his grubby face. Thankfully, the handlers didn't see this and Merren deliberately stepped forward to attract Aran's attention. He turned groggily, noticing the movement and almost made to step towards her. Would he realise what they were trying to do and keep quiet? She motioned for him to be still before quickly returning her full attention to the Talent in the shadows.

The owner had continued his study of Carrick, now noticing the honourable face and the air of respectability. Indeed, as they chatted, he could see this man was clearly someone to respect, someone of a high calibre yet limited means, he mustn't forget that. It would be an honour to do business with him. Yes, yes, an honour...

"Why sir," the owner enthused. "I'm sure we can come to an agreement that will suit you... I mean us both."

He found himself liking the man even more as they shook hands, such good manners. "However, it is rather unusual to sell outside of an auction. There will have to be an extra charge for such a transaction," he felt strangely guilty for saying this and wanted to say something else to reassure the Hallorn gentleman.

"That's fine," Carrick replied, not wanting to push things too much. Nudging the will of others wasn't his specialism and to add to the problem he didn't have the money to buy all five slaves. He was already applying quite an amount of persuasion and the owner was no fool; too much and the man's instincts could begin to cut in. He tried not to look at the guards. "I have two hundred in my purse here," Carrick said brightly, but he felt the man's mind lurch and the smile slipped somewhat. Obviously, a bad offer, but nearly all the money they had. A glance over the owner's shoulder checked that the Talent in the shadows was still completely distracted. Carrick pushed a little more and the smile returned to the owner's face.

"Then perhaps two hundred and twenty would be a more suitable offer?"

"Hmm," the owner was struggling subconsciously. "You're... you're, clearly a man of... honour," he began haltingly, "and... it's such a pleasant day."

Even Carrick wondered where that comment had come from. The man was squeezing at his chin thoughtfully, his tongue wanting to say something, but some part of his mind still wanted to try for a better price.

"Two hundred and fifty!" Carrick quickly offered, pressing a little more. They'd have to worry about food when that problem arose. Kellim always had money, but he was a long way off yet.

There was a long pause that seemed to last an age. The slow cogs of the owner's mind turned. He had to be given time, but even so, Carrick couldn't help a glance at Merren and Bryn. Thoughts of a forced exit from the warehouse and the city's formidable walls came to mind. The owner's head suddenly filled with the image of fighting, arrows and long sharp spears. Carrick stole himself. He was losing focus. With an effort, he calmed his nerves, abandoned caution and pressed harder. The owner suddenly seemed to have been given the go-ahead from deep in his subconscious and his face changed from a picture of extreme concentration to one of relief. With that he took Carrick's hand in a firm and decisive shake, offering him a broad smile.

Carrick quickly handed him the purse and made to edge away. "If you don't mind. I'm in a bit of a hurry," he said, trying to free his other hand. "My cart is just outside. I wonder if you would have the slaves loaded."

"Don't mind…bit of a hurry, slaves loaded…of course," the owner beamed. "An honour sir." He clapped his hands and pointed. "You two get that lot loaded onto this fine gentleman's cart. Well, don't just stand there can't you see I'm- I mean he's in a hurry!"

The people in question snapped to and the slaves were roughly turned and pushed and shoved onto the cart. Bryn made to block this rough handling, but Merren, still focusing on the Talent in the shadows, motioned anxiously and Bryn reluctantly sat down, his fists clenched hard around the reins.

"And now that our business is complete, perhaps you and the lady would care to join me in a small drink," the owner offered. "After all it has been such an honour…"

"Most kind…err, but big rush." Carrick held up his hand and edged away, "Must be off. Stars and tides wait for no one and all that sort of thing." With that, he turned on his heels and made for the doors. Merren was already on the cart. Carrick reached it and leapt on. Bryn stirred the team into movement and they were off.

"Sir, where do you want this lot putting?" One of his workers was talking to him. "Sir... sir!"

But the owner's head was in the clouds, watching the departing cart. "Such an honour," he was mumbling dreamily. "Such an honour."

"Sir, the slaves!"

"The slaves?" It suddenly occurred to him. "Oh, let them all go. Let them all go," he repeated with a magnanimous wave of his hands.

***

Kara was not prone to maudlin thoughts, but it had rained for three days now and she was wet and less than warm. Pidone was a hot country, she liked the heat, so what was going on with the weather? She reined in her mount to look up at what could have been ribs from some great beast. The two curving structures would have once made a ring, perhaps thirty or forty feet across, part of the Pidone field line, she guessed. Now they stood half-buried and broken; redfern and cliffwhite fixing them to the landscape. The metal had rusted decades ago and the gilded decoration stolen long before that, leaving them stark against the sky. She looked far into the distance, but couldn't see any others. Come to think of it, she hadn't seen many in all of her travels; few remained from the time of the Panids when the field flowed freely. She walked the mount closer to the chalky cliff edge and looked out across the Tana Sea. They'd been following a small slave ship for some time as it hugged the coastline, taking advantage of the lack of patrols. The crew couldn't be more than ten. Ten slavers out at sea were fine, but now their ship had moored and was sheltering in a small bay. There were villages in the area too small to be marked on maps, they would be easy targets. The small and overworked group of soldiers she accompanied had just deployed to search the area. They were one of the few left patrolling the coast of Pidone. The great forest, which stretched the full length of the country's eastern coastline, provided too good a hiding place for slavers and needed constant policing. As a group the patrol was a long way from any support and deployed like this, they and she were vulnerable. Now was the time, for once in her life, to listen to that small voice of common sense and re-join the patrol. She could handle two slavers, but any more and she would be in trouble. She turned her mount only to lock eyes with the first of two, armed figures coming out of the woods ahead. More noise made her look behind as another stepped out of cover.

"Bollocks." She glanced both ways, trying to judge ability and position, three slavers presented with a petite, unaccompanied and seemingly defenceless Hallorn woman.

Chapter 3

Jai stood listening to the night. Behind him, the fire crackled, ahead only the lonely call of a mooneye made a sound in the deep desert. There was no wind, no moons, just stars and the chill night. The events of his old life meant he knew the Ugasi, a great expanse of arid desert that dominated the remote northern reaches of Amaria. Starved of rain by the North Amarian Mountains and with temperatures that ranged from hot to freezing, it was a difficult place to exist in and yet its people did. There were no great cities in this dry place, its capital Karna had been built on the shores of lake Myta at the southernmost extent of the Ugasi. Few roads and little in the way of vegetation marked the landscape. The people who lived here were nomads and had always been viewed as inferior by the rest of Amaria, but Jai preferred their direct but generous nature. Travel further south and you were treated with indifference and arrogance matched only by the sharp-featured people of Urukish.

They'd put enough distance between themselves and any possibility of pursuit by Varin, bought mounts at a small village and continued across the Ugasi. Far to the north of Calk they'd finally come in sight of the Western Amarian mountain range and sold their exhausted animals. Heading south, they'd been forced to continue on foot and found no other villages large enough to have spare mounts.

Jai had to admit he was tired; they were all tired, months of constant travel and poor sleep had taken their toll. Hopefully, the pass would force them to ease their pace and provide a distraction. He'd had too much time to think. The Ugasi made you do that, the monotonous terrain, the barren landscape, nothing to distract. Only your thoughts, the glaring sun and the cold. But now it was dark out there, dark like the cavern. The images came back as they always did, the same events playing over and over in his mind, the same sickening feeling of helplessness and aching loss. He flinched, his expression playing out every terrible second. The sudden crash of rock, the realisation and then Kellim's hand dragging him from the abyss as his hand reached desperately to...

"Jai," Kellim griped his shoulder and brought him back.

Jai turned sharply and it was a moment before he fully registered where he was.

Kellim was speaking "... come back to the fire. It's small, but provides a distraction."

It did. The fire cast flickering shadows on the rocky outcrop and illuminated a circle of ground, an island in the absolute dark. Kellim had thought it safe to light a fire, a welcome comfort and the promise of a hot meal.

"Do you think he just let us go?" Lewan asked.

"Indeed," Kellim began. "At first, I believe he intended to attempt our recapture, but we weren't pursued for long."

"Let me get this right," Jai said, trying to catch up. "At first you think he didn't want us to escape?"

Kellim nodded. "He has removed himself from his Order, hidden away and against strict laws somehow developed his ability to draw on the field. A man previously so devoted to his Order does none of that lightly. He has an objective and needs uninterrupted time and space to reach it. We became a threat to both."

"Something must have changed shortly after we left?" Jai concluded.

"Apparently." Kellim stroked his beard thoughtfully. "Quite what, I don't know. I am also intrigued by something else I sensed far bellow the cellars. It may need investigation at a later time. So many questions and so very few answers." His thoughts found their way to his lips.

"That was a lot of risk for almost nothing," Jai said irritably.

Kellim inclined his head. "We at least know more than his Order," he corrected lightly. "And we are by no means any the poorer for our detour. Certainly, things might have been far worse without this young man's help." Lewan smiled self-consciously as Kellim patted him on the shoulder.

"You did a good job," Jai said, allowing his mood to be clipped by Kellim.

Lewan tried to turn the attention away from himself. "You and Kellim had everything under control. You didn't need me there to help."

"I wouldn't be so sure about that," Jai said. "You sorted the courtyard guards and planted lots of those copper balls of Kellim's. They created enough chaos to give us a chance."

"Spheres," Kellim corrected.

"Didn't they," Lewan enthused. "I've never seen anything like them before. They were amazing! I wouldn't have believed something so small could help create that much damage. And the guards! They didn't know what hit them. It terrified the ones near me and then when you hit the main gate." Lewan mimicked the explosion with his hands. "Boom!" he rocked back laughing.

The young man's sudden excitement was infectious and the other two found themselves laughing. The relief was sudden and the laughter broke the tension.

"They proved themselves a useful way of carrying out several tasks right under Varin's nose." Kellim seemed quite pleased with himself. "He believed me to be unaccompanied and a bit of a doddering old fool."

"Well, he got that wrong. So, what's next?" Lewan asked.

Kellim picked up a stick and poked at the dying fire. "We should think about sleep. We have a long journey still. Cali will be worrying about us and eager to see her brother, so we must also catch up with Carrick and Merren."

"I'll take the first watch," Lewan offered, suddenly eager to make time move quicker.

"I'll do that," Kellim replied. "I've much to think about. You rest, I'll wake you when it's your turn."

"Okay," Lewan said, settling himself down. "Though I'm wide awake now. It'll take me ages to get to sleep." The young man wrapped himself in his blanket and settled down. "Night Kellim, night Jai."

"Sleep well," Kellim replied. He looked over at Jai, who pointedly started counting on his fingers. As he reached his ninth, a loud snore rang out from the bundle of blankets.

"I think I can remember being that young," Jai whispered.

Kellim chuckled. "You're not that much older."

"I'm twenty-six," Jai corrected as if it made a world of difference. "He's still a kid, only just reached twenty."

"Twenty-six is still young, my friend," Kellim corrected. "I, on the other hand, am considerably older…"

"Understatement."

Kellim gave Jai a withering look, though inwardly he was pleased to see some return of Jai's questionable humour. "As I was saying, I am somewhat older, but can still remember being that young. However, I cannot remember ever snoring that loud."

They worked their way down the edge of the Western Amarian mountains eventually arriving at an Amarian gate fort. The substantial structure was being enlarged and renovated and would only allow limited access to the old spice trail. Its gates had been reopened days earlier; having been sealed for the better part of a century. The trio and their packs were searched with detailed efficiency and Kellim felt the need to apply subtle weight to his explanation when asked their reasons for being in Amaria in the first place. Eventually, they were allowed through and set foot on the rough trail. Jai in particular had spent too much time with his thoughts and Kellim was glad that the change in terrain was about to become more of a distraction.

The old spice trail wove its way steadily southwards through the western range of the Amarian mountains, which in turn marked the border with more fertile lands in Ildra. The track was cut into the steep slope on one side of a deep ravine, it offered impressive views and was an ancient and once well-used way through the mountains. However, the path was precipitous and loose underfoot, easily providing the distraction Kellim had hoped for. As the trio progressed deeper, they found it had also been diverted around several boulders too massive to move. At one point the way ahead was completely blocked by a recent rock fall; forcing them to clamber over the unstable mass. Despite this and the frost of the early mornings, they made good time.

They crossed a mountain river several times as it continued its task of cutting the ravine deeper. Eventually, it would join with others and become the mighty river Ild. The bridges were serviceable if a little rickety. But when they reached the final crossing, they found the bridge had collapsed, providing Jai with a probable explanation for the lack of Amarian or Ildran patrols.

"It is just a short distance," Kellim felt the need to point out. "I've carried out transports like these for, well, a long time."

Jai still didn't seem convinced and looked down at the foaming water, too cold, deep and fast to risk. He groaned in resignation. "Let's get it over with then."

Lewan looked at him. "I still don't get why you hate this so much."

"I just do," Jai muttered and stepped over to the remains of the bridge.

Lewan could see Kellim trying not to smile. But still couldn't understand what all the fuss was. "What's to be afraid of?"

"Come on Kellim. Do what you have to and get us over there," Jai urged.

Kellim walked over to him and focused his will.

Jai turned to Lewan. "Have you seen what happens when it goes wrong?"

Lewan looked at him. "Wrong? What do you mean goes wrong?"

"Stand closer if you would," Kellim beckoned the young man over.

"What can go wrong?"

Jai felt the tell-tale prickle of his skin as Kellim drew on the field.

Lewan persisted, "What do you mean, wrong?"

"Ready," Kellim signalled his intention.

"Bits everywhere," Jai gestured dramatically.

"Wha…"

They walked on for two weeks; a journey made shorter by Kellim's transports. The climate had gradually grown warmer as they'd headed south and dropped altitude. Jai had lost count of how many times they'd made the uncomfortable transits and Kellim had pronounced him well and truly cured of his phobia. Jai had decided to say no more about it, ever.

"That was the last transport," Kellim assured him.

"You've said that every time," Jai finished rolling up his sleeves and shouldered his pack, before walking on after Lewan.

Kellim was about to follow but the smile slipped from his lips and he turned abruptly to check the way behind.

"Anything wrong?" Jai asked, coming back to where Kellim stood shielding his eyes from the sun's glare.

"I think we're being followed. Not by Varin's men," Kellim quickly added as Jai tensed and Lewan appeared, wanting to know what was up.

"A patrol, no way, not even the Amarians could get the bridge fixed that quick?" Jai thought it unlikely even before Kellim shook his head. "Any ideas then?"

Kellim tugged at the short beard on his chin. "I've never been good at this sort of thing. It's not a strength of mine and all these rocks and bends make it very difficult." He pulled a dissatisfied face. "Now, if Merren were here she'd have a much better idea."

Jai looked about them searching the surrounding slopes for signs of movement. He shrugged off his bow. "I'll backtrack a bit and see what I can find."

"And I'll go on ahead," Lewan offered.

"No, we're quite safe. The trace is fleeting and I believe, a long way off. There are no other tracks in this part of the pass so we should continue."

"If you're sure," Jai was not fully convinced Kellim was telling all but knew better than to push the old Panid. As the other two set off, Jai shouldered his bow and once again looked back along the path. There were no sounds, nothing moved, it was a lifeless place. He paused a little longer and then, deciding he was being too cautious, took a quick drink, poured some of the water over his head and jogged after the others.

By midday, the pass began to open out and the steep walls started to fall away until eventually they rounded a long bend and found themselves looking down onto the fertile lands of Northern Ildra. Rolling grassland stretched as far as the eye could see. Clumps of gnarlwood trees marked the remnants of the once great forest that had stretched across the whole of Northern Ildra. The Great War had all but destroyed it along with most of the wildlife that had roamed this land. Below them, straddling the path, a fortress was under construction. Once complete, its extensive walls would close off any free entry into Ildra from the pass. Several military tents formed a large camp near it. Keeping a low profile, they watched as a small patrol of soldiers set out on the path and began the climb to their position.

"We will have to risk a transport," Kellim said. "Our presence here may not be welcomed."

Jai nodded. "We've been in the middle of nowhere for a long time, things have moved on faster than we thought. Looks like Segat's tightening control of his borders as well as everything else. If we can keep clear of any patrols, we should be alright. We'll have to avoid the city of Ippur and stick to the smaller roads. The locals won't give us away, I hope."

"I'm sure they will remain welcoming. It is the patrols that concern me. I hadn't expected to see soldiers until we reached central Ildra. Seeing them here may be a sign that Segat's threats now have some weight behind them."

With a good line of sight, Kellim was able to transport them well past the fort and they remained alert to the possibility of further patrols as they moved on. The military activity signalled yet another change in Ildra. The presence of the Emperor would be felt by his subjects and free movement across its borders was to become a thing of the past. It was some time before they paused briefly to eat, a grove of gnarlwoods providing cover. The trees were smaller than usual and marked their most southerly extent. Kellim patted a trunk noting the progress they'd made.

"I know it's a while off yet, but a softer bed and a proper meal are things I've missed." Jai stretched, before hefting his pack onto his back and stepping back onto the path.

"Indeed," Kellim agreed. "In addition to time spent with Harun and Hatice."

"Yep," Jai said looking at Lewan, a smile spreading across his face. "You've hardly mentioned her."

Lewan blushed slightly. "You mean Cali? Err...well... we get on and she's good company and..."

"You like her," Jai interrupted, "and I think she likes you too." He ruffled Lewan's hair. "It's good to see you smile," he relented, not wanting to embarrass the young man too much. "Come to think of it, you do a lot of that around her."

"She makes me want to smile, but I'm not sure what she thinks about me. I mean I don't talk much and she probably likes people who have a bit more to say and ..." his shoulders slumped. "It's...oh, I don't know. It's just nice being around her." Lewan tried to flatten his hair.

Kellim smiled. "I'm quite sure she appreciates you for who you are. Remember it is often she who seeks you out, and even though I'm well past all that sort of thing, I would say that is a good sign. I too am happy to see you smiling." He turned to Jai. "Indeed, I'm happy to see you both smiling." The point was not lost on Jai and a brief shadow of guilt passed over his face.

"Come on my friends, the path waits," Kellim gestured. "We have more walking to do until I can speed our progress again."

They bought mounts from a farm on the very outskirts of Ippur and made good time in the increasingly warmer climate, days quickly adding up into weeks. Level terrain meant Kellim could make regular transports, which cut their journey time greatly. The tracks were straight and easy-going, flanked on either side by wide expanses of grassland, grazed by herds of horned animals and milkies. Here and there small huts, used by herders, sheltered from the warm sun under quill and even the occasional spine tree. They spent one night in a ruined town. There were many like this in Ildra. Destroyed during the Great War and then abandoned because there was no one left to come back.

Kellim had wandered off and Jai, concerned by the Panid's unease, eventually went looking for him.

"You alright?" Jai asked.

Kellim stood on a slight promontory looking down on the ruins of the town. A low wall and an arch marked what might have once been a balcony of some sort.

"They would've had a nice view," Jai tried to make conversation. The old man seemed lost in his thoughts.

"They would have," Kellim replied distantly. "I was here when the first of the Elementals were used. Two sides pushing in different directions and Ildra trampled beneath their feet." He shook his head.

"Segat would do us all a favour if he thought about those times," Jai said.

"He would," Kellim sighed and turned away from the view. "But they never do. There is always a new fool."

Over the next few days, Kellim was forced to subdue their presence on several occasions as patrols finally started to interrupt their progress. As they journeyed on, the land became more heavily cultivated and was dotted with small holdings and larger farms. The river Ild, which had splashed and tumbled through the pass, had grown into a wide waterway busy with sail ships and would continue its way across the whole of Ildra, eventually exiting into the Cian Sea. More days of walking and several transports brought them just short of a large market town, the home of the local garrison, here they headed further south and onto quieter roads.

The final stretch of their approach hadn't gone unnoticed by friendly eyes and so Harun and Cali came out to meet them well before they reached the farm. Harun was a tall broad man, typically Northern Ildran in appearance with his dark eyes and brown skin, fashionably sporting an Ildran earring and multiple toe rings. He was a farmer who had worked hard, with his wife Hatice, to make their holding a success. There was no pretence about him and he was as generous as he was good-humoured. He stood waving from the gate to the farm as Cali, unable to wait any longer, ran to meet them.

Lewan waved back equally excited as the young woman headed towards them. One of Hatice's daughters must have loaned her a dress, he thought. She wore the loose-fitting garment well on her slim frame and had adopted the Ildran women's taste for intricate gold leaf skin patterns. As she ran, she struggled with the hand-printed material for an instant, when it threatened to trip her, but still managed to keep waving with her other hand. As she got closer her face lit up and those brown eyes, that had dazzled him from the moment they'd met, sought his.

She hugged them all warmly. "I'm so relieved," she said enthusiastically, a little out of breath as she stepped back to look at them. "It feels like you've been gone for ages. The farm's been really busy. We've had so much to do, you won't recognise the place, and I have so many questions to ask."

"Are you feeling better now?" Lewan asked, still guilty they'd been forced to leave her behind.

"Fine, my fever went ages ago. I can taste things again." She played down his concern. "You all look exhausted."

"We've loads to tell," Lewan replied. "You've cut your hair," he said suddenly noticing it was much shorter.

Cali blushed slightly. "Do you think it looks alright? I mean it's not too short. It kept getting in the way and I got sick of it. Is it too short?"

"It's great," Lewan said brightly, flattered by her interest in his opinion. Cali beamed and took his arm, the two-headed off and were quickly lost in conversation.

Harun greeted Kellim and Jai as they reached the gateway. "A warm welcome my friends." He grasped each firmly by the hand, his accent heavy as he spoke Koan. "We are all much relieved to see your safe return. Cali has been especially anxious. Lewan is a fortunate boy to have such a clever and pretty girl so interested in him."

"Try telling him that," Jai commented as they watched the two head towards the farmhouse.

Putting a large arm around Kellim's shoulders Harun led them in. "Hatice is eager to hear your news and has hot drinks and your favourite biscuits ready as we speak. There is clean water and clothes, good beds and the food, let me tell you about the food she has prepared. You have never seen the like of it and the smells, such aromas. I am amazed you could not smell them as soon as you entered the valley. I am indeed the most fortunate of men to have a wife so beautiful, so intelligent and with such skills." He stopped and turned to look at them all. "And of course, my family is complete again." Eventually, they reached the farmhouse and Hatice came out to greet them.

The room was full of life, a dozen conversations mingled in an air of ease and good humour. Hatice's beautiful hand-woven rugs covered the floor they sat on and oil lamps decorated the plain walls with a warm glow. Cali had eaten her fill and was chewing on what, she had promised herself, would be a final piece of bread. At last, she'd been able to enjoy a meal now that Kellim, Jai and Lewan had returned. For a short while, she had taken simple pleasure in the company and the evening, but as always, her thoughts turned back to her brother and she longed for news of him. Though Kellim had done his best to reassure her, she still couldn't help but worry and hope that he was safe again. Had Carrick, Bryn and Merren managed to catch up with the slavers? Would they have rescued him? Was he unhurt? She stopped the trail of thought, knowing full well she would imagine the worst and tie her stomach in knots. Instead, she deliberately focused her mind on the room and its occupants. Harun and his wife, their mutual respect and the life they had carved together were both touching and enviable. The cornerstones of a large family, something she had never known.

She watched as Kellim chatted with those around him and how they listened and hung on his every word. The man was such a mystery, among the last of the Panids, he was a link to a distant and very different time. She wondered at the things he had done and seen and at the secrets he kept deep inside. She knew something of the Panids and the Lantriums; the Great War was a source of many stories, its heroes, heroines, the notorious Four, the terrible battles and the great victories. Stories the man, sat before her, was a part of but was so reticent to talk about.

Her imagination wandered, her talent subconsciously lifting images from the minds of the people around her. She drifted through memories, emotions, images and then at the very edges something else, a faint whispering. She jumped, suddenly aware Kellim was looking at her, but then he too was distracted, looking sharply at the window above. He got up quickly and at first, she thought he was coming over, had he heard the whispering too? She knew her habit of dipping into the minds around her was rude, but she couldn't help it. It just, sort of happened and it was all so interesting. But he walked straight past and left the room, clearly intent on something else. Her eyes met Jai's who had also registered his sudden departure. Jai winked reassuringly and looked back to his food. Clearly, he hadn't heard anything. Cali watched as Kellim headed for the back door. She wasn't overly concerned, always feeling safe in his presence. What would it have been like to have a grandfather like him, wise, quietly confident and watchful of those about him? Nothing like the image he often portrayed as the harmless, slightly distracted old man. She had seen right through that pretty early on. There was a lot to Kellim, a lot she'd love to know. The odd accent always hinted at something different, a tantalizing remnant of a time long past. Then there was Jai. She knew he was from Cian, but little else of his past. Tall, brown-haired, brown-eyed and handsome; he'd do for an older brother. In her village, her girlfriends had been immensely jealous, and Cali had made the most of the status his occasional visits, with Carrick, Merren and Bryn, had brought. She watched him a little longer. He was in the room and not, all at the same time. She had noticed he was often like that, withdrawn and moody, it seemed out of character and she'd seen only glimpses of the joker everyone said he was. Something had happened several months ago before she and Aran had joined the group, that much she'd gleaned. Something none of them had come to terms with, and in a demonstration of uncharacteristic restraint, she had not pried.

Then there was Lewan. She was glad he'd shaved off the patchy beard he'd grown in the last few weeks, while he, Kellim and Jai had been away, and approved of his whim to let Hatice cut his brown hair very short. The heat here meant most Ildran men wore their hair like that or even shaved it off. She'd liked Lewan's easy-going nature from the start, his willingness to try new things. His quiet confidence and honesty made him easy company. When they'd first met, she'd found herself wanting to know more and more about him and spent an increasing amount of time with him. He was always glad to see her and had often come looking for her when they weren't busy. He made her feel valued. It was a good feeling. His ready smile and brown eyes put flutters in her stomach but despite all of this Cali was confused by her feelings for him and not a little scared. Still vulnerable from the trauma and upheaval of recent events her instincts had told her that friendship was by far the safest and most sensible option and that a friend was what she needed. Then he'd left with Kellim and Jai. Sick with a fever, she'd remained on Harun's farm and began to realise just how much she missed Lewan, how much he'd come to mean to her. Did he feel the same way? Was she just a friend or the sister he'd never had or...? She became exasperated. Stop overthinking things, girl.

On the other side of the room, Lewan looked up as if somehow sensing her thoughts. His warm smile lifted her spirits. He leaned back, jokingly patting his stomach and puffing out his cheeks, she laughed and then acknowledged the chunk of bread in her hand and stuffed it into her mouth. At that moment everyone in the room looked up as one of Harun's sons announced the arrival of dessert and the gathering made appropriate noises of delight and pleasure as a small procession of dishes were carried into the room.

Outside in the shadows surrounding the house, tall, pointed ears listened to the muffled cheers that drifted out into the chill night and a keen intellect tentatively probed the very edges of the minds inside.

"Why did..."

The man-sized creature spun round in sudden alarm, hackles raised, razor claws extended. Kellim stepped out into Issa and Lissu's soft radiance seeming somehow unreal in the cool half-light of Koa's twin moons. The creature took a step back and glanced warily about it for others.

Kellim held up his hand. "I apologise The Faithful. It wasn't my intention to startle you."

"The Faithful was listening, listening very hard and quietly," it replied by way of an explanation. As it spoke it clicked the tips of its taloned fingers together, a mannerism peculiar to The Faithful when it felt uncomfortable. "It is good to hear Kellim of Eln's accent, a reminder of a different time."

"You didn't announce yourself on the spice trail," Kellim continued. "I had been aware of your presence for some time?"

"The Faithful followed from much earlier," it announced proudly and finally straightened, allowing its arms to settle to its sides in a stance signalling respect.

Kellim quickly altered his posture, somewhat out of practise with The Faithful's peculiarities.

"You were not followed far after the fort. The Faithful assumed to help, but this was not needed. You transported away. The Faithful followed. You transported again and The Faithful followed. Not easy." The monster seemed proud of this. "The Faithful did not seek to announce itself as it was better, more helpful to watch from a distance." It smiled revealing a set of needle-sharp teeth.

"Then I thank you for your help. I had no idea you were in the Ugasi. Our paths have not crossed in a long time." Kellim relaxed his will, reducing his link to the field. The creature, like many of its kind, adopted unusual names. Signalling a need to associate, distance, or even elevate themselves from their creators in an effort to fashion an identity of their own. An identity completely belonging to them, but at the same time, quite sadly Kellim found, only exposing their inner needs and desires. All of his dealings with their kind were edged with unease and a sense of guilt. Their creation, the war and what had followed troubled him deeply. Even now, decades later, they reminded him too much of the failings of his own kind.

"Accident, The Faithful was wandering in that area not looking for you. There were others with you. Two men The Faithful does not know and now the girl. She is special. You do not know this." The Faithful announced with some satisfaction and was pleased by Kellim's surprise.

"Cali was not with us at the fortress at Aurt and spice trail. How did you know about her?"

"The Faithful sensed it. Traces around you and the other two, faintest traces. The Faithful knew you would return for her and so The Faithful followed. And now you are pleased to see me. This I also know."

Kellim smiled. "And as always you are right." The Faithful's words about Cali had piqued his interest. "You said she is special. How? In what way?"

"The Faithful does not know this yet," it said folding its arms to mimic Kellim with a snort. "The Faithful wishes to be of more help, but is unable."

"Indeed," Kellim reassured. "You've opened my mind to ideas I've been too distracted to see. I'm very grateful. Will you come in and join us? Harun would be honoured. Your kind are still held in high esteem in this part of Ildra. You saved many from the Elementals."

"That is good. It is good that they remember. Most of The Faithful's kind are gone. But it would not be right to come in, not now. There is a task to complete and The Faithful can be of use. The Faithful must learn more about the girl and will seek The Beholder."

Yet another name from the distant past, Kellim thought. Many memories resurfaced bringing images, and emotions both chilling and exhilarating. For a while, Kellim was lost amongst them.

The Faithful's eyes widened. "Yes," it gasped. "A long time. Such power. A great sacrifice, a bird that can no longer soar."

"You read me too well, but I still have wings and can glide on the lesser currents."

"The Faithful does this too. But perhaps the Panid Kellim can do more than just glide." The Faithful watched the old man for a sign that its insight had caught him off guard. Kellim merely smiled.

"Secrets, secrets. Always secrets," it said, awkwardly raising its hands and clicking the very tips of its talons together.

"It has been a pleasant surprise to find you in Ildra," Kellim said. "I have missed your counsel and insight."

"The Faithful thinks you must be careful here. The golden fruit that is Ildra turns sour. It would not be wise to linger too long." At this The Faithful bowed graciously, by way of ending the conversation and began to turn, signalling its eagerness to be on its way.

"Will you find me, or may I look for you once I'm free to do so?"

"The Faithful will find you," it said abruptly, having considered the conversation ended. Time was now being wasted with unnecessary questions.

Kellim inclined his head, realising his error in the protocol. The Faithful was already walking into the shadows. Kellim stood for a time watching as the lone figure gradually faded into the night. Were the other remaining Panids' Children abroad in the world again? Kellim was both excited and disturbed by this, shadows from the long silent past returning to trouble him. How many of them were still alive after all this time? What significant event had drawn this one out of hiding?

The farm, as always, woke early. The air was cool and a light mist hung over the fields as livestock drank at tranquil watering pools. Harun and eight members of his family had been out for hours working the fields. Lewan and Cali had joined them; glad to be of help. Kellim had promised to look at two of Harun's animals and had just finished coaxing a ligament to heal by reasserting its form field. He left the stables wiping his hands, shirtsleeves rolled up and looking quite at home. Jai and Harun's two oldest sons had been working on repairs to outbuildings. They hurried to complete the job before the sun rose and its heat made such tasks arduous. The men hefted the last roof truss into place as the sun began to leave the confines of the horizon. Securing the beam into its bracket and hammering in wooden pegs they jumped down off the walls and laughing and pushing raced to the farm's small lake. Brood birds and milkies scattered in all directions. Clothes were quickly discarded and the fresh water provided a welcome reward for their efforts and a chance to let off steam.

Jai closed his eyes enjoying the cool water as it seeped into his aching muscles; unaware of the passage of time he let it wash over him. He drifted; the stillness of the water helped keep his thoughts away from guilt. Finally heading for the shore, he realised his clothes had been taken. Up at the house, the two brothers were laughing and waving them in the air.

"Jai," Harun greeted diplomatically, trying to behave as if nothing were out of place. "I see you have finished the repairs on the barn and made a fine job of it." He looked up towards the house, raising his voice. "You are a good influence on my lay about sons!" His words were not wasted and they shuffled rather shame-faced into the house. "Come, it is time for breakfast," Harun continued, wishing the group now gathering behind him would go.

The group in turn stood fascinated by Harun's attempts to carry out this conversation, wondering just how long he could keep it up. Two of the girls cupped hands over their mouths trying not to giggle, Cali was trying not to look and the others were trying not to burst. Jai, for his part, was trying not to move his hands.

"What?" Harun finally demanded of the sniggering crowd. "Have you never seen a naked man before?"

"Not like him," blurted one of the girls before everyone erupted into laughter. There were sudden shrieks as Jai, laughing at his own expense, inadvertently raised his hands.

Breakfast was set under the shade of a huge breadvine. The food was hot and delicious. Plates and bowls crisscrossed their way up and down the table as people helped themselves and passed them on to the next. Amidst the clatter, the conversation covered the morning's work and what needed doing before the full heat of the day.

After the meal was eaten new tasks were handed out and the workers departed. Kellim sat with Harun and Hatice feeling settled and at ease.

"How much of the madness has found its way to the north of Ildra?" Kellim asked.

Harun rested his hands on his stomach. "Even Segat cannot shout this far, my friend; there are few here who would strain to listen even if he could. Some have left to seek glory and we will miss their hands come the harvest. There are more soldiers and a new fortress, but so far, they are uninterested in us; we are poor and, in their eyes, ignorant. If that is the worst of it, life here has changed little."

"Many in the south of Ildra are listening," Kellim warned. "I'd hate to see that change come here to the North. You and your fathers have been a much-valued constant in my life. I worry there is more to come." Kellim was concerned for the safety of Harun and his family. If it were in any way possible, he would have stayed on the farm till the threat of war faded.

Harun nodded. "We are one country built from many nations and our heritage has never left us, my friend. But the blood of Southern Ildrans is mingled with that of the Urukish and they have lost sight of that heritage. True Ildrans do not understand Segat. He speaks with an Urukish heart and tongue. The

UruIldrans keep themselves to the magnificent cities of the South. Here in the North, we will continue to be a feature of this land, remember our heritage and welcome you as part of our family." He smiled and then looked more mischievous. "Of course, I do not say this because your visit has brought strong and much-needed hands."

Kellim chuckled. "We've all been glad to help and glad of this place. But…"

"Surely my friend, you are not thinking of leaving yet? You have only just arrived," Harun interrupted.

"I'm afraid so," Kellim exhaled heavily and sat up. "As much as it pains me to say, we will have to leave by the end of next week. We need to meet with Carrick and Merren and get Cali and her brother, Aran, to Naddier. I'm also concerned by the number of patrols; I would not want our presence here to put you in any danger."

"You will have to avoid travel by sky ship," Harun warned. "The sky lanes and the ships are also patrolled. Our neighbours were refused passage no less than three days ago. They say the ships carry soldiers now."

"Why were they turned away?" Kellim asked.

"They are Cian by decent, they are good people and settled here more than thirty years ago. But not long enough to be trusted by the military it seems."

Kellim had been hoping to make the journey easier and faster across Ildra by using sky ships. But this news made things difficult. "I can hide my presence on a ship, but not Jai, Lewan and Cali's. We will have to continue on the roads and I will have to hasten our journey as much as I can."

"Jai will not be pleased," Hatice laughed. "I will give you extra clothes and provisions. Your skin and hair are dark enough to blend in, but your features are not Ildran and that will attract attention."

"It will be a long journey for you." Harun noticed the sudden change in Kellim, the unconscious signs the Panid always displayed when he was preparing mentally to leave. "I wish your stay could have been longer."

"You know I've always considered this my home and would stay much longer if I could. Cali and Jai in particular need rest and I can think of nowhere better."

"She is a resilient girl," Hatice smiled. "I have grown to care very deeply for her and have enjoyed her company. She talks freely and openly and that has aided her healing. She is ready for the challenges ahead I have no doubt. But Jai, he worries me a little. Stran's death has affected him deeply. We have spent some time together, but he is unwilling to talk. He has always played the joker and that mask hides a past he is reluctant to share, and now, a hurt he is unable to set down." She shook her head in concern.

Kellim nodded. "I too have struggled to get him to talk. But the past few days at least have seen a welcome change in him."

"Yes, he is brighter and much improved since you left for Amaria. It will take time Kellim. Guilt can be a persistent companion," Hatice comforted.

"He does blame himself. But there was nothing he or any of us could do. It was dark, we were deep underground. The field was weak and would not respond. I..." Kellim broke off.

Hatice reached across the table and held his hand in both of hers. "You did all and more than could be expected. There is no blame to be placed here. Do not seek to find it a home. This you must tell Jai."

"Yes, indeed yes," Kellim cleared his throat. "This break has come at a good time, for all of us."

Harun poured more of the hot sweet kinti and handed it to Kellim. "Rest, and good food work wonders. You have carried the burden of care for too long and we have been glad to share it. It is good that Merren, Carrick and Bryn will soon be with you."

"Yes," Hatice agreed. "Particularly now that your responsibilities grow," Kellim looked puzzled. "You have of course noticed the growing bond between Cali and Lewan?"

"Clearly not as much as I should have."

"There you have it. For all your ways and talent, a farmer's wife sees far more." She wagged a finger comically at him. "The union ceremony of course will be here." Kellim was about to speak and then realised Hatice's game. "Perhaps," Hatice chuckled. "Perhaps that is a little far in the future, even for me to see."

Chapter 4

"What rot is this! Are you insane?" Ritesh spat the words, toppling his chair as he stood. Other members of the Corumn began voicing their outrage and the meeting broke down into an exchange of insults. Mia Svara and Chancellor Nirek remained silent and seated, watching as Ritesh leaned on the table to glare across the room at Varin, his anger no longer contained, his voice rising with each sentence. It now echoed beyond the chamber and would be heard in the hallways outside. "You have only your interests in mind! Don't insult our intelligence with this talk of enhancement. To push against The Field's Cap is an offence and a fool's quest!"

The patience of both men had worn thin in the preceding hours, and now the last fine threads of civility snapped. "Sit down," Varin snapped. "And the rest of you, gawping like halfwits. Unthinking puppets of the crown, it is your short-sightedness that erodes the influence of the Amar Order. I present you with vital information regarding Segat's intentions to invade Amar, and you talk of envoys and delegations. That UruIldran dullard posing on the throne of Ildra must be controlled and contained!" Varin was astounded by their obstinacy, how could they be so blind? "Once our influence prevented the actions of egotists. Now you simper and fawn like servants, instead of commanding for the greater good of Amaria."

"The greater good!" Ritesh interrupted. "You talk of nothing more than your hubris. Segat may be arrogant, but he is no warmonger. Not even an UruIldran could want more than the vast ranges of Ildra and its natural riches." He paused for effect. "Unless of course, someone was exerting an influence."

Mia Svara continued to observe. Varin had been a respected member of the Amar Order and her tutor at one point. When Nirek was made Head of the Amar Order of Talents, Varin had opposed many of the new Chancellor's changes and especially his decision to re-establish links with the other Orders from across Koa. Varin's increasing extremism had marginalised him and cost him a great deal of respect. He'd left without any warning only to return now, over two years later, following a request to meet with the Amar Order's governing body, the Corumn. The man before them was changed. The black hair was prematurely grey, the brown Amarian skin had an unhealthy pallor and his features were now harsh and etched by pain. His long soodrey jacket and narrow trousers, so much a part of his pride, were now loose and ill-fitting.

Varin took another step forward. "You would have our kind at the beck and call of every ruler on the continent, the guard hounds of every dictator and potentate. We are commanded to advise instead of being entreated. Viewed as servants rather than masters and all because they think us impotent, shadows of what we were. No longer a power to be reckoned with, or an unknown quantity to fear and respect." Uncharacteristically Varin's voice was shaking with emotion. This meeting had been a humiliation. He had not expected so much change, the Panid's copper spheres would be useless. The old Corumn had gone, those he could control and those whose support he had felt assured of had 'stepped down'. The minds that ranged against him now, were open to Chancellor Nirek's idea of change. They were moderate in their views, outward-looking, younger and powerful. They would not accept the way forward Varin's research could offer and he wasn't strong enough to manipulate them all, even with the aid of the Panid's copper devices. He hadn't prepared for so much change, he'd been overconfident, come here too soon. All of his efforts, all the suffering and for what?

"That's it, isn't it," Ritesh's voice was shrill. Spit flecked his lips. "That's what eats at you. Your pride! You've always thought yourself above us all and especially the talentless. And now the proud Varin must follow their orders, call them majesty and bow with humility. It devours you, doesn't it? You may fool yourself, but not me." Ritesh was triumphant as he closed in for the kill. Words he had wanted to say for years rose to his lips and before an audience of their peers, how rich how satisfying. "You've always hated the fact that I have risen in our Order and not you. Perhaps it is time you learnt why that is, Varin. Do you know why so many times you have been overlooked? Do you!"

"Enough of this," Chancellor Nirek interceded. "The Corumn is not a place for personal recriminations or the settling of grudges. Ritesh, take your seat and calm yourself." Nirek could see Varin had straightened, colour rising on his face, the man seemed unstable and could be dangerous.

"No Chancellor, it is time he knew!" Ritesh was well aware of Varin's weak spots, he had twisted a knife in them on many an occasion, but with hardly a reaction. "That calm exterior fools none of us. We are all aware of the frailties lurking in that troubled mind of yours, your inability to move with the times. Your outspoken views made you a laughingstock. No wonder you ran away to hide your shame. The fact that you have returned, after all of this time, with this ludicrous talk of defying The Field's Cap and extending your powers is..."

Nirek slammed his hand down on the table. "You go too far! This is not a stage for petty bickering and point-scoring. Be seated! Both of you!"

Ritesh was breathing heavily, he stood for a while glaring, enjoying the fact that Varin was apparently struggling to contain himself. "Of course, Chancellor Nirek." Ritesh calmed his voice and inclined his head towards the Order Head as he picked up his chair and lowered himself into it. Varin turned away, his back rigid and fists clenched.

Mia Svara had remained silent throughout the whole of the meeting. Varin's words had touched a chord in her and she found herself unsettled by the truth of them. She was not entirely happy with the speed and range of the changes Chancellor Nirek was pushing through. She had never liked Nirek and agreed to take a place on the Corumn in order to keep him in check. She had recently taken her position along with several others. The change in the makeup of the Corumn was considerable and would not have been expected by Varin. With the support of the Empress, Nirek had been able to make sweeping changes to the Amar Order of Talents. Changes Varin would have thought impossible. Despite this, he had tried to win them over, offering greater power and a chance to raise the Order above all others. But this new Corumn, unlike the old, had no such interests. His reputation and achievements were of little consequence to them. Mia Svara could sense his growing desperation. He truly believed he was right and had clearly suffered much in the past two years for an Order that no longer wanted him and, if anything, was embarrassed by him. To make matters worse Ritesh had begun to see an opportunity, a chance to settle old scores. Ritesh's envy of Varin's abilities had always obsessed him. This was no carefully hidden secret; Mia Svara knew this; everyone knew this. Deep down he knew Varin to be superior and had tried for years to raise himself above the man he both loathed and yet desperately wanted to be. Mia Svara now feared Ritesh's goading had gone too far and Nirek seemed unable to control the situation. Varin was becoming unstable, his growing anger hinted at a raging will, barely held in check. His unswerving loyalty to the Amar Order was wearing thin. If he had been able to develop his powers, they could be in danger and Mia Svara wouldn't allow herself to be placed in such a situation. "Now would be a suitable time to adjourn the Corumn, before it is allowed to run away with itself," she spoke calmly. "We should reconvene tomorrow and discuss matters further."

Irritated, Nirek was about to correct Mia Svara's remarks when Varin began speaking.

"I have learnt much recently from an old man," Varin spoke quietly and kept his back to them.

"What-" Ritesh snapped. "What are you mumbling at?"

Mia Svara looked quickly to the Chancellor, sensing a change in the field, but didn't have time to react. Varin spun round and as he did an array of copper spheres spilt onto the floor. Activated by a thought he used their stored field energy to seal the doors and freeze the minds of those present. The five were fixed in their chairs, able to see and hear, but unable to move or focus. Varin slowly walked the remaining distance to the table.

The air filled with static and their minds filled with a dull roar as he drew unopposed on the field.

"Perhaps I have not wasted my time in isolation," Varin was saying, his voice strangely calm. "Unmonitored by you I have pushed against the boundaries of The Field's Cap. Forced myself to endure its agonies so that now I can draw deeply from that endless sea. Far deeper than any here." He sat down on the table and leaned closer to Ritesh's face. "And perhaps during those tortured moments, when I pushed myself beyond reason, my mind may have become a little abraded. But through it, I have achieved clarity of intention and understanding that has always eluded you, Ritesh. Has it never occurred to you that perhaps I was overlooked for reasons other than those dreamt up by your insecurities? Could it be that the Amar Order raised you to your current level because it saw a man who could be manipulated? A man whose blinding pride wouldn't allow him to consider the fact that he was being used."

Varin enjoyed the moment as the flicker of doubt took seed in Ritesh's eyes. But the aching stab of failure soon returned and with it the whispering. He had failed. The bleakness of this realisation stretched before him; it was time now to abandon this. The Corumn wasn't the clutch of ageing separatists he'd left behind. Powerful as he now was, he couldn't hope to take on this new Corumn and the current attitude of the Amar Order. Even Mia Svara seemed set against him. The plans that had consumed his every waking moment had failed. The Amar Order of Talents had been his life but now wouldn't listen, wouldn't give him a chance. They no longer needed him. What did he have left?

Activity some distance away pulled him back to the present. Forcing some semblance of control over himself he leaned forward again and looked directly into Ritesh's eyes.

"You spoke of the frailties of my mind," Varin's voice was flat, emotionless as he searched the face before him. "How strong is yours I wonder?"

Ritesh's forehead began to bead perspiration, fear now clear in his eyes. Satisfied, Varin picked up the small copper orb in front of the man whose eyes darted between it and Varin's face.

"A clever little device. Did I tell you of Kellim's visit? A far greater mind than yours Ritesh. Only he stopped to wonder why I had left the Order and removed myself from the world. Only he suspected I had an ulterior motive for leaving. He failed to find answers but left behind the means to bring forward my visit here. Unfortunately, they cannot help me reach my original goal, but may still furnish an opportunity to settle old scores."

He juggled the sphere between his fingers. "They can be constructed to contain a surprising amount of energy. A mere thought, one hardly detectable, can activate them." He stood up and turned to look at Mia Svara. "My congratulations, your sensitivity is indeed impressive. I feel some pride in your achievements and my contribution to them. I suspect, my dear, that without these I would not have been able to deceive you." He looked at Nirek. "Or hold the Corumn in my hand, albeit for an all too brief period. But as for you Ritesh, how should I mark the occasion of my visit, indeed should I mark you, leave you with a permanent reminder of your frailties..." Varin suddenly broke off and glanced towards the doors. "Ah, there we have it. Your rescuers approach."

There was a series of shouts from outside the heavy doors as the first of a series of blows struck them. Varin swayed, placing a hand on the table to steady himself. He remained there for seconds concentrating, focusing, drawing deeper. The dull roar in the heads of his captives grew to new levels as he pulled in more field energy. The doors stopped shuddering and the noise outside became distant, but the whispering persisted. Eventually, he lifted his head, touching his top lip with the back of his hand, he was perspiring heavily. When he next spoke, his words were an effort.

"You are... fortunate today Ritesh... very fortunate," and with that, he was gone.

***

Segat, Emperor of Ildra, First of the Urukish bloodline, Ruler Englorie, looked out across his capital; Hass, First City of the Sun. It dazzled the eye with its beauty, its art and above all its gold.

And it was all his.

Thirty years of political intrigue had finally paid off and allowed his family to claim ascendancy to the Ildran throne. The sacrifices and crippling expenses had been worth it. It was only now, at this point, this turning point in Ildra's history, that he paused to enjoy his achievements. He had rid himself of all true threats to his throne. He had made Ildra stronger, making it one country, no longer a rabble of states with a figurehead for a monarch. He had built monuments, roads and an economy to rival Selarsh, proving himself an equal to any ruler in Koa. He had achieved all this in the first three years of his reign alone. But had he rested? Had he sat back on the riches of Ildra and grown fat like his predecessors? No, it was then that the visions had started, providing the inspiration that would lead him to where he was now. In just two years he had made Ildra a military force to be reckoned with, a country on the brink of empire. All of this from vague images and a voice that had danced at the edge of this mind's awareness, offering him a way forward to true greatness. He was convinced it had been the voice of the great Queen VaCenet, speaking to him in his dreams, an ancestor to be proud of, one to model himself on. Many in his family had baulked at his vision for the future and even criticized and mocked him. Their words had condemned them and now, none spoke out against his vision. Now he would alter history and bring meaning to the title Emperor. Selarsh, Kiashu, Hon, Neath even Akar would fall to the power of his armies. He gazed to the east, spitting a curse on the winds to Amaria. Let them entreat, let them talk of new beginnings, let them cower behind the high walls of The Hand, he would come and bring with him a lesson in contrition. DuLek would be avenged...

There was a knock at the door. "Enter," he snapped churlishly. The Aide to the Chamber stepped in and bowed. "F-forgive me your Imperial Majesty. The Head of the Ildran Order of Talents begs to remind you, Sire, that she awaits your pleasure." The man kept his eyes lowered, the tremble in his voice evident.

Segat noted VaCalt's use of her title with an amount of irritation but delighted at the grudging politeness of her message. He knew she would be seething inside. It pleased him to waste her time; to remind her of her position. She had even resurrected and awarded herself the title of Potent, an ancient Urukish term for Head of the Order. The Potent, he used the word derisively, overrated her importance to him and her growing conceit would have to be clipped. He smoothed down the embroidered gold of his tunic and adjusted two of the jewelled rings on his fingers. Nothing, but nothing was more important than the whim of the Emperor, no matter how trivial, no matter how petty.

Segat turned back to the city, sharp Urukish features held high above the people. Perfectly styled hair cut short with intricate designs cushioned the fabled Ildran crown. It caught the sun as he looked down on the city, how magnificent.

The aide stood trembling at the door, waiting for a further fifteen minutes before Segat spoke again. "Tell VaCalt I will see her now. Tell her it had better be important."

"Sire." The aide bowed again, scuttling to leave the room. It didn't pay to bring unwanted news to Segat's ears.

Segat kept his back to the door, listening to the sound of the servant as he rushed away and then to the sweep of long robes as VaCalt approached. At seventy-three there was no hint of infirmity in those steps. No lessening of strength, ambition or resentment. Segat knew little of VaCalt's past. There were plenty of stories. Rumours of her ruthlessness, her drive, even tales of time spent in the forbidden North, studying at The Mammoth Temple in Kemarid. The telling of such stories would have been interesting but he would not pay her the compliment of curiosity. She entered the room, the air of outrage she emanated was palpable and still, he made her wait. Helping himself to some sweet fancy from a multitude of golden bowls that presented the very best of Ildra's chefs.

Finally, dabbing his mouth with a soodrey cloth, Segat favoured her with his attention. He still needed her, or rather, he corrected himself, needed what she could make the Ildran Order of Talents achieve. She was as hungry for power and position as he was for prestige. They shared the same UruIldran heritage, the main reason he had supported her rise to Head of the Ildran Order and allowed her to be known as Potent. Her features had lost none of their sharp angles, her skin and hair were still dark, her eyes darker yet, a window into the strength within. She had more drive and stamina than a woman half her age. Her talent was unparalleled and her ambition, her ambition needed a leash. "What is it VaCalt?"

"Your Imperial Majesty," she bowed stiffly, her face and her irritation disappearing under the amber yellow of the soodrey cowl she wore. "They are complete. The Talent DuChen awaits your pleasure and remains under guard as you commanded."

"He has remained in complete isolation and shared his knowledge with no one?"

"His knowledge is secure, Sire. The wards are impenetrable. I have seen to them personally. It is as you commanded." VaCalt was now certain of Segat's intentions. "DuChen lives purely to serve."

"And you VaCalt? Does that include you?"

"Of course, Sire. I devote my every waking instant to your service and…"

"Spare me VaCalt," he waved a hand irritably in her direction. "I will see them now, and make sure DuChen, their creator, is present." Segat turned his back on her and returned his attention to the distraction of food.

***

VaCalt's voice stabbed into DuChen's head like a blade forced between the lid of a sealed chest. This illegal communication was an effort even for her. "I have told the Emperor all he needs to know," she said hurriedly. "You will only facilitate the imprinting. You will say nothing. Do nothing to attract his attenti…" the voice in his head was smothered. He tried to extend his mind but hit a wall before he could draw on the field. Then VaCalt pierced his consciousness again. He flinched; the pain was terrible. How was she able to get past the wards? "DuChen! When the imprinting is complete, you will attempt to leave at the earliest opportunity. Venat will meet you at the agreed place. Is this clear, DuChen?"

"Y-yes," his voice caught in a dry throat.

"Make no mention of this. I am all that stands in the way of your death."

He nodded pointlessly. She was gone and the wards and other form fields imprisoning him re-sealed before he had time to draw a trembling breath. He rubbed at his shaved head, now slick with sweat, his nerves turning his stomach in knots. His commitment to the task of creation and eventual success was meant to advance his position. Not endanger his life. He looked at the fruits of his labours. The two figures stood motionless, shrouded in purest white, the cloth masking their form. He couldn't see their eyes but knew they would not be watching him. He knew who they had been and what they now were, his creation. Unlike every Talent on Koa, he had no reason to fear them, but he did fear the Emperor and what Segat could do to him. He wrung his hands and began pacing, short desperate movements. What could he do? Why had he gloated at the failure of the other Summoners? He should have left, his task complete, and ran. But how could he have known this would be his reward. When Segat ordered the confiscation of his research that morning, the work room became his prison. Not even VaCalt, as Potent and Head of the Ildran Order of Talents, had been allowed entry. He stopped his pacing and tried yet again to draw on the field, nothing. Nothing! The room was sealed. He clenched his fists to his head. Why hadn't the danger been obvious? Segat wanted a personal guard immune to the powers of his country's Talents. DuChen was their only creator and minutes from now Segat would no longer need him. Why, why, why had he not realised this for himself? Why had he been so arrogant? He clutched at his stomach, suddenly feeling sick. With shaking hands, he tried to pour a drink and gulped at it sloppily, before slumping into a chair and hugging his sides. A noise from the room outside made him freeze. He could hear soldiers and General Immed.

VaCalt walked quickly, DuChen's breakthrough had implications that could change everything. The creatures he had created nullified the field around them, virtually rendering them immune to attack from a Talent. One touch de-stabilized living form fields. Anyone, talented or not, would literally break down into raw materials with no pattern to support them. She had not been allowed access to him or his research, and so she needed him. She needed what was in his head. Segat saw only his own protection. VaCalt saw both her downfall and her salvation. The latter would bring about the elimination of any Talent who stood in her way, and the pre-eminence of the Ildran Order of Talents, all-powerful, unchallenged, with her as Potent. She had to have that information; its loss could not be allowed to limit her. She walked into the heavily guarded and warded chamber outside DuChen's room. Her hands clenched as she was searched. Finally, the guards stepped away, but she maintained her glare on the man in her way. If General Immed felt the burning gaze on his back, he made no sign of it. The UruIldran General stepped forward as the door was opened for him, but turned at the threshold and gestured. "After you VaCalt."

VaCalt refused to look at or acknowledge him in any way. Instead, she stood as if oblivious to anything around her.

Immed smiled, sharp features pulled taught by the action. "Of course, you prefer to walk in my shadow."

VaCalt's eyes moved to fix his. "Remember what is in there General. And who will profit in the eyes of the Emperor." She spoke with unveiled contempt.

General Immed stepped forward. He knew about her Order's aversion to body contact, its ritual cleansing and obsessive observances. It pleased him that she stiffened as he moved his face closer to hers. "I am very aware of what is in there and the momentary status it may bring you…"

VaCalt interrupted. "Then you will be aware of what they are capable of doing to those who fail him. Do you not fear their gaze and the cold touch of their hands about your throat,

Immed?" She met his gaze, unaffected by his proximity. The General lifted his head away, but it was VaCalt who now stepped closer, pressing herself to him. "Do you not feel my touch, General." She pushed past him.

"Tell me VaCalt," Immed said as she stepped away. "Who will they be watching as we enter?"

VaCalt didn't falter, didn't alter her pace, she knew who those things would be watching. The chill slid down her neck like a knife.

Chapter 5

Lewan pulled on another layer. It was getting cooler; they'd all noticed it more after the heat of central Ildra. It now seemed so long ago and he wondered how much longer Cali could contain herself. She was understandably nervous about seeing Aran and with each passing hour, her impatience grew. She'd been itching to gallop her mount, but Lewan had suggested it wasn't a good idea. The animals had carried them a long way from Harun's home in the east of Ildra and they were now tired and needed rest. More importantly, there was also the ever-present threat of patrols, the group had encountered and avoided several and Kellim had stepped in on numerous occasions to dampen anything other than perfunctory interest. The contact had heightened their sense of unease and kept The Faithful's warning foremost in Kellim's mind.

Now, after weeks of travelling, they were only miles away from Kagash, a large town on the border of Ildra and Sancir, here there would be more patrols and probably a garrison to avoid. Having journeyed on the River Ild they'd re-joined the roads at lake Dal and headed northwest. They'd ridden through farmland, dotted with small settlements and shaded groves of quill trees and increasing numbers of gnarlwoods. A regular feature had been large kilns and great stockpiles of bricks; all made from red Ildran clay. Everything in Ildra, it seemed, was constructed from them.

The North gave no hint of the country's immense wealth. The larger cities were in the South; closer to the border with Selarsh and its coastal ports. Lewan had never been there, but Kellim had told him stories. The southern cities were grand, ostentatious and decorated with pure gold. He had told him of great vaults piled high with treasures from the country's mines and about an Ildra that had never harboured ambitions beyond its borders. But looking about him now, he could see signs, even this far north, that they travelled through a country poised on the brink of hostility towards its neighbours.

Kellim had told him about some of the events leading to the start of the Great War, the devastation of Urukish, the evacuation of its people into Ildra and their longstanding devotion to the memory of their beloved Princess DuLek. The south of Ildra had absorbed the Urukish population and there were many UruIldrans alive today; their sharper features hinting at an Urukish heritage. For thirty years Segat's Urukish family had risen in stature amongst them and stories of how this had been achieved abounded. One by one, claimants to the throne had disappeared, whole dynasties had been wiped out and the few that remained had gone into hiding. Segat had assumed the throne just five years ago, consolidated his position and now only Prince Immar remained, all other claimants to the throne were dead. Segat's climb to power mirrored VaCalt's; both stories were littered with ruthless accounts of the extreme lengths each was prepared to go to.

The Orders had been formed a few years after the Great War. The Ildran Order of Talents had placed importance on service to others, ritual and remembrance of the past. But later, the growing UruIldran influence had begun to change these core beliefs. The changes were subtle at first, gradually moving the focus. Until VaCalt was made Head and entitled herself Potent at the start of Segat's reign. Then, the changes become brutal and extreme, turning dedication to fanaticism and remembrance to bitterness.

The north of Ildra had continued its daily existence in ways unchanged for centuries and so the countryside had remained peaceful and was populated by friendly locals untouched by the character of the South. Lewan could see this way of life was under threat, it was being squeezed in the grip of its Emperor, moulded into a state of existence more to his liking. He peered over his shoulder to check that Kellim and Jai were right behind.

The two men had been talking, planning the border crossing and their journey into Sancir. At Kellim's request, Cali reined in her mount and they paused at the side of a crossroads. The Panid climbed down stiffly and went to speak to a man sitting by the roadside, they seemed to know each other. Watching the traffic, Cali realised just how much it had increased, it now seemed crowded in comparison to the roads of the last few days.

She felt suddenly nervous. "Where did all these carts come from? It's like they sprang out of nowhere. Just like the patrols."

"The traffic's been on the increase for a while, you've had your mind on other things," Lewan pointed out.

"Who's that Kellim's talking to?"

"I'm not sure," Lewan peered at the man. "Kellim often talks to what seems like random strangers, though I'm sure they're not really."

Jai leaned forward. "He's just checking the way ahead and how safe it is for us to enter the town."

"Do you think it might not be?" Cali asked.

"We're just checking, best to avoid surprises," Jai could see she was nervous, he wasn't so sure about their chances of getting to the inn without trouble himself. But wasn't going to worry Cali or Lewan for that matter. "We'll be fine. It's just to be on the safe side." Jai looked back to the road.

Cali could see now he was more alert and that his hand hovered closer to where his sword was buckled. She looked at the steady stream of traffic passing them by. All of the people, all of them strangers. "Do you think it will be much further?" she asked Lewan.

"Not far at all now," he checked ahead, taking a drink from his water pouch before offering it to her. "If you look that way, you can see the start of the town. Just up ahead there. I think there's a tower too. Can you see it?"

Cali shielded her eyes and peered through the haze in the direction Lewan was pointing, "Oh yes. I see it. Is Kagash a large town?" she asked. "I've never been anywhere that could be called a city. Rel was small, well it was a village really and we hardly travelled anywhere. It just wasn't the done thing. If anyone went ten miles, they were called adventurous. Of course, now, after all the places we've been to, I'd be positively worldly." Cali was aware that Lewan was smiling. "I must seem so backwater to you, such a country mudger," she stopped for a second. "Or is it because I'm babbling and haven't paused to draw breath?"

Lewan laughed. "That was pretty impressive and no you're not a mudger. Maybe just a bit nervous. Kagash is quite big though. But I don't think you could call it a city. It doesn't have a port tower and cities tend to have at least one."

Kellim returned and exchanged a few brief words with Jai.

"Okay you two," Jai said. "Let's get moving. Stay close." He looked again at Kellim, who nodded. "There's not an easy way to say this, but there might be a bit of stuff ahead. Erm, things that won't be easy to look at. Just keep your eyes down and ride."

Cali looked at him.

"We'll be fine," Jai reassured as best he could. "Just remember what I've said."

They rode on, if Cali had been urging her mount on earlier, now she hung back slightly and Lewan's mount moved forward by a head.

"It is a lot busier," Cali said, looking increasingly unnerved by the traffic, and by whatever Jai had been hinting at.

"It's a busy town," Lewan said. "Lots of people from other countries but not as many as there used to be."

Cali hadn't noticed the lack of diversity and now began to take more note of the people around them. She caught bits of conversation, which reminded her of an observation she'd made and hadn't gotten around to asking about. "I thought I'd hear more languages as we travelled. But no matter where we've been everyone talks the same."

"What do you mean?" Lewan asked, waving half-heartedly at an annoying insect.

"Well back home. The village didn't get many visitors from other countries. We saw a few people from Pidone and Cian, but that was it. And now I've been all over the place and everyone seems to speak the same."

"As far as I know most countries speak Koan. I suppose people have travelled from one place to another for so long that it makes sense for trade and all. Only places like Kiashu…" he paused for a moment to think, "and Lagash refuses to teach it as the main language and as for Ciad, well no one's heard from them for decades."

"Oh, I know about Lagash," Cali said. "Isn't there a long-standing joke about Lagash being… you know, the bottom end of the continent?"

"Yep. But those aren't the words I've heard." Lewan laughed and then pulled a face as he swallowed the insect. "Blah!" he spat. "I don't know why it got that reputation…" he picked at his lips for bits. "I suppose there isn't a reason to go there."

"Shinpur!" Cali said suddenly. "Shinpur doesn't encourage the speaking of Koan."

"Not officially. But they do all the same. It would affect their trade empire..." Lewan steered his mount as they overtook a cart. "I suppose money is just as important to them as it is to Selarsh."

They rode on a little further, moving past slower traffic and avoiding some of the more careless as it clattered by. The manoeuvring kept them occupied for a while. Then Lewan noticed that Kellim had ended his conversation with Jai and seemed deep in concentration while Jai now watched every movement around them. Lewan realised why as they passed a group of Ildran soldiers. They were inspecting a cart and the owner was being handled roughly. Lewan's and the group's disguises were good enough for passers-by, but not up to inspection by patrols. Kellim seemed to be doing something to subdue their presence. Cali had gone very quiet and Lewan struggled to think of something to keep her talking.

They eventually settled behind a large wagon and several people driving a sprawling herd of milkies; that typically yapped and glared at every passer-by. The commotion offered some cover and Lewan relaxed enough to think up a distraction.

"Did you say you'd never known your parents?"

"Sorry, what was that?" Cali asked.

"Did you know your parents?"

"Not really," she replied. "Orla said our mother died giving birth to Aran, he's a year younger than me. Our father blamed Aran for her death. Blame he couldn't let go of. And then one day after a fit of rage, he upped and left. Might have gone back to Kersel. We never saw him again. Orla, the midwife who delivered us, took us in. She had talent herself and recognised it in us." Cali thought for a while and Lewan glanced over, concerned she may be upset. "Oh, I'm fine. I was still young and don't remember him really, Orla said he was a sad and bitter man," she smiled gently, catching his look. "Life continued after he left. I don't remember missing him. Orla was very busy. We had to fend for ourselves most of the time and I think she kept us at a bit of a distance, now that I think about it. Don't get me wrong. She was kind, taught us what she knew and gave us a stable childhood, but was very clear that one day we would leave the village and go to Naddier. And that's about it really," she shrugged lightly. "It's always been just me and Aran." Mentioning his name made her stomach lurch in anticipation of seeing him again and so she made herself keep the conversation going, she needed the distraction. "What about you? Don't you come from quite a big family?"

"Yep, three older brothers and one younger. I came from a small farm outside of Naddier and hadn't even been to the next village until Kellim, Jai and Bryn passed through one day. It was just after my seventeenth birthday and so it sticks in my mind."

"How did they end up at your parents' farm and how did you end up going with them?"

"They were heading back from somewhere. I can't remember where now, but they needed a place to spend the night, it was raining and just that little bit too far from the city. They ended up staying longer and sort of helped out. You know how Kellim is about farms." Lewan had to break off while they worked their way past a cart that had shed its load. There was a lot of shouting and people waving their hands at each other, but no one was doing anything.

"That's not going to get cleared in a hurry," Lewan shook his head. "I'm glad we met that sooner rather than later." He looked back at the growing confusion as a patrol of Ildran soldiers approached. He glanced back at Jai, who gave him a reassuring wink. He was beginning to feel uncomfortable now and could sense it in the others. He kept an eye on the road ahead but still tried to keep talking. "Anyway, erm, they told me about their travels and adventures. We got on well and the more I listened the more I wanted to see what was out there. We heard so little of the world and I guess I realised what I was missing. It all sounded exciting. All those places I'd never seen or even heard of."

"So, what happened?" Cali asked, relying on her mount's road sense to keep them out of trouble.

"They left and suddenly my life seemed so dull and boring and just…" Lewan shrugged, pulling a face. "Just so full of nothing. Do you know what I mean?"

"Yep. I couldn't go back to my life before, even though this has been frightening and scary and all sorts of other things. Life back in Rel would be unbearable now. So, tell me the rest. They'd left, and you were feeling miserable, what did you do?"

"Packed a bag, snuck out and ran after them. I almost didn't find them. They'd gone on a long way towards the city, the roads were busy like this. I'd just about given up and said to myself I was only going to carry on to the next junction in the road. But there they were. I shouted and they must have recognised me and waited. Kellim wasn't happy. But I pleaded and went on and on and on. And then he seemed to consider things and changed his mind. Funny that, talking about it now just made it jump into my head. I should ask him what made him change his mind. Anyway, Bryn still wasn't very pleased."

"Why?"

"Because I'd left without telling my parents. He marched me right back and said that I could come if my family agreed."

"And they did?" Cali asked.

"They were reluctant at first. But I kicked up such a fuss and, in the end, Kellim persuaded them, saying it would be an education and it would give me advantages and all that sort of thing. And here I am three years later."

"That makes us the same age." Cali smiled back and then there was an awkward moment. They both looked at each other for a little too long, blinking in the brightness. Wanting to say things, but not wanting to be the first, in case the other wasn't thinking it too. Then Jai's mount was at her side.

"Just keep riding," he said to both of them.

Cali heard and then saw the crowd to the right of the road and then the large numbers of Ildran soldiers there. She was about to ask Jai what was happening when something to her left caught her eye and she gasped.

Tall posts, twelve feet high had been driven into the ground at the roadside. Hanging from shackles nailed to the top were people. Filthy, half-naked, dead and dying, hanging by disjoined arms for all to see. The smell became terrible as they drew nearer and she had to hold her hand up to her mouth.

Jai reached over and took her reins, keeping his mount close to hers and guiding it along. Lewan touched her arm, she flinched at the sudden contact but held eye contact with him. Jai moved them on quickly, only once glancing back at Kellim.

The gruesome sight seemed to stretch before them forever and Cali held her nerve and fought the urge to retch. She wanted to know why they were there? What they'd done? But couldn't speak for the smell. One of the people they passed cried out suddenly and she had to blink back tears. She couldn't bear the thought of the suffering, what those people had been put through and how pathetically helpless she was to do anything about it.

"The gates." Jai's quiet alert pulled her from her thoughts. They were passed the poles and working their way through the traffic and the crowds. She could see the walls of the city ahead of them. Kellim wordlessly moved to the front. Cali noticed that the Panid seemed harder to focus on, she couldn't explain the effect. Even the guards seemed interested in anything else but them. They edged forwards seemingly unnoticed along the queue of carts and people waiting to enter the town. At the gate, they were forced to pause as a group of guards blocked the way. But then the soldiers moved to a man complaining about the way his cart was being searched. Cali looked away as one of the guards struck him and he fell to the floor. It was only once they were through the gatehouse that Cali realised, she'd been holding her breath.

Jai released her reins. "Well done," he said. "That wasn't easy."

"Let's get to the inn," Kellim looked exhausted. "We'll go this way; it should be quieter than the main road."

Jai dropped back and offered Kellim his water pouch, the Panid accepted it gratefully.

"He'll be okay," Lewan said gently to Cali. "We're inside now, it should be a bit easier."

Kagash wasn't big enough to be called a city. It was more like a town that had sprawled. Its markets were the main reason for this, pulling in all the local growers as well as farmers from across the border. It was a colourful place and the cultural differences between the farmers from Ildra and Sancir made it interesting. The buildings they passed were typically Ildran, large and blocky with sloping sides. Each one seemed to have its own gnarlwoods decorated with colourful Ildran lanterns.

The journey through the dusty hotchpotch town took some time and the group became silent, each feeling a mixture of fatigue and anticipation, so it was a relief when finally, they left the crowded street and rode into the courtyard of a building that grandly announced itself as the finest inn in Kagash. The owner was an acquaintance of Kellim's and so their stay would go relatively unnoticed.

Cali practically threw herself off her mount when her brother and the others came out to meet them. She'd been worried he'd be changed, that somehow, she wouldn't recognise him. That he would be different outside as well as inside. He seemed taller, he'd clearly lost weight, and his characteristic mop of hair had been shaved but was growing back, though, like hers, it was now dyed black. Despite all this it was him! She called out his name even though he was running towards her smiling and laughing. They collided in a mass of arms and laughter that eventually turned to tears of relief as emotion overcame them. The others hugged in greeting, picking up from where they'd left off with the banter of relief.

"Where's Jai?" Bryn asked in amongst the excitement and chatter of the reunion. Kellim looked round and then pointed in the direction of the inn's stables.

"He's still not right then?"

Kellim shook his head. "Better, but not his old self."

"I'll catch up with you," Bryn headed over, eager to talk to his friend.

Kellim watched discretely from amongst the group as Bryn strode over to Jai and grabbed him into a hug. The conversation that followed appeared to be a difficult one for Jai, who spent much of it looking at his feet, or anywhere to avoid Bryn's searching gaze.

"Well at least Jai is nodding now," Carrick noted.

"I can't stand here anymore," Merren said as the others began to make their way in. She headed over, hugged Jai and drew them back to the inn and the others.

As they sat together that night, sharing a meal, it became clear to Cali that this group was more like a family. The sharing of news, banter and leg-pulling was something she'd seen at Harun's but hadn't fully been a part of. It felt warm and comforting and the evening had passed quickly. Having her brother safe and with her made it almost perfect.

The meal over, the conversation had turned to more serious issues. Kellim related the events leading to their meeting with, and escape from Varin. "All I can say is that Varin must have been at Aurt for one or perhaps two years," he concluded, looking at Jai and Lewan to see if there was anything further to add.

Lewan was asleep and Jai shook his head. "You've pretty much covered it, except for Varin's reasons for being at Aurt."

Carrick leaned forward, folding his arms on the table. "I wonder why he left Amar? We know little of the Amar Order but what we do know highlights Varin time and time again. The Amar Order seems to have been his life's work."

Kellim looked at Cali and Aran, aware that some of this conversation would be meaningless to them. "It would help you to know something about the history of Amaria and Koa. I think you already know that during the time of the Panids there were two places of learning for Talents, the Lantriums, it's old Koan for guiding hand," Kellim explained with a hint of irony in his voice. "One Lantrium was based at Gillern across the river Naddier. The other in Urukish…"

"Urukish?" Cali interrupted. "But Urukish is nothing but jungle and isolated cities."

"Indeed, it is, but that wasn't always the case. The war changed much." Kellim purposefully left no gap for Cali's inquisitive nature to fill with questions. "After the fall of the Lantriums, during the Great War, the remaining Talents were forced into forming Orders. Each country was to have one, overseen by its ruling government or monarch. Amaria now has one of the four largest, centred at Amar, the country's capital. Varin is known to have been one of its longest-serving and most respected members. It is rumoured he wanted to see the Amar Order return to a position of dominance both within Amaria and across Koa. I suspect his views will have put him increasingly at odds with the new political tide in his country."

Bryn nodded. "That in itself could be reason enough for him to leave."

"So," Cali said thoughtfully, "what is so bad about Varin wanting his country to return to the way it was?"

Merren explained. "Amaria was a powerful country with huge influence across the east of Koa. When Emperor Karna III spoke, everyone listened and few argued. He got used to hearing only his voice and believing only Amarian opinion mattered. His way was the right way, the only way. When Nebessa's internal problems began to destabilise the East, Karna decided it needed an Amarian government and invaded. Kiashu and Ciad were taken soon after and Akar made the mistake of objecting and so it too was annexed and became part of the Amarian Empire. To make things even worse, the death of DuLek, the Urukish royal ambassador was also attributed to Emperor Karna's arrogance. His actions, in collusion with four of the Panids, were blamed for starting the Great War and Amaria was not allowed to forget it. After the war, his surviving son, Emperor Rasna withdrew his armies and closed the country to the rest of the continent by way of self-imposed atonement for the mistakes of his father. After Rasna's death, Essedra gradually moved the country forward. Her first challenge was to wrestle back control of her court. Then she faced a similar challenge in curbing the power of the Amar Order of Talents. They'd got too used to self-rule and had vast influence, more so than the crown. It's taken her decades of political and more unorthodox action to reform the hierarchy of her country. With the result that Amar now seems determined to offer the hand of friendship to those about it. That pace of change has taken on a new momentum with Essedra's appointment of Nirek as Head of the Amar Order of Talents. He was only too happy to serve and take up the title of Chancellor that accompanies the position. I wonder if Varin is aware of just how much his Order will have changed in his absence?"

Cali sensed that Merren had left out a lot of details to save Kellim's feelings and avoid an awkward disagreement over the actions of the Panids at the time of Emperor Karna III. She had noticed his mild unease as Merren related past events.

Kellim for his part had listened with a solemn expression on his face. "The gift of hindsight is a wonderful thing. At the time, events were not so clearly defined and action to stop Karna was clouded by other issues. The reality of that time was far more complicated, grey and not so black and white." There was a hint of the defensive in his tone. "As indeed things are now. We are dealing with a lot of greys as if looking through a mist. We can only guess at the glimpses of things we see. The change in Amar would go some way to explaining Varin's departure. But he wouldn't be the type to give up easily. There will be another reason for his leaving."

"You think he had a plan?" Bryn looked at Kellim. "One best put into action, or at least thought through, away from the eyes and senses of his Order?"

"Indeed. On meeting him I was taken aback by the extent of his abilities and was surprisingly aware of his mind, even some distance from the fortress."

Bryn looked puzzled. "You're saying he's changed, developed his ability. Is that possible?"

"At this time, I'm not sure what to think. Our escape from Aurt was a close thing, and not what I had anticipated."

"Ah yes," Carrick smirked unable to resist the opportunity, and the chance to lighten the mood. "We've heard a lot about Kellim's copper balls of late."

"Careful now Carrick," Jai warned. "I've had my hands slapped already."

Kellim rolled his eyes as the others laughed. "I prefer to call them something more suitable. I see your sense of humour hasn't developed in the months we've been apart, Carrick. I did notice that the other children staying here have long since gone to bed, perhaps you and Jai should retire."

Carrick attempted to look contrite. "I'm sorry Kellim. How would you prefer we spoke about your balls? I mean…"

"Spheres," Jai helped. There were more sniggers.

With an air of considerable dignity, Kellim cast his gaze over the smiling faces. "Kellim's…" he paused for effect, "mighty balls. If you don't mind." He managed to hold his expression for a short time before the laughter forced him to join in.

As things calmed it seemed like a good time to get some sleep and some of the party made their excuses and went to their rooms. Kellim, Bryn, Carrick and Merren remained. They talked at length but were unable to reach any further conclusions beyond the need to gather more information. After much debate and a certain amount of toing and froing, the next leg of the journey was eventually decided on before the conversation finally headed in an inevitable direction. Bryn closed the map, each fold watched by the others in a growing silence that signalled it was finally time to talk. The tavern was empty, the staff to bed and the fire pit nothing more than rippling embers. The wind made the only sound, the quiet matched the turn in their mood.

"It's been six months," Bryn said with a heavy sigh that acknowledged the expectant silence. "Five since you were able to get word to us."

Carrick nodded. "We haven't been able to talk until now."

Kellim stroked his beard thoughtfully. "There hasn't been the opportunity my friends. This is the first time we've all been together long enough to sit down and draw breath."

Merren shook her head. "I still feel we should have made time. We could have done more to help when we left Cali with you, Lewan and Jai."

"A chance to reorganise our numbers only," Kellim reminded her. "We had journeyed from Akar, only then learning Varin's behaviour demanded attention in Amaria. You were chasing Aran and needed to head south. Cian offered an all too brief meeting place and urgency dictated an immediate departure." He sat back in his chair, a slight smile on his face. "Hatice reminded me not to dwell on events beyond our control. It would serve us all to heed her advice, but first, you need to hear all that happened in Akar."

For the first time, Kellim was able to tell them fully of the events in Akar that had led to Stran's death. A loss they had all been forced to put aside when the simple task of taking Cali and Aran to Naddier had been complicated by slavers and Varin's unexplained behaviour had demanded an investigation. Thinking back to their journey through the cave system in Akar, seemed like a revisiting of distant events and, at the same time, not. The memories and emotions the recollection stirred were still raw and at times Kellim struggled.

Bryn gripped Kellim's shoulder offering support words alone couldn't fully convey. "You did well to keep Jai and Lewan going." He wanted to say more but didn't trust his own emotions.

Merren cleared her throat. "You said Jai's taking a lot of risks."

"Yes, he has an alarming disregard for his own safety, while at the same time being overprotective of us," Kellim responded. "He seems determined to prove himself and, I fear, make up for what only he sees as his failure in the caves."

"Then we'll have to keep an eye on him," Carrick said. "You especially Bryn, you're his closest friend. Did he say much out there in the yard?"

"Only that he was ok," Bryn scoffed. "And that we didn't need to worry. Oh, and get this one," Bryn added irritably. "Could we stop talking about it? It's him to the core, always trying to make up for his shortcomings. Faults no one else sees."

"That sounds like Jai." Merren could see Bryn was frustrated but knew Jai would probably never want to talk. Jai fostered the image of a rogue; flippant and hot-headed. But underneath he was a fiercely loyal friend who cared a lot more than he was able, or willing to express. His attitude had always been a quirky contradiction but had now become a struggle and one he was fast losing ground against.

"I want to help but don't know how. It's frustrating, he's definitely *not* ok," Bryn picked up his glass and took a long drink.

There was a pause, a collective internalising of all that had been said. Kellim felt, for now, it was time to move the conversation on. "What of your journey?" he asked, looking at the others.

"Not exactly one of our best," Merren began wearily. "From Cian, we intended to head south into Hon in the hope that we would reach its capital, Kals, before the slavers' ship did. However, we ran into trouble shortly after Esra."

"We were attacked by brigands, a few hours' ride from Cian's capital," Bryn added dryly. "They were a poor excuse for trouble, but held us up nonetheless."

"Brigands, that close to Esra?" Kellim was surprised. "Cian is a safe country to travel through. The south of Koa hasn't seen that kind of behaviour since the aftermath of the Great War."

"Tensions have continued to grow in the South," Carrick said. "Most of Hon's armed forces have moved closer to its borders with Ildra. Cian has done something similar, so the roads and coastlines are left to take care of themselves. Highway people, brigands and slavers have free rein."

"That said the brigand's hearts weren't in it. They'd been hired," Bryn added.

"What do you mean?" Kellim asked.

"Any brigands out for themselves don't take risks, are usually well prepared, know the area and are ready to fight. These were none of those. Any half-whit who can pick up a sword is trying to get in on the act; they think it's easy money."

"We figured they'd been paid by slavers," Carrick added. "The unrest caused by Ildra is allowing slavers to hunt elsewhere or hire others to do it. There seems to be an increasing amount of this happening along the coasts of the southern countries and there's little left there to enforce the law. It's an unsafe area and there are some reports of it starting to spread. The attack on Cali and Aran's village in our own country is unheard of. That's why we decided to head north and meet up with you rather than journeying near the coast. We thought we'd avoid further trouble and possibly get some idea of troop movement around the Ildran borders."

"You'll see what it's like," Merren said, "when we cross back into Sancir tomorrow. On the way up we've seen a lot of military movement and it's kept the roads clear of trouble. But getting into Ildra wasn't easy and we should be prepared for tomorrow; leaving may be complicated."

Carrick nodded. "A few more weeks and I don't think anyone will be moving across Ildra's borders."

"There seems to have been an increase in the momentum of change," Kellim noted. "There is a build-up of strength across Ildra and a more visible troop profile. There is now a fort on the Ildran's side of the old spice trail and a considerable upgrade to the newly opened gate on the Amarian side. I think you are right Carrick. Our exit may be timely."

Merren yawned despite herself. "I think we'll all breathe a sigh of relief once we cross into Sancir and we can make some shortcuts. It's been a long journey and I'll be glad to get Cali and Aran to Naddier."

Merren's last sentence seemed to trigger a decision in Kellim's mind. "There is something else I must tell you," Kellim began rather mysteriously. The others looked at him. "The Faithful found me."

"What!" all three echoed.

"As in the Panids' Children?" Bryn asked, sitting forward in his chair. "None of them have shown their faces for at least eighty years. What did it want?"

"It was aware of Cali. Yes, Cali," Kellim repeated himself in answer to the questioning faces. "It had 'sensed' her and seems to be under the impression that she is special in some way to its kind."

"Did it say more? In what way special?" Carrick was slightly perplexed.

"It knew little and left to search for The Beholder to learn more." Kellim pulled on his beard thoughtfully. "The Faithful's type were designed to multi-task. Amongst their many abilities, we attempted to weave in something of the Seer's discipline. Though this rarely worked. Only a few developed skills and so they had some insight into matters beyond the immediate. The Faithful was particularly skilled in this area, as I recall, and I have learnt to trust its intuition."

"You make them sound like objects," Bryn commented, slightly surprised by Kellim's description. The old man rarely talked about the Children and when pressed often changed the subject.

Kellim cleared his throat, but there was a long pause before he finally replied. "To our shame, that's how we viewed them. Tools to accomplish a task; tasks considered unacceptable for a Panid. Even with the Meta, it gradually became clear that these self-sustaining form fields were more than just automata. It became increasingly evident in the Children. Those that survived long enough showed the ability to think for themselves and eventually developed emotions. It was at this point that some of our numbers became uncomfortable with their use and objected."

"You mentioned that some time ago. Eth, Etefu, Tebeb and you fought to prevent their continued creation," Bryn said.

Kellim was becoming uncomfortable with the conversation and chose to look at the dying embers of the fire, rather than the searching faces of his friends. His next words were voiced as an admission of guilt. "I was not so quick as the others. During the Great War, I fought in many battles and had seen the almost endless loss of life. The fighting was brutal and took a terrible toll on all forced to endure it. The war had to be brought to an end and I saw the Children's continued use as a way to achieve that and so closed my mind to what I knew to be true." Kellim paused again, clearly distracted by memories. "It was only after I'd worked alongside a small group of the Panids' Children that I saw how they'd developed and what they'd become. I finally accepted the truth and aligned myself with Tebeb and the others. As a result, we were increasingly excluded from decisions and given tasks, which in retrospect, kept us out of the way during the final months of the war. The Panids planned much in that time and made many decisions we were not a party to..." For a moment it seemed like he might say more. "Hmm, perhaps I've said enough. Another time maybe." Kellim looked up, offering an apologetic smile for his reluctance to continue.

"We don't judge you," Carrick offered, hoping to ease the older man's discomfort.

"Not in the least," Merren said as she gently squeezed Kellim's hand. "Talking about the Panids' Children as a current issue as opposed to a historical fact is a new and unfamiliar experience for us. And here we are. All this time nothing and now two of them pop up in a conversation. Could things possibly become more interesting, or should I say complicated?"

Carrick sympathised. "I think the latter. We'd better keep a close eye on Cali," he said more seriously. "I'm not happy about the Children's interest in her. I was beginning to think we should find an easier way across the border, but the season draws on and we're going to get less daylight. I think the quicker we get to Mel Akor and catch a transport to Naddier the better."

"Indeed, it's a risk crossing here, but it is direct. I feel a certain amount of unease and I think, Aran will also need watching," Kellim added thoughtfully.

"Why's that?" Carrick put down his drink.

"As much as I dislike complicating things further. I've detected traits in the boy I've not seen since the time of the Panids."

"Even this early on," Carrick's eyebrows lifted.

"There is great potential there. Something more than an Adept," Kellim confirmed, "but he'll need the correct training if he's to reach his potential safely."

"If that's the case," Carrick began, "I want you to spend as much time with him as you can. We may need to be unconventional in our approach to training these two. If only for their safety."

Chapter 6

They set off early the next morning to leave through Kagash's west gate. Officials, forcibly backed up by soldiers were monitoring the traffic in and out of Ildra. The once free flow of trade that kept the market town alive was being choked. As the queues lengthened tempers frayed and arguments broke out as farmers clashed with soldiers. The group took an opening to leave as one such disagreement flashed into a brawl. The violence acted like a whirlpool, dragging others into its core and the group had to push their way through as panic spread and the gate was left unattended. Hidden amongst the surge of people they left Ildra, entering a neutral area clogged with traffic. At the Sancir border, they presented their papers to the soldiers now stationed there. Even with Kellim's subtle intervention, this once-easy procedure took far longer. Once through the checkpoint, they passed a large military camp. Trees were being felled and a makeshift fort was being erected. The size and extent of the camp made it all too clear that change had arrived and the peace, so long taken for granted, was now very much under threat.

Once clear of the border, and given time to leave the stress of the crossing behind, Cali had noted how obvious it was that they'd entered another country. Before, the changes had been gradual; changes in climate, landscape, buildings and people evolved as one region of Ildra overlapped and then separated from another. Here the change was more immediate and all because of one obvious thing. Travel in the north of Ildra generally relied on a network of dirt tracks, here in Sancir they built roads. Excellent roads of stone that made progress easier and faster. Over the next few days, they made good time and put a lot of distance between themselves and the border. The countryside had changed rapidly from the flat plains of Ildra to the rolling wooded hills and fields they now travelled through. The movement of troops and regular patrols dwindled. General traffic thinned out gradually and they passed several carts belonging to refugees fleeing Ildra before the border shut. Quill trees had long since given way to gnarlwoods and copper beams. Sancir's geography was sufficiently different to alter the climate in a relatively short distance, so it was mild and nothing like the heat of central Ildra or even the north where Kagash was located. It was also much wetter throughout the year, which added to the more abrupt change in vegetation. Cali noted the effect this had on the people; the way they dressed and on their architecture. Sloping roofs instead of flat ones shrugged off the rain and stonewalls were favoured over red brick. The men's clothing changed to shirts and trousers and the women's to longer fuller skirts; clothing similar to the styles favoured in seasonal countries like Hallorn.

"The roads are still fairly busy," Cali said. "Do you think we'll have any more trouble with Ildran patrols or slavers?"

"We won't meet any Ildran patrols," Merren reassured. "And as for slavers, we're too far inland," Merren said this and then wondered if the statement still held any truth.

"Would we have any warning if we did?" Cali asked.

"Well, Carrick, Kellim and I are keeping a bit of a look out?"

"In what way?"

"If you're focused you can pick up on people's intentions."

"Can you actually read people's minds?"

"Not really and I'm not sure I'd want to," Merren admitted. "But you can sense emotions and glimpse images, which can be helpful. But it takes a lot of focus."

"I think I've been doing that, without realising it," Cali admitted.

"What do you get when you try it?"

"I don't so much try, as it just seems to happen. I get nothing much beyond emotions. Some people seem to give off strong feelings, some weak and a few that do something a bit strange."

"Let me guess, a kind of pushback."

"Yes, exactly. It felt oddly embarrassing, a bit like being caught peering in through somebody's window and them slamming the shutters."

Merren smiled. "That's a good analogy. Those are the ones with latent talent. They aren't strong enough to warrant development. They mainly don't know they have it, but their minds subconsciously attempt to defend themselves."

"Does everyone have talent?" Cali asked. It was a change to have someone happy to answer her questions. Orla had always been more guarded and usually too busy.

"I don't think so," Merren frowned slightly. "Most people have abilities of one kind or another. The ability to run fast, see well, throw and catch or learn a new skill quickly. Our kind of talent is just one amongst many. Some have a little and don't know it. A few have enough to make a living from it but are largely untrained, and then some people can focus their will to a far greater extent and draw deeply on the field."

"Does everyone with real talent get discovered? You know for training and everything?"

"Probably not. It's a big continent and not everyone has access to a village healer or a local practitioner. Because of Orla you were both identified at an early age and received some guidance to help you understand your abilities. She kept us in touch with your development until we thought you were ready for Naddier."

"I remember you visiting from quite early on. Orla said we should think of ourselves favoured by fortune. But wouldn't explain what she meant by that."

"There are two schools or academies in Naddier. One for Talents of moderate ability and one for Talents of very high ability, we call them Adepts. They can focus their will further than any Talent and so draw more from the field. Carrick and I are Adepts and you and Aran show promise in that direction. The first for a long time to enter into our disciplines," Merren smiled. "It's an interesting coincidence that you're brother and sister too."

"I hadn't really thought about that." Cali considered it briefly, but then saw Merren's expression change; she instinctively followed her eyes to a mounted figure.

"Is everything ok?" she asked.

There was a pause. Merren looked back over to Carrick and then Bryn, who signalled he'd seen him too.

"Sorry, Cali. It was an UruIldran. Interesting you brought the subject up just before we saw him. I sensed his anticipation, which made me look for a face."

"I didn't even notice," Cali admitted, looking back over. Bryn was still watching him. "What do you think he's doing?"

"Possibly after the Ildran refugees, we passed, or rather someone of importance amongst them. Many need to escape Segat for one reason or another. Segat's family along with all the others in Ildra, who had a claim on the throne, were in competition with each other for the better part of thirty years. Over that time the number of claimants has shrunk. Segat assumed the throne five years ago and now only one other survives."

"Would he make a better king?" Cali asked.

"Possibly, his family were well respected. Segat will be desperate to find him and be rid."

"Do you think they might have been amongst the refugees we saw? The ones you think that UruIldran was after?"

"No, I think they'll still be in Ildra. Prince Immar is too well recognised to attempt such a busy border crossing."

Cali had one last look back. The mounted figure was gone and Bryn was looking forwards again. "You said disciplines. I mean, you mentioned disciplines what are they?"

"Didn't Orla tell you any of this?" Merren asked.

Cali shook her head. "No, should she have?"

Merren laughed, not surprised by Orla's lack of progress on that front. "We agreed she would the last time we visited."

"Orla was very busy that month. Lots of babies being born. But then she's always busy."

"Orla is an interesting character. I've a lot of respect for her."

"Why do you say that?"

"Did she tell you where she came from?"

"Not at all. We just assumed she'd always lived in Rel."

"Orla came from the North," Merren said.

"As in Kemarid and Agant, that North?" Cali was surprised.

"Yes. When we talk about Koa, we're only really talking about the southern, western and central parts of the continent. Lont, Agant, Coth and Kemarid form the north of Koa but we talk about those countries as something separate. Chances are they have a different collective name for their lands, but no one knows what that is. And as for Orla, hers is quite a tale. Not one she spoke of often, which explains why you didn't know. Talent of our kind is a corporal crime in the North, punishable by death. She'd have been used to keeping her talent under the lid. I imagine it's not a habit you can break easily and the threats she faced would have been very real. It must be difficult to unlearn habits that kept you alive. You were fortunate in that she supported you quietly, didn't try to shape you, or drum information into your heads."

"All this time and we didn't know. I'm glad you told me. We just looked at our lives with her, in one set way."

"The way she told you. You weren't to know. You asked me about the disciplines. Do you still want to know?"

Cali nodded. "Absolutely."

"It's nothing complicated. There were ten original books in the time of Mennem. Those books are now lost to us. The ten books focused on a specific discipline and its use of the field. Talents now study one of those disciplines. The Discipline of Summoners, the Discipline of Shapers, Speakers, Healers, Conveyors and so on. Each can access and use the field, the ambient energy we all draw on, differently."

"You're a Convoker, aren't you?" Cali asked.

"Yes, and you probably will be. That's where we think your Talent lies. But it's not nailed with iron. Only time and you will bear that out."

Cali tried out the title in her head, it sounded unwieldy.

"Carrick heads the Discipline of Conjoiners, though sometimes they get named double-handers and other things, nicknames. Keeps their feet on the ground."

Cali looked puzzled. "Double-handers?"

"There aren't many of them, as they have some ability in all ten disciplines, one for each finger, so double-handers, but he's lazy and tends to stick with the abilities of the discipline I head. They're all just names. It doesn't matter how you access the field, just that you use it with understanding, the best of intentions and a healthy amount of respect for others."

"Aren't some of the other disciplines rare, I mean not many people have those talents?"

"That's right, there are very few Summoners in comparison and currently I know of three other Adept Chanters and I think four Adept Speakers in the whole of Koa. There hasn't been a true Seer since the very first Panids. Even the Conjoiners have no real ability in that discipline. I think the best Carrick's managed on that front is guessing who comes in through the door first."

"But there's still a Discipline of Seers?"

"There is, but it's research only. A few people are involved, all the time hoping a Seer will be born but I wouldn't place such a burden on anyone."

The following day the road passed by a greater concentration of fields and farmsteads and then began to climb gently back into open woodland. Some of the precisely laid curb stones had been lifted by gnarlwood roots, red ferns and other shrubs softening the edges. Occasionally wild fruit bushes offered the chance for a sweet snack. Kellim managed to spot these well before everyone else and at one point had them all picking the dark fruit. The road continued to climb and the woodland became thicker. The wind had picked up slightly, stirring the leaves and branches, there was a chill to it.

"I've got used to the wind always being warm," Cali noted. "This one feels more like the winds we got at Rel. It sounds like a distant waterfall."

"The sound of rustling leaves does sound like that," Merren agreed, combing a hand through unruly hair.

"That sound makes me think of a ruin near where we lived."

"Why's that?" Merren asked.

Cali pursed her lips as if it would help pull up the memory. "The tower was up on a hill just outside our village, there was always a breeze off the sea it seemed. We went up there to play when we were young and I liked to sit up there and watch the sun rise or set, whenever I could."

"It sounds nice."

"It was. Trees had grown up around it and whenever I hear that sound it makes me think of the tower. I think it was very old. It had a sense of age."

"It sounds like a watch tower. A lot were built during the Great War. I wonder how many more are still around slowly slipping back into the landscape."

"It seems a bit of a shame really," Cali said.

"I think most people alive after the Great War wanted to distance themselves from anything to do with it, and as time passed its relics were either torn down and reused or simply forgotten."

They rode for a while, Cali listening to the wind and watching the rope trees ripple. "There weren't always disciplines, as in groups, were there?" Cali said, a question from the previous day still left unanswered.

"That's right, the disciplines came about as a necessity after the Great War. Before The Field's Cap, the Panids could draw on the field and use the full range of disciplines. They had particular strengths but were able to use all of the disciplines because of the abundance of the field. And like us, the Panids' ability to focus their minds determined how powerful they were."

"I can't imagine how different it must have been then," Cali said wistfully.

"Very," Merren agreed. "When The Field's Cap was put in place and the field became restricted. Talents found they could only access it, to any useful degree, through one particular discipline. So, schools for each of the disciplines were formed to focus on developing them independently. They didn't have to start afresh, but a lot of the rules had to be rewritten and new limitations understood because of the lack of field energy. It took a long time for them to get to grips with what they could and couldn't do, along with the rest of the continent. It would've been a time of considerable change for everyone. Not a good time. You should ask Kellim about it. You might have more fortune getting him to talk about the past. There's a lot I'd like answers to."

"You said Talents are very limited by The Field's Cap. Is it the same for the remaining Panids?"

Merren laughed. "That's one question, I've tried no end to get an answer to. Kellim and the remaining Panids are a bit of an enigma."

"How many Panids are left? What happened to the others?"

"There are four left, though one of them hasn't been seen for decades. The others were either killed during the Great War or sacrificed themselves to create The Field's Cap."

"Sacrificed!"

"It required a huge amount of potential to set it in place. At least that's what we think. Very little is known about it and even Kellim doesn't seem clear about the construction of The Field's Cap, how it worked, or what it was."

"Kellim doesn't know!" Cali said, surprised by the information.

"He doesn't, none of the four remaining Panids were told."

As the day wore on Bryn began looking for suitable places to sct a camp. That seemed to be one of his roles in the group. They'd seen other travellers setting up their camps and before it was too dark Bryn found a spot just off the road. Everyone fell into a routine, even Aran and Cali had their jobs and before long the mounts had been seen to, firewood collected, shelters and bedding set out and the fire lit.

"My turn this evening," Kellim said and headed off into the woods to hunt.

The light had just reached a point where it was too dark to read and Aran's legs had gotten tired of sitting, so he closed his book and went to stretch his legs. Jai nodded as he left.

"Don't stray too far," there aren't any predators left in this part of Sancir, but there are plenty of holes. Don't fall down one."

Aran promised to keep his eyes open and headed off in roughly the direction Kellim had left earlier. He wondered if he would meet him coming back and walked on, picking his way through red fern and huge gnarlwoods, the smell of loam filling his lungs. There were noises in the undergrowth that said the night shift of animals was beginning its time in the forest and that his rather noisy presence was an inconvenience.

He took his time and ambled on, but eventually decided he'd gone far enough and there was no sign of Kellim. With the light dimming, he decided to turn back until his eyes caught a view that had been hidden by branches. It looked like a wall. A substantial one, or at least, the remains of one. He knew there were ruins dotted everywhere across Koa. Most of them left over from the Great War and some from earlier still. He carefully ventured over and climbed a section of the wall for a better view. Throughout this part of the woods, he could see the remains of what must have been a town. Stone buildings in various states of decay, the woodland having grown up, around and through them. What had this place been? He caught himself asking. A busy town perhaps, not too far from the road. Where had all the people gone? A noise behind him made him jump and he nearly fell off the wall as he turned.

"Sorry about that," Kellim said. "I seem to be in the habit of surprising people and..., well let's just leave it at people." He held up his catch. Two fat birds of some description hung from his hands.

Aran was about to ask him what they were when Kellim turned back to the ruins. It was his turn to be surprised and without a word, he crouched and beckoned Aran to do the same. Leaving the birds, Kellim crawled silently towards the wall and gestured for Aran to follow after holding a finger to his lips. Aran did as he was told. Keeping low behind the wall, Kellim was intent on something and after a while, he pointed to a patch of undergrowth at the edge of the ruins. He held his finger to his lips again and Aran felt his use of the field. It was some time again before a creature stepped cautiously out from behind a large copper beam tree. Aran's breath caught in his throat and he clamped his hand over his mouth to stifle the gasp. The creature faltered, looking about and sniffing the air. It was some time again before it stepped clear of the tree, light from the twin moons catching its snout. It raked at the ground with huge, clawed hands and lifted something to its mouth.

Aran had never seen anything like it before. In a vague way, it had the build of a person. It had stepped into the light on two legs but for now, stood on all fours. Its arms being longer, because of the huge hands, meant it could probably move on two or four limbs. Its skin was mottled in greens and browns, its eyes dark and constantly searching. The snout was blunt and armed with tusks. Aran looked at Kellim. The old man mouthed Panids' Child back to him. So many questions and yet Aran could do nothing other than stare in wonder.

The creature stood motionless; its vision fixed on a more distant point than the trees in front of it. Caught up in the moment, Aran only vaguely noted the direction matched that of their camp. The Child sniffed the air again and took a silent but cautious step in that direction. Perhaps it would have taken another, but something seemed to prevent it, almost as if a silent voice had stayed further progress. Then the creature's head moved sharply to stare directly at them. Aran quickly looked at Kellim, the old man was surprised. For what seemed like an age the Child hovered in indecision. Aran could only guess but it seemed to him the creature recognised Kellim and would have come closer, but something prevented it. The something, a silent inner voice from the past perhaps, won out and with silent grace, unexpected from its ungainly appearance, the Child turned and quickly disappeared back into the night and the deep woods.

Aran turned back to Kellim again. "That really was a Panids' Child," he whispered.

"Indeed, it was. It was searching," Kellim added thoughtfully. "It sensed us. I thought my efforts to hide our presence adequate, but I was mistaken." Kellim looked puzzled and surprised in equal measure and then, noting Aran's intent gaze, lightened his expression. "Not to worry," he dismissed. "I can only begin to wonder how it got this far south. There are few left, and they keep themselves to the quietest and remotest places of Koa. Away from people and the trouble we bring."

Aran was about to ask his questions but Kellim was already moving back to his birds. "Come on, these won't pluck and cook themselves and by now Jai will be beyond hungry."

He grabbed the birds and marched off in the direction of their camp, Aran stumbling in the dark to follow him and keep his feet on the track Kellim's seemed to have no problem finding.

The old Panid paused only to say. "Keep this to yourself for now."

Kellim winked at him but even in the shadows of the night, Aran could see there was an amount of concern on the Panid's face.

Aran was lost in his thoughts for most of the next day. The image of the Panids' Child was in his mind but the events of the night before now felt like a dream. If Kellim was still troubled by the meeting he showed no signs of it and no one else had mentioned it, so Aran assumed Kellim was still keeping their find a secret.

Carrick called them all to a halt at the top of the hill. The view stretched across a small valley of fields and woodland to the hills on the other side. Many smallholdings were visible and the road could be seen winding its way past them before beginning a zigzag ascent of the other side.

"This is the start of them," Kellim said, he could hear Jai muttering to himself already. "We could save ourselves several days' travel."

Carrick lowered his navigation lens. "The clearing at the road's side is still there and the traffic's not too bad. If we judge it right, there shouldn't be any problems." He collapsed the brass object with a satisfying click and turned. "Kellim, would you take Lewan, Bryn and Jai and provide us with a marker? Merren and I'll bring Cali, Aran and the mounts. We can swap for the next couple and share the work."

Cali edged her mount over to Aran. "Have they said anything to you about how this is done?"

"I thought you'd have asked already," Aran said. "Didn't Kellim do it when you were in Ildra?"

"Several times, but I never got the chance to ask, it was usually to avoid trouble."

"Do you remember Orla talking about being able to put yourself in more than one place and then decide which one you wanted to be at," he gestured. "To move yourself from one place to another, so long as you could see where you wanted to be or knew where a marker had been placed?"

"I remember her saying you had to be careful," she replied. "You link points or something."

"That's it," Aran nodded. "Kellim said you link points and kind of slip from one place to the other. He also said that this is the way all Talents used to get around before The Field's Cap. Apparently, there was also a network of things called transport platforms."

"Transport platforms?"

"A raised stone area, type of thing. There were always two, one for arriving and one for leaving."

"Type of thing? Kellim used those words, they don't sound very technical."

"I can't remember everything he said. Can you remember everything Merren's told you? The Field thingy was your last one."

"Okay, okay," Cali held up her hands. "I won't interrupt. Look I'm all ears." She cocked her head and affected a look of intense interest.

Aran looked at her. "As I was saying…"

"Still listening."

"Are you sure we're related?"

"I've wondered that loads of times. You were talking about the transport platforms."

"I was," he shook his head. "It was an unbroken rule that the arrival platform was always kept clear, so it was safe for Talents to transport to. And if you stood on the leaving one you sort of communicated with where you wanted to be. If it was a long way, you did it in stages, transporting from one platform to another."

"I suppose they can't do that anymore," Cali mused.

"I don't think so; The Field's Cap prevents it."

"Not enough energy to go any great distance."

"Aran, Cali," Carrick called over to them. "You should watch this."

They headed over and Carrick explained as Kellim began the process. They could feel the subtle alterations in his concentration and the effect it was having. Kellim made it look easy as, with practised skill, he focused his will, drew on the field and selected the point he wanted. The four men disappeared, leaving a dull feeling in the air and almost instantaneously reappeared on the other side of the valley. Just visible in the distance, Lewan signalled and Cali and Aran waved back.

"He made that look so easy," Aran said in admiration.

"He's had a good bit of practise," Merren said as she guided the mounts over to where she wanted them. "Remind me to tell you about the first time we tried it."

With that, she focused her will. Cali and Aran could sense the dull roar in their heads and feel the quality of the air change around them again.

"See you on the other side," Merren said and was gone along with their mounts.

They could both pick out the change in air pressure this time, caused by the larger movement of animal flesh.

"Are you ready?" Carrick asked. "Stand close, I'd rather we didn't collide with our mounts over there."

Cali and Aran did as they were asked and before they knew it found themselves on the other side of the valley.

"Still in one piece," Jai greeted.

It proved a short ride to the other side of the hill where they found themselves looking across another valley, very similar to the last. After a brief pause, while they located the distant road, they prepared for the next crossing. A short time later they were on the other side of the second valley, having waited for a set of five carts to reach the top and crest the hill. Cali had noticed that any travellers who witnessed their actions were only reasonably interested and stopped briefly to see what she assumed must, in these parts anyway, be a reasonably common site. They transported two more times until a short ride brought them to the lip of a much larger valley.

"We've been fortunate with the weather," Merren was saying. "It's been a clear day. Any haze and we wouldn't have been able to see safely across," she handed Carrick's navigation lens back to him. "As it is, this one's going to be a bit of a stretch."

"We'll have to double up. How about you Kellim?" Carrick asked.

"I should be able to manage this along with the mounts."

"They've done well," Bryn said patting one on the neck.

"Alright," Carrick rubbed his hand, "Merren and I will take Bryn and Lewan. We'll have a quick rest and then the three of us can pull Jai, Cali and Aran across."

The transports went well and after Kellim, Merren and Carrick left with Bryn and Lewan. Jai, Cali and Aran sat down to wait. The traffic had thinned as the afternoon wore on and now the road was quiet. One cart rattled past, loaded with barrels for one of the local inns.

Jai looked at his timepiece. "Right, it's time. They should be ready and looking for us."

"I'll do it," Aran offered and collecting the navigation lens, went to look across the valley. He skimmed the patchwork of fields and then followed the road to the point where he expected to see the others standing waiting.

"Jai," he called back.

Jai came over to join him. "Are they ready?"

"I can't see them. I might be looking in the wrong place." Aran handed him the lens.

"There's the outcrop," Jai puzzled. "No sign of the mounts either." He searched the area again, before lowering it and then re-checked his timepiece.

"I was looking in the right place, wasn't I?" Aran asked.

"Yep, they aren't there," Jai scanned the hillside one last time.

Cali came over "Can you see them?"

"No. Something's not right," Jai's brow furrowed. He thought for a moment and then something caught the edges of his hearing. He turned back to the way they'd come, looking at the denser woodland. Then to the road ahead, it was clear and the woods there were too open to hide anything. His hand had moved to his sword. "Get onto the road," he said calmly. His eyes went back to the denser woodland behind them. "Start walking. No questions. There's a cart some way ahead. See if you can catch up with it."

He'd heard a bow creak, there was no mistaking it. Without altering his gaze, he slowly drew his sword and moved to block the way. The woods had fallen silent, there was definitely someone out there.

Cali and Aran had begun walking, glancing back over to check on Jai. His stance had altered. Aran didn't know much about swordsmen, but he could tell when a man was preparing to fight. He ushered his sister on and started checking the woods to either side.

There was a sudden movement in the bushes and an arrow caught Jai's side as it tore past. Another ripped through the air as he leapt for cover. There was a log crack and a great movement of branches. Then the greenery erupted as a huge two-legged creature erupted from the undergrowth. It was clothed and dressed in leather armour; the only things familiar to Jai's eyes. He was stunned, vital seconds passed as his brain struggled to make sense of just what was lumbering towards him. It threw its bow aside and drew a massive sword. Jai recovered himself in time to block the blow. The impact jarred his arm painfully. He was able to avoid the next blow. He parried several more. Each was heavy and brutal, straining his back and shoulder muscles. The creature was at least half his height again and massively built. With the quickest of glances, Jai checked Cali and Aran were clear and only just managed to avoid the next strike. It bit deeply into the tree beside him. Jai took the opportunity and swung. The blade found flesh and the creature bellowed in pain. He made ready to swing again, but the creature freed its sword and brought it humming round in a wide arc. Jai leapt back from the point. The thing swiftly brought its sword back to cut down. Jai parried the action, spun and brought his sword round and down with all the momentum he could. He hoped to knock the weapon out of his opponent's hand. It didn't work. Instead, Jai's sword was lifted into the air and he was thrown back. He landed well enough to thrust low through its defences. The creature roared and abandoned caution. It swung its sword down onto Jai's and made to grab at him. He stumbled back and rolled. His sword spun out of his hand and he landed on the road. Winded, he struggled to right himself before the creature got to him. He had just enough time to draw a knife, but not enough to throw it. The creature focused its will and sent Jai spinning into a tree. There was a crack and he dropped to the floor.

Satisfied the man was no longer a threat The First of the Three touched its side with a grimace and looked at the blood on its hand. Discarding its sword in disgust, it paused in concentration and then headed down the road.

"Can you see Jai?" Aran gasped as they ran. Where was the cart? He looked ahead, hoping somehow that Carrick or Merren would appear round the next bend.

"There's no sign of ... It's that thing!" Cali suddenly shouted in alarm. "It's coming!"

Aran glanced back, fear gripped his stomach, it was after them. "We can't outrun it!"

"The woods, into the woods," Cali struggled for breath. "That might slow it down."

They left the road and headed into the trees; both hoping they would make it harder for the much larger creature to follow them. But red ferns, tangle bush and uneven ground threatened to trip them with every frantic stride.

They leapt and ran with the sound of the creature crashing its way behind them. Panic threatened to overtake them as they struggled on. They couldn't look back; one wrong foot and it would be on top of them. The crashing was getting closer and they could hear its heavy breath. Both felt it focus but didn't have time to react. The tree directly to their left exploded, throwing them sideways and off their feet. They struggled to get up. Aran called out as the creature grabbed hold of his ankle and lifted him clean off the ground. His arms flailed in the air as he tried to reach for something, anything he could use as a weapon. Cali grabbed a branch and swung frantically, but with little effect. Aran was yelling at her to run. The creature knocked him unconscious, cast him aside and turned back to Cali. She swung again, knocking its hand aside. Then, as if from out of the air, Jai was on its shoulders. With a cry of rage, he drove his knife deep into the creature's neck. It screamed, reaching back to knock him clear. Jai struck again and again as the creature flailed about, finally grabbing hold of him. Jai stabbed at the arm, but the creature didn't let go and dragged him over its head. He thrashed madly trying to break free. It grabbed at his knife arm, hanging him in the air, his legs flailing. Cali swung at its leg snapping the branch.

"Run!" Jai yelled as the creature's hold tightened. He kicked out, but it swatted his foot aside and took hold of him with both hands. It shook him savagely and Cali reacted. There was a great rush of unfocused energy. Trees erupted and the creature was knocked off its feet. Jai hit the ground as Cali stumbled forwards, her head suddenly filled with excited whispering. The creature recovered quickly as Cali struggled to focus again. This time it deflected the weak blow and retaliated, knocking her out.

The First of the Three straightened, looking about it. As the whispering retreated, satisfaction spread on its heavy features, this was her; it had The Purpose. Pressing a hand to its wounds it grimaced painfully and concentrated. The blood stopped flowing and darkened. It kicked Jai out of the way angrily and walked over to pick Cali up, throwing her over its shoulder with a grunt of discomfort. Turning, The First of the Three, headed back to the road now some distance away. The crack of twigs under its feet provided the only noise in the otherwise silent woods. On reaching the road it looked up to the other side of the valley searching for signs of its brothers. It was about to take a step when the air behind it exploded. It stumbled, nearly dropping Cali. Small branches and other debris were blown aside as Merren appeared. She faced the Panids' Child, a tight grip on her fear.

"Put her down," she compelled.

The First of the Three dwarfed her, its voice was like a land slide. "That has no effect. A Panid would have known this. Step aside minor Talent. The whispering directs me to The Purpose only."

Merren had no answer and instead, she took a risk that could leave her vulnerable. Cali disappeared. The creature grasped clumsily at air and in frustration released energy. Merren struggled to redirect it. Stone paving shattered to her left. They both refocused. The field responded and they pushed. The air cracked as the blows met. Merren braced herself against the road. The First of the Three shouldered the force but kept its footing. Wills locked and both pushed harder. The air between them began to distort and bend.

Aran came to, looking for Cali, he was drawn to the road. Keeping low he'd scrambled to a point behind Merren and almost crawled over his unconscious sister. He tried to rouse her, cupping his hand over her mouth when she came to. Her sudden panic faded when she saw him. He took his hand away, gesturing for her to look. The air between Merren and the creature now warped and bulged, there was no sign of the others. Cali and Aran had no choice but to stay hidden.

The First of the Three was straining forward, its heavy features contorted in concentration. Merren stood, fists clenched, the distortion whipping leaves and branches into a swirling cloud. It became pronounced and unstable as the two focused more and more energy at each other. Merren sensed the field was reaching its limit. Soon it would fade and she would be left defenceless. Alarm forced her to act. The distortion reached a wild peak. Merren dug deep. The distortion lurched and wheeled out at The First of the Three. Bones and road slabs cracked under the blow. The creature fell. The maelstrom dissipated and Merren was left on unsteady legs. When the creature failed to stir, she flopped to the ground, exhausted. The woods had become silent and leaves fluttered back to the ground. She caught her breath, unable to take her eyes off the body.

Cali and Aran struggled to take in what they'd seen and it was a while before either moved. They helped each other up in a lingering silence that made the whole thing seem unreal. Neither could speak, even as they finally got their legs working and made their way to Merren.

"Are you hurt?" Aran asked, anxiously glancing at the fallen body of the creature.

Cali had taken a cautious step towards it. "Is it dead?"

"I'll be fine, just a bit shaky." Merren got to her feet and stepped forward unsteadily to draw Cali away from the body. "It's not getting up again."

"What is it?" Cali asked, unable to take her eyes off the huge creature.

"One of a group, they named themselves The Three." Merren stopped suddenly. "Where's Jai? Wasn't he with you?"

Realisation suddenly struck them and without speaking Aran raced into the woods. Cali clutched at Merren's arm and led her after him. "He tried to stop it, but then it came down here after us. It nearly had us when Jai sprang out of nowhere. He leapt on its back. It was terrible. Jai was trying to keep it away, but it shook him hard and then I reacted and I can't remember what happened. I must have…"

"Here! He's here!" Aran was shouting, relief in his voice. "He's ok." They quickened their pace as much as Merren was able and arrived to find Aran pulling Jai's arm across his shoulder and heaving him up off the floor. He was covered in cuts and dirt. A gash had bled a large stain into his shirt.

"I'm sorry, I couldn't… it was too…"

"They're fine." Merren stopped him. "You're hurt. Aran help him to that log. Let me have a look at the damage."

There was a noise on the road behind and for one dreadful moment, they all thought the same thing. Instead, Bryn's booming voice echoed urgently through the woods. He came crashing across to them, sword in hand. He was flecked with blood and his face was ruddy from exertion.

"You took some finding," he breathed heavily as he reached them, and then sheathed his sword. "Kellim and Lewan can't be far behind me." Cali smiled bravely and Bryn instinctively hugged her before reaching out to Merren.

"Carrick's safe, he's trying to find our mounts," he said as he held her.

She hugged him tightly. The sudden relief made it hard to speak, Merren wanted to say more but couldn't trust her voice.

Breaking the awkward moment Bryn turned to Aran. "Are you alright, no injuries?"

"I'm fine, but I think Jai..." he turned to where the man had been sitting.

Jai had slumped onto the ground. Bryn rushed over, propped him up and checked for a pulse. "Unconscious," he said with evident relief.

Once reunited Kellim had attended to injuries while Merren and Carrick kept a constant check on the area. They'd all been brought up short by the attack. Kellim quietly blamed his complacency, feeling he'd put them all in danger. The Panids' Child he and Aran had seen was a smaller and timid creature. He had not expected to see any more Children, let alone be attacked by them. They were all badly shaken and what should have been an easier journey through Sancir had now taken a very different path.

"I believe you'll live," Kellim said to Jai after a final check on the work he'd done. "The rib bones are mended, but the area will feel tender for a while yet. Try not to stretch the stitches." He fixed him with his eyes. "That means no risks."

Jai nodded, trying to avoid the piercing stare. "I promise," he relented when Kellim didn't look away.

Kellim looked at him a while longer, making sure the message had taken hold and then started to clean his things.

Jai reached for his shirt. "Look at that," he complained, holding up the tattered cloth, "That was my favourite shirt."

"You have more I assume?"

"Yeh, the one I wear when I'm not wearing this one." He went to get up and then quickly sat down again. "Did that a bit too fast."

"Don't be in such a hurry," Kellim warned. "You've had a good crack on the head."

"May have knocked some sense in," Bryn said coming over and sitting down. He picked at some grass awkwardly before saying, "Sorry we couldn't get to you quicker."

Jai sat forward with a wince. "I think you had other things to think about."

"Merren sensed them," Bryn explained. "The instant we came out of transport. We had just enough time to get into the woods, hoping they'd carry on and not see us. They'd been hiding on the other side of the hill waiting for us to pass. Carrick thinks they'd picked up on our transporting and were expecting us to show up soon after. When we didn't, they came looking for us. They had four mercenaries with them. When one of The Three transported himself away, we feared he might stumble across you. Then the others started looking on our side, which startled the mounts. They saw us and we had no choice but to fight. It was some time before Merren could get to you."

"Did you manage to find out anything?" Jai asked.

"Nothing. Only one of The Three escaped."

"A dangerous move, unless he had a marker placed somewhere," Kellim added absently. "They weren't interested in us," he looked up from what he was doing. "The First of the Three left quickly to find you."

"He wasn't interested in me," Jai said and then lowered his voice. "The second it came out of the woods it was looking for Aran and Cali. I was just in the way."

Kellim nodded, keeping his voice low. "Then they were after Cali. This is more than just the simple interest The Faithful hinted at."

"You think there is something in what it told you?" Bryn asked.

"It appears so," Kellim concluded and got up to return the medical pack to his saddle. He passed Merren and Lewan, not wishing to disturb their conversation with Aran and Cali. The two had been badly shaken, but now seemed calm and ready to move on. Kellim stowed his medical bag and went to stand beside Carrick, he waited for the man to open his eyes, not wanting to disrupt his concentration.

Carrick finally looked up. "There's nothing hiding out there. I've swept it again and again. Did you say The Faithful would find you?"

"Yes, and with some badly needed answers, I hope."

"The sooner the better." At that, Carrick got up. "We aren't ready for this Kellim," he kept his voice low. "If this is a taste of things to come, we're going to be hard-pressed."

Kellim nodded. "I'm afraid a hundred years of peace is no preparation for what may be ahead of us. But you and Merren are fast learners," Kellim tried to reassure him. "You'll both meet the challenges to come with your usual fortitude." He patted him on the shoulder.

"Let's hope so."

"Ready to move on?"

Carrick checked the sky. "We don't have much of a choice if we want to make Leet before dusk."

Kellim brightened his expression. "We'll extend our stay. It will be a safe place to gather ourselves before continuing and, if I remember correctly, they make excellent pies."

Chapter 7

The Leet was an old travellers' inn, hundreds of years old and off the main highway. It was quieter but had a reputation for good food and so Kellim knew it well. While the others sorted their rooms, Aran and Cali helped Kellim stable the mounts. He took them with him as he set wards about the inn; hoping the simple task would assure them of their safety over the next few days. They talked and Kellim steered the conversation, allowing them to air any worries about the attack. He knew all too well that any such feelings, kept inside or hidden away, would only come back to trouble them further. He knew it wasn't a cure-all but it was a start.

"Do you ever get scared?" Aran asked, still troubled by the vulnerability he'd felt in the presence of the Child.

"Often," Kellim smiled. "I wouldn't be here if I ignored such a useful emotion."

"It's just that all I could do was tell Cali to run and then I was unconscious and couldn't do anything. I left her…"

Cali took his hand, squeezing it tightly. "You did what you could."

"But I have to keep us safe, *you* safe." The guilt Aran had felt suddenly welled up inside him, he could feel his emotions getting the better of him, and felt all the more foolish for it.

"You've always done that," Cali reassured, wishing she could rid him of the guilt he carried for the loss of their parents. Even as a young child, he'd been very protective of her. Fearing he would lose her too.

"You both acted with courage," Kellim said simply. "You faced a threat few have encountered in living memory and had the presence of mind to act in each other's best interests."

"But we left Jai behind," Aran said.

"You followed his orders," Kellim reminded. "You respected his judgement and attempted to reach safety. That gave Jai time to recover and in turn, come after you. His actions then gave Merren time to find you and stop your assailant. All of those actions contributed to an outcome. Great or small, the chain would have been broken by the absence of any. Do you see that now?" Kellim looked at them both in turn.

Cali accepted his reasoning, seeing the sense in it, but Aran was struggling with something far older and deep-rooted. Kellim knew he would need to speak with him again.

"We're a part of something now," Cali reassured Aran.

"Indeed, you are," Kellim smiled. "Far more than links in a chain. You are family and I for one feel stronger and grateful for that. Neither of you is alone. Orla is still with you, make no mistake there, and now you have all of us too." Kellim wove the last of the form fields and winced as he got up. "Too far down for these old bones." He looked at them again and smiled. "They'll do their job so you can both sleep safely tonight."

Their meal finished, the first night found them all in their beds early, tired from the journey and needing sleep, the second night did the job Kellim hoped and put some emotional distance between them and the effects of the attack.

The third day found them more at ease, the inn was quiet and the fire warm, they spent it in the lazy distraction of food, allowing the meals of the day to mark its course. The next day's journey planned, Kellim came over to where Aran was sitting dozing by the fire.

"Care to stretch your legs for a bit?" Kellim asked when one of Aran's eyes popped open. "I want to check my wards and thought you might like to try setting one yourself."

They left the inn, heading into the woodland that surrounded it and found the first of the markers. Kellim had intended this to be the starting point of a conversation, an opportunity to check on Aran, but the young man beat him to it with a question of his own.

"Will they come back? The Children I mean."

Kellim brushed his hand through the form field, and for an instant, a section of the wards showed themselves, faint threads no higher than his kneecap. Kellim straightened and looked at Aran. "I must accept the blame for that ambush, I underestimated the threat. It has been far too long a time since my last dealings with the Panids' Children. It is surprising to find how something so vivid, can become so faint. If they do return, these will give enough warning. We were unprepared; they will not find us so again."

"Do you think the one that's left might come back?" Aran asked.

"It is a possibility, however unlikely."

"I think that's what bothers me," Aran admitted. "The thought it might come back and that again I won't be able to do anything."

"Would it help if I taught you a few things? Just enough to hand back some control of your concerns?"

Aran nodded. "It would, a lot." He seemed to brighten at the thought but then came the question Kellim knew both Aran and Cali would want an answer to. "Why do you think they attacked us?"

Kellim, started walking, for some reason the action had always improved his ability to organise his thoughts. He knew he was treading a fine line between the truth and not wanting to worry Aran unnecessarily. "I have to be honest with you Aran. I don't have any definitive answers. I would prefer to wait and see what The Faithful can tell me. Will you be patient and trust me until then"?

"Well err, yes, of course. I'm not sure what I'd do with any answers you might have, to be honest. It's more to stop my imagination from getting the better of me. That thing did seem interested in us, or am I being stupid and imagining things?" There was a certain amount of hope in his voice, hope that Kellim would say it was just that, a figment of his imagination, that the creature was acting on nothing more than basic animal instincts, like any predator needing food.

Kellim worded his answer carefully, he didn't want to lie but saw no benefit in frightening Aran. "They may have some interest in new Talents. Why that is I couldn't say and I'm still at somewhat of a loss to explain their actions. Those Children remaining have kept themselves to the quiet places, lost in all but children's tales."

"There are others? I mean more than the ones we've seen in Sancir." Aran hadn't considered the thought. He'd always been told stories, like any youngster, the tales had been a part of his childhood. But he had never thought for one minute they still existed. It was one thing to be scared by a story, their reality had been another thing again.

"Yes, there are others, but as to how many are still alive, I cannot say. The numbers should be small now by now," he said this with less conviction than he would have several weeks ago. "Like the Panids, few survived the Great War. The one we saw on its own in the woods was of a type used in the war as scouts. Fast, secretive and intelligent. Able to defend themselves but otherwise gentle. The Three are different again. You only saw one of them but would have found all three identical. They and the others of their type were created as escorts for the Panids, protectors skilled with weapons and some field use. As you learned for yourself, they are not gentle. How they survived the years following the Great War I do not know."

They walked further, and Aran felt he had enough answers for now. The chance of learning to defend himself made the prospect of another attack somehow less threatening, he wouldn't be helpless. Kellim's quiet confidence made a huge difference and as they walked and chatted, he began to feel less worried about the rest of their journey.

They completed their check of the wards, and Kellim showed Aran how to set one for himself. When all was done Kellim didn't seem ready to go back in just yet. The morning was clear and bright and it was good to be outside after the smoky warmth of the inn. It was late summer in this part of the continent and autumn would eventually catch up with them during their journey south.

A bronzed leaf settled on the fence. Kellim picked it up. "The copper beams turn early; they are always the first to herald the distant approach of autumn." He looked out over the enclosed field.

Aran leaned against the fence. "Were there many Children?" Aran ventured.

Kellim turned his attention away from the meadow and the condition of the crop growing there and leant back against the wooden fence. "At the start, very few, but as the questionable knowledge was perfected, they were created in their thousands, and far outnumbered the Panids."

"I always thought there were lots of Panids like there are lots of Talents now."

"The Panids were a comparative rarity. Fifty, if I remember rightly. Most chose to live in the Lantriums when they were created. A few preferred to be away from the intrigue that inevitably follows a large grouping of people."

"That's not many. Weren't there many people with talent then?"

"Not many, and we still don't know why that is. There were other lesser Talents, but they were mostly untrained. They used their basic abilities to make a living in the towns and villages."

"Weren't any of the other Talents jealous?"

"Some may have been, the Panids were held in high esteem. It would be difficult for someone with an average ability not to want more. And after Mennem left the Panids guarded their position carefully."

"That doesn't sound fair."

"It wasn't. The Panids, we," he added. "Were too distant from the rest of Koa. Too removed from the real world and its difficulties. As the same can be said for the privileged of today."

"Why did Mennem leave?"

"I wish I knew," Kellim said, his voice heavy with regret. "It would have made his leaving easier to bear."

Aran would have liked to know more, but it became evident Kellim felt he'd said enough about the past.

"We still have some of the morning left. Why don't I show you a few useful defences?"

Carrick stepped down from the awkward stairs that, for some reason, were hidden in what felt like a cupboard.

Merren made the same manoeuvre of descending the half spiral and ducked under the door lintel. "Three nights and I still haven't found an easy way to do that."

"It's busier tonight," Carrick noted.

Merren looked. "We've done well to have two quiet nights." The inn was far from packed, but there were more people in the bar eating. It was dimly lit by candles and a fire, which offered light for those who needed it and shadows for those who preferred a more inconspicuous stay. The room smelled of pipe smoke and ale, which wasn't necessarily bad once you sat down below it. Old beams stained dark by the years and wooden floorboards muffled sound and occasionally creaked underfoot.

"I think that must be our table over there in the dimly lit corner," Merren pointed to a large wooden one with a handwritten sign on it saying *Held at the landlord's discretion.*

Carrick looked over. "Which of the dimly lit corners would that be? Do you want a drink?"

"Yep," she replied looking at the kegs behind the bar. "What's on tap tonight?"

"Leet Ale, Kagash Kri, Bara Lek and Eris Mash." Carrick looked at Merren expectantly.

"Bara Lek. I haven't had that in ages," she said, leaning on the counter.

"Two of the Bara Lek," Carrick motioned to the innkeeper.

"Make that four," Jai added, appearing behind them with Bryn.

"You look better," Merren said to Jai.

"Aches and pains," Jai dismissed. "Kellim gave me some more of his stuff, though why it has to taste so bad, it'd be much better if it tasted like this." He pointed at the barrels.

The innkeeper put four large tankards down. "Shall I add it to the tab, sir?"

Jai's hand hovered over his drink. "Whose name is it in?"

Bryn answered before the innkeeper could check. "Mine."

"In that case, we'll have another round." All four tapped mugs. "Down to the bottom," Jai saluted.

Merren gave him a wary look and then relented. "Down to the bottom," she took a breath and all four focused on emptying their tankards. The mugs hit the bar at the same time and the innkeeper had four more waiting.

The second drink lasted longer as they recounted old memories and past events. Tales from many years on the road in times that now seemed very different.

Bryn steadied his drink as someone pushed behind him. He turned and watched as the big man was followed by three others. They dragged two drinkers from their seats and pulled in more chairs. One of the group shouted to the innkeeper.

Jai had stopped drinking, angered by their treatment of the travellers. "The UruIldran we saw on the road," he gestured, pointing out the Urukish features that distinguished the big man from Ildran.

Merren looked to Bryn. "I'd have thought he'd be gone by now. Not pushed fortune with the Sancir patrols."

Bryn nodded. "There'll be money involved. After someone important and hasn't found them yet."

"We can hope for that," Carrick added.

Jai had stepped forward. "Whatever he and his mates are up to, they should show more respect. I'll ask them to move."

"The two travellers have found seats." Bryn put a hand on his shoulder. "They're fine."

"Not the point. You don't treat people that way. I'll be Mr Polite," Jai added.

"You?"

"It's my other name."

Bryn gave him a weary look. "You've so many. I've lost count." Bryn looked at the Urulldran and the mercenaries with him, as Sanciran law dictated, they'd left weapons with the innkeeper. "Just forget it, Jai. They're not worth the trouble. You always end up swinging the first punch and then I have to rescue you."

The group began jostling the landlord as he took over their drinks. One hit the floor, spraying ale everywhere. More people moved away. The large Urulldran started shouting as he wiped his clothes down.

Merren watched as Jai put down his drink and headed over. "Is this a good idea?" she asked.

Bryn shrugged. "Maybe a thump will do Jai some good."

Merren wasn't convinced. "He's had one already."

"Yep," Bryn said brightly. "And look at how much better he is."

The landlord returned. Carrick turned back to the bar. "We'll need more drinks and maybe a bandage."

Jai reached the table and pulled over a chair. The big Urulldran looked at him. Jai sat, picked up the sign from the next table and placed it on theirs. "This table was already taken."

The group continued to stare at him without expression. Jai picked up the sign, reading it out in less than perfect Ildran.

Carrick looked at Merren. "What did he say?"

Merren was concentrating. "I think it was, this bed is me, though I could be wrong, my Ildran's not good."

Bryn finished his drink. "It's better than his. I hope he doesn't try anymore."

Merren's hand lifted. "No, he is."

The UruIldran had said something to the others and they all laughed. A few more phrases were exchanged and then he stood up. "You think I am a dock?" the UruIldran spoke Koan.

Jai's brow furrowed in thought, "Do I? I meant co…"

"Perhaps it would be good for you to sit elsewhere Cian." The big man's accent was heavy.

Jai shrugged. "No, here is good and you can stay if the travellers don't want their seats back."

The UruIldran looked at his men. "And you're going to make us move."

"My friends might help," Jai pointed. "Though the big one said I should be polite." The UruIldran looked over. Merren offered him a dry smile, but Bryn had noticed something and put his glass down.

The UruIldran's face remained expressionless. "No. You will go," he talked as if speaking to a child.

Bryn's fist ended the big man's move and the knife skidded across the floor.

"I saw him!" Jai complained as the table erupted.

"I've always liked this inn, it's not the best but it's quiet," Kellim was telling Aran and Cali. "And the food is go..." They pushed passed the onlookers.

The innkeeper had leapt over the bar and was frantically shouting about damages. Other travellers were making rapid exits, but still carrying their food. Carrick and Merren were standing at the bar occasionally ducking flying objects and Bryn and Jai were at the centre of the fight.

Cali and Aran stood agog.

"Dear me," Kellim tutted.

"Should we do something?" Aran asked urgently.

"Yes. It will hold up dinner."

Kellim stepped forward, rolling up his sleeves he headed for the fracas. The room became filled with the now familiar static feel of field use. One by one the mercenaries and the UruIldran vanished until only Jai and Bryn remained and both stumbled as their respective opponents disappeared.

"Gentlemen," Kellim greeted.

Bryn and Jai straightened, somewhat disorientated and stood breathing heavily, still glancing around the room.

Jai finally looked at Bryn. "Be polite, he says. You always throw the first punch, he says." Bryn had folded his arms, a bemused expression on his face.

Chapter 8

It had been two weeks since they'd left Leet. Carrick, Merren and Kellim had continued their vigil. Bryn, Jai and Lewan's hands had never moved far away from their swords and Cali and Aran had ridden in the centre of the group, wishing they could do more to contribute. It had been a long, tense ride and all were relieved when at last they crested the hill and came in sight of the city of Mel Akor. This truly was a city, a rich city of grand buildings and wide streets, of parks and bustling markets. But all were dwarfed by three immense port towers. They were not unlike giant stone trees with colossal buttresses transferring their weight into the ground like roots. Each was a huge octagonal structure that reached two hundred feet into the sky. Their plateau-like tops were crowned by long wooden suspension bridges that cantilevered outwards, forming jetties for sky ships to moor at. A cascade of ropes and cables hung from the towers like vines; lifts transferring cargo and people constantly ascending and descending them. Around them, large ships and small boats glided and manoeuvred like great birds.

They worked their way quickly through the busy city, despite Cali's habit of stopping to look at anything that caught her eye. Aran noticed some interest being shown in their progress, or rather that of Kellim's. They had travelled in relative anonymity but now, closer to Hallorn, it seemed the Panid was well known. His passing was noted with interest and respectful gestures. The old man seemed untroubled by it, occasionally nodding politely. Eventually, the street they'd been riding down opened out into a vast paved area that surrounded the base of the towers.

Warehouses and administrative buildings edged the square. Aran's neck swivelled from one thing to another as he struggled to take in as many of the sights, sounds and smells as he could. The square was a mass of activity. Carts and people transported goods to and from the warehouses and towers, clusters of market stalls sold produce straight from the ships, queuing passengers collected tickets and goods were loaded onto platforms that rose at an alarming rate to the summit of the port towers.

They unbuckled their things from the mounts before Jai, Merren and Lewan led them to the local dealer. The animals were tired and would be too big to take with them. The money they'd bring would go some way to refilling Kellim's rapidly shrinking purse. Bryn and Kellim were near one of the lifting points talking to an officer and Carrick sat with Cali. Aran's attention was drawn upwards as a shadow rippled over the square. Shielding his eyes, he watched as the fifty-foot ship cleaved through the air, its hull long and slender. At the back, two sets of large horizontal and vertical fins kept the craft stable and allowed it to manoeuvre. They were called sky ships, but their resemblance to the sea-going vessels was scant. The silhouette it presented from the ground was more like that of a wide sword.

"They used to be a lot bigger," Carrick noted his interest.

"It's still amazing," Aran continued to watch as the vessel slowed and began manoeuvring towards one of the moorings.

"How does anything like that stay up in the air?" Cali asked,

"They have a field engine," Carrick explained. "Though it has no moving parts and no physical substance. Basically, it's a form field that draws in the ambient field and uses it to keep the vessels in the air."

"You could go anywhere you liked. Fly as high as you wanted," Cali said wistfully.

Kellim smiled. "There are limitations. Go deep enough underground and the field becomes defused. A Talent can not draw on enough of it to do anything. Travel high enough and the same thing happens. Even before The Field's Cap was set in place sky ships were limited. Field engines work best where the field is focused, forcing them to fly at relatively low altitudes. The higher you try to go the greater the chance of dropping out of the sky. But we will have no such problems on our journey."

"We're actually going on one like that?" Aran asked.

"One of Bryn's as it happens," Carrick replied. "Our friend has several that fly between here and Naddier. We're fortunate this one is almost loaded and aiming to sail later today."

"Bryn owns ships," Cali's surprise was quite evident. "If someone had said, guess what he does for a living, that wouldn't have been on my list."

"Looks can be deceptive," Carrick told her. "He was a very successful merchant. Set up his business from scratch and built it into one of the biggest in Naddier."

Aran tried to picture Bryn without a sword, dressed like a merchant. The image didn't work. "But he's not a merchant anymore?"

"Bryn got bored and went looking for adventure, his sister was happy to take over. That's when Merren and I got to know him, about fifteen years ago now, I think."

"How did you get to know Jai?"

Carrick was about to answer when Merren, Jai and Lewan returned. "I was just about to explain how we met Jai." He gestured towards him with a wry smile. "Would you like to take over? I'll leave it to you to decide which version they get."

Jai scratched self-consciously at the stubble on his chin. "I wish I could say I rescued them from a blood-thirsty horde, but the truth is Bryn helped me with an argument I was losing, badly." He winced at the memory.

"Losing?" Aran grinned.

"Let's just say I got into a discussion with two guys who thought they were getting something for free. I'd have won if their mates hadn't joined in." He seemed quite convinced by this. "I was about to make a hasty exit when Bryn came along."

"It was a brawl," Merren butted in. "A street brawl. Don't let him spin you otherwise."

Jai looked back at Aran. "I was in the habit of getting into trouble a lot in those days." He pulled at an ear slightly embarrassed by the admission. "I suppose you could say Carrick, Merren and Bryn showed me a different life."

"Right folks!" Bryn shouted over from the lifting point. "Let's get going."

"I hope you've got a good head for heights," Jai pointed at the platform and its lifting cables. "It's a fast, high ride."

Aran followed the thick cable up, craning his neck to see its end in the mass of wooden structures way above them and started to feel less enthusiastic about the whole thing. "Are they meant to wobble like that?"

"You can let go now," someone was saying. "Hey Aran, you okay?"

Aran opened one eye in the direction of Jai's voice. "Are we there yet?"

Jai smiled. "Yep, we're there. It's over and it's totally safe."

Aran opened the other eye experimentally and took a careful look around. No drop, just the lift housing around him and the open deck of the port tower. Only the passing clouds and the lack of horizon revealed they were some distance up in the air. The others were carrying their packs off the lift.

"It's ok," Jai encouraged. Aran released his grip on the railing and as casually as possible picked up his bag. Jai stepped off and waited for him. "See it's just like any other port. But instead of the sea, we've got sky. You can't see the drop."

"Yes, but it's still there."

The deck was enormous and stretched off in all directions like a natural plateau. There were wooden buildings, small warehouses, cranes, carts and cargo. Amongst all this, people worked or made their way to and from ships. Some way off, moored to the suspension platforms that radiated outwards were several craft. They were like conventional ships, in that they had a hull, deck, masts and sails, all of which seemed very delicate and slender, but as he got closer to one, he could see the hull was quite different; being shaped to allow the craft to travel through the air and not water. The huge array of fins at the rear of the ship were unlike anything Aran had seen before and he marvelled at their design. Bryn was leading the others onto its deck and shaking hands with a man Aran assumed was the Captain. When the Captain saw Kellim he bowed and then shook the Panid's hand heartily.

Bryn introduced the others, "… and this is Aran, and of course, you know Jai."

"It's a pleasure to have you all on board," the Captain said. "Your sister will be glad to see you return home safely. Though you seem to have had a rough time of it."

"We've been on the road a long time. How has Mel Akor fared of late?" Bryn asked.

"The city officials have one eye to the East and the other fixed nervously on their profits. The markets are struggling; the unrest means people are less inclined to take risks and hardly anyone is brave, or fool-hardy enough to venture into Ildra. We've heard tales of whole ships being confiscated and members of the crew being held indefinitely for questioning," the Captain said sceptically.

"What time do you intend to set sail?" Bryn asked.

"Before noon, sir. We're nearly loaded and I want to make the most of the prevailing winds."

"Good. Then we'll get out from under your feet."

"The boy here will show you to your cabins and I'll have you informed when we're about to leave. You might enjoy the view." Again, he acknowledged Kellim with deference. "Sir, ladies, gentlemen if you'll excuse me." At that, the Captain took his leave and the young lad, he'd indicated, showed them to their cramped accommodation.

After what seemed like a brief opportunity to rest, they assembled on deck, chatting in twos and threes as the Captain shouted commands and the crew sprang to activity. The gangways were hauled in and ropes untied. A call announced the ship was free-floating and the Captain turned to his Master Conveyor. Aran had been aware of someone drawing on the field and he could now trace it to this man. It was then that Aran realised the ship was under his guidance as it slowly glided out into the open air. Once clear he manoeuvred the large craft into the correct attitude, where it hovered calmly. He felt the Talent release his will; leaving the ship's field engine to do its job. With a signal from the Captain, the ship's arrays of fins were deployed. Further orders sent the crew scurrying to release ropes and climb the angled masts to unfurl the ship's sails. At first, they rippled and billowed in the wind, but more orders soon had them under control and with a soft thud they caught the air and went taught. The ship lurched forward slightly, heading away from the port tower and out over the city. Once clear of its walls the Captain issued more orders, more sail was set and the attitude of the huge rear fins were altered; the ship began to climb higher into the afternoon sky, picking up speed as she did. Aran watched everything, making a mental note of the procedure and the commands that accompanied certain actions. His concentration was only broken by his sister's shout of delight.

"Amazing," Cali said excitedly as she turned to Merren and Carrick, the view stretched to the distant and faint horizon. "Absolutely amazing!"

The rest of the day seemed to pass quickly and as night fell the stars came out, clear and bright against the deep of the sky. The air was particularly still and the night peaceful. The ship skimmed its way over a fog bank, leaving a swirling wake behind it. Jai leant out on the ship's bulwark, lost in thought, catching glimpses of the dark landscape beneath them. Aran walked over to him and was about to lean on the side, but then changed his mind.

"You alright?" he asked Jai, not wanting to intrude.

Jai breathed in deeply, looking back out over the side. "The world seemed a bit different the last time I was on this ship." His tone hinted at regrets.

Aran wasn't sure what to say next but had some idea of what Jai meant.

"Well," he hesitated, feeling a little awkward, "if you ever want to talk, I've been told I've got a good ear. I know it's probably none of my business and you'd probably talk to Bryn or Merren or…"

Jai interrupted before Aran tied himself in more knots. "Don't put yourself down. Funny I've said more to you than any of the others, don't know why but you're easy to talk to. I'm not too good at this sort of thing, you've probably guessed that by now."

"I just wanted you to know I sort of understand. I can imagine what it's like to lose someone important. Having family means a lot to me."

Jai turned back to look at the view and was silent for some time. "A lot's changed since we set out on this ship from Naddier. There's a lot I wish I'd said but didn't. If I think about it, talk about it too much…" he stopped himself. "Sorry, it's difficult."

"It's fine. Look you know where I am. As I said, I'm a good listener."

Jai cleared his throat. Looking at Aran. "I haven't asked. You and Cali haven't exactly had an easy time. How are you holding up?"

Aran accepted Jai's attempt at diversion and thought for a while, trying to make some sense of things. "Not sure really. It's all happened so fast I don't think we've had time to let it all sink in. I think once we get to Naddier and have time to sit still the enormity of what's happened will hit us."

"Do you miss your home?"

"It might sound strange but no. I, my…" he faltered not sure how to explain, not wanting to voice words that had troubled him all his life.

"Cali told me about your father. What he blamed you for. That must have been hard on you."

Aran only nodded. Jai could sense a similar struggle going on in Aran's head, self-blame. He wanted to reach out, hug him and say it didn't matter, to let it go. All the time wishing, he could do just that.

"It's difficult," he said, finally looking at Jai.

Jai managed a laugh that was half muffled by irony. "It is."

They watched the mist slip away beneath the ship, revealing a half-lit landscape dotted with the lights of farms and small villages. "What about your time on the slaver's ship?" Jai asked. "You okay about that?"

"I talked to Carrick and Merren a lot, and that helped. I don't remember much of it. We were drugged and so it's all a bit fuzzy really, like a kind of dream." He paused for a while, seeming a little uncomfortable. "Don't laugh, but I still get nightmares about it."

"Don't be embarrassed. You got through it. And sometimes you just have to give yourself space. It's like you have to allow yourself to take time and come to terms with what happened. Talk when you need to and not, when you don't." Jai shrugged slightly, feeling odd about handing out advice. "Don't hold feelings in, thinking no one will understand."

Aran smiled.

"What?" Jai asked.

"Was that advice for both of us then?"

Jai laughed. "Yep, maybe I should listen to myself more often. I give good advice." He patted Aran on the back. "Come on," he pointed to the stairs leading below decks. "If we can smell dinner so can Kellim. We'd better go and make sure he doesn't eat it all."

The next few days slipped by uneventfully. The crew lost their awe of Kellim and along with their passengers fell back into a daily routine that dictated life on board. It provided a chance for the group to relax and talk without the pressures of the journey. Carrick and Merren were particularly glad of the rest after days of constantly searching for possible threats. Kellim now took over this duty and Aran marvelled at how he continued his daily interactions with them and the crew but still maintained his vigil. He took every opportunity to talk to Kellim about the skills he would need to master. Kellim enjoyed this hugely and used the time to teach as well as assess the young man's unrealised abilities.

"I know how to use the field." Aran began setting his question in context. "And I'm getting a bit better at using it."

"Given the short time you've had, I'd say you're doing well, don't underestimate yourself," Kellim encouraged.

Aran smiled. "And I am getting better at using it."

"That sounds better." Kellim winked at him. "The loss of a few words makes quite a difference."

"As you and Carrick have taught me things, there's been one question I've not asked. A bit of a basic one I think."

"What is the field?" Kellim asked it for him.

"Exactly. Why haven't I asked that before now?"

"We've been somewhat on the busy side of things. And in truth, it's not a necessary piece of information. A fish cannot tell you what the sea is, but it uses it nonetheless."

"I think it would still be useful to know."

"And indeed, it is."

"I know it's a kind of energy, but where does it come from?"

"It is a kind of energy. A potential. The inner sea, the lake of facility, the field, the source, the song, the spark, the flame. Its list of names goes on. It comes from out there." Kellim gestured towards the sky. "It is a part of the vast expanse beyond the sphere on which we exist. Unseen, it forms the greater part of the fabric of this reality. Its substance passes through us all, passes through everything. Mostly with no effect."

"Passes through us?"

"Indeed. Its basic essence is so inconsequential that it permeates everything unnoticed except for Talents and field trees of course. How can I put this?" Kellim rubbed his chin. "Let's go back to the sea. Think of the field as water and people as sieves. Water passes through a sieve and does not change it. The field passes through people without consequence or effect. Talents are nothing more than people with a finer mesh, so not all of the water passes through. Because of that, they can gather the field and make use of it."

"And an Adept has a finer mesh still," Aran guessed.

"That's right. They have and can gather more and therefore use more of the field. I would say it's as simple as that, but of course, it isn't."

Aran was also fascinated by the ship and how it was operated, chatting often with the Captain and the Master Conveyor. Both were happy to answer his questions and show him how things worked. The Master Conveyor explained his role, and with Carrick's permission, tutored him on control and the skills required to move and manoeuvre the ship in port and when the wind dropped. He also explained the function of the different parts of the ship and the differences in its layout and decks compared to a sea-going vessel. Aran was excited when the

Captain offered him the wheel and the chance to steer the ship. From then on most of the crew allowed Aran to take a turn at the wheel offering him suggestions and giving guidance.

Getting up early one morning he was surprised to find Merren there. She handled the wheel as well as any of the crew; the same casual ease that belied considerable skill. It turned out she had spent a year working on board a sky ship and was quite proficient. It seemed to Aran that each day he spent in the company of this group of people he found out something new, something that never failed to surprise him. She stepped aside as he approached and let him take the wheel.

"It looks like almost everyone's up early this morning," she said and pointed to the mid-deck.

Lewan and Cali were sitting there, they'd spent a lot of time together on the ship. Talking endlessly, finding out more about each other and simply enjoying each other's company. It was clear that the bond between them was deepening and Merren watched its progress. They seemed well-matched and very comfortable in each other's company; she was pleased to see them happy.

"You're enjoying this aren't you?" Merren asked with a smile.

"I am," Aran replied. "I think I could live a life on a sky ship. There's so much to do and it's all so interesting."

"It is. You should try it when the weather's not so good."

"Jai was telling me about some of the trips you've had on a sky ship. Some of the storms."

"That's the difference with a sky ship. You don't try to sail through them. You either go around or land."

"Just as well a sky ship doesn't have a keel."

"It's awkward enough because of the fins at the rear but if it's a bad storm these ships can't cope. They're not as strong as a sea vessel. Can't be because of the weight involved."

"Jai talked about having to land and some of the trouble that brought."

"You two are getting on well."

Aran smiled awkwardly.

"I think you're good for him," Merren said. "He seems more comfortable dropping his, 'I can cope', front when he's talking to you."

"I'm not sure I'm doing anything much, except listening."

"I think that's the best way with Jai," Merren said. "You understood that from the start, which made it easier for him to talk."

"Well, I err,"

Merren smiled again. "Accept the compliment. It's not blind skill. You've talents in many areas, not just with the field."

"I suppose I'm not good at taking compliments."

"It takes practise," Merren said with an amount of irony. "For all of us. If you're ever stuck just try, thank you that's very kind of you to say. You acknowledge the compliment and offer one in return."

"I wouldn't have thought of that," Aran said.

"I'm sure you would have, you're a fast learner."

"Thank you that's very kind of you to say," Aran grinned.

Merren laughed. "Told you you're a fast learner."

On the third day, they passed over the Sancir border and finally into Hallorn. Carrick and Merren had continued to teach Aran and Cali the skills they would spend the rest of their lives mastering. The two had picked things up quickly. Later that afternoon, they waited as Bryn placed a leather satchel atop a large crate on the fore deck, with a nod to Carrick he walked back over to the mid-deck where Lewan and Jai were sitting against the bulwark enjoying the lazy warmth of the sun.

"We safe here, do you think?" Jai asked dryly, as the tall man came over.

"Better here than over there," he pointed to where the others were stood and noticed Kellim had seated himself discretely up on the wheel deck to watch the proceedings.

Thirty feet away, close to the stairway that led to the wheel-deck, Carrick was talking to Cali and Aran. Merren was sat on the steps to the wheel deck watching intently.

"Remember what I've said. Always brace yourselves. Let the ground or something else around you take the weight, not you. This won't need you to, it's too light, but it's a good habit to get into." He pointed. "Focus on the bag, get a feel for its form field and then picture it in your hand and draw it to you. You need to form that connection between it and you. You will get a sense that it's in many other places." He waved his hand. "Ignore them. The trick is to maintain your focus on where you want it to be. If you don't, it will end up in any one of a trillion other locations." His expression gave a small hint at the possible dangers of transporting. "Okay Aran, you first."

Aran stepped forward to shouts of encouragement. The few deckhands working nearby stopped to watch. Following Carrick's instructions, Aran readied himself.

"Focus on the bag," Carrick reminded.

He did as he was asked and was surprised at the result. He'd followed Carrick's lead, while he'd demonstrated, but now that he was doing it, he could actually sense the form field, the framework that gave the bag its shape and governed every facet of its existence. Aran focused his will, sensing the field's response and thought about the satchel in his hand and only his hand, linking the two and the distance between them. Then suddenly it was there, sitting in his open palm.

"Impressive," Carrick said, looking at Merren in mild surprise, she seemed equally encouraged and glanced up at Kellim.

The Panid inclined his head, his expression giving some hint of his satisfaction.

Carrick patted Aran on the shoulder. "Well done, do you think you can do that again?" Before Aran could say one way or the other the bag was back on the crate again. "Have another go."

Merren sat forward slightly; Aran had managed the task with exceptional ease. She watched as the young man focused again and there it was, effortless and in his hand. Aran grinned, obviously pleased with his success. Clearly not a fluke Merren thought. She looked up at Kellim. He winked in response.

"Okay, Cali. Your turn," Carrick directed.

Cali walked forward accompanied by another good-natured round of applause. She gave the three-man audience a quick bow, took up position and gathered herself. Calmly she concentrated, focusing the field's energy on the bag at the far end of the deck. She found its form field, but couldn't quite bring it to mind as clearly as she wanted. She frowned slightly and focused more. Images of the bag in different places flashed through her mind too quickly to register. She focused more, drawing on the field. Kellim got to his feet, a faint noise disturbing his senses, a distant sound like whispering. Bryn, Jai and Lewan realised, at about the same time as Carrick and Merren, that things weren't quite right. The deck behind Cali creaked alarmingly and it was only Carrick's quick action that knocked her out of the way as the bag appeared right where she'd been standing, but still on the crate.

Cali sat up indignantly and then saw the crate. "Oh. Maybe I could try that again?"

"Good idea," Carrick agreed. "Remember it's just the bag you want."

They flew across Hallorn, a low mountain range to their left and a forest stretching beneath them. The Captain had decided to keep his course westerly rather than north-westerly with the intention of joining the Gillern field line. The slight detour would pay him back in time as the field line would greatly speed up their journey to Naddier. Cali said good morning as she passed him. The morning was fresh but clear. She spotted Bryn down on the fore deck sharpening his sword and walked to him.

He was sitting on the famous crate. She rolled her eyes at the thought. He smiled and patted its top.

"Don't worry," she said brightly and sat next to him. "I've practised lots since then."

"Never crossed my mind. Breakfast's out in the Captain's cabin if you're hungry."

She considered the thought.

"There's still a good choice, Jai and Kellim aren't up yet."

"I'll take the risk," she replied. "I want to see the sun come up."

"Then you've picked a good morning. It should be a good rise."

Cali looked about, not sure of her bearings.

"This side," Bryn offered.

"Will you come and see it?"

"Not this morning. I've a few things to do. But one of these days I want to take you and Aran to where I live. There's a place I think you'd like. Best sunrise spot in all of Hallorn."

"Yes please," she said.

"Did you sleep alright?" Bryn asked.

"Yes, thanks, out like a candle."

"Good," Bryn had been concerned by her early rise and wondered if her restless nights had returned. "Well, I'm going to have to leave you with the sunrise." He gathered his things. "See you at breakfast."

Cali watched him go and then looked about her. The morning watch was on and the Captain had headed up onto the wheel deck to speak with the Conveyor. Cali felt completely at ease this morning, possibly for the first time in nearly a year. The attack in the woods seemed like an age ago, a distant dream, something not fully real. As for the attack on the village, that could have been a lifetime ago, so much had happened since then. She understood now what Kellim had meant by time brings its own healing. As usual, he was right and it had.

The sun hadn't risen yet. Whether sitting on the hillside near her village or watching the sun go down on a warm evening, sunsets and sun rises had always been a passion. Following Bryn's suggestion, she made her way to the edge of the deck and rested her hands on the bulwark. The sun was just announcing its imminent appearance in rich bands of colour and the world seemed to open out before her. She stood soaking up the view. She was aware of her brother's approach even though he hadn't made a sound.

"I know you're there," she said foiling yet another attempt.

"Thought as much," he shrugged. "But worth a try."

"You're just in time."

They stood side by side, as they had on many occasions, watching the sun's steady climb into the sky, washing out the earlier colours and lifting the horizon to a hazy blue.

"They're never the same," Cali said. "Even when you watch them from the same place time and time again." Cali paused remembering her earlier thoughts. "Do you think we'll change much?"

"I suppose we already have." Aran turned slightly to look at his sister. "You okay?"

"I think so. I was thinking about it earlier. Now that we've stopped running and had time to rest, everything seems better. Sort of distant, as if it never really happened. Merren said it often feels like that; it's a way of dealing with things." She looked thoughtful. "Even our village."

"It does. Do you think Orla is ok?"

Cali smiled. "You know her. She'll be as busy as ever." Cali linked arms with her brother. "I'd almost forgotten something Merren told me back when we were travelling here."

"What's that then," Aran peered at her.

"About Orla," and with that she told him the scant facts of Orla's history in the far North of Koa and the perspective Merren had offered of their childhood with their guardian. They talked for some time with Cali offering what she'd had time to think over since she'd been told. Cali's words brought memories into Aran's head and the two began piecing together a slightly different perspective of their childhood, as one memory triggered another.

"So, I think we need to talk to her. Learn more about her past and maybe thank her more than we have for all she's done for us," Cali said once they'd had time to let things sink in.

"Yep, I think so and we should probably..." Aran broke off midsentence, as something caught his eye. "What's that?"

Cali glanced at Aran's scrunched up face and then turned to look into the distance. "Looks like a tower of some kind. And next to it a ring. But it's huge."

"Yep, just floating in the air. I thought I was seeing things."

Neither noticed Kellim's approach and gave a start when he spoke. "It's the Gillern field line." Both looked puzzled. "Where to begin," Kellim pondered. "The surface of Koa is where the field's energies are more concentrated. As I said before, go higher or lower and the concentration dwindles. At the surface, the field is, in some ways, like the sea and indeed the air. It can pool or forms currents that flow along a continuous path. The continent is crisscrossed by them. Some short, some long. Some are so weak they are barely detectable, others much stronger. The Gillern line is by far the strongest and used to flow from Naddier through Gillern and onto Mel Geth, near Sancir's northern border."

Aran looked at the circle now glinting in the morning light and at the slender tower to its side. "So is the ring a part of the field line?"

"No, we placed the rings along the length of key lines, they have their own field engine to stay aloft," Kellim explained. "The ring's job is to concentrate the energy; a bit like banking in the sides of a lazy stream to make it flow faster and stronger. The rings were placed at intervals along the lines to stabilise them, sometimes they are spaced closer, sometimes more distant, depending on the natural strength of the current. And there my analogy to a stream must end as the lines flow in two directions.

"Are there any others," Cali asked.

Kellim shook his head. "There were many, but this is one of a few still strong enough to use. When the field was capped, the lines became weak and most of the rings fell out of the sky.

Every now and then you come across one half-buried in the ground."

Aran could now see people at the top of the tower and the glint of a navigation lens. There were two other ships moored to pylons; tall wooden structures with what looked like a spiral stairway down their centre. A small village nearby, probably catered for the needs of the ships that docked there.

"What's the Captain doing?" Aran asked as the ship began to descend.

"After the Conveyor has checked with the tower, we'll join the line."

Shouts went up from the Captain. The sails were drawn in and the tilted masts lowered closer to the deck. Aran could sense the Conveyor was now moving the ship. The great metal ring floated serenely in the air and as they drew closer, Aran could make out its highly decorated surface. They must have received permission to enter and so the ship was carefully manoeuvred in line with the centre of the huge ring. There was a slight jolt as the ship's field engine began channelling the energy of the line. A shout came from below decks, the Captain responded in the affirmative and the ship began to move smoothly forward. The vast arch of the ring passed overhead and the ship began to pick up speed.

"The line will power the ship's progress almost to Naddier. A relic of the Panids' ingenuity," Kellim noted as he headed up to the Captain.

The next two days of good, but cooler weather marked their smooth progress through the skies of Hallorn. The irregular passing of the rings became a part of the journey as they rushed through them. The first touches of autumn had reached the forests below, and only the evergreen of an occasional field tree defied the season. The rare trees' last natural refuge being the few remaining field lines. At last, the forests gave way to a patchwork countryside of fields and villages that sent wispy tendrils of smoke up to meet them.

On their final day, shortly after breakfast, Lewan's excited calls brought them all up on deck. Just visible in the distance they could see the coast and the shapes that formed the great city of Naddier. The immense port towers became discernible first, in the north of the city and then its huge walls. Eventually, its towers and turrets came into view. The sky was busier with other ships now, some larger than theirs and some smaller, others just distant dots heading towards and away from the city. As they approached activity began to build on board and the crew made the ship ready for the final leg of the journey.

The excitement levels built. For some the thought of returning home after almost a year's travelling, for Cali and Aran the wonder of seeing one of the greatest cities on the continent for the first time, and for Jai the thought of returning without Stran.

Bryn pointed out new things to Cali and Aran as they passed over them, his estates to the east of the city and the nearby ruins of Gillern. "The original home of the Western Panids, the Gillern Lantrium," Bryn pointed to the extensive ruins below and then looked over at Kellim.

"Indeed," Kellim walked over to admire the familiar sight as they passed through the last of the rings. "They're not much to look at now, but in its time Gillern was a place to take the breath away, even for those of my kind who lived and worked there. It was truly a wonder that demonstrated one of the better sides of the Panids. I would that you all could have seen it." Kellim looked back across the vista, a smile touching his lips.

Aran studied Kellim, his developing respect and admiration for the Panid were only deepened by the old man's wisdom and fascinating past. He'd learned so much but wished he had the nerve to delve deeper, and then he noticed his sister. Her lips were doing the thing they did when her mind was building up a wall of questions. And before he could stop her, the dam broke and the flood headed towards Kellim.

"Kellim," she began, her voice light. "You say my kind. I've noticed that a lot, as if the Panids were sort of, well different to everyone else. Were they? I mean, are you?"

Several brows raised and then the eyes beneath slowly turned to fix their gaze on the Panid.

"Hmm," he pondered for a time before answering, his eyes returning to the ruins as they slipped away. "I was unaware that I did that. You have a good ear, Cali." It was clear that Cali expected an answer and was quite oblivious to Kellim's notorious evasiveness. Her gaze held, unwavering, searching for further nuances to question.

To everyone's surprise, but Cali's, Kellim responded. "From the very start of our training, our masters told us that we were different. Set apart from the peoples of the continent; we had talents few others possessed. But a sense of responsibility and duty was impressed upon us. As the years passed, we were increasingly treated with respect by the people of Koa, until awe greeted our every action. We were treated like royalty. No," he corrected rather sharply. "We were held above the Kings and Queens of the time. It was difficult for the Panids, for all of us not to be affected by such exaltation. It is not something to be proud of."

"There you did something else," Cali jumped in. "That's another thing. The Panids, you sometimes talk about them like you weren't one, or wanted to distance yourself from them."

"Perhaps a coping mechanism for the deeds of my kind that I'm ashamed of. You're quite right. I have attempted to distance myself from those actions over the years." Kellim laughed to himself. "Young lady, you have given me food for thought. Keep asking your questions."

With that Kellim excused himself.

"Well," Carrick breathed, "you've got more out of him in a few minutes than I've been able to in years."

Cali watched Kellim head below decks. She wondered about the wonders he would have seen. She wondered about his deeds; deeds that had made him recognisable across the continent even now. She wondered about the time when the Panids were in their Potent. A time that was now long gone, his people had died out and he had been left behind. She wondered if he was lonely.

It wasn't long before they could see the city clearly; the roads and canals that led to it, its immense sky ports and the great sea harbour beyond. High-fortified walls punctuated by four towered gates surrounded the city. The largest of which was the east portal, providing access to the city's heart via the Grand Bridge that arched its great width over the River Nadd. The city was organised and structured with set districts, large open squares and parks. The present city had benefited from the singular vision of its designer, some four hundred years ago. Her plans had allowed for rapid expansion, meeting the demands of both the burgeoning sky ship trade and Gillern. Three times it had outgrown its walls, which had then been cleared and turned into three concentric avenues that now encircled the city. Because of its relatively rapid expansion, the buildings were of one architectural period that lent the city a continuity of style few others could boast, and now all new buildings, by law, followed that original style.

The others had left to gather their belongings, but Aran lingered watching the distant ruins of Gillern. Forehead creased, he finally turned to see Bryn looking at him.

"Why in ruins?" the tall man anticipated the question. Aran nodded. "Destroyed to save the city. That's the reason why Naddier came through the war relatively unscathed."

"Had Gillern always been the home of the Panids?"

"Pretty much. I think the Lantriums were built to meet the needs of the Panids as their numbers grew, one here and the other in Urukish. Before that, the history of field use isn't documented. There weren't many books about then. Too expensive to make. Most of the information got passed on in stories and folk tales, something else that's been lost over time."

"You said as their numbers grew," Aran puzzled. "Weren't there always the Panids?"

"Nope, before the Panids there were very few field users." Bryn thought for a while. "The few history books we still have, talk about the six tribes that left Nebessa and the six Talents that were first born in their communities as they colonised the rest of Koa. They were spread out across the whole of the continent. I think we now call them The Cunning Ones but, in their time, they were known by all kinds of names. Fields Masters, Elementalist, Metagists, Clever Hands, Calismets and The Dry Folk. Anyway, the list goes on. There are a lot of myths surrounding them. Their age, for instance, they were supposed to be thousands of years old. But then something happened and they disappeared. We don't know why and the books we do have were written a long time after all of this was supposed to have happened. The next bits of history talk about Mennem. The first of the Panids. I think he lived to a great age too. He was something like one hundred years old when he got around to searching out and training a second. It was hundreds of years after that when they trained others. Bringing their number to eight. The name Panid probably stuck then as I think they often get called the Original Panids. It's all a bit vague with little in the way of evidence to support it. A lot of books that might have helped were destroyed in the Great War."

Aran nodded. "Is there anything left to say what happened next? Something about the rest of the Panids?"

Bryn paused to organise his thoughts, attempting to piece together scant pieces of information he'd read years ago. "There was then a gap as the eight Original Panids learnt about the field from the set of special books and the disciplines detailed in them. I think there were only eight books finished then. Eventually, there'd be ten. At that point, the tales say the Panids each took an apprentice and passed on what they knew. That's where Kellim, Eth, Etefu and Tebeb come into the story. The apprentices spent years with each of the eight Panids, learning all eight disciplines.

There weren't any true Seers then, or something like that, and the idea of a Conjoiner, like Carrick, wasn't a thing because all of the Panids used all of the disciplines as the field wasn't restricted." Bryn explained. "I said it's all a bit vague. Anyway, the apprentices in turn eventually trained others and the number of Panids grew. It's not clear when the Lantriums were built. Certainly, Lue-Esh was the first and possibly before there were a lot of Panids. I think it was meant as a centre for learning, not just for Talents. Might have been some kind of library before Mennem and the original Panids turned it into a Lantrium. You should read up on it, if you get the chance at Naddier. But, as I said, there isn't much."

"Are there any other places where there might be more information?" Aran asked.

"You'd have to try the libraries at Amar, Ippur or New Kallian. Failing that you'd have to venture into the far North. The Mammoth Temple and Dothica are supposed to have ancient libraries. You could try asking Kellim of course. Cali might have loosened him up a bit. I think he'd talk to you. I know he has high expectations and will want to help you all he can."

Their ship was efficiently docked and as cargo was being unloaded the party said their goodbyes to the crew and made their way down the tower, Aran's least favourite part of the journey. Once he was up in the air, he was fine, but somehow being anchored to the ground, at this height, was unnerving. They were met at the base by two carriages, which took them through the busy streets of Naddier.

The architecture was refined, and the streets were orderly and clean. Copperbeams lined many of the avenues, their bark matching the warm tones of the buildings. People thronged the streets; Aran had never seen so many in one place. Faces from Hallorn and a host of other countries; some he could place and others quite unfamiliar, their clothing and appearance hinting at the city's diversity. Aran examined his clothes; he hadn't noticed how tatty they were. He looked again at the smart citizens of Naddier and decided he definitely needed new ones. There was a shout, someone near the roadside had noticed Kellim. Aran watched as eyes quickly sought out the Panid's progress.

"I wondered how far we'd get," Jai nudged him.

"Is he really that well known?"

Bryn nodded. "There are whole books about him."

Aran was just adding to his list of must-reads when Bryn pointed at something.

"There, not many people see one of those in their lifetime."

"His very own statute," Aran stared at the figure overlooking the square they'd just entered, he craned his neck to study it for as long as he could. But all too quickly they moved on and Aran had to settle back in his seat. It was odd seeing someone you knew in a different light. He felt proud to know Kellim and favoured by fortune to have him as a friend and teacher. But he wasn't sure how he felt about having to share him. It was difficult to piece together in his head, to understand the odd feeling. Aran felt he had a family. He was slowly allowing himself to accept that and what the people in that family meant to him. This was the first time he'd had to think beyond the group and the bonds that tied it together. That some of his family meant a great deal to others, people he knew nothing about. He was a small part of something far bigger. It unsettled him that things might change, that he might lose something he'd let himself get used to, that others might have an equal or even greater claim on the friends he naively thought were his. He felt foolish for being so insecure. His friends had obligations and Kellim even more so. He couldn't imagine being famous, all that attention, being many things to many people and the responsibility that it would bring. He'd struggled with the tiny amount of attention his abilities gained him in their village. Always happy to help, but never wanting the embarrassment of praise or being the focus of attention. He was glad to be the unimportant member of this family, but not so unimportant that he ended up forgotten. It was a sobering thought and he looked up from those thoughts at Jai.

"You'll get used to it," Jai said as if reading his mind.

"At last," Carrick said. "That's the main academy." He pointed out the large complex of buildings set in their own grounds.

"Aren't we going in?" Aran asked, a little puzzled as they drove on.

"We're based in a smaller place called the Adepts' Buildings just a little further down the road."

They arrived at a long attractive building, its walls punctuated by columns and elegant pedimented windows. The carriages left the bustling street, entering a gatehouse halfway down the building's length. They emerged into a large quadrangle, encompassing a wide, grassed square edged with gnarlwood trees. The stone buildings surrounding it stood no higher than two storeys, making the space feel bigger than it was.

"I wouldn't have guessed all this was in here," Aran said. "You could pass by and not even suspect."

"I think that was the general idea," Carrick explained. "It's a welcome escape from all the noise out there. The city can be a bit much at times."

As their ride came to a halt in front of the main entrance, Cali's head suddenly popped over the back of the carriage in front. She waved at Aran, full of excitement. She'd be loving all of this he thought. Brother and sister, opposite and equal.

"The place seems quiet," Carrick noted to Bryn as he stepped out of the carriage.

"Yes, I expected it to be busier," Bryn's eyes narrowed. "I thought Durnin would be here to greet us."

"Probably nothing," Carrick said, too tired to jump to conclusions. He let Jai get out next and looked at Aran. "Well Aran, here we are. Home."

Chapter 9

Even now, months later, Varin couldn't lift the feeling of despondency that hung on him; a weight that dragged at his every movement and clouded all thoughts of the future. He'd sat at his desk all morning, hardly moving, staring at the wall. Only the whispering registered in the grey landscape of his emotions. His appearance at Amar had been a failure. The rejection of his proposal and his inability to influence the Corumn had been a humiliation. He hadn't been strong enough and now that humiliation gnawed at him from the minute he awoke to the end of the day when he finally succumbed to sleep. He had always controlled his emotions, but now they persecuted him. He grasped his head; the whispering had allowed him no peace. Wearing him down to desperation. Were the stories about this place true, would the ancient fortress claim him?

Standing up, he lurched from his desk, crossed the room to the window and clutched at the sill. He stifled a sob and straightened. Bitter regret twisted in his stomach; all was lost. He looked down, the drop from here would be enough. He sat on the sill and made to swing his legs out but the whispering flared in his mind, forcing him back. He stumbled, clutching at his head and fell against the desk, weeping uncontrollably. The sobs racked his body until, emotion spent, he collapsed to the floor.

In the silence the whispering returned, this time a soft sound, quietly bringing with it the awareness of another mind. It was something on the edge of his thoughts, a presence he could not identify. It slowly filled his head, smothering his anger, easing the loss, calming his thoughts and bringing an offer of hope. It spoke gently to him and somewhere deep inside he began to listen. His eyes grew heavy and he drifted.

It was of no surprise when two weeks later he sensed the approach of twenty riders, three of them attempting to hide the party's approach. He'd know his Order would find him eventually; his crimes could not go unpunished. The Amar Order demanded loyalty; frowning upon any who questioned their vows and dealing severely with those who broke them. He allowed them to continue their approach and was flattered that Mia Svara was among them. Transporting himself to the battlements he looked out across the glaring plain to the approaching riders, their armour glinting in the high sun. Let them come, what had he to fear from Adepts? His thoughts had been moved in a new direction and the more he'd accepted this change the more his dark mood lifted and the whispering retreated. He had the growing seeds of enthusiasm and an insatiable desire to answer questions that now slid unsolicited into his mind. It was nearly time to leave; to find answers to those burning questions. He needed only a day to finish what he wanted and destroy anything that might hint at his intentions. He concentrated, feeling the field respond easily as if rewarding his present thoughts.

He appeared thirty feet in front of the group with a dramatic rush of air that sent grit and dust spiralling. The startled mounts offered him vital seconds , to assess the situation before a powerful blow struck the air before him. He turned it aside, allowing the energy to dissipate behind as he responded and Asav was hurled clean off his mount, ribs cracking as he hit the sand. The armed men and women had brought weapons to bear and the second Adept, Oresh, had focused, ready to retaliate. Mia Svara swung around commanding them to stop. The soldiers faltered and reluctantly lowered their bows as she repeated the command. Oresh held his will in check. Glaring defiantly at Varin, he lowered himself from his mount and then walked back to where Asav lay groaning.

Mia Svara had suspected from the start that Varin would outmatch any group who found him. Unable to sense any hint of his presence she had been convinced the fortress was deserted. She was as shocked as the others by his sudden appearance, but unlike them had kept her wits. Now she would have to take her time if there was a hope of gaining anything from this encounter.

"Hold," she snapped before nudging her mount forward in a deliberate move to distance herself from the group's failings. Varin's will wrapped field energy around him like a wall of granite. He was more powerful than she had suspected. She was both intimidated and exhilarated by the forces he commanded.

"It would seem we are at a distinct disadvantage," she said finally.

"You are, but I am honoured by your presence." Varin inclined his head, his focus never wavering. As his student, he had always respected Mia Svara and even liked her. While the others sweated like roasts in the heat, she sat atop her mount cool and collected, how typical. She was a striking woman, black-haired and dark-skinned, like all Amarians. She had worked hard to have her talent noted above her beauty and her unfavourable origins in the North of Amaria. She was a realist; this too he had admired about her. She was also intelligent and devious beyond measure. "I see, as always, you are armed," he noted the discharge rod attached to her belt. "Until now I never understood your preference for those things, when your talent is so far beyond the need for such primitive devices." Now he could sense the reason why. How had she hidden it for so long and yet remained in control?

Mia Svara stiffened.

"My respect for you has increased considerably Mia."

She noted his use of her name, the more familiar abbreviation she seldom tolerated. A remnant of their once close relationship and now a sign that his new insight into her ability would go no further. If he had continued as her mentor, would she now be standing at his side? "You are a difficult man to find Varin," her voice had lost its edge. "The Corumn would have you held firmly in its grasp, but now I realise we will return to Amar empty-handed."

"Empty-handed," Oresh interrupted in outrage. "We will have to carry Asav a long way for treatment. How dare you attack us!"

"Fool," Mia Svara turned sharply to glare at him. "Would you have us all lying in the dust with Asav?" Oresh bristled at her tone but said nothing more and returned his attention to the Adept's care. Mia Svara turned back to Varin. His face was unreadable. "I expected to find Aurt empty," she said conversationally.

"And yet it is not. But had you arrived a day later."

She glanced over towards the fortress. "Aurt is much restored. You have been here for an extended period."

"Time enough."

"You seem much recovered since our last meeting."

"Do I? Tell me, how is Ritesh?"

"Ritesh is a fool," Mia Svara took advantage of Varin's apparent curiosity. "The Corumn was wrong to ignore you and now there will be a price to pay. Segat has plans for his country, or should I say intentions to extend his borders. Amaria herself is under threat." She watched his face for a reaction, some hint of his involvement, but found none. "Of course, this will be of little interest to you." She added a deliberate hint of suspicion to bate him, but there was no bite. "You were able to sense our approach," she tried a different line, but again to no avail. The conversation evaporated in the dry air of the desert. "I suspect you would be unwilling to tell me your plans," Mia Svara asked wearily.

Varin smiled slightly. "You already know my response."

Mia Svara mirrored his thin smile, much to her irritation she was running out of things to say as she tentatively probed the very edges of his mind. "Your abilities have grown considerably. Asav was foolish to act." She pushed a little deeper, daring the risk.

"He is a good man," Varin appeared genuine. "I regret my reaction. You, as always, were restrained, controlled." Varin's eyes narrowed as he looked about her person. "What else have you brought with you?"

Mia Svara didn't want him searching too far, or too deeply. "I have been fortunate," she began quickly. "Fortunate enough to come into the possession of a useful artefact. Shall we say it provides me with a back door out of any situation I might find difficult."

"Ah, of course, Eltram. Many have hoped to acquire one of his Follies. You are full of secrets Mia and have overcome more than even I was aware of. I hope your endeavours meet with success."

She inclined her head graciously. "I have much to thank you for." The words hid her relief.

Varin paused for an instant. "But you are quite unwise to attempt such cunning with me?"

Mia Svara flinched, painfully. "Quite," she managed, between gritted teeth, "I allowed my emotions to distract me."

"Your attempts at conversation nearly caught me out. Try entering my thoughts again, Mia Svara, and I will reach into that exquisite head of yours and release the chaos you work so hard to hold at bay." He let the thought hang in the air between them. "Now I sense you all wish to leave." The sentence was an instruction. He turned and started to walk away. "Make no attempt to enter Aurt. I will deal with any intrusion most severely."

Mia Svara watched as the haze gradually enveloped him. She hungered for such ability. She even envied the freedom it had given him, but not the cost. He was a danger and grudgingly she listened to her sense of duty; to return to Amar and with all possible speed.

Chapter 10

Merren and Jai stood sheltering amongst the columns of the main entrance to the Adepts' Buildings, watching the mounted rider emerge into the academy's inner square. Rain bounced off her coat and dripped from the building's eaves. The gnarlwoods around the green hung heavy in the downpour.

"It's been a year since we've seen her," Merren noted and then looked at Jai. "Would you like me to tell her?" she added gently.

Jai shook his head slightly. "No, I'll do it."

Merren didn't linger on the subject; with time on his hands, his mood had dipped since their return to Naddier. "She looks tired."

"Hmm, tired and wet."

"I think this has settled in for the day." Merren looked up at the low grey sky.

"At least she's back and safe," Jai stepped out into the rain, heedless of the soaking he'd get. Merren watched after him.

"Hey there, Reds, you're late!" he called.

"I'm never late. Just not on time," Kara grinned and leapt down from her mount, long, red hair flicking water in all directions, feet carelessly splashing as she landed with feline grace.

"Still adding the fire then," Jai indicated her hair.

"A girl's got to look her best. Am I glad to see you. You big hunk of man." She stretched on tiptoes and threw her slender arms about his shoulders in a tight hug. "We're both soaking," she laughed, stepping back and then her expression changed. "What's wrong mister?"

"Later," Jai answered uncomfortably. "Come on let's get out of this rain."

He took her pack and the mount was led away as they climbed the steps. Kara looked questioningly at Merren as she went to hug her.

Merren shook her head subtly. "Glad you're back."

"I had a right run-in with a band of slavers. It was a close call but there are a few less of their kind of scum floating about on the seas around Pidone. You wouldn't believe the trip I've had."

"You, us and some of the others it turns out. You're the last to return. Ressca only arrived back yesterday," Merren said, taking her arm.

"We've got a lot to catch up on then. The weather's been miserable. Four weeks I've been out in this. It's moped over the east coast of Pidone and then followed me here," Kara complained. She grabbed Jai's arm. "It's good to be back though."

He'd always liked this room. Polished floorboards and pale walls were decorated only by light and shadow from the tall windows. It was airy and unchanged since Allim's time. It gave him a sense of continuity; Durnin liked that. He'd sat in this room, at this very table, first as an Adept and now as the Head of the Naddier Order. With him sat Kellim and nine Adepts, the heads of Naddier's Disciplines. They ranged in age from Ren at thirty to Ressca now in her sixties and onto Kellim whose age was always a point of conjecture. There should have been ten but Naddier, like all the Orders had no Seers. This meeting was the first time the Discipline heads had all gathered in over a year. The atmosphere was tense and so he'd allowed them time to share news before asking each to share their reports.

"There's nothing more you can add about Varin?" Durnin asked Kellim finally.

"Indeed, little that is definite beyond what I've just told you. His mind and his lips gave little away. I gleaned some images of his departure from his Order and the work on Aurt, but nothing more. It was evident he'd improved his talent considerably, that is indeed the only thing I can attest to with certainty."

"Why subject himself to that kind of torment?" Durnin puzzled. "What does he hope to achieve with this extra power?"

Ressca, the head of the Discipline of Makers spoke. "Just that. Power! From what Kellim has suggested it would follow that if powerful enough he could apply persuasion and bring the Amar Order in line with his views. Certainly, the Corumn during Varin's time were old and would be vulnerable to manipulation by a strong mind."

"We've always heard rumours," Ren, the head of the Discipline of Speakers continued. "Varin wanted the Amar Order to return to its position of authority. A role the Order was being made to distance itself from, mistakes of the past and all that. I've heard talk they're thinking of renaming themselves as the Amarian Order. Such is their will to change."

"Absolutely," Ressca said. "We know he wasn't happy about the direction the Empress was set on. But is he aware of the sweeping changes made to the Corumn? Mia Svara's appointment for instance?" Kara let out a snort of derision at the sound of the woman's name, which Ressca ignored. "Things have moved on at a considerable pace since Chancellor Nirek's appointment. No more doddering Adepts easily manipulated by an augmented will."

Durnin was inclined to agree. "Our intelligence tells us the Order at Amar has long been plagued with in-house politics and power struggles. The Old Corumn would have been open to a rise in their authority over the crown and the surrounding countries. The current one would not."

"Perhaps, given enough time to develop his abilities," Ren suggested. "It could be possible for him to force the new Corumn to agree to his views."

"It's possible," Ressca agreed, "but would his loyalty to the Order make such action unacceptable in his mind?"

"Loyalty to the Amar Order not necessarily the Corumn," Ren corrected.

"You said it looked like he'd been at Aurt for a while?" Kara asked.

"Possibly two years, even longer. Aurt seemed much restored," Kellim recalled. "Seemingly, he wanted to work unobserved and I suspect is unaware of the changes made to the Amar Corumn. His isolation was complete."

"That's a long time," Kara warned. "He could do a lot in two years."

"Then we may need to warn the Corumn," Durnin interjected.

"Indeed," Kellim nodded.

Ursa, the head of the Discipline of Summoners cleared her throat impatiently. "Amar should be left to itself if you ask me. They are not to be trusted as enemy or ally. Should we not be more concerned by Segat? Amaria is a long way from here. Ildra is only two borders away!"

"I assume you mean the current unrest?" Ressca noted the tetchy nature of Ursa's words. "The Hallorn Crown is certainly concerned. When Perin heard I was in the city…"

"You really should be more respectful," Merren scolded her lightly.

"Nonsense I've known the King all my life," she dismissed. "I was returning here via Oren and was commanded to attend, pass on what information I had and ordered to bring details of Perin's latest troop deployment to Durnin. He believes the independence of Selarsh is in jeopardy. Yes, I thought that might rattle you all a little. Hon and Cian are very edgy and have been moving troops for some time. Perin's sending out envoys left right and centre to Cian, Hon, Selarsh, Sancir even Urukish. He's as worried and alarmed as they are by what's going on in Ildra. His spies are everywhere, sniffing out any bit of information they can."

"There you have it," Ursa asserted. "Our problem is more immediate than this second-guessing of Varin's actions. It is clear to me at least, that our attention needs to be directed to Ildra and the sooner the better."

Carrick leaned forward from where he had been listening. "Varin and Segat. They may not be two separate problems, just two parts of something more complex."

Ursa waved her hand dismissively.

Carrick continued. "I don't know about the rest of you, but it seems to me that King Perin is handling Segat, I want to know exactly what's going on in the Amar Order?"

"As Talents that should be our next move," Durnin said decisively. "We'll pay them a visit. Relations with them are greatly improved. I'll send word. Whether they accept, or not, maybe telling in itself. It'll certainly test this new policy of openness. They've talked about hosting a meeting of the Orders. Now would seem like a good time to encourage them to do it. Unity amongst the Orders of Koa could help dissuade Segat."

Ursa wasn't happy with this decision. "We must act early with a show of force, rather than more talk. Segat has made much of his desire for a coastline and the restoration of pre-Great War borders. We also know Segat is UruIldran and is a direct descendant of The Urukish throne. The feud with Amar's royals has never been settled and Segat has made no secret of his desires to avenge the assassination of Princess DuLek."

"For us to act alone and too soon would be a mistake," Ressca argued.

Ursa wouldn't be dismissed. "And to act too late would invite disaster."

Durnin sat up in his chair. It was time to move things on. He held up his hand to block Ressca's reply. "We will gather as much information as we can about both sides of this puzzle." He looked around the table expectantly. "Good. I will set wheels in motion and task some of you with this undertaking. Ressca has brought word from Oren and I must head there to meet with the King. I leave for the capital tomorrow and will pass on what we know. Hopefully, I'll bring back answers to some of our questions." Durnin set his hands on the table. "Is there anything else before I close this meeting?"

"In that case," Kellim began, "there is indeed something else. My apologies Durnin, I was unaware of your summons. I've held onto this information in the hope of learning more, but now I must tell you what I know before you leave." Kellim considered his words before continuing, unintentionally creating a certain amount of suspense. "It would appear the Panids' Children are abroad in the world again."

His announcement shocked the gathering and he was asked several questions at the same time before Durnin could calm everyone.

"And I thought I'd created a stir," Ressca said dryly when the room finally became silent.

"Tell us what you know my friend," Durnin said.

Kellim proceeded to tell the gathered Adepts of his contact with The Faithful, his sighting of one of the Children in the woods of Sancir, of the attack by The Three and the possible link to Cali.

Fennick, the Head of the Conveyors was taken aback. "With all respect Kellim. You were going to keep this from us!" He looked at Carrick and Merren with equal concern. "You were attacked. It could happen again to anyone in this room or worse to one of our Talents. Did it not occur to you to warn us?"

Kellim held up his hands. "We believe The Three were after Cali. The Faithful itself considered her to be of some importance to the Children. They had no interest in us whatsoever. Until The Faithful finds me we can only speculate as to why."

"Does Cali know about any of this?" Kara asked, peeved none of them had told her either.

"No," Merren answered. "There's no point in worrying her. The experience with The Three was frightening enough. She's recovered from it and we're unwilling to put more pressure on her and her brother. They've been through enough." Merren was a little more contrite. "Perhaps we should have told you immediately, but as Kellim said, the interest was in Cali and not Talents in general. We have no answers beyond that."

"I suppose you had your reasons," Fennick accepted. "I'm simply worried we've become soft in the years of peace since the Great War. We're heading into unsettled times and I fear we're going to be tested further. If we are, shared knowledge will help us all. Is there anything else we should know?" He looked at Kellim who shook his head.

"Then," Ressca said, "let us hope we can make ourselves ready for whatever comes our way and that Cali is resilient. You must keep a close eye on her. The young have a habit of bouncing back right up until the moment they snap. I agree with you, Fennick." She folded her arms and rested them on the table. "We are none of us, apart from Kellim, used to war let alone a continent full of monsters. And yes, Ursa, we must keep an eye on Segat."

"Their like hasn't been seen for a long time," Durnin said. "Kellim, I believe you and Kara are the only ones amongst us to have seen them or met them. I certainly haven't in all my sixty-five years. Should we be worried?"

Kara shrugged. "Don't think you could call mine a meeting. It was a bit one-sided. It died before I could help and then I studied its form field."

Ressca tutted and rolled her eyes. The others had turned expectantly to Kellim.

He spoke, as always, with reluctance. "They have become the stuff of storybooks. Bedtime tales told to make small children behave themselves. The Three were relatively minor creations. I assume they have survived this long by remaining hidden. They attacked when we had Cali with us and were isolated. The odds of that happening again are remote. But now I can't be sure how many of them are still alive," This seemed to irritate him considerably. "We thought them all accounted for. But whatever the number, it cannot be large. While Cali remains here, she is among a great number of Talents. The remaining member of The Three would be unwise to attempt another attack. To worry would achieve nothing. To be watchful and guarded would be wise."

"Let's hope you're right," Fennick said, not entirely convinced.

Ursa sat forward. "It concerns me Kellim that you failed to report this. May I remind you, that we are equals around this table and not subject to the remaining Panids' censorship. Knowledge of this nature is extremely valuable to my discipline and could be put to good use; we could create our own Children and be at an advantage if the current unrest becomes hostile."

"My intent was not to censor information, merely to pause until I had fact rather than speculation." There was an edge to his voice seldom used and all the sharper for it. "I'm increasingly convinced their focus is Cali, they have no interest in you or the rest of us," he continued as Ursa bristled. "And further to this, you would be unwise, no, foolhardy to attempt a re-creation of any of The Panids' Children."

Ursa had gone red. Again, she went to speak.

"You don't trust us, Kellim." The new voice was almost apologetic. All heads turned to find who was speaking. Edara the quiet head of the Discipline of Healers had a habit of saying little, but often with greater impact. "We must seem like children to you, ignorant of so much, dabbling with the field. Fumbling awkwardly on its lesser currents when you have soared."

Kellim smiled at the quote. "Attrius," he identified its originator. "A wise man but a little creative when it comes to a past he didn't experience first-hand." Kellim looked at Ursa, she returned his gaze in the uncomfortable silence. "I'm in no position to judge anyone, talented or not and make no mistake the Panids were not without fault. But the Children were the stuff of nightmares, a fire that laid waste to the nations of Koa. You cannot imagine the sheer terror one felt in the presence of an Elemental, even those of one's own creation, Ursa. Their power was immense and the field roared unchecked through their being. To attempt to rekindle that spark would be an invitation to slaughter."

Nobody spoke, a chill had struck the room. Kellim's eyes were haunted, hinting at the visions he had witnessed and the true terror of the Great War's final years.

Durnin cleared his throat. "I think now is the time to conclude our meeting."

One by one the others left, leaving Kellim to sit alone. He was only too aware, that at one time or another, all of the Adepts in that room had longed to live in the times when the field was unrestrained. Many of them had spoken all too freely of how they would have done things differently. He got up stiffly. Had they learnt from the Panids' mistakes? He doubted it.

Chapter 11

Segat sat forward on his golden throne and absently rubbed the end of the arm. He found it reassuring that no matter how often he did this it would never wear. He noticed his stomach, pressed against the belt of his uniform and straightened, allowing the gold, braided material and polished buttons to fall back into place. Segat liked his uniform, he had never served in the army, but he felt it lent an air of greater authority in the presence of his generals and members of the Ildran Order. He fiddled absently with his earring, his thoughts drifting a little longer before he became aware that General Immed had finished talking and that VaCalt now spoke and had been, apparently, for some time.

"…I strongly urged Most High, that the Panid be kept alive. He may prove to be of yet more use. He h…"

Segat waved his hand dismissively, making the strange tutting sound the court understood as shut up. VaCalt bowed stiffly and stepped back from the throne. General Immed noticed she did not step back to join the others of her Order or the generals gathered in the audience chamber; she stood slightly apart, perceptibly closer to the throne.

"Useful to who, VaCalt?" Segat met her gaze as she straightened.

"Why, to you, Most High. As Head of the Ildran Order of Talents, it is my only desire." VaCalt bowed again.

Segat snorted. "The right answer, VaCalt. But then you always have the right answer. Don't you VaCalt?"

She merely lowered her head and kept her thoughts to herself. There was something in his tone, something in the way he kept saying her name. What did he suspect? Her eyes unwittingly glanced at The Imperial Guard.

"Yes, they are there, aren't they, VaCalt, and DuChen is dead and his knowledge with him." Segat referred to the twin figures who stood behind and a safe distance from him. Even in the Ildran heat, they were shrouded in material from head to foot, rendering them amorphous. Only their gloved hands showed. Intricate embroidery in gold thread concealed the flesh beneath.

"I rest soundly, Most High, knowing your safety is assured at all times by their presence." Her response only showed the faintest trace of tightness. She could unravel him like a cheap carpet. Melt him and the throne on which he sat but instead, she had to watch her every move, consider every response for fear this fool on a golden pedestal would decide that he wanted her dead.

Segat turned, bored of the game. "And you Imalt?"

The Adept Summoner bowed deeply and stepped forward from the assembled Talents to stand in the privileged attention of His Highness. "Most High, your health and continued reign are always utmost in my thoughts and actions. I aspire…"

"I think, Imalt," Segat interrupted, "you aspire to VaCalt's title of Potent, Head of the Ildran Order."

Imalt bowed deeply again. "My only wish is to serve, Most High. In whatever capacity." He gave VaCalt a sideways glance.

VaCalt kept her eyes fixed on the throne, at the discoloured gold caused by Segat's interminable rubbing. He sullied everything he touched.

"A safe answer Imalt. You are proving to be more useful than others give you credit for." He looked at VaCalt. Her eye remained downcast. "Yes Imalt, I must congratulate you, because of your actions we are closer to finding the usurper Immar and his bastard brother."

VaCalt looked up sharply, Segat's eyes had not left her. Segat was playing them against each other and she was losing ground.

Segat smiled, taking pleasure in her discomfort. "I may have another task for you Imalt, you have pleased me greatly. Be careful VaCalt I feel the wind of change stirring my hand." Then he caught sight of Ducat. "You would rid me of this pretender to my throne, wouldn't you, Ducat?" She bowed and stepped forward awkwardly. Segat was morbidly fascinated and disgusted by her in equal measure. What passed as thoughts in that unbalanced head he wondered? What amusement could be gained from provocation? "Speak up, Ducat. Don't be shy."

Her answer was to bite her hand, drawing blood she offered it up to Segat. "My blood is yours, Most High."

Segat looked at the dripping liquid, quite taken aback by the action and then tutted her away. His clever tongue had no taste for this. His mood spoilt, he stood, doors opened and he left the room, The Imperial Guard following, an extension of the cloak that swept behind him. Ducat returned to the assembled, flashing her eyes at VaCalt for some hint of acknowledgement. VaCalt looked on with distaste.

Chapter 12

The weeks rolled on, autumn had arrived, and the weather had remained especially mild for the time of year. Autumn and winter in northern Hallorn were more like one season and could be cold, but rarely saw snow. Travel further south and the locals called it the storm season and hardly noticed a drop in the warm Hallorn climate there.

Cali had watched the season approach and take hold of the gnarlwoods on the green of the Adepts' Buildings. It was odd, she thought to herself, how attached to them she'd become. Perhaps they reminded her of Rel and the lane of gnarlwoods that led to the village, always a welcome sign of home territory. They made her feel safe, silent guardians who had always been there and always would be. Now she had the gnarlwoods of the green to look at and in turn to imagine them keeping a watchful eye on her. She laughed at herself for being so sentimental. Her room also gave her the perfect vantage point to watch the comings and goings of the academy. She'd watched Durnin leave and return from his visit to the capital and she wondered what the city was like and how different it would be to Naddier. Bryn had left to visit his estates and see his sister, taking Jai with him. Kellim had left soon after and was gone for weeks, returning in a sombre mood with news Merren would say little about during their lessons. She wondered too at the many visitors to the buildings. Who they were and where they'd come from? People from Hon, Urukish and Akar. The list went on. Some were greeted by the staff, others by the Discipline heads. Even Carrick and Merren had entertained visitors and it seemed odd, somehow, to see them in such a different role. The seemingly constant comings and goings told her two things, that something big was happening and that she didn't have a clue what it was.

A small part of her missed their final trip on the sky ship. The time they'd all spent together had been special to her, despite the long journey before it and its tangle of events and experiences. It all seemed so distant now. Even their arrival at Naddier felt like such a long time ago.

She and Aran saw Merren and Carrick every day to work on their talent. Aran had also spent time with Kellim and was growing in confidence. Their abilities grew with each passing week. The routine was set and with it, the days passed. Carrick insisted that they ate their evening meals together as often as possible. This usually worked out at two or three nights a week and was particularly enjoyable when they were all there.

As she watched now, she could see Lewan heading across the green. She smiled and the fluttering feeling she got in her stomach returned. She'd been worried when they'd first arrived, that he would disappear, melt into the background and that she would be left feeling a fool for letting him into her heart. He hadn't. He was as dependable as ever, even turning down the offer from Bryn to visit his estate, just so he could spend time with her. Over the weeks their relationship had developed. She had been relieved that Lewan and Aran got on well and they spent many evenings joking and laughing with some of the other students. They walked, they talked, he showed her the city and sometimes they just sat; it was enough to be in each other's company.

Today was her day off from studies and Lewan was taking her out. She saw him wave at Kellim. They spoke briefly before Lewan crossed the road which ran the perimeter of the green. It wouldn't be long before the door would open so she quickly checked herself in the mirror and then heard Lewan bounding up the stairs.

"Morning!" he greeted.

"Hello you," Cali said hugging him. They kissed. She looked at him still smiling, holding on to his waist. "A whole day. Just you and me."

"I know. How will we cope?" Lewan said flopping back onto the bed as Cali pushed him over. He sat up quickly and grabbed her, she shrieked with laughter and collapsed on top of him. They laughed and hugged. Cali rested her chin on his chest and peered up at him. He looked back, meeting her gaze, a gentle smile on his face as he combed her hair back with his fingers.

"You growing this?"

"Yep," she nodded. "Thought I'd have a change. I couldn't get used to it being short."

"I like it," he grinned raising an eyebrow. "I prefer it longer, like it was when we first met."

Cali laughed again. "That was the intention."

It was sometime before they finally made their way out of their building and once clear of the main gates, they nudged their mounts into a gentle trot amongst the busy traffic. Leaving the centre of the city, the main road led them past estates where Naddier's great and good chose to show off their wealth with conspicuous houses and their equally grand gardens. It was a pleasant and comparatively quiet road, lined with trees. They trotted on in conversation until the quieter road re-joined one of the busy main avenues leaving the city. Both were glad when they finally left its walls behind for the surrounding farmland, now green with the season's crops.

"It's lovely. So peaceful after the city, even with the sky traffic." Cali breathed in fresher air and looked out across the countryside. "We should come out here more often." She reined her mount in and it took advantage of the break to graze on a patch of fern grass at the roadside.

"Yep, it's great. You should see it in the warm season when all of these fields are filled with crops. It just goes on forever and ever." He gazed about him with unguarded pleasure.

Cali watched his face, fixing the moment in her mind. She wanted to touch him and would have kissed him had the mounts not been in the way.

Lewan's face lit up anew. "And when there's a breeze. The sound it makes." He settled back in his saddle. "One day I'd like a house out here and maybe some land."

"Your parents are farmers?"

"Yep, it's in the blood."

Cali listened as Lewan described his plans. She watched his face, his eyes and his smile. She loved his mannerisms, come to that she loved everything about him. The thought struck her. She loved him. She really did. Then she realised Lewan was staring at her.

"I'm being boring," he apologised.

"No, no. You're many things, but you're never boring. Do you think there will be room for two people on this farm of yours?"

"Depends who's asking?" he smiled.

She sidled her mount right up to his, leaning over to kiss him. "You are so not boring." She stroked the side of his face still looking into his eyes.

"I love you," he said, hoping he hadn't spoken too soon.

"I love you too," she replied, pouring how she felt into the words. He grinned, his whole face lighting up and kissed her.

Their ride took them to Gillern and the Lantrium's ruins. They tethered the mounts and set out the picnic they'd brought. Both hungry, they enjoyed the food and then set to exploring.

"I wonder what it was like," Cali said as she looked for clues to the ruins' previous appearance.

"Kellim doesn't say much," Lewan replied, his arm resting across her shoulder. "But what he has mentioned makes Gillern sound amazing. You can see the ruins but they tell you nothing of what it must have been like."

"The hill the main ruins are on," Cali frowned. "It looks out of place. I mean I can see the hills behind aren't that far away but this one's in the middle of a level area. Just seems odd."

"Kellim said the Panids raised it out of the ground themselves, that's why it looks out of place, and then they built the Lantrium on top of it. A huge palace of glass and golden stone. I think there was a lake here then too. With the hills as a backdrop, it would have looked incredible. He said it was lit at night so it could be seen for miles. Kellim also said the wonders didn't stop on the outside and that once inside visitors would have seen all kinds of incredible things. Like indoor trees and meadows of flowers found nowhere else on Koa. Some of its windows looked out onto views in other countries, don't know how that's possible but that's what he said."

"No wonder people came from all over to see it and the Panids were admired so much," Cali said, trying to picture the Lantrium.

"Come on," Lewan said, taking hold of her hand and leading her to a tower. They climbed its spiral stairway and eventually reached the top, exiting through a narrow arch they both had to duck to get through.

"You can see for miles," Cali said, looking out across the view in delight.

Lewan put his arm around her waist and pointed into the distance. "This was built so you could get a better look at the ruins but I think the view beyond is better. Can you see that wooded area over there, right in the distance?" Cali nodded. "And the shapes just to the right of it? Well, that's Bryn's estate."

"Really."

"It goes from there, right over to the coast," he pointed, guiding her view. "To that point there where the flat-topped hill is."

"It's huge. I hadn't realised how big it was. We must have flown over a part of it."

"Now look over there. Do you see the road and that little farm next to it? That's the one I always wanted to buy. What do you think?"

"I think it looks perfect," she said resting her head back on his chest.

***

"Come in Kellim," Durnin greeted. "Come and sit by the window. It's a fine day and a shame to be inside."

"Indeed, it is. I have only just returned from Gillern."

"I see, keeping an eye on Cali?" Durnin asked.

"Yes, but from a discrete distance. I stayed until they were safely back in the Adepts' Buildings. Ressca," Kellim greeted the other Adept sitting by the window as he took a seat. "The gnarlwoods are looking quite magnificent this year."

"They are. We have a new gardener, one more interested in plants than sleeping." Durnin offered him a hot drink. "Carrick and Merren should be along soon." Durnin's study was a simple room. Uncluttered, light but not austere, it reflected the dependable nature of the man it belonged to.

Ressca put down her cup. "How was your other trip? We haven't had time to talk."

"Uneventful," Kellim sighed. "I headed as far north as I was able, while we waited for word to arrive from Amar. I hoped that The Faithful would find me."

"Why north?" Ressca asked.

"It was generally believed that The Beholder had headed for Lont and the mountains close to the border of Coth. I thought she might have settled there. I at least hoped to intercept The Faithful as it headed south. That said I'd barely entered Northern Sancir."

Durnin shook his head ruefully. "It seems strange to be talking about these creatures as living things."

Ressca nodded. "To us, they're just the stuff of stories, words and illustrations." She made herself more comfortable. "Your words in our first meeting were a stark reminder."

Kellim made a non-committal gesture. "The Children were created out of desperation. Created to win a war that had spiralled out of control. Most were monsters and giants with formidable weapons." He sat forward-looking at them both directly. "They were designed to terrify, to overwhelm. With each generation, their powers grew and became harder to control. Then came the Elementals. The final battles were desperate harrowing affairs. After the war, the Children that were still alive struggled in a world that no longer needed or wanted them. Some were allowed to disappear, living out their lives in isolation, but many had no understanding that the war was over and continued the purpose for which they had been made."

"To kill, to destroy, to usurp," Durnin said soberly, with a glance at Ressca.

Kellim stroked his beard, momentarily distracted by his thoughts. "It took those of us left a long time to track down most of them and end those fearful times. Was I trying to warn you against their resurrection?" Kellim drifted off staring out of the window.

Ressca watched him. "Whether that was your intention or not I think we should treat it as such and rely on the insight of one who has experienced them first-hand. I, unlike Ursa, would not be one to debate you on that matter."

Kellim looked back from the window. "It would seem the past, I thought best left behind, has decided to return, whether I like it or not. There are many things that should be left undisturbed and perhaps more that were kept secret from me. Those unknowns trouble me the most. We may be past the time for warnings."

Kellim's words were ominous and despite himself, it was a while before Durnin could break their grasp. "Speaking of returning." Durnin began. "Were The Three amongst those allowed to live out their days in isolation?"

"They would have been considered too dangerous for that." Kellim concentrated as he tracked back over ninety years. "They were listed among those destroyed right at the end of the war. Clearly, they were not. You will appreciate it was almost impossible to keep track of everything after the continent was devastated." He looked at Durnin. "There may yet be others out there we had thought to be long gone."

Durnin sat back in his chair with a long sigh. "We've enough to worry about as it is. I'm also concerned about Cali's place in all of this. She's an Adept but I sense nothing beyond that." He looked at Ressca. She indicated she had reached the same conclusion.

Kellim sipped thoughtfully at his drink. "It's not unusual for abilities to lie dormant and unannounced. Her brother on the other hand clearly has the makings of something beyond an Adept. I could understand the Children's interest in him more than Cali," he stroked his beard. "But I trust the words of The Faithful."

At that point, the door opened and Carrick and Merren walked in. Ressca laughed. "Do you always plan to appear at the same time?"

"Years of practise," Carrick said with a wink and pulled up a chair.

"We do it on purpose," Merren added as she sat down.

"It unnerves people," they both said and then looked at each.

"That's never happened before," Carrick chortled.

"You unnerve quite a lot of people," Ressca said with a smile. "I've been hearing about some of your recent exploits. Your names keep popping up in some high-ranking circles. There's been quite a lot of talk."

"Some of it good I hope," Merren laughed.

"And you," Ressca accused Kellim. "Something about vanishing Urulldrans in a bar room brawl in Sancir."

"Indeed," Kellim said. "Gossip is always prone to exaggeration."

Carrick turned to look at him. "Yes actually. What did you do to them?"

"Transported them," Kellim replied casually.

"Where?"

He thought for a moment, "Ildra, Amar. Somewhere on land." There was a moment's hesitation. "Probably."

Durnin chuckled. "You're all as bad as each other. Speaking of Amar, Carrick and Merren I want you to go there. Kellim, I was going to ask you to accompany Ressca and me on another visit, but now I think you'd be better off heading to Lont. Let's give The Faithful every opportunity to find you."

"In that case, I'll head for Neath and make my way up into Lont. It's wild and empty there. The Faithful will feel more comfortable meeting me in those places."

"You aren't going alone?" Merren asked. "You know how they feel up there about Talents."

"I will ask Bryn and Jai to accompany me if I may. Their companionship would be most welcome and Jai is in need of a distraction. I suspect Lewan will want to stay here."

"You might be right," Merren smiled.

"Amar it is then," Carrick accepted. "Cali and Aran can stay here and continue their lessons with some of the masters. I'd have liked them to come, but they'll be safer here."

"Past and current events taken into account, I think that's a good idea. We can keep them out of harm's way and allow the odd discretely supervised visit beyond the city walls," Durnin added.

"I wonder if Kara would come?" Merren said. "I'd have asked you Ressca, but it sounds like you're off on a jaunt yourself."

"I'd be happier with a little extra support," Carrick agreed.

"I imagine Kara will be only too happy to go with you." Durnin guessed. "It's always hot in Amar and she had quite a cold and wet time of it in Pidone. As for Ressca and I, we'll be heading back to the capital at the King's command. He is considering further diplomatic talks with Segat in a final attempt to dissuade him from making any kind of a move against Selarsh. The King wants some experienced diplomats and a strong arm to support him."

"I'm amazed he asked you as well Durnin," Carrick gave Ressca a sideways glance. "I'd have thought Ressca alone could supply both of those."

Ressca gave him an imperious look. "Absolutely right young man. So, watch yourself and mind your manners."

"There have been new developments?" Kellim asked.

"We were sent word in the early hours of this morning." Durnin was irritated by the timing. "I wish they'd built Naddier closer to the capital. I've not long since got back. All this travel is taking up a lot of valuable time that could be better spent. I'm sorry," Durnin paused, he was under increasing pressure and had slept little over the intervening weeks. "Yes, my friend the threat grows. There have been considerable troop movements in the south of Ildra. The borders are closed, trade is reeling from the impact and Segat has made the first of his demands known to Selarsh. He will see this meeting as a small victory if it goes ahead. King Perin is sure peace rests on a balancing point. Normally he wouldn't consider such a thing, but he sees it as a last chance to avert war. He is a great man and wise enough to salve such flattery on Segat's ego to secure the peace or buy time; Segat has been army building for years and we need to catch up."

Kellim was still uneasy. "You must be careful. Emperor Segat is set on a path we can still only guess at and is at best unpredictable. As for VaCalt, as Head of the Ildran Order, she will take any opportunity she sees."

Ressca was slightly dismissive. "Really Kellim, we're not exactly first season flowers."

"VaCalt alone would be a threat to your safety," Kellim warned. "She's one of the oldest and most powerful Talents alive. She is experienced and ruthless."

"That's why I want Ressca there," Durnin added.

"I'll take that as a compliment, though a dubious one at best."

Carrick looked at Durnin. "There's more here than greets the eye," he said suspiciously.

Ressca looked at Durnin and Durnin shrugged. "Okay. You might as well know."

"Intrigue," Carrick noted.

"That's not the half of it," Ressca replied archly.

Durnin looked at them collectively. "This goes no further," he warned, his face less than its normally jovial self. "We believe the UruIldran you saw in Sancir was one of many searching the Ildran border for the Duke of Crath and the remaining claimant to the Ildran throne. The Duke did all he could to stop Segat from reaching the throne. He's been sheltering Immar and his younger brother and moved the Princes days before Imalt's people raided his house and killed everyone found there, only the

Duke's nephew escaped. The Duke and the Princes are still at large in Ildra and we are making efforts to rescue them; the meeting will also provide a distraction while we attempt this."

"How old is Prince Immar?" Kellim asked.

"Twenties, not entirely sure."

"Not a child then, Segat would see him as a threat." Kellim stroked his beard.

"If we can get them out, there is a chance of winning Ildran support to overthrow Segat from the inside. Another reason for buying time."

"Where is this meeting happening?" Merren asked.

"On the border between Ildra and Selarsh," Durnin replied. "A good place to be when smuggling fugitives."

"This meeting between King Perin and Segat, is it just a ruse?" Merren continued.

"It's real enough," Ressca replied. "And it's also convenient."

"Of course, all eyes will be on Perin and not a fugitive sneaking across the border."

Ressca nodded. "We're hoping to get the Duke, the Prince and his brother in one go."

"It's a risk," Merren said.

"Of course," Ressca agreed, "but things are desperate. I'm aiming to have something up my sleeve, just in case. Segat has made it a little easier. He agreed to the meeting but with strict limitations on those present. Equality on both sides, and more usefully no ships or troops within a half-mile of the border. Segat wants to appear confident and show that we pose no threat to him. He's being quite off-hand about the whole thing. He wants certain things and is putting on a show of confidence. It's the best chance we have. Coming down to it, it's the only chance we have of getting near Prince Immar."

"What have Segat's demands been?" Carrick asked.

"Segat wants recognition as an equal, he wants a personal apology from Essedra for the death of the Princess DuLek and he wants the corridor of land, through Selarsh, reinstated giving him permanent access to the Ashra Sea."

"He doesn't want much then. Surely King Perin wouldn't support that, even if Selarsh agreed," Merren scoffed. "Or are we back to buying time?"

"Just that," Ressca confirmed. "But we've some intelligence regarding Segat's personal guard and the development of other weapons. A meeting may also give us a chance to dismiss or gain some knowledge of these right from the fountain's source, so to speak."

Ressca could see Kellim was still concerned and despite her bravado knew well enough to listen to the Panid. "We've put a lot in place, but will discuss our preparations further. We will be careful Kellim, but it is worth the risk."

"Then I will say nothing, other than be on your guard. Information can be taken from both sides; it could also be an opportunity for the Ildrans." Kellim looked expectantly at Carrick and Merren.

"Yes," they began in dull unison. "We will be careful too."

"That's twice," Carrick noted. "We've been spending too much time together. Kara has to come with us."

Ressca looked at them. "You want to be around Kara and Mia Svara in the same building? It would be bad enough the same city, or country."

Merren pulled a face. "I'd forgotten about that. Kara will just have to behave herself."

Durnin chuckled. "Don't worry, there will be lots of other people there for you to place between them." He looked quite pleased with himself. "A little diplomatic one-up-man ship finally convinced Chancellor Nirek to follow through with his idea to hold a meeting. Every Order in Koa will be represented. It should be quite an occasion." Then Durnin looked them all in the eye. "This includes you too, Kellim." He wagged a finger at the Panid. "Heed your own good advice. I don't want any risks taken. Do you hear me? I'd like you all back here and in one piece."

Aran sat watching the flames in the fire, he'd just finished a letter to Orla and was thinking of the nights in their tiny cottage in Rel. Shadows dancing on whitewashed walls, the smell of herbs and the milkies she kept in a small pen at the back of the living area.

"Hello, Kellim."

The Panid paused for an instant, the boy hadn't looked around. He didn't question the insight. "You seemed deep in thought."

"Just thinking of Rel, I've written Orla a letter."

"Good, don't forget your roots."

Aran looked at him questioningly.

"Roots, where you come from. How you began and who helped you as you took your first steps on life's journey."

"What were your roots?" he turned to face Kellim, sensing this might be one of those times when the Panid was willing to talk about his past. Aran had learned to recognise the right moments, the quiet times when he could slip in a question and find out more about his mentor and friend.

"Mine were as humble as yours," he said looking into the flames. "And like you, I ended up travelling further than I ever thought I would."

Aran found his eyes drawn to the fire as if the memories Kellim was about to relate would show themselves in its flickering light.

"I left my parents' care to be schooled in field craft. I was apprenticed to a powerful Talent. You would know him as the first and greatest of the Panids. To me, he was simply Mennem a friend and a mentor. There were eight Panids at that time and eight apprentices. I was one of them."

"Was that at the Gillern Lantrium?"

"No, no, the Gillern Lantrium hadn't been built then. Talents of any real ability were still a rare thing. Only the Lue-Esh Lantrium existed."

"In Urukish?" Aran asked.

"Yes. Lue-Esh was a city in Urukish. A great city with one of the most important libraries of the time. At some point, its fortunes along with the city's took a turn for the worst. Mennem got involved and saved the library and with it the city. Sometime after that, he and the other seven Panids turned it into the first Lantrium. A long time later the eight Panids took on eight apprentices, as I've said, and we moved in too. It became a place of great learning and we were eventually joined by others. The Gillern Lantrium came into existence when the number of Panids reached fifty, it was built as a place of protection for the Panids of the West. We pulled it out of the ground in a show of defiance, quite childish really, to make a point that we were more than just tools to be used by kings and queens as they saw fit. We were to be independent and safe. There to help but not to be commanded. We split into two groups, looking back, that was the first of our mistakes. The distance created a lack of communication and therefore understanding. What the West needed the East did not. What was important to the East was not so in the West. It didn't seem like a problem at the time. Much later, after Mennem and the original Panids had left, it all began to come apart. We didn't realise at first. In fact, things seemed to continue as they had. We achieved much until our divisions became evident and all was torn asunder by pride and ambition." Kellim blinked as a log crackled and sparks spun up the chimney. "They used to say, well before my time, I hasten to add, that flames were a gateway, the reason why we see so much in them. They are quite mesmerising."

But Aran wasn't watching the flames anymore, his mind was quickly putting dates together. His eyes grew wider as he tracked further and further back in time.

"I have a book you might like to read. If I can find it, and if it hasn't crumbled to dust at the bottom of a pile somewhere."

Kellim turned slowly to look at his young friend, a slight smile on his face. "Your sister has a direct approach when it comes to interrogation. You, young man, are far subtler and trick even the most secretive of individuals into talking more than they should. Keep it to yourself, if you would."

"O-of course, certainly. I wouldn't, I mean I couldn't..." Aran felt suddenly self-conscious, worried he'd upset the Panid.

Kellim winked at him. "It's a useful skill."

Aran scratched at his ear, self-consciously. "Jai said something pretty similar to me a while ago."

Kellim nodded. "He plays the fool, too well sometimes, and even convinces himself on occasion. You are a rarity; someone he trusts fully and will open up to. Even Bryn has to wring his troubles out of him. I think you will be good for each other."

"I hope so," Aran said absently and then added. "He's a good friend."

Chapter 13

The grand pavilion had been erected exactly on the border between Ildra and Selarsh, a neutral location agreed upon by both parties. A ruined town lay nearby, a reminder of the consequences of failed negotiations. Some distance behind it, two Ildran ships hovered in the sky, and deeper into Ildran territory a vast military camp sprawled across the countryside. The conditions of the summit were met, but a sign of intent had been placed within plain sight.

King Perin knew of course this was a risk, forty years on the throne had encompassed many mistakes and taught him just as many lessons. Emperor Segat was looking for status and redress for the perceived slights on Urukish and Ildra. Insults his ancestors had bitterly held onto through centuries of history. All of this, for what amounted to recognition. A rank Segat had not earned and blame that should not be borne by people three generations removed from the actions of an Amarian Emperor. Both seemed trivial, almost petty, but Perin had to try even though the effort, the risk to others and the chagrin involved rasped at his bones like an iron file. Prince Immar was on the verge of capture, running out of support and places to hide, and foremost in Perin's mind, if war came, he had to be certain that he had tried every reasonable route to peace before committing his people to a conflict that would claim the lives of thousands. He glanced behind him towards Selarsh, six of his royal guard rode in ceremonial formation and behind them were three Adepts. In the air, a pre-agreed distance from the meeting point, two Hallorn ships hovered. On Perin's left, General Caiddin straightened at the first sign of movement near the pavilion. On his right, Ressca rode with her eyes shut.

"I'm not asleep, Sire."

"I didn't think for one minute you were, Ressca." Perin returned his gaze to their objective. "How many?"

"Six, so far, General Immed, two Talents and three others, two of which could be his commanders and the third is a servant."

"One Talent for each pair, though I doubt the servant is included in that," Caiddin noted.

Ressca nodded. "Optimum numbers for transport. Any more people and it becomes harder for the Talent to guarantee their escape. We're playing the same ratio in our grouping."

"Segat?"

"I've searched as far as I dare, but I suspect VaCalt and the Emperor are still in the camp."

Perin laughed, all be it with little real humour. "I expected an amount of petty politics, he'll keep us waiting."

"A little man elevates himself on the tolerance of others," the General added, irritably.

"Now, now, Caiddin you know the game as well as I," Perin reminded.

"I apologise, Sire. I have little patience for such political games."

Ressca looked at him. "I agree with Caiddin, Sire. We are dealing with a petulant brat."

Caiddin laughed. "Don't temper your words Ressca." The General wasn't about to admit his unease, but inwardly he knew they were riding into a situation fraught with traps, political, physical and otherwise. As they approached, he checked his timepiece, judging the dash at full gallop to the cover of the sky ships. His men and women had been drilled, each was a volunteer, all with a clear understanding of the sacrifices expected of them should things go awry. His timepiece struck the mid-point of the day. Their people should be in place, waiting for a sign from The Duke and Immar. There was a lot at stake here. Too much for his liking.

Ressca looked at him. "It's time," she noted. "The Duke's is a small group; they should have a chance of crossing the border to our people."

The General wasn't so sure. "Our people, two Talents and two soldiers. It doesn't present many options."

"Two Talents was all I could spare."

There was a blare of trumpets, announcing their arrival. They passed the sentries and came into a clear area trampled to dirt by foot and hoof alike. Caiddin's eyes sought the guards, the hiding places in nearby trees, entry routes and escape routes. He'd planned for every possible eventuality and then planned for the improbable. Beyond that lay Ressca's domain.

The elaborate pavilion rippled in slow waves of gold and purple, extravagant Ildran banners snapped in the hot breeze, the gilt symbol of its Emperor flashing in the sunlight. Caiddin took it all in and looked at his King, his circlet also catching the light, a more fitting symbol of humility and a sovereign.

Ressca was all too aware of the Ildran's choice of a pavilion. She remembered visiting the arena in Magor as a child in the company of her father. Over fifty years ago now, and the last time the questionable spectacle was held. A brutal source of entertainment for such a seemingly civilised nation and an experience she had not enjoyed. The pavilion ahead matched those surrounding the vast stadium, housing the champions who sought glory and freedom. Was it a conscious choice, on Segat's part, to draw the comparison? A subtle reminder that life and liberty were again at stake. She heard Perin take a deep breath, without looking she could sense the mental change within him. Their candid conversation was over, the man she rode beside took practised control of his emotions, heightened his senses and unfurled the mantle of authority about himself. It was a transformation even Kara would be pressed to match, a change in presence that was almost palpable. Perin's mount moved ahead and began to strut, as it now carried the King of Hallorn into the arena.

They were shown into the pavilion, a familiar smell of canvas still pervaded the air, despite the expensive resins that burnt in gilded braziers. Rich carpets and tapestries along with every other comfort, the immense wealth of Ildra could provide, were present in abundance. General Immed of Ildra and his commanders stood in line in the centre of this. As King Perin entered, they executed a perfunctory bow.

"Where is Segat?" Perin demanded.

General Immed was about to greet the King and his entourage, offering introductions but instead cleared his throat, possibly embarrassed or angered by the demand. His apology was delivered with control. "Your Majesty, the Emperor has asked me to make sure you are made comfortable and want for nothing. The Emperor intended to be here personally to greet you, Sire, but is detained by important state business." Immed was far from happy. The Emperor should have been present, if he wanted to appear equal, he had to be seen observing the correct protocol, one that would set the right tone, one of control and authority. Now, they appeared unorganised and Immed was forced to play host like some servant. Introductions were made in an atmosphere of growing impatience. Eventually, all were seated in the stifling heat of the tent. Servants set out food and drink, all of which remained untouched.

Into this walked VaCalt, closely followed by two more Ildran Talents, Imalt and Venat. She strode to her seat with no intention of acknowledging the King of Hallorn.

If Perin was further irritated by this, he let no sign of it show. General Caiddin, on the other hand, stood with a force that shook the table. "The Potent forgets her place. You are in the presence of the King of Hallorn and will show due deference before taking your seat."

"I am quite aware of who is present, I bow only to my sovereign and will sit when I am ready."

"Aware of whom is present, but ignorant of your place under them," Caiddin returned angrily.

VaCalt stopped abruptly, the chair half pulled out. "I am the Potent, the Head of the Ildran Order of Talents, second only to the Emperor himself, I am ignorant of nothing. Least of all your reasons for being here..." She and the chair now blocked Imalt and Venat who were brought up short in the confined space.

"You would be advised to remember that you are a long way from Hallorn."

"If not ignorant," Ressca began mildly, "then absent-minded. You seem to have forgotten General Immed, doesn't he outrank you? We will make allowances for your advancing years. As for the plural, I am aware of only one reason for our being here. Your imagination is getting the better of you, VaCalt."

VaCalt glowered at Ressca and then at the King. "Does his Majesty know how to keep his servants in order?"

Perin regarded the Ildran Potent, his expression difficult to read. He neither spoke nor withdrew his eye contact.

VaCalt was having to brace herself against the chair until Imalt and Venat had sense enough to move back or sit, they of course were waiting for her to take her seat. It would appear as if she was awaiting permission to sit down. It was becoming a strain, Perin knew this.

"You may sit now," Perin said.

VaCalt had no choice, it was sit or fall. He had timed his words perfectly.

Caiddin sat, a smile playing on his lips.

"The General is amused," Imalt bristled.

"I would have applauded," Caiddin replied, "I've not seen a more impressive entry in some time."

Imalt was about to spit out a retort, but VaCalt spoke. "The Emperor is here."

Segat marched in, dressed in a military uniform and cape. He strode his way straight over to Perin. "King Perin, it has been years since we last spoke." He offered his hand while the King was still seated, his head lower than the Emperor's.

Perin however did not offer his until he had stood. "I trust our talks will meet similar success in the furtherance of sovereignty and the continuation of peace. Shall we get to business, Segat?"

"Yes, yes. Sovereignty and its current imbalance interest me greatly. I have no doubt peace is foremost in both our minds and I wish for nothing more than its continuation when an agreement is reached on the issues we will discuss this afternoon." With that he turned to his chair, holding out his hand as he sat. The servant quickly approached with a goblet. Segat began to drink, heedless of those around him and while documents were hurriedly placed in front of all those seated.

Perin watched the man who had served the wine and now scuttled about with the papers. Did every servant live in this state of constant fear? Perin wondered as he watched his anxious movements and flustered activity. He looked at the bound papers that had been set before him, Segat's demands, Perin assumed, gilt-edged and worded with equal lustre he had no doubt.

Caiddin looked only briefly as the servant placed his documents on the table, he was more interested in numbers and quickly counted heads. The Ildrans were missing two. He glanced questioningly at Ressca, was something amiss? She stiffened slightly and his gaze returned immediately to the entrance. Two figures entered, shrouded in white they appeared to float to their place behind Segat.

Caiddin went to stand.

"What is this Segat?" Perin asked, gesturing for Caiddin to remain seated.

"My personal guard," Segat replied and gestured at Perin's. "We did agree on particular numbers."

Ressca couldn't hold her tongue. "Numbers no civilised person would allow to encompass those abominations."

Segat's hand slammed down on the table, spilling his wine. Red-faced he stabbed a finger at her. "You dare to address me directly!" The figures began to move, their shrouds hissing as they brushed against the carpet.

The Hallorn Talents came to their feet.

"Call them off Segat," Perin barked. "I said, call them off, now!"

Segat looked at Perin, any sense of cordiality gone. He struggled to regain his control and at the last minute, some unspoken signal from him halted the shrouded figures and they returned to their post.

The Talents sat, after a quick gesture from Ressca. She was all too aware that VaCalt had been watching her, she could sense the satisfaction as she now began scanning the pages of the Ildran demands. Ressca kept her outward appearance calm and pushed down her growing unease. She'd seen some information about the shrouded figures, but the reality of them was something else again. What she could sense was abhorrent and it had shaken her. Those things had to be destroyed. Did Segat realise the possibilities they offered him? More to the point, did VaCalt? Hallorn and all of Koa were lost if either of them did. Kellim's concerns about the wisdom of this meeting returned to her thoughts just as a messenger entered and discretely handed a note to VaCalt. While she read it, Ressca quickly leant towards the nearest of the Hallorn Talents and whispered. "See what you can find out."

Bellim nodded and with an unconscious glance at the shrouded figures, quickly left the tent. VaCalt's eyes followed his exit.

Segat swallowed, he could still feel his face burning, Perin however had regained his calm in an instant and this aggravated him further. He had wanted to appear composed, in control, a confident monarch, the equal of Perin. Inwardly it was taking all of his control to remain seated, the urge to upturn the table, to vent his embarrassment and frustration, was compelling. He was surrounded by enemies, Hallorn and UruIldran alike. He glared at General Immed and then at Imalt and Venat, they looked down, not wishing to meet his stare. Let one of them cross me, fail me. He heard the movement of his guard, the soft murmur of their linen coverings. Segat became aware of the silence in the pavilion and glanced at Perin. The Hallorn King sat with an air of expectation, one that suggested his impatience and one that suggested he was not used to this level of ineptitude. Proceedings had ground to a halt.

"Imalt. Imalt. We are waiting!" Segat's temper ignited afresh.

"Your Majesty," the Adept quickly got to his feet, hurriedly opening the document as he stood and began to read. "King Perin," he stiffly inclined her head. "We are here to ensure the continued peace and prosperity of the nations of Koa. At this time, some obstacles obstruct Ildra's absolute right to land taken from her at the end of the Great War. Many of our people are forced to live on land their ancestors knew as Ildran but is now held by Selarsh. Tens of thousands have suffered the loss of a link to the sea, our seafaring brothers and sisters have lost a living that has scarred generations..." Imalt continued, no more impressed by the words he read than anyone else in the tent, except perhaps the Emperor.

During Imalt's reading of the protracted documents. Bellim returned, speaking briefly with Ressca. She kept her expression level, her emotions were harder to calm, and she feared, all too easy to detect. They'd failed, the Duke of Crath had been captured. Immar and his brother were being pursued, and her people and Caiddin's had paid for it with their lives. Was Segat aware of these events? She suspected his reaction would have been immediate, driven by emotion, he had proven himself quick to anger. No, if he'd known about this, they would have been confronted by now. She sensed VaCalt's hand at play. If Perin planned to place Prince Immar on the Ildran throne, why wouldn't VaCalt? The Prince could be a substitute for an Emperor who was unpopular, increasingly irrational and hard to manipulate.

Ressca realised her attention had been elsewhere when Imalt finished reading and with a bow took his seat. Segat stood and began addressing the gathering. VaCalt was looking directly at her, she could read the UruIldran's expression as if printed on the pages in front of her. Ressca and Caiddin had made provision for the situation they were now in. The question was, would it outmatch that of VaCalt's?

Chapter 14

Amar, the first city of Amaria was a complete contrast to Naddier. Devastated at the start of the Great War it had been rebuilt in a simpler, modern style. Sharp towers of amber stone and burnished metal domes dominated the skyline. Graceful metal bridges crossed the many wide canals. Seven new port towers, only one of which was complete, were being built in a new part of the city as Amaria opened itself to the continent. The great palace of the Empress, the Revered Essedra of Amar stood atop a hill in the city's centre, its myriad spires stabbed the sky like a crown, its white stone glistening in the heat of the sun. On a second hill stood the buildings of the Amar Order of Talents. Her father, Emperor Rasna, had wanted the Order Building to be placed above the people but had ordered the hill diminished by one hundred feet so that he and his palace would always look down on the Order, a constant reminder to all Amarian Talents of their change in status.

Carrick, Merren and Kara's journey had taken them by sky ship over the crowded skies of Hon, Selarsh and Urukish. A more direct route across the Cian and Amarian Seas was seen as too great a risk for the comparatively delicate sky ships. The strong winds there made the journey dangerous and was the territory of stouter sea-going vessels. However, once they'd entered the calm air over the Bay of Amaria, their ship had been able to head south for Amar. The preferred route would have taken them directly over Ildra, but its air space was now off-limits.

They now sat in an open-top carriage surrounded by twenty mounted soldiers in full, dress uniform. They'd progressed through the city taking in some of its most impressive sights.

Carrick exhaled heavily, wiping his forehead. "The heat. It's like being in an oven."

"It's lovely," Kara stretched out further on her seat and then pulled irritably at the soodrey dress that caught on her legs.

"So different to Naddier," Merren noted. "I suppose they're used to it. Look, those children running. I'd melt if I walked too quickly." She smiled as the children ran alongside the carriage waving and shouting. "Aran and Cali would have enjoyed this. It's such a contrast to home, the sights, the smells, the sounds and the people."

"Yep," Kara opened an eye, "but not worth the risk considering the trouble you had getting them to Naddier."

"You're right, they're safer there," Carrick agreed. "And the more they learn the better."

"Studies," Kara groaned.

Merren laughed. "It's been a long time since we had to do all of that. And here we are the teachers, not the pupils. When did that happen?"

"Speaking of time," Kara asked. "How much longer is this tour going to last?"

"The longer the better," Carrick said. "I'm in no hurry to be cooped up inside."

"It's a historic moment. This is history in the making." Merren pointed out.

"There's that word again. I'm more interested in the present."

"Present, past or future," Kara complained. "This dress is a pain. It's too long. What if there's a problem or I have to run? This thing'll have me doing cartwheels." She tugged again at the expensive soodrey.

"Durnin did say dress to affect," Merren reminded her.

"Well, we all have and it's still a pain. There's going to be a lot of showing off, isn't there?"

"There's always a bit of position sorting. Who's more senior, who's this, who's that? We've had worse to put up with."

Carrick smiled. "Durnin's devious hints seem to have prompted them into something really big. The great and the not so great will all be there. Just sit back and let them play their games, Kara. We've nothing to prove. At least we got an escort."

"I noticed none of *them* came down to meet us though," Kara noted. "No Chancellor Ritesh, no members of their Corumn and certainly no Mia Svara."

"Come on now," Merren scoffed. "You expect her to come and greet us."

"It would give her more time to admire the view from the top of that perfect nose of hers," Kara mimicked.

"They've been so insular; hung up on internal political wrangling, what can you expect?" Carrick sat back and watched the ever-changing display of life in the city. This was what he missed, a chance to mix with people and learn from them. He was tempted to stop the carriage and get out and walk. But they were here for a reason, and as Merren had mentioned earlier, they weren't the students anymore, they were the teachers and now, it seemed, the diplomats. However, their destination was still some way off and he could make the most of the ride. The streets teamed with life, the colourfully dressed people of Amar lived their lives on the roadside, buying, selling, washing, eating and even getting a haircut. Brown-skinned, dark-eyed heads turned as they passed, equally interested in the strangers that were still a novelty to the city. And still, they smiled in greeting, the rest of Koa had more than one thing to learn from these people.

"Do you think they'll be stood on boxes so we have to look up at them?" Merren asked dryly.

"Don't be silly," Kara corrected. "They'll be stood on stilts."

The carriages began to wind their way up the hill to the Amar Order's buildings, offering glimpses of spectacular views across the city as they climbed the tree-lined road. Finally, their honour guard passed through an imposing gateway and clattered into a vast open courtyard. In its centre stood a fully-grown field tree. The great dome of its branches spread to make full use of the ambient field. Carrick wondered how they'd managed to keep it alive. It was rare now to find specimens anywhere away from the strongest remaining field lines. One this big would need a lot of energy. Its burnished leaves showed no signs of distress and would look magnificent at night when the leaves revealed their gentle glow. The carriage crossed the courtyard and approached the main entrance. The Chancellor, Ritesh and Mia Svara were waiting to greet them.

"You're both wrong," Carrick said. "They're stood on steps!"

***

Bryn was startled as Jai scrambled to his feet, leapt over the boulder and drew his sword.

"Jai!" He grasped at thin air in a vain attempt to yank him back to cover.

Unable to pinpoint their attackers Kellim directed the field, shattering several random boulders in an attempt to create a distraction. Swearing under his breath Bryn heaved his tall frame from cover and raced into the narrow canyon. Using a pause in the arrows, Kellim risked a look over the rock. Jai had engaged a small group. Bryn was bearing down on others. The men and women were hastily dropping bows to draw swords. Kellim hit out three times, disabling a third group and sending an archer reeling before she could fire.

Three people down, Jai turned to meet two more scrambling over the icy rocks to get at him. He drew his knife and charged with both blades. The two men faltered, taken aback by the move. The nearest tumbled forward as the knife hit him. Jai leapt and blocked the second's sword. Using his momentum, he followed through with his fist and hit him in the face. The man stumbled back, hit the ground hard and lost his grip. Jai sent the sword spinning off to the side. Fixing his footing he made to finish the job, but Bryn's shouts registered. The sword missed the man's throat by a whisker.

"Alive!" Bryn was shouting as he ran over. "We need one alive!"

The man glanced at the knife lying inches away. Jai considered letting him grab it, but Bryn arrived and brought his foot down on the man's arm.

"Are you trying to get yourself killed?" Bryn asked heatedly, kicking the blade aside.

"It worked didn't it!" Jai snapped, his sword tip still at the man's throat. "What did you want to do? Sit behind the rock all day?"

"That was foolhardy and you know it!" Bryn said angrily and sheaved his sword.

Kellim blew on his fingers to stir some warmth into them and walked over. "The other three are unconscious," he looked at Jai and Bryn. "Let's see what this one has to say." He deliberately stepped between them.

"We'll talk about this later," Bryn said ominously, glowering at Jai before stepping back to allow Kellim through.

Jai stared back stubbornly, his breath steaming in the cold air.

"If you would be so good as to remove your blade," Kellim asked patiently. "He's not going anywhere." Jai looked at him and then lowered it. His mood had taken a darker turn since they'd returned to Naddier, Kellim put it down to too much time to think. On their journey north, Bryn had become increasingly frustrated by Jai's risk-taking and there had been several arguments. Both pots now appeared torrid, perhaps now would be a good time to allow them to boil over.

Jai sheathed his sword and stalked off to find their packs. A few flakes of snow swirled in the air behind him.

"I've had enough of this," Bryn growled and went after him.

Kellim mused briefly at transporting their swords away but instead, he looked at the greying sky and then turned back to the man he'd fixed to the frosted ground.

Bryn caught up with Jai. "Just what is it you're trying to prove!" he demanded.

Jai continued to check their packs; his back turned. "Nothing," he replied, roughly lashing two together.

"Then is it us, or just yourself you're trying to get killed!"

Jai froze, his knuckles white on the straps.

"Well!" Bryn demanded.

"Just forget it," he said irritably.

"Forge…" Bryn's anger boiled over. "Curse it!" he shouted. "That had to be one of the stupidest things you've done. And you've done some bloody stupid things!"

"I didn't ask you to follow!" Jai shouted, getting to his feet to face Bryn.

"What!" Bryn was incredulous. "I was supposed to sit there, while you…while you…" he struggled to calm himself. "You could have got us all killed! But Jai has to be the bloody fool!" He took a step forward. "I could have been pulling arrows out of your dead body!"

"I don't care if I get killed!" Jai bawled in Bryn's face. "Don't you get it? I should be dead!" Jai stabbed at his chest.

The expression on Jai's face took Bryn aback. He looked desperate. His eyes were filled with guilt. Neither spoke. Bryn stepped back easing the tension.

Jai was breathing heavily trying to get a grip on his emotions. "It should have been me; I should be the one dead. Stran should be here now," he ranted. "It was my fault! If I'd gone first, it would have been me. That's why I have to be the first! Now and every time!"

Bryn stood open-mouthed. "I…" words failed him. He knew Jai was struggling, but all this? How could he have missed all this? Looking now it was clear. He could read it in the man's eyes, the guilt burning there. Eating at him from the inside. "W…why didn't you say. We could have talked." Bryn gestured helplessly. "I could have helped. You're the closest thing I've got to a brother, Jai. One death is enough. Did it ever occur to you how your death would affect us?"

Jai stood and eventually, his shoulders slumped, his anger spent. He sniffed, shaking his head slowly and dragged a hand across his eyes. He felt stupid, embarrassed by the loss of control.

"How could a rock fall be your fault? You all took a place as you climbed. You could just as easily say it was Kellim's or Lewan's fault. Or-or mine for not being there. For going with Carrick and Merren." He put a hand on Jai's shoulder as if in some way it would help the words sink in. "But in reality, it was no one's fault. Not Kellim's, not Lewan's, not mine." He tried to catch Jai's eye. "And not yours." Jai nodded dumbly. "It was a terrible thing, but it wasn't your fault."

There was a long silence. "I miss him," Jai's voice choked when he finally spoke. He looked up. "I miss him and I can't let it go. I feel pathetic even talking about it." He rubbed at his forehead.

Bryn instinctively hugged him. "I know, I know," he held his friend until he could feel the tension in him begin to ease. Eventually, he let go of Jai so he could look at him. "You can get through this, but without the risks. You don't have to sort things on your own," he searched Jai's eyes.

Jai nodded and wiped the tears from his face,

"And no more risks?" Bryn waited. "Jai," he prompted.

"No more risks," Jai mumbled at last.

"We'll talk properly when we get to… Well, when we get to wherever we're going," he sighed heavily looking about them. "It's getting colder. Come on," he stirred Jai into action. It was time to move, not dwell. "Let's get our stuff, see what Kellim's managed to find out and build a fire."

The Panid's shout startled them both. Bryn pointed a finger in Jai's face. "No more risks," he warned hurriedly. A split second later they were both running, swords drawn, Bryn leading.

***

Cali waved as she spotted Aran. He was sat on a bench under the cover of one of the ancient gnarlwoods that edged the green of the Adepts' Buildings. The trees had been bare for some time, the storm season was well underway and dark clouds threatened rain.

"Morning," she called as she got closer. "You're up early."

"Lessons," he made a face. "What about you?"

"Thought I'd get up for the sunrise. This is a good spot to watch it from," she stopped to look about, getting her bearings. "It's supposed to be spectacular this time of the year but the clouds will hide it."

Aran patted the seat for his sister to join him. "You always did like sunrises. I remember you getting up early when we were younger."

"Such a peaceful time," she snuggled in close. "And the whole day ahead to look forward to." She suddenly delved into the bag she'd been carrying. "I'd forgotten," she said cryptically, pulling out a parcel and handing it to her brother. "Present, Kellim left it for you ages ago." Aran looked puzzled. "Go on, open it," she urged.

He battled with the paper and string. "Have you been fiddling with the form fields of this or something?" He gave up on the knot and managed to slip the string off, releasing the paper. "Kellim must have found it. He promised me a book about the time before the Panids." He turned the ancient text over in his hands, admiring the cover.

"He gave me one about the Panids' Children," Cali pulled another book out of her bag. "He said, knowing more about them would help."

"Have your nightmares come back?" Aran looked at her.

"No, I've not had one for ages."

"What about those dreams with the whispering sounds?"

"Gone. They weren't frightening, just odd. Stop looking at me like that. I'm fine."

"Did you tell Merren?"

Cali shook her head. "No, there was no need. Just daft dreams."

Aran looked at her suspiciously. "You know we're safe here, right?"

"Really, I'm okay." Cali looked at the distant cloudbank, hoping it would break and allow a view of the sunrise. "Lewan says it's going to rain again today and that it's cooler than normal."

"Tell me about it," Aran shuddered, barely looking up from the book. "I've never been anywhere this cold."

"Well, cool's probably more accurate. I'm not sure you could describe this as cold. It'll get milder once the suns up." Cali tucked her hands in her pockets and watched for the first glimmers of red. "Been here long?"

"Nope," Aran shrugged.

"There, the sun's just coming up." Her stomach gurgled.

"You had breakfast yet?" Aran asked as the noise came again.

"No. Any idea what it is?"

"I could smell bread as I passed the kitchens. But that was a while ago."

"We can go and have a look in a bit if you like," Cali said.

Aran nodded. "Has there been any word?"

"No. Ursa said they should be in Lont by now and that not even Kellim could send from there. It would be nice to know something; they've been gone ages."

"Yep, about a month." Aran did a quick mental calculation. "If it's cool here, it must be freezing up in Lont. They'll probably have snow. Now that would be something to see."

"Merren, Carrick and Kara will still have hot weather." Cali looked at the sky now lifting to misty oranges beneath the clouds. "The start of another day. I wonder what they're all doing."

***

The ornate hall echoed with the conversations and occasional laughter of those assembled. Light streamed in through elegant arches and a warm breeze brought the distant sounds of the city and the dry heat of the day.

The combined talent and experience in the room were considerable and with it came an equally impressive amount of posturing, speculation and gossip. Most of the Orders were represented, though Kara suspected curiosity had a lot to do with that. Amaria hadn't opened its doors since the end of the Great War. With that in mind, she wondered if Ciad would follow suit and was looking for a representative from its Order. She'd searched the multitude of heads and found none that looked Ciadran. No doors in the Enclosure yet, she thought to herself. She gave up the search and went back to watching the others.

Clothing, accents and skin colours were diverse reflecting the many nations present, though all spoke Koan, only slipping into their native tongue to pass an aside. The interplay between the Talents was entertaining, some quite open and friendly, some guarded, others caught up in games of one-up-man-ship. The members of the Amar Order were particularly interesting. They were as guarded with each other as they were with everyone else. The orchestrated front, put on for this audience, made her wonder just how draining this place must be. Just then two figures caught her eye as they entered. The Chancellor and Mia Svara made no such pretence. It was clear they didn't like each other and no matter what weren't going to pretend otherwise.

Merren and Carrick circulated, catching up with acquaintances, gathering information and passing on Durnin's regards. The role of Talents had changed since the Great War, demanding more of a focus on diplomacy. It seemed that the wind was on the turn, and Segat's threats would bring with them a greater demand for field use. This fact coloured their conversations, most of the representatives they talked with questioned their Order's ability to rise to the challenge. There was a degree of uncertainty and shared anger at the growing demands and unreasonable expectations placed on the Orders.

"Ah, the famous, or should I say, infamous brother and sister." Carrick and Merren turned to face the heavy accent that addressed them. Drassique, the Head of the Akar Order was a large man, wide around his middle and wider in his opinion of himself. He sported a large, curled moustache, which perfectly matched his flamboyant appearance. The large-brimmed hats he wore meant he was never lost in a crowd. His leadership of the

Akar Order was considered unconventional but despite this, he was generally respected if not always trusted.

"Drassique," they greeted. "It's been a long time."

The big man laughed, brushing his moustache with a flourish. "Is there an echo in here?" he shook both of their hands, his voice a rich drawl. "Yes, ten years and how they have flown." His manner of speaking and the expressiveness of his face hinted at an urge to appear on the stage.

"That long," Merren added mischievously.

"Of course, I have an excellent memory for dates and events. Particularly the more scandalous ones," Drassique rumbled theatrically.

"Oh, now surely you can't still hold that against us," Merren grinned.

"You were only too happy to have our help at the time," Carrick added.

"Hmm. You still have it then, I assume," Drassique noted with interest, twiddling the tip of his moustache.

"Wouldn't be without it," Merren replied.

"Safe in your rooms perhaps?" Drassique made a pretence of looking for a member of his Order.

All three laughed. "Now, now Drassique let's not make a scene like the last time," Carrick waved a finger. "Finder and keeper."

"My dear chap, I wouldn't dream of it," Drassique waved his hand expressively. "Especially in such vaunted company. I've never seen so many Heads and Adepts. Almost every Order must be here, with a few notable exceptions," he added as an aside.

Merren nodded and looked about them. "I hoped we might see Ciad represented."

"I doubt very much we will ever see a Ciadran face again," Drassique said. "The Enclosure is no less formidable now than it was at its completion. They are isolated as indeed are the people of Dallene. Though their barriers are formed by water and ancient beliefs."

"A troubled island," Carrick noted.

"Increasingly so," Drassique brushed at a moustache thoughtfully. "Their links with the rest of Koa ebb and flow as much as the tides that encircle their island. I would have been surprised to see them represented here today."

"Even the best of us can't ignore an excuse for a good nose around," Merren said.

Drassique took on an imperious look, his tongue firmly in his cheek "I of course am here to foster inter-Order relations and professional development in the spirit of kinship and mutual trust," he gave a slight bow.

"Impressive," Carrick encouraged. "What does that mean?"

"I have no idea," Drassique admitted roguishly. "But I've heard it said a lot when Order Heads don't want to admit the real reason why they're here."

"And what's that?" Carrick wondered if he was thinking the same.

Drassique gave him a wary look and lowered his voice to a conspiratorial rumble. "Come, come now even you must admit to concerns about national character traits reasserting themselves."

Merren nodded. "You mean the Amarian Elite and their character traits."

"The Elite, if you want to put it that way are the ones with the power. They are the face of their nation."

"That's a bit of a generalisation," Merren warned.

"Then you haven't considered it. That, my dear, dare I say it, is very Hallorn."

"I didn't say we hadn't considered it," she said with a faint smile. "And what do you mean very Hallorn?"

Drassique laughed. "This is how things began with Karna III. Let's all be friends, but with Amar in charge, oh and don't mind us while we help ourselves to your land." He pinched the air and popped it into a pocket. "Amarians have always considered themselves superior."

"Certain Amarians." Carrick was inclined to agree to a point. "Essedra has shown herself to be different."

"Same bloodline," Drassique shot back.

"New ideas."

"Not if you ask Essedra's oldest daughter. Jalsa Treya's disposition favours her great grandfather's."

"The family name bears enough scars to remind them of past mistakes," Carrick added.

"Scars dealt by Hallorns, who have always seen themselves as guardians of the law and arbiters of right and wrong."

Carrick chuckled. "That was the Gillern Panids, who just happened to be in Hallorn," he corrected. "You have us all pinned down, don't you?"

"Of course," Drassique swept a hand across both sides of his moustache.

"And the people of Akar?" Merren inquired. "How would you label them?"

"Clear-sighted, truthful and…"

"Prone to stereotyping," she finished for him.

Drassique chortled. "How insightful, for a Hallorn," he added with a wicked grin.

Merren gave him a wry smile and then turned to follow his line of sight as his expression changed.

Drassique glanced back to see if they were all looking at the same thing. "Could there be a more obvious proclamation of what we've just discussed?" He was referring to Mia Svara who had just come into view. "She is the personification of Amarian superiority, devious, highly intelligent and cold. Quite the most exquisite creature. I wouldn't trust her as far as…" he paused. "Isn't that Kara just off to her left?"

"Oh no," Merren groaned.

"Are we at a safe distance?" Drassique craned his neck for a better view.

Carrick smiled. "Perhaps under the table would be better."

Kara had just finished a conversation with Glytta, the Order Head from Ronce, and turned to find a drink, but instead came face to face with Mia Svara. The tall dark-haired woman seemed equally pained by the coincidence. Bollocks, Kara muttered, how could she have missed her? The bloody woman stood out like a column of flame. She was notorious for wearing striking red soodrey of a style favoured in northern Amaria only. A deep red as eye-catching as Kara's hair, though neither would have admitted to any common ground. The South of Amaria had always regarded the North as its poor, less sophisticated relation and admitted few Talents from that area. Mia Svara had been a rare exception and took every opportunity to remind the Order of its ignorance. Kara suspected it was a constant struggle facing such prejudice and held begrudging respect for her but on that point only. Beyond that, she couldn't stand her. Kara stretched a smile across her face and locked it in place.

"Kara."

"Mia."

"That's Mia Svara. You are well?"

"Fine, and you, Mia Svara, are you well?" Kara inwardly kicked herself, she'd meant to keep up the Mia thing, knowing the woman hated any shortening of her name, save by a select few.

"Quite." Mia Svara did not attempt to hide behind a smile. "I see Merren and Carrick are as popular as ever. Though everyone must be disappointed by Kellim's absence. And I see you have made... an effort."

"Well, you lot all seem so hung up on petty gestures I thought I'd play along. And you? Still wearing red."

"Crimson," Mia Svara corrected.

"Right, like a bruise."

"And your hair, the gushing cascade of blood from a more serious wound," Mia Svara smiled. It didn't sit well on her features. "And I see you are wearing shoes. Did you have help?"

"They're sandals," Kara snapped.

"You know the difference, well done."

"Tell me," Kara could feel herself getting irritated; it annoyed her even more that Mia Svara remained so cool. But she was determined to even the score. "Is that the same dress or do you have a wardrobe full of them? What shall I wear today?" Kara tapped a finger on her chin. "Oh yes, the red one. At your age, it must make things so much easier."

The temperature in that part of the room plummeted. Mia Svara turned stiffly to take in the rest of the hall. "This must be very interesting for all of you," her tone even, if a little tight.

"Interesting?" Kara asked.

"Why, to see Amar of course. Quite a wonder compared to where you've come from."

"You must be very proud, such a lot of domes. I suppose if you keep practising you might eventually get one right." Kara was sure she could hear smothered laughter coming from somewhere nearby.

The doors to the hall closed, a small handbell was rung and, much to Kara's relief, everyone was asked to be seated. A quiet hum of expectation filled the airy room. Servants attended to the needs of the guests only to melt into the background as Chancellor Nirek, Head of the Amar Order of Talents rose from his chair. He waited until all eyes turned to him. "Colleagues, might I take a moment to savour the historic implications of this gathering. None of us here can be immune to its significance."

Kara made to scratch her nose looking side-on at Merren and muttered, "Blah, blah, blah. Posture, posture, posture."

"I would ask those of us assembled here today to make a vow to meet again on this date, each year, to strengthen the bonds that unite us and herald in a new era of cooperation." The Chancellor was satisfied as the hall filled with applause.

"Some of us have been doing that already," Kara muttered as she clapped politely.

"And now..." Chancellor Nirek began, his expression darkening.

"Here it comes," Carrick whispered. "Will he address the rumours or keep us all shut out? We need to see a change if we're to trust them."

"...in the spirit of openness, I must bring to your attention recent events in Amar. Several months ago, our Order was attacked." There was an audible gasp of surprise in the hall and the Chancellor waited for it to settle. "Varin, one of our Discipline heads attempted to take control of the Corumn." Again, the room was filled with voiced concerns and questions.

"How is this possible?" a member of the Jedesyut Order demanded, his accent a marked contrast to the Chancellor's. "How is it possible that one man could hold and control such high-ranking Adepts? No one has access to that kind of power since The Field's Cap was put in place."

"Colleagues," Chancellor Nirek raised his voice in irritation at the interruption. "If you will allow me to continue." Slowly the hall became calm again. "In self-imposed isolation, Varin has found a way to access the field to a greater degree. It was his intention to take control of the Corumn, setting in place his own agenda for the future of the Amar Order. However, he was unaware of the recent changes in its membership and was unable to bring his plans to fruition..." Yet again a wave of questions and conversations interrupted the Chancellor.

Merren exchanged a glance with Carrick. "That's a start," she conceded.

In Order to answer some of the many questions being directed at him, the Chancellor continued to speak, forcing everyone to fall silent again. "We were aware of his desire to see Amar return to its preeminent position of influence in the east of the continent. This idea was of course flatly refused."

"We'll have to take your word for that," Drassique voiced the concerns of many. "This Varin of yours seems to have designs on altering the landscape of power in the east of Koa at a time when Segat has the same idea. Personally, I find that very interesting, I'm not one to believe in coincidence. Might I also ask what the Amar Order is doing to bring him to heel?"

"That is in hand," the Chancellor spoke bluntly. "You can rest assured however that Varin will be made to answer for his crimes."

"So then, my dear Chancellor, is he still at large?" Drassique pressed.

"The matter is in hand," the Chancellor repeated irritably. "I raised the issue becau…"

"Then we have nothing more to worry about," the Head of the small Selarsh Order said dismissively, her accent lending a clipped tone to Koan. "Drassique you're clutching at air, Varin has merely taken an opportunity to act while all sensible eyes are on Ildra. It's time we moved on to other business. Isn't the current unrest in Ildra the real reason why we are all here? Surely this is a more pressing issue than this delusional Adept of yours."

Many voices rose in agreement.

The Cian Order Head spoke. "We border with Ildra too, but I am reluctant for the Orders to become overly involved in continental politics. I would prefer to leave that to the ruling houses or governments. The Great War came about because of the interference of Talents. We can't put ourselves in that position again. It has taken us a long time to claw back respect."

"Ildra is the overriding concern and Ildra alone!" The Selarsh Head reiterated. "Segat's actions threaten our existence, our reputations will count for nothing," Again many voices rose to support the words of the Selarsh Head.

"If I might," Mia Svara spoke before the Chancellor could respond. "Make no mistake that Varin is a power to be reckoned with. There are none here who could best him. He was able to overpower the Corumn and has since developed his powers further. It would be foolish to dismiss him before considering any connections he may have formed with Segat."

Carrick spoke, "Varin's plans appear complex and could still be very much in operation. As Talents isn't this our collective responsibility. Varin must be taken out of the equation."

"We have all noticed that the Ildran Order has failed to send representatives to this meeting," the Pidone Head stated. "The diplomats have their work set before them. Varin could hamper their efforts. I agree, in part, with Mia Svara of Amar and Carrick of Naddier. Varin can not be ignored by any of us."

"And that is why," the Chancellor began, bringing the attention back to himself, "we have sent a contingent of our most powerful Adepts to find Varin and put an end to any further threat he may present."

The discussion continued for several hours even before the day's agenda could be started. In the middle of a particularly heated debate, the doors to the hall swung open and a member of the Empress's staff entered. He hurriedly found the Head of the Amar Order and handed him a note. Chancellor Nirek accepted it, with a look of irritation at the messenger. As he read it, his expression changed.

"This is confirmed?" he asked the messenger urgently.

Those seated nearby noted the tone of his voice and stopped talking.

The Chancellor pushed his chair back and stood, he looked shaken. Conversations died as the gathering turned towards him. He looked at the message again, before passing it to Mia Svara.

"I..." he seemed uncharacteristically at a loss for words, looking at the concerned faces about him. "I have terrible news," he said at last. "I have just heard from Her Imperial Majesty that Ildra has invaded Selarsh and Urukish." The room erupted in disbelief and outrage. Some of the delegates were on their feet and those from Selarsh and Urukish were already heading for the doors. He raised his voice to continue. "And that forces are advancing on Hon."

Chapter 15

Bryn and Jai skidded to a halt as a bristle of arrows met their sudden approach. Kellim stood watching the man he'd been questioning scramble up the sides of the pass, but then a smile touched the edges of his lips as he spotted a familiar figure. Bryn and Jai watched in disbelief as The Faithful hurried down from the ice-covered ridge, shouting excitedly in its strange voice.

"No, no, lower them, lower them! This is good. This is a good meeting! They are not the other one." Reluctantly the bows were lowered as The Faithful continued its insistence and hurried to greet Kellim.

On reaching the Panid it stopped, and composing itself, bowed. Kellim quickly followed with the appropriate response.

"These people are with you?" Kellim was a little surprised.

"This is so. The Faithful has joined them and now protects The Beholder once again. The Faithful is sorry you were attacked. You were mistaken for another." It tapped the tips of its talons together, a nervous smile on its face. The smile was intended as a friendly gesture. Jai found the array of teeth on show unnerving.

"Do you have news for me?" Kellim asked. "The Children's

interest in Cali is my chief concern."

Again, The Faithful tapped its talon tips together and seemed to be considering its thoughts.

Bryn watched somewhat bemused by this strange habit. It appeared it had a lot to think through. Perhaps it was considering where to start. "This doesn't look good," he commented under his breath to Kellim.

Kellim waited patiently knowing better than to interrupt its thought processes. The Faithful had many quirks, the same as any intelligent being. Finally, the creature stopped its cogitations.

"None that The Faithful can share," it replied.

Jai rolled his eyes. "You're joking."

Kellim knew the creature would filter out anything irrelevant to the question, no matter how dangerous or fascinating, but hadn't expected the filtering to be so complete. He did notice the scorched patches on the creature's fur and several recently healed scars. "You've been hurt. What happened?"

"Now is not the time for this. You will follow?"

"Apparently so," Kellim was left with no other options. "Then yes, you should lead on my friend." The Faithful bowed, welcoming Kellim's use of friend and turned to head up the path.

Kellim checked the stance and disposition of the people arrayed about the ravine before moving. Some were starting to make their way along the rough path; others remained. He made his way carefully over to Bryn and Jai.

"That was worth the journey," Jai commented dryly as he rubbed his hands together in an attempt to get some sensation back into them.

"Are all the Panid's Children like that?" Bryn asked as he too began to wonder if the effort of getting here had been a complete waste of time.

"No," Kellim replied. "And there will be others, so might I suggest you both close your mouths and try not to stare. Be aware that they can be sensitive and mutual respect is of paramount importance to them. Oh, and they don't like to stand around once a decision has been made." Kellim gestured after The Faithful then turned and began to follow it.

"What about our packs…" Jai turned to see their belongings had already been collected.

Bryn started walking up the path into a sudden flurry of snow and noticed the sky; the weather was pulling in. If they were delayed, returning to Naddier could be difficult.

They climbed to the top of the ridge by which time it had begun to snow in earnest, this made the already slippery path a harder prospect. Now they had to watch their footing and try to keep up with The Faithful. Through the building blizzard, Kellim could just make out the Plain of Coth, a distant expanse beyond the mountains. He pulled on his heavy hood, glad of the protection the old but favourite coat provided.

The Faithful marched onwards as the weak winter sun faded. "Keep up. Keep up. You will be warm soon," It assured, its fur now coated with snow.

Distracted from his thoughts, Jai looked at the creature, even his short and brutal childhood had included tales of the Panids' Children. None of them had happy endings and most involved nosey girls and boys being carried off and popped into a cooking pot. He'd been frightened by such stories as a very young child. Warnings from an embittered mother whenever he showed any of his father's traits. She had clung to the injustices of life and blamed his father's shortcomings for all of them. Had she affected him so deeply that even now he held onto guilt, a familiar and safe feeling, despite its destructive effects? He was forced to reflect on Bryn's words and as they trudged on, he finally allowed himself to accept the truth in them. He'd needed something to force an end to a destructive cycle. Mainly because Bryn had pointed out the effect his actions were having on others. People he cared about. Perhaps he'd been ready and, at that moment, let go of something, dropped a burden he shouldn't have carried. Now all he had to do was apologise, stop feeling stupid and possibly avoid being eaten.

The Faithful led them some distance along the ridge and then down into a small valley easily overlooked by any travellers willing to brave this remote and desolate part of the world. They descended steps carved out of the grey rock, making their way past terraces now planted with over-winter crops. The snow was laying and covering everything. Only an icy stream remained free as it splashed and tumbled its way noisily along the bottom of the valley, before disappearing into a small cave just visible through the driving snow.

The wider steps finally gave Bryn a chance to walk alongside Jai. "Were you told stories about them too?" he inclined his head in the direction of The Faithful, breaking the awkward silence between them.

"You can't see anything around here chopping root veg, can you?" Jai was glad to answer.

Hearing their voices Kellim paused and turned to look at them. "Gentlemen, remember your manners," and then speaking quieter still, added. "Of course, they will eat you both first. You have far more meat on your bones." With a knowing look, he resumed his descent of the steps.

"Stay close," Jai teased, gripping Bryn's arm.

"I preferred you when you were miserable," Bryn said dryly and then cuffed Jai on the back of the head for good measure.

They entered the small cave the stream cascaded into, which quickly opened out into a large well-lit tunnel. As it climbed up into the interior of the hillside, they came to a set of steps flanked by smooth walls. It became obvious that the tunnel had been worked to make it more uniform and accessible. Water from the much higher mountains must have once tumbled this way and joined the stream they'd left behind. Eventually, the steps led to a large cavern whose access was controlled by a high wall. Men, women and a creature, they only caught glimpses of, patrolled its battlements and watched as they entered through the gateway at its centre. This cavern led to an enormous space in which a small village had been built. Buildings had also been carved out of the chamber's steep sides to a height of about thirty feet, leaving the ceiling to continue for at least another twenty into the powerful light above.

"How are they lighting this?" Jai asked, his mouth open as he turned to take in as much as he could.

"And how have they kept it all hidden?" Bryn asked, turning to look at Kellim.

"A lot of the Children were given abilities. Some are talented. Though I'm unsure how they managed all of this so far underground." Kellim shielded his eyes as he scrutinised the light source above and speculated about its creation and maintenance. "Of course, we are not deep underground; we have travelled upwards inside the hill and as a result, the field is still strong here. Most interesting."

The Faithful walked back to them, impatient to continue. The people accompanying them had continued onwards and disappeared into the streets below. "Hurry, we must hurry. We are expected. Collect your packs. It is impolite to keep her waiting," The Faithful fussed before heading down the steps to the narrow streets below. They shouldered their packs, still gazing at everything about them and followed.

The streets were made busy as the occupants of the buildings went about their business.

"Tell me The Faithful. Who are these people?"

The dispossessed, the homeless, like the Children," it answered not turning or slowing, its claws clicking on the paved street. Some of the people stopped to watch as they passed, far more interested in the three strangers than The Faithful.

"Are there many more of the Children here?"

"Several," The Faithful seemed evasive, unwilling to give exact numbers away. "Less than there was. Some chose to join the Adept whose name is Varin of Amar."

"Joined Varin?" Kellim was shocked.

"The choice was not theirs. She will explain. We are nearly there."

They didn't see any more of the Children but passed several buildings of considerable size accessed by openings designed for beings quite different to people. The Faithful led them to a wider street that gently sloped upwards towards the side of the chamber, ending at a set of wide steps that climbed to a large, highly carved building of arched openings and many columned levels.

The Faithful ushered them in as they reached its main entrance. Inside was comfortably furnished and far from austere. They walked into what looked like an audience chamber. Its plastered walls were painted with scenes from the Great War and showed battles the Panids' Children had played pivotal roles in. The floor was scattered with rugs and cushions of varying sizes, small tables and chests. Several braziers burnt sweet-smelling resins that gave the room a smoky atmosphere. It was a peaceful place and the three felt immediately at ease.

The Faithful bowed deeply as a figure entered. Kellim quickly followed suit and gestured with a discrete hand for Bryn and Jai to do the same. They did, trying to see who or what it was they were greeting.

"Please, there is no need for such formalities." The voice was that of a woman's, but deep and gravelly. "Kellim, your reputation has not diminished. You are a part of history itself." The Beholder walked over to greet him. "I am pleased that time's embrace still touches you lightly. Your journey has by far been the longest. It is good to see you again."

Kellim took the hand that was offered him and held it warmly between both of his. The soft light glistened in his eyes as he looked at the diminutive figure before him. When he spoke, his voice was emotional. "Your presence inspires and moves me as always Maga. I realise now it has been too long and for that, I am truly saddened. Your wise counsel has been sorely missed."

Still holding Kellim's hand, she turned to the others. Maga bowed to The Faithful. "Your quick action and insights have increased the debt of gratitude we owe you The Faithful."

The Faithful straightened, positively glowing from the praise and then immediately bowed again in reverence. The gesture was graceful and contrasted greatly with its outward appearance. "The Beholder is most kind. The Faithful is deeply honoured."

Bryn watched as the woman walked toward him. She was all of four feet tall and appeared to be in her sixties. Though he knew she had to be much older. He had not expected her to look so much like a person and wondered at the difficulties this must have brought her in the past. She was dressed in many layers of clothing, interspersed with jewels and trinkets of no great worth, but clearly of personal value. She seemed a little uncomfortable in their company. What was she thinking he wondered?

"You quickly size me up Bryn of Naddier," she smiled and walked over to him. "But do not worry we are all safe from the past here and the insecurities of others." He was surprised by her words and that she knew his given name. Kellim had talked of her on one or two occasions, but this was his first experience of her abilities. Her large brown eyes seemed to read every shadow of thought in his. This fascinated him.

"Your forbearance is a source of endless comfort to your friends and especially to Merren." Bryn started slightly at the mention of her name. "Watch over them all," she whispered for him only to hear. "They will need you more than ever if what might be, unfolds..." she stopped herself and smiled apologetically before taking his hand. "Watch over them, keep them safe."

"I- I will," Bryn answered somewhat bemused and a little unsettled by her words. She smiled again before moving on to Jai.

"Jaitan of Cian you have at last released a burden." Without thinking, Jai lowered himself to one knee as she took hold of his hands. The Beholder looked back at Bryn. "You were right, it was not his fault, and now he has been able to listen to you." She nodded before turning back to Jai. "It was time to let go of the past. To remember what you have gained and been gifted by one so special to you. Do not linger on what you have lost but carry forward what you have been given. You will need both eyes on the road ahead and when you are ready there is one who will need you." Jai swallowed, his emotions beginning to surface again. "Do not hide them. They are the source of your strength." The Beholder watched Jai intently for some time, finally nodding at an unspoken understanding. The room was still when she finally turned back to the others. Her voice broke the silence. The air stirred and time seemed to move on again. "I have much to tell you. But first, Kellim, I think we should listen to your stomach. Food, yes that is a fitting way to welcome you." Maga walked over to him, took his hand and led him out of the room.

Jai got to his feet and fell into step with Bryn. The big man looked at him. "Jaitan?"

"I didn't choose it," Jai replied defensively.

***

The speed and force of the Ildran invasions had found Selarsh and the city-states of Urukish ill-prepared. Hon fared no better. The border forts had done what they could to be ready. Catapults had been armed and walls strengthened in the short time available. Despite the early movement of troops, Hon had a relatively small army and its Order was a minor one. News of Ildra's forces and their size had reached them and it was with a sense of dread that the border forts waited for the first sight of the advancing Ildran army. News of its ferocity and the terror unleashed by its Talents reached every ear. Each man and woman assigned to Hon's defences had said goodbye to friends and family before urging them to join the thousands of refugees now fleeing the coming invasion.

Near Pell, the border fort waited, hands gripped swords and bows, eyes fixed to the east, ears listening for the drums, the pounding heart of the advancing army and the sound of the leviathan's approach. But there were no drums, no pounding feet; no dark stain to blight the horizon. Instead, the skies brought a silent terror; a hundred sky ships casting a creeping shadow over the ground that swallowed everything beneath it. Stunned soldiers were jerked into action by their commanders and the catapults sprang into action, creaking and groaning as each hurled huge boulders into the sky. Arcing through the air one struck home, shattering the hull of an Ildran ship. It pitched forward and began to fall from the sky. A great cheer went up from the walls only to die as the first echoing booms cracked the air. Sulphurous smoke bloomed like flowers from every ship and seconds later destruction rained down on the fort. The armada sailed overhead, barely slowing in its progress towards the capital.

***

Her Imperial Majesty the Revered Essedra of Amaria looked to the neat formal gardens. Close to one of the fountains, her second daughter Princess Urvasi sat splashing her hands in the cooling water. She had considered a future marriage for the little girl with Segat, tying the countries together, stabilising the Urulldran bloodline. But not even Essedra was prepared to make such a sacrifice. A short distance away, under the shade of a bower tree, her eldest daughter, Princess Jalsa Treya, sat scowling. She would someday marry a Kiashan prince. Essedra and King Osen-Zay of Kiashu wanted an alliance that would help to ensure peace in the east of Koa. But Jalsa Treya, even at this young age, was a concern. At times Essedra wished Urvasi was her eldest and next in line. Jalsa Treya was headstrong and proud, more like her great-grandfather Karna III. She needed to learn humility, compassion and patience. That journey would be a long one and Essedra was uncertain of its outcome. The progress Essedra's country was making had to continue, leaving the past and her ancestors shortcomings so far behind that they could not reassert themselves. She needed time. Time for her daughters to grow up, mature and continue that progress. Until then, Essedra knew she would have to live a long life. To reign on the throne of Amaria until her days were spent and Jalsa Treya had learnt what she needed, what Amaria needed.

Essedra turned reluctantly from the arch, allowing the fine curtain to float back as she moved to stand behind her chair. Resplendent in a gown of the finest soodrey, she was a symbol of her country's prosperity and power. Every decision, every word carefully considered, she had ruled for 50 years and steered her government and country to a position of power and wealth matched only by Hallorn and Akar and surpassed by Ildra alone. Leaving behind the isolationist views of her forebearers she had slowly but firmly nudged her people into a new age, but now this.

"You say a powder was used in the attacks, Chancellor Nirek?"

"Yes Ma'am," the Head of the Amar Order of Talents answered. "It is a mixture of chemicals and minerals. Mixed in the right proportions its destructive powers are considerable. The barrels would have been indistinguishable from any others loaded onto the ships." Nirek shook his head. "None of the Order delegates would have been able to sense the danger they and their ships were in as they returned home from our meeting. The powder has to be ignited to release the energy stored in its components. Exactly how this was achieved remotely we are still uncertain."

"Carrick."

"Yes Ma'am?"

"Does your Order have knowledge of this weapon?"

"Yes. Like most of the Orders, we have considerable knowledge of the volatile properties of various combinations of minerals, chemicals and compounds, though our abilities to manipulate the field have always negated any need to develop the use of such primitive weapons. The prevailing peace since the Great War meant that they were still considered redundant, despite the limitations imposed by The Field's Cap."

Essedra nodded. "But it would appear Emperor Segat and VaCalt, the Head of his Order of Talents, have a different view. A view that has us scrabbling to gain an equal footing against this powder weapon. I can defend my borders against an open attack, but this more subversive, this more cowardly approach will require us to learn new skills if we are to prevail."

Her chief advisor, Lord Atma spoke. "Ma'am, we are exploring the possibility that spies exist within our ranks, informants who supplied departure information allowing the barrels to be placed on the correct ships. All cargo is now checked by sight as well as talent and we can once again guarantee the safety of our shipping."

The Empress moved to stand behind his chair. "A vital guarantee, but one that we should have been able to provide to the visiting Orders. These subversives within our walls must be captured and made to pay publicly for their acts." Essedra released her grip on the back of the chair. "The loss of so many lives." She was also aware of the humiliating blow this had delivered to her and her country, so much of her work undone.

"Indeed Ma'am," Atma inclined his head. "A disaster that could have been far worse. If the ships had exploded over the city the death toll would have been far greater."

"How many were lost?" The Empress asked.

"Out of the forty Adepts, twenty-eight are dead and six are seriously injured. Those delegates forced to delay their return home, due to the dangers of attempting a flight over Ildra,

Urukish or Hon, were the fortunate ones." Atma looked at the information before him. "Four hundred crew members were also killed or injured. At your instruction, their families have been duly compensated."

"How does one compensate for the loss of a life," Essedra said. "It has been a long time since I felt this helpless."

Atma turned in his chair to look at her. "You have never been that my Queen," he said gently.

Essedra patted his shoulder. Carrick made some pretence at looking at papers but was surprised by the familiarity between the two. But then Atma had been by her side right from the start of her reign. How could they not be close?

"I am interested in Segat's order of invasion. It was my understanding he wanted a coastline and that Selarsh was to provide it."

"We can only assume, Ma'am," Atma replied. "That the damage dealt the countries surrounding Selarsh will persuade them to surrender. Segat would want as much of its infrastructure intact as possible."

"Ma'am," Carrick noted a detail in the information before him, "six of the Adepts were Order Heads. This appears to have been timed to create the maximum amount of confusion, chaos and terror across Koa. Segat begins his invasion and deals a blow to his adversaries, strong enough to wrong-foot their response."

The Empress nodded. "We are confused and weakened. Just how I would want my enemy before I attacked. This is only the beginning." She turned her attention to Chancellor Nirek.

"Speaking of wrong-footing; Varin still eludes capture? Has there been any word from Ritesh?"

"I'm afraid not, Ma'am," the Chancellor answered uncomfortably. "His last dispatch came from Neath before his ships attempted to follow the River Tybe through the mountains of Lont. The largest of their vessels was forced to remain at Bara, it being too large to navigate the gorge. We are unable to cast any light on why Varin is heading into the North or how close Ritesh and his people are to capturing him."

"What are their chances?" she asked.

"I would not like to say," Chancellor Nirek admitted reluctantly. "Navigating the gorge will be fraught with danger in itself. If they survive the journey, they will have to pick up Varin's trail and contend with any hostiles. That would all take time. Our concerns could of course be unfounded; they may have him and be attempting to return as we speak. But that will force them to skirt Ildra's northern border again."

"Do we have any news from King Perin of Hallorn?" Essedra asked.

"Only this morning, Ma'am," Merren began. "He is on route to Oren after the talks with Segat broke down. Their attempt to free Prince Immar was discovered. A confrontation followed and lives were lost but King Perin evaded capture. It seems Ressca had made some unorthodox provisions to aid an escape should it be needed. All other initiatives connected to the meeting have failed. The Duke of Crath is a prisoner and we can only hope Prince Immar and his brother are still free."

"We have a lot of unanswered questions," Essedra took her seat. "Lord Atma, shall we move on to a subject that may furnish some answers. Our borders, are they secured yet?"

"Work progresses well at the Hand and the northern gate to the Calk spice trail is now complete. The Ugamas Pass has been further reinforced due to the increased activity there."

"Activity?"

"The Ildran sky navy is testing for weak spots Ma'am."

"And do we have any?"

"No Ma'am."

"A definitive answer at last. We seem to be making progress. Now, tell me what news from Hon?"

Chapter 16

VaCalt scrunched up the report and then struck the desk. As Head of the Ildran Order of Talents she would not be undermined. She had worked hard to make the title of Potent mean something. Power, authority, respect and fear. Any loss of what she had worked so hard for burned her like fire. The flickering candle caught her eye. It was a reminder and flattening her hands on the surface of her desk she brought the anger under control. She rose and walked to the candle, where it stood with a metal bowl atop a wooden stand, rolled back the loose sleeves of her amber robe and distracted herself with the ritual; one of a few she now allowed in the Ildran Order. She ran her hands through the candle flame and washed them in the bowl; following the set order she had been taught as an initiate. She still remembered her harsh mistress, even now after so many years. Finally, VaCalt smoothed water over her shaved head and allowed it to run where it might, taking her unwanted thoughts with it. The sensations distracted her and focused her mind on the present. And so, when a knock begged entry, she calmly permitted it.

"Potent," her initiate spoke respectfully, eyes lowered. "Venat awaits your pleasure."

VaCalt did not answer and completed the ritual. The initiate waited silently. She would have waited all day if expected.

VaCalt dried her hands and returned to her desk. "Send him in."

Venat entered and bowed deeply. "Potent."

VaCalt nodded in acceptance and gestured for him to be seated. She pushed the paper to him. "Read."

Venat smoothed out the sheet, making sure its condition did not affect his expression. He read quickly so as not to irritate, and then chose his words carefully.

"His highness…"

"Imperial Highness," VaCalt corrected. Referring to Segat in any other way now meant certain death, and while she had no respect for the man, she would not let herself, or anyone she found useful, be caught by words.

"Potent," he said gratefully. His Imperial Highness's latest whim was being vigorously enforced. Segat altered the way he was to be addressed almost as much as his mood. "So, his Imperial Highness has indeed set Imalt a task." He put the paper down. Imalt was VaCalt's only challenger for the position of Head of The Ildran Order of Talents. He had grown in favour with Emperor Segat and was therefore a threat. "But in your wisdom, you had him followed at all times by Ducat?"

"And that was so but we now have a second traitor to watch," VaCalt kept her voice calm. She would never allow anyone to see her in less than a state of perfect control. Even Venat her most trusted.

"Ducat has aided Imalt? But surely not, she has been desperate to prove herself to you, to earn your favour."

"Ducat has proven herself to be no more than a fool or an opportunist."

"She allowed him to leave unfollowed?" Venat was deeply unsettled by this.

"She denies it, but it is clear her allegiance has been transferred to Imalt while he basks in His Imperial Highness's favour."

"His Imperial Highness doesn't give you the respect and favour you deserve; you were with him from the start," Venat soothed. "Without you, his ambitions would not have been realised. Your abilities, your foresight and your daring have set Ildra and our Order on the path to greatness. Does he not realise this? Does he forget the latest blow you have delivered Amaria and the Orders, a plan of sheer brilliance?"

VaCalt nodded in modest acceptance of his words. "His Imperial Highness is ever looking for the next victory. He needs me, Venat, but he is insecure and increasingly paranoid. He continues to play Imalt and myself against each other and keeps us all in line with his personal Guard."

Venat's face flushed with emotion, as did any Talent at the mention of the personal Guard. "Their existence confuses me..."

"And terrifies," VaCalt noted ominously.

Venat met her chilling gaze for an instant and then looked away. "I do not understand why he forced us to create a guard immune to the field, a means by which we could destroy every Talent that opposes us, but has so far sanctioned the creation of only two such creatures."

VaCalt shook her head. "You do not understand?"

"But, Potent, the continent would be at our feet, the Orders decimated," Venat added uncertainly.

"Do not think for one minute that His Imperial Highness had any thoughts of using them to bring the Koan Orders to their knees. His thoughts had one aim and one aim only, his protection from us. Once certain of their unswerving loyalty he had the pattern book and their creator destroyed. You were not here. DuChen did not die easily."

The Adept shivered, he'd heard reports of the event. "Why did he not use them to destroy the Panid Tebeb as well? His knowledge ultimately made their creation possible."

"And that is why I have summoned you here. Up to now, I have been able to persuade His Imperial Highness of the Panid's usefulness, but he may well change his mind and order the Panid, Tebeb, dead. He is still of great use to me and must be kept alive. His Imperial Highness is currently distracted as he pushes our forces outwards. Now is the time to move the Panid out of the palace. You will take him to Magor. You have a house there that will serve well enough as a prison. What the eye does not see the mind will forget."

"As you wish, Potent." Venat lowered his head in acceptance of her wishes.

"I will see to it that you have access." VaCalt picked up a pen. "The rest will be your doing."

My responsibility, Venat suspected, should Segat become aware of these actions. "I will not fail you."

"You will leave as soon as is reasonable. Make your plans, but not in my name. You will also instruct your initiate to join the search for Imalt. I want to know where he has been sent."

"I-I was hoping to keep him at my side. His training is almost complete and…"

"That is why you will send him in search of Imalt. I have watched his skills develop with interest."

Venat swallowed his words; there was no use in arguing, nothing to be gained by her displeasure. "As you wish, Potent."

"Go now," she dismissed. "I have much to do."

Venat respectfully took his leave.

VaCalt completed the document she had been working on and then signed it with a certain amount of satisfaction. With Imalt gone his followers were vulnerable. Two were already dead and with this document Ducat would find herself a part of the advanced forces heading for the Amarian front, a fitting reward for treachery. As for Imalt, the favour he was now enjoying would be turned to VaCalt's advantage. He was far from Ildra. She knew that much and had scouts searching for his exact whereabouts. His absence would allow her free reign to manipulate His Imperial Highness and strengthen her position. She would suggest the use of powder weapons again. The gift she had presented the Emperor would now begin to pay its way. It was time the Hallorns had a taste of smoke; Naddier needn't think itself safe. A successful attack would turn His Imperial Majesty's eye back to her.

The arm of the Ildran Order was reaching ever further west. Her hand grew ever stronger and she had a new card to place on the table, her greatest achievement to date. Summoners loyal to her were close to achieving their goal, the creation of an Elemental, a Fury. A child of the Panids not realised since the Great War. His Imperial Highness would be indebted to her. He had his heart set on further weakening Amaria; she would utilise her spies in the Amar Order and be only too happy to grant him this wish.

***

Kellim stood at the cave entrance looking out onto the snow, the valley's surface now even and soft. Blue shadows crisscrossed its surface, sharp and clear in the twin moons' light. Everything was still, as if asleep. He should have felt calm, but his thoughts could not wander far from the news of Amar and the powder attack on the Orders. Even though Maga had informed him of the disaster days ago it prayed on him, he felt frustrated at not being able to help and worse, concern for his friends gnawed at him.

He turned to Maga, who sat with her own thoughts. He felt a little uncomfortable and any attempt at small talk seemed contrived. His relationship with the Children had been a complex one. On many occasions, he had been forced to make choices he was still troubled by.

Maga, by contrast, showed no sign of her earlier discomfort. "Winter has closed in upon us. It would be far too dangerous, even for a Panid, to attempt to travel," she tried to ease his unspoken thoughts.

"Indeed," Kellim had forgotten The Beholder's window into his inner emotions. "Even Varin will have to wait the snow out when it reaches the Plain of Coth." He turned. "Did he find your valley?"

"No. The Guardians found him before he could get any closer, though not before he convinced some of my kind to join him."

Kellim was surprised to hear the word Guardians used in the present tense. "My list of questions has just increased considerably."

Maga smiled, she could see his thoughts as if they were her own. It would have been more efficient to anticipate the questions, but she had learnt an etiquette that made others more comfortable with her abilities. "Then you should ask and make the list shorter."

Kellim stepped in from the cold. "I believed there to be no more Guardians. How many still survive?"

"Only two. They were more than a match for Varin." She considered her words. "For the time being anyway."

"Only two out of the original one hundred. The night used to shine with their radiance. Their final clash with the Fury was the turning point of the war," he noted absently.

Maga nodded. "I am much relieved that it was the Guardians and not the Fury that survived." The two were quiet for a while, distracted by their memories of that time.

Maga eventually looked up. She seemed to have made a decision, a question of her own to ask. "You eventually sided with Ethre, Tebeb and Etefu and spoke out against the continued creation of my kind. Why was that?" There was no hint of accusation in her voice.

"Hmm, yes," Kellim was distracted by the question. "The Panids had become arrogant, egotistical, I was troubled by this.

In the western conflicts during the middle of the war, I worked closely with The Faithful and other Children. My perspective was further altered and I was forced to reassess my original perception of them. My desperation to end the war blinded me to the truth. But my decision to side with Eth and the others had its consequences, which we are only now beginning to fully realise. Much was kept from us in the final stages of the war. Answers to questions and events that now trouble us greatly."

"You spoke of being blinded to the truth?"

"I believed your kind to be a necessary tool that would bring about the end of the war. But all too quickly many of you became more than the tools you were created to be and couldn't be directed without concern for your well-being. The Panids would not accept this. Once I saw this for myself, I was forced to think differently." He couldn't hide the regret in his voice. Kellim looked up at the moons. Issu and Lissa looked back, cold and distant in the deep night, they reflected his guilt. "Did you know, before the War, the Panids were working on a grand plan? Issa and Lissu were to be their first objective. I was telling Aran about it. To walk on the surface of another world," he was still excited by the idea. "It was quite within their reach and then to the worlds beyond. They thought there was nothing beyond their ability, but there was much beyond their understanding."

Maga nodded. "The Panids were powerful and their knowledge was vast. They were the masters of the field. Much responsibility rested on their shoulders." It was strange, but even now there was a reverence in her voice when she spoke of the Panids.

"But creating life simply to use it as a tool?" Kellim still couldn't come to terms with their view. "That surely is something best left to nature and the natural wisdom of selection over time. The Panids didn't feel the need to consider the consequences of the Children's creation and all involved suffered because of this."

"You regret our existence?" Maga asked quietly.

Kellim caught the subtle tone in her voice, an unsure child asking a parent if it was unwanted. "Forgive me, Maga. I'm in no position to lecture. The Panids acted and the Children brought the war to an end, but at a cost. Many of your kind have enriched us and led fulfilling lives in their own right but others didn't. I regret only that which was forced upon them."

Maga nodded slowly, satisfied with his answer. Knowing his thoughts, the instant he had them, somehow wasn't the same as hearing the words spoken.

"You had other questions," she reminded him.

"Yes indeed," Kellim thought for an instant, glad of the subject change. "You said some of the Children have joined Varin?"

Maga's expression hardened, her disappointment in their decision clear. "Yes. He came looking for us in the belief I would help him in a new quest that obsessed him. I only became aware of his approach when he was a short distance from the valley and sent several of our community to bar his way. Not all of them returned. His will is strong, he pandered to their desires and fears and they gave in to his control." She folded her arms. "The thoughts of those renegade Children are now lost to me.

Only the arrival of the Guardians prevented him from convincing more to follow him. The people that attacked you thought he had returned. It took a little time for me to get word to them."

"What could his quest be, that requires your help and the risk of manipulating the Children?"

Maga made herself more comfortable on the small boulder, her feet barely touching the ground. "It is difficult to know for sure, he has worked hard to hide his mind from me while at Aurt and then quite suddenly became almost unreadable after his failed meeting with the Corumn in Amar. I am now only able to gain glimpses of his thoughts. I believe he is looking for clues to the location of The Field's Cap and I surmise he intends to head for Dothica where he may find written information. I now suspect he wanted that information from me. I of course only know it exists and of its location because of your thoughts and that of the other two remaining Panids." She paused in thought. "If Tebeb has any other knowledge I cannot tell. His mind was lost to me long ago."

Kellim, Etefu and Eth had searched for Tebeb over the decades, but to no avail. The thought was a depressing one and distracted him despite his unease surrounding Varin. He eventually pulled himself away from Tebeb and thoughts of his lost friend. "The location of The Field's Cap. Then, Varin's plans have indeed changed."

"Yes," Maga agreed. "Originally, he intended to manipulate his Order. You know he is unhappy with Amar's current place on the world's stage?"

Kellim nodded.

"You know he has pushed against the constraints of The Field's Cap and that he has become powerful. Perhaps even a match for you."

Kellim's unease had grown with each confirmation. But he was not prepared for Maga's speculation.

She simply nodded in recognition of his thoughts. "He was using Emperor Segat as leverage, placing thoughts and ideas in the Ildran's head. Segat was to make threats only towards Amaria, though convincing enough to unsettle the Amar Order. Varin then intended to take advantage of this, to use it to help him sway the minds of the Corumn. You do not know that he acted hastily, bolstered by a chance find, a capacitor left behind by you at Aurt."

Kellim flinched at the news. He sat slowly, as the full impact of his mistake took hold. He went to speak, his stomach sickened by his careless stupidity.

Maga held up a hand. "Your error only brought forward his actions. The traces of probability I see in the field were not set in place by your oversight. However, they have inadvertently contributed to his current search."

Kellim pulled himself together. He would have to push aside his guilt. Self-pity would not put this right.

"I am sorry Kellim," Maga, watched him carefully, all too aware of the impact her words were having on the Panid.

"Please continue."

Again, she nodded. "You now know he was unaware of the wide-ranging changes in the Corumn. The capacitors were meant to aid his entry into the minds of the old members of that inner group. Once in he would use his enhanced talent to place ideas in their heads and steer their actions. Slowly setting the Amar Order on the path he wished it to follow. But the members and minds that now make up the Corumn have changed. Too many younger, powerful minds not even he could hope to control. He barely escaped and returned to Aurt." Maga paused allowing Kellim time to think.

"Without Varin to control him, Segat has taken the ideas planted there as his own and they have moved beyond empty threats. He wants to avenge the death of Princess DuLek and expand his borders. Ultimately, he will settle for nothing less than the downfall of Amaria, and with it the rest of Koa. I cannot see his plans, though I have tried endlessly," Maga said bitterly. "His thoughts are still partly masked by fields set up by Varin to prevent my sight."

Kellim considered the implications of this. His thoughts turned to the peace that had lasted for so long and the lives that would be devastated by the coming war. Yet, despite all of this, he was deeply unsettled by Varin's intentions to find The Field's Cap. "Do you have any insight as to why he seeks The Field's Cap?"

"I can offer no help. The minds of those who conceived and worked on it were also masked from me at the time of its construction. I have no knowledge of The Field's Cap's, beyond that which I can read in your thoughts, and I am unable to catch any clues from what small opportunities I have had to see Varin's."

Kellim drummed his fingers on his chin as he thought out loud. "Eth, Etefu, Tebeb and I were allowed to know of its location and its purpose but we were not a party to its construction or how it achieved this. There may, of course, be other things stored along with The Field's Cap, though I find this unlikely, as the Panids were not ones for creating artefacts. Only Eltram did this in the dim past, but Varin could only be aware of him as a fable, a myth." Kellim thought a little longer. "The Follies, if they still exist may be locked away with The Field's Cap. I know of one that could be used to influence the minds of others. Perhaps it is the circlet that he hunts for. I may know little about The Field's Cap or the Follies, for that matter, but I do know that an Adept, even one as strong as Varin, couldn't hope to overcome the knowledge and arts of the Panids and gain entry into the chamber where The Field's Cap is housed." Kellim stopped fiddling with his beard. "And yet despite that, I cannot eliminate him as a potential threat."

Kellim got up and began pacing as he searched through his memory for anything he may have missed. Maga sat quietly, her eyes lowered, listening to the thoughts in his head. It felt like days long gone when she was at the beck and call of her masters. For all that was wrong with it, she couldn't stop the feeling of nostalgia for those days. She had a role, a use, a purpose and a part of her reached for that time and those feelings.

"Is there anything else you can tell me, anything I have missed or not considered that would allow me to place Varin at the bottom of my list of problems?" Kellim asked finally.

Maga looked up. "I am aware that his Order is pursuing him and feel they are close to catching up with him."

"Is Varin aware that his Order is set on his capture?"

"He cannot be certain, but he knows of old that his Order does not tolerate behaviour like his."

"That might explain the renegade Children," Kellim concluded. "They could be used as protection for Varin against his Order. Is a confrontation imminent?"

"As you know my insight relies on the thoughts of others and can only hint at future events when collective intention raises their probability." She relented "That said the minds of those pursuing him are confident of his capture."

"Then we must hope their beliefs are not misguided and that Varin's endeavours to locate The Field's Cap will end there." Kellim seemed momentarily relieved by this, but then began pacing again.

Maga's expression changed. She sensed something new entering his current thought process. "You are concerned about Cali and the Children's interest in her."

This brought him up short. "My mind is full of questions with no answers. So many threads force me to look for a pattern to explain all of these events and an overall grand design. If I had a Seer's ability, I would be able to trace them, follow them to their most probable conclusion. I feel there is an architect at the heart of things, someone who ties all of this together. But there are so many threads my mind pitches from one problem to another." Kellim raised his hand in exasperation and shook his head, he hadn't confirmed her last statement. "Yes, I am aware that Cali is of interest to the Children. The Faithful described her as special and alluded to a role in their future. I wonder at Varin's involvement in this."

"That idea came into being before Varin had any contact with the Children. He is not the originator."

"Do all the Children believe Cali to be special? You for instance?"

Maga frowned. Realising that she would now be forced to reveal a secret. "No, the belief lies only with the Children who chose to wander the shadowed places of the continent and not join us here." She felt bound now to explain. "After the war, the few Children left, split into two groups, those who chose to wander and those of us who chose to settle here. And now we are split into three with a renegade group under Varin's control."

Kellim shook his head. "We thought we had a record of all of the Children remaining after the war. We only knew of the ones who chose to settle. I now know others survived that we thought were dead." He looked at Maga unwilling to hide his disapproval. "You choose not to share this information."

Maga held his gaze defiantly, though it was clear she was uncomfortable even now to face the disapproval of a Panid, no matter how moderate. "Yes," she said stiffly.

"And allowed Children like The Three to remain, to wander the shadowed places of the continent?" He used her words deliberately. "You know their nature. The job they were created for. Did you stop to consider the implications of your choice? The danger it would place others in?"

Maga looked down, cupping her hands in her lap. "I made them promise. Even the thought of a transgression and I would reveal their whereabouts. The threat of losing their freedom and ultimately their lives was enough. They kept their word."

"Until now," Kellim was exasperated.

"Until now," Maga admitted unhappily. She went to explain, but Kellim had turned away and so she sat in silence.

Kellim was more shocked than angry. He was struggling with feelings he'd avoided for decades. The sacrifices he'd made were now standing on foundations and beliefs he was increasingly unsure of. After the war many of the Children simply ceased to exist, their form field's life span being limited. But some of them must have lived on beyond their designer's expectations. Some like The Faithful and Maga were allowed to go out into the world with the certainty they posed no threat. Others could not move beyond their original purpose, unable to leave the war behind, they were a danger. At the time, Kellim could only justify their destruction in terms of securing a future. He, Eth and Etefu had been forced to seek out and destroy the Children who posed a threat. It had been a disturbing time and they had all struggled with it. He was beginning to think the solid peace they'd paid so much for was nothing more than a veneer. To find out now, that other Children had survived and, at any point, could have reverted to their original purpose, or fallen prey to the will of a Talent, was disturbing. How many of the Children still out there might believe Cali to be a part of their future? What threats would she have to face? "Should I be more worried about the wandering group of Children, or Varin's renegade group?"

"It is the wanderers who believe Cali plays a role in their future, but the threads of possibility lead me to believe that the renegade children may join them if released by Varin."

Are you aware of the origins of this belief? What or who has led the wandering Children to think that Cali is of some significance to them?" Kellim kept his voice even.

"I cannot see where this belief came from." She was glad he was speaking again. She disliked the silence of a Panid.

"Can you tell me of the whereabouts of those Children who pose a threat to her?"

"I cannot."

Kellim sighed. "Cannot, or will not?"

"Please believe me Kellim I have only once lied to you and even then, acted with the best of intentions. I cannot tell you where they are, as they too have been hidden from my view."

"Hidden," again Kellim felt his sense of unease grow. "But not by Varin."

She closed her eyes in concentration and it was some time before she spoke again. "I have focused on this much. Earlier, you spoke of an architect at the heart of things, someone who ties all of this together. There could be another mind at work, someone unknown to me, controlling the wandering Children and powerful enough to block my sight. The only hint I have to his or her identity is a strange sound, or sensation, that hovers on the edge of my consciousness."

"A sound?" Kellim pressed.

"I can best describe it as a whispering, or rather the hushed voices of many."

"Whispering," Kellim mouthed.

"You heard it at Aurt," Maga saw the images Kellim now focused on. "The whispering is also linked to Varin; he hears it too."

Kellim had been grasping at threads and now it seemed they had stumbled on one, perhaps the one that tied many together, the whispering. Who was the source of it? What was their intention?

Kellim at last felt he had made a step in the right direction. Now he had four very clear threads. One led to Aurt, he still had questions about the traces of familiarity he had sensed deep beneath the ancient fortress. Another led to Varin, to capture him would eliminate any threat to The Field's Cap, offer support to the Amar Order and provide answers about the whispering mind. A third led to Segat and war, a war Kellim could help bring to a swifter end. The fourth led to Cali, she was perhaps in greater danger than he'd thought. There was a mind focused on her, perhaps the same whispering mind driving Varin, pushing the wandering Children to seek her out.

Cold sense indicated one as the priority, feelings drew him in another direction and curiosity and a sense of foreboding drew him to the other two. Four choices, and four places to be. He turned again to look at the snow, pristine and glittering in Issa and Lissu's light, a blank expanse with no answers.

***

Ritesh had led the contingent of ten of Amar's most powerful Adepts and a force of fifty heavily armed soldiers in five newly build Imperial sky ships. They had flown to Aurt to add what evidence they could to Mia Svara's findings and from there, traced Varin's steps to the Ildran border. Several of the Adepts had subsequently found routes into the country. At Ritesh's instruction, they had followed Varin's trail with some difficulty, eventually finding some evidence that he had stopped at Ippur and possibly its library and records repository. The trail had then headed into Neath and from there into the mountains at Bara.

Upon the Adept's return and at great risk, they'd managed to navigate the old spice trail through the mountains from Amaria. The trail led south, but they had struggled north following its less-used passage into Neath. From there they'd travelled through the comparatively narrow and uninhabited area of Neath that edged the north Ildran border. Progress had been slow, but they'd picked up Varin's trail again at Loch and taken on supplies before heading north to Bara. There, they'd been forced to send their larger ship back, after all attempts to get it through the gated pass, had failed.

If the journey along the spice trail had been difficult the one through the mountains into Lont, and the forbidden North, had proven disastrous. Only the certainty that they were closing on Varin had convinced them to attempt the journey. The decision proved to be a costly one, reinforcing the long-held belief that the mountain range, which stretched the full length of the continent, was all but impassable. It had taken them weeks to manoeuvre through the narrow canyons of those mountains in Lont.

Centuries ago, one route alone, far to the east of their position, had been discovered through the mountains into the

North of the continent. Known as The Marauders' Way it had offered a possible path through the range fraught with treacherous thermals and eddies. Over the years the jagged base of the pass became littered with wrecks and eventually, all attempts stopped and the vast range was left to divide the continent. As the centuries passed, merchants and envoys were sent across the Sibura and Segen seas into the North, they had all failed to return. Ultimately, interest in the North dwindled and was replaced with myths and tales of its barbarous and blood-thirsty people and so the countries of the North and South of Koa had developed quite independently of each other.

Only three ships had survived the journey through the mountains of Lont, themselves badly damaged and suffering a loss of crew. They now faced the prospect of continuing the search through hostile territory. They emerged from the mountains above a vast area of forest in the land of Coth, one of the four countries that made up the forbidden North of Koa. Here they were able to set down and make repairs, a danger in itself, as it was believed the North regularly patrolled its border. It was only through fortune and the need to find open ground that they eventually rediscovered Varin's trail. It was a testament to the skills of the group that they'd been able to trace one man's journey over such a huge distance. Ritesh was now confident of their ability to find and capture Varin and eagerly anticipated the encounter. This was to be his final mistake.

That morning the ships flew very low over the Plain of Coth in order to track Varin's trail more easily. They were on high alert and if discovered by the Cothican military would have two threats to contend with. The sky was an even grey and it was clear the first snow was on its way, all the more reason to capture

Varin and return before winter completely closed in and left them stranded in a hostile country.

Too late the Adepts become aware of a massive pooling of field energy. They had no time to react. A lance of directed energy suddenly tore through the first ship, cleaving its hull. Its bulk erupted and fell with a baleful wail. On impact, with the ground, its sides crumpled and wood ruptured and shattered, killing all on board.

A second but far less powerful blow hit the next ship's aft section. Its manoeuvring fins were shredded, making it unstable and it began to list and lose height. This ship carried the bulk of the contingent's armed force. Those that could, clung in desperation to the deck as other soldiers fell screaming to their death. The ship began to turn out of control as the icy wind caught its flailing sails. The hull brushed against treetops, dipping alarmingly before striking the ground. The vessel shuddered as its momentum forced it forward, gouging a ragged trench. A wave swept through the slender hull causing it to buckle and split along its length.

The third ship attempted to escape and began to alter course in a wide but cumbersome arc. The Captain bawled and yelled commands at a stunned crew, while archers rained arrows on any area that could be considered a hiding place. Still in shock, Ritesh and eight other Adepts attempted to locate the source of the attack, but they were not given the chance. Three Children appeared on deck in a blinding flash of light intended to stun and confuse.

In the ensuing chaos, the Children immediately headed for the biggest threats and attacked the Adepts. Three were killed before they even had a chance to pick themselves up. In desperation, Ritesh headed to the fore deck to gain vital seconds and focus his will. One of the Children followed him. Leaping on all fours, it resembled a huge feline standing six feet at the shoulder. It launched itself at him, but Ritesh was able to deflect it with an equally powerful blow. The Child crashed into the main mast but quickly recovered as Ritesh worked to defend himself.

Another Adept from the Discipline of Changers had time to transform and descended on the second Child, savagely ripping and tearing at its armoured hide. The two fought brutally, rolling across the deck and crashing into crates. Soldiers were unable to help for fear of striking the Adept. Some were crushed as the two creatures thrashed and struggled. The fight raged around the deck, scattering anything that got in the way. The beasts lunged and tore at each other, trying to sink teeth into the other's throat. They reared on hind legs, claws ripping and tearing, teeth bared, guttural roars and snarls drowning the chaotic sounds elsewhere. The fight was savage and protracted, but eventually the smaller Adept, weakened from loss of blood, began to tire.

The words of a Speaker kept the third Child aloft and two soldiers nervously stood guard while she concentrated. Aware they were one of the last pockets of resistance, she spoke quickly, the words a blur, moving the Child towards the edge. It thrashed its jagged sword wildly, cursing as it floated towards the bulwark. Deep in concentration, the Speaker prepared to lift it over the rail and send it plunging, but an unseen blow shattered the vertebra in her neck. The Child hit the deck, quickly recovering to attack the soldiers. The fight was short-lived.

Shortly after, Varin appeared on the deck and paused to appraise the situation and gather his strength. All of the Adepts were now dead bar Ritesh, Varin had made it quite clear that he was to be left. The deck was still, bodies were scattered amongst crates and broken barrels, blood-coloured everything. Below deck Varin could hear the second of the Children finishing the crew, the desperate shouts of the men and women seemed distant and detached. Up on the wheel deck, the third Child cleaned its sword, on the clothing of a fallen soldier, before taking the wheel. The ship had followed its wide arc but was now beginning to drift towards the mountains. A mass of grey cloud was rolling down from the high peaks, a curtain of white devouring everything beneath it.

Battered and sweating Ritesh had been able to keep the first Child at bay and managed to inflict several injures that now drained it. The two stood, eyes fixed, tensely waiting for the other's next move. Ritesh may have been able to kill the creature and help the remaining crew, but Varin reached out, invisibly sweeping him up off the deck and into the air. Ritesh struggled, looking at the Child in confusion. Slowly it began to crouch, lips curling back over sharp teeth as it prepared to pounce. Ritesh writhed, desperately trying to break free and focus his will, but to his horror, he found he could do neither. The Child saw its chance and made to leap.

"No," Varin snapped. The invisible blow sent the creature rolling across the deck. The ship shuddered as the third Child forced it to gain height and steer away from the mountains and the snow. Bodies began sliding down its sloping decks. Seemingly unaware of this, Varin watched Ritesh as he realised his fate. The struggling had stopped, and the Adept hung there, his breath coming in short gasps as the storm approached. Varin stood motionless, gaunt and physically exhausted, he leant heavily on his staff, but he still commanded the field and with the cold uncaring strength of metal held Ritesh in the grasp of his will.

Fatigue settled on Ritesh as the first of the snow began to fall. His mind began to drift, fogged by the thinning air. The shadow before him faded into the dwindling light as his vision blurred. Swirls of snow swept the deck and Ritesh's thoughts drifted with them. He no longer felt cold and images began to dance through his thoughts, people, places; flashes that became sparking light caught on the surface of the vast river Am. The view from his study was one that never failed to bring him peace. He thought of the elegant towers and buildings, of the sun adding its golden glow to the burnished domes. He closed his eyes and for the last time surrendered himself to that light.

The ship was silent, debris swirled with snow in great eddies, caught in an icy wind that rolled and billowed the sails. Varin's face was a mask as he let Ritesh fall and turned away. There was no exaltation, no satisfaction. Nothing. He would now progress unhindered, head further north to Dothica and continue the quest. With those thoughts, the whispering receded into the blizzard.

***

The day had brought a leaden sky and a biting wind that whipped at the falling snow so that at times it was horizontal and at others lapsed into disarray. Kellim subconsciously braced himself against each gust as they tugged and pulled at him. He stood staring down through the mountains and blizzard towards the distant Plain of Coth. He sensed Maga's presence before he heard her unsteady footsteps through the snow.

She came to stand beside him. "Ritesh and his people are too distant. You could not have reached them in time and would have been too exhausted to help." She watched with concern as Kellim struggled with his feelings. The wind tugged fiercely at both of them. "Varin has fashioned himself a staff," she could see Kellim tense.

"Is he able to use it?" he asked.

"Yes, as we speak a sky ship falls to the ground."

Kellim turned to look at her.

"I said he was powerful."

They stood in the snow and wind, Kellim only able to guess at events on the Plain of Coth the flakes sharp and angry as they caught his face. Maga stood huddled in her layers, witnessing the confrontation through the eyes of others. Thunder rumbled through the clouds and lightning lit them from inside. The storm raged overhead and stretched as far as they could see. For a time, it dominated in every direction but slowly the boiling clouds left the mountains, their energies now focused south. Any sense or sight of the Plain of Coth's direction was obliterated by distant walls of snow. At last, the wind about them subsided and the white flakes drifted without anger.

"It is done," Maga said. "And you have decided your next steps."

Kellim nodded slowly. "To be in four places at once."

"They will all give their best."

"Of that, I have no doubt," Kellim replied a note of regret in his voice. "We should return to your valley, as it is, it will be night before we reach it."

"It is a long time since I have left its security and isolation," Maga said.

"I'm grateful for your company." Kellim acknowledged the effort she would have made in following him.

"You intend to remain with us until winter is over," Maga said.

"Yes. I must sit on my hands until then. That will be hard."

"Then perhaps you can occupy them with this." The gently falling flakes seemed to coalesce over her hand as Maga produced a metal staff seemingly from nowhere. Its length exactly matching the Panid's height. She held it out at arm's length, her hand on a narrow wooden band that encompassed it.

"Mennem's." Kellim stared at it.

"Mennem's gift to you," Maga corrected.

Reaching out Kellim faltered and looked at his hand, the last of the wind tugged at it sharply. "Does the wind know something we don't?" he asked. "Is this unwise? These hands were a lot younger the last time I held it." Kellim was still staring at the rod.

Finally, he took hold of it, the wooden band moving to meet his grip. "It seems heavier," he said testing its weight. The long rod vibrated in his hand, reaffirming their link and the snow was instantly diverted around Maga and Kellim.

"It knows its owner," she smiled, sensing the staff's awakening and the change in the field around them. "You have never truly been content to glide on the lesser currents."

Chapter 17

"They're all dead!" Kara was stunned. "That's a bit over the top, isn't it?" She lowered herself onto the window's sill still wondering if she'd heard Carrick right.

Carrick closed the door behind him. "They lost contact with Ritesh two weeks ago after he'd set course through the mountains beyond Bara. Up until then, they'd managed to keep up some form of regular contact."

"So how has this news reached Amar?" Merren asked.

"One of their sky ships was too big to get through the gate pass at Bara. They waited at Bara and then sent two Talents to investigate when Ritesh and the other ships didn't return. Even with transporting it took the two Talents a while to locate the wreckage and return." Carrick related the rest of the information he'd been given. "The big sky ship just got back. I happened to be in the right place to be a party to its news."

"So, Varin's strong enough to direct raw field energy." The idea was shocking. Merren stood up looking at her brother. "That's something no one has been able to do since The Field's Cap. None of us can do that or at least not to any useful degree." She thought again. "I wonder if Kellim could."

"Kellim's always kept such things to himself. I don't know and we can't rely on his being able to," Carrick shrugged at Merren.

"This lot," Kara gestured referring to the Amar Order, "are up against it. That's a big chunk of their Adepts wiped out and the Ildran Order has always been heavy with talent."

Merren was still looking at Carrick. She had a notion of the thought that was creeping its way into her brother's mind. "Still no news from home?"

Carrick shook his head, trying to avoid Merren's enquiring gaze. "Nothing's getting over Ildra or any of the occupied central countries."

"We're stuffed," Kara interrupted.

"Segat's several steps ahead of everyone. I've a nagging feeling there's more to come."

Merren sat down on the arm of Carrick's chair. "I'd be happier if we knew what was happening in Naddier and had some word that Lewan, Cali and Aran are safe." The other two nodded. "No news and all this waiting. I can't sit around here doing nothing."

Carrick exhaled heavily puffing out his cheeks. "Well, we've got four choices. One, stay here and watch the border along with the rest of Amaria. Segat will need to consolidate his position in the west before making another move, but sooner or later he's going to head this way. Two, head north and see if we can track down Kellim. And yes, I know that would be like looking for a drip in the rain, but at least we'd be doing something. Three, try to find a way through occupied territory to get back to Naddier. Or four, see what we can do here to help, as Kara said they're shorthanded."

"I said they were stuffed," Kara corrected.

Carrick looked at the timepiece on the wall and got up. "I'll leave those options with you. I'm off to get ready for the ceremony." He paused before closing the door. "See you later."

"There is a fifth choice," Kara added deviously.

"Oh, yes," Merren responded, her eyes narrowing.

Kara smoothed down her dress and folded her hands neatly. "We could always wind Mia Svara up some more."

***

The transport platforms stood in a seldom-used courtyard of the Adepts' Buildings in Naddier. Cali and Aran had been to see them for no other reason than they'd been part of a lesson. The platforms had once been at the heart of every city's communication and travel networks, allowing almost instantaneous transport of people and goods. In order to function, they required unlimited use of the field. Since The Field's Cap had been put in place this energy had been greatly restricted and made most of the platforms unworkable or unsafe. Across the continent many platforms had fallen into disrepair however, the then Head of the Naddier Order had been adamant that at least one of the city's platforms should be maintained and over the years this custom had been continued. Durnin kept up the tradition considering it important to preserve links to the past. The stonework had been maintained, the rules governing their safe use had been taught and the Discipline of Speakers had replenished the form fields that carried each platform's unique identification and marker signals. In the decades of continuous peace, since the war, it had never been considered that the platforms, so carefully maintained, could provide direct and unmonitored access to the centre of the Order.

Rain fell undisturbed through the midnight air, making the platform's surface wet until a large figure appeared. The rain drummed on its back before it quickly moved to the shadows. The rain continued to fall.

Cali watched the downpour, noting the different sounds it made on the paving and the trees. Despite the cool air, she had the window open, it was pleasant to be sat somewhere warm and dry looking out into the weather, feeling the cooled air and listening to the hiss and drip of water as it fell to the ground or trickled along guttering. She'd only stirred and closed the window when Lewan woke and complained about the draft. With a last look at the rain, she fixed the image in her head and climbed back into bed, snuggling against him.

The frantic knocking at the door woke Cali and Lewan with a start. Lewan leapt out of bed, grabbed his trousers and stumbled to the door as Aran threw it open.

"Get dressed," he ordered, trying to catch his breath.

"What's going on?" Lewan asked, quickly pulling on the rest of his clothes.

Aran turned to check the stairs behind him before stepping into the room. "Something's got into the buildings."

"Something!" Cali said scrambling to dress, alarmed by her brother's expression.

"They think it's one of the Panids' Children. It's caused a huge amount of damage." They looked at him incredulously. "It's killed several people! Two of the Discipline heads are attempting to stop it."

Now dressed, Lewan was looking for something he could use as a weapon. He'd left his sword in his room. He settled on two of the fire irons. "Where are we headed?" he asked, checking the view from the window, now aware of approaching shouts and movement outside.

They quickly made their way down the stairs from Cali's room and stepped out into the chaos. The few Adepts, who weren't away from Naddier, were herding terrified students and other staff out through the main entrance. Suddenly two enormous explosions cracked the air. There were screams and calls of dismay, students ducked while others looked for the source of this new threat. For long seconds everyone faltered, not sure what had just happened or what to do next. It became clear that the detonations had come from the main academy buildings. A second set of explosions shook the ground and lit the night as a vast balloon of flame boiled into the sky. For an instant, the rain became orange.

Panic broke out anew and the rush for the gatehouse increased as several crashes reverberated from nearby buildings and a double set of doors burst open. Despite the darkness and confusion Cali and the others instantly recognised the eight-foot figure that stumbled onto the scene and began heading in their direction. They saw Ren leading another Adept to bar its way. Lewan began struggling through the throng to join them, shouting at Cali and Aran to get to safety. The two were torn between wanting to help and escape. Ursa saw them hesitate and quickly headed over.

"I want you both out of here. It's after…" she broke off, but Aran caught the look in her eye and nodded.

"Come on Cali," Aran urged but she was still looking in Lewan's direction.

"He'll need our help," she said desperately and took several steps.

Aran grabbed her arm and made to follow Ursa. "Come on!" he shouted as she resisted. "We have to go. Lewan knows what he's doing. We don't. We'd get in the way," he added, trying to make her see reason. Eventually, she nodded but still managed one last anxious look as they ran to the gatehouse.

Exhausted, The Second of the Three made its way forward, sweeping its sword in wide clumsy arcs at the fleeing figures before it. Ren fought his way through blind panic and managed to flatten himself to a wall. The other Adept was knocked over by the crowds, but managed to scramble to his feet as the creature closed. The Second turned to follow his movement and focused its failing will yet again. The impact hit the Adept full in the back and sent him sprawling into puddles. Ren saw his chance, spoke the words of power and levelled blows that hammered at The Second. Its footing was swept away. It fell heavily on the wet paving, its sword skidding away. Injured and tired from its previous confrontations, The Second struggled to gain its footing. Ren spoke again, his words drawing what little heat there was out of the air and the body of The Second. The paving crackled and popped as the temperature plummeted and the rain on its surface became ice. With effort, the creature struggled to its feet, confused and increasingly unable to function. It bent over, clumsily groping about for its sword. Lewan arrived in time to knock it further out of reach. The Second drunkenly swung at him and Lewan evaded the blow, but not the area of intense cold. The creature fell again as its body struggled to cope with the paralysing loss of heat. Lewan resisted the urge to deliver a blow; frostbite had already caught his arm. He backed away from the growing area of ice, ignoring the pain, ready to act should the creature get back onto its feet. All the time Ren continued to speak the words that chilled the air. The Second made some efforts to raise itself, feet slipping, movements sluggish. Exhausted and groggy its strength failed and it collapsed. Ren drove the temperature down and Lewan stepped back cautiously as the painful chill reached him. The Second became still, its breathing growing shallow until finally, it stopped. The creature's skin became pale and began to turn white, the rain above it was falling as snow. Silent feathery flakes alighted on the last of The Three. Lewan looked to Ren, waiting for confirmation that it was dead.

"Keep back from it," Ren warned. "The air around it will freeze the blood in your veins."

"It is dead, isn't it? I mean it looks dead," Lewan called, trying to detect any motion or sign of its breath. His billowed in the night air, but nothing came from the lifeless giant. At last, confident it was dead, Lewan turned and walked over to Ren. "Where are the academy guards?"

"Something must have happened at the main academy buildings." He pointed. "Look the sky's orange, there must be a big fire."

"Was it after Cali?" Lewan glanced back at the body.

"I can't be sure, but it seems the most likely reason why it's here."

Merren looked across the sea of heads that bobbed in conversation or craned to look at the surroundings. She walked with Carrick and Kara down the central aisle of the palace's grand hall past slender pillars that rose into the air, fanning at their tops into a pattern of intricate design that supported the high ceiling. The glass walls flooded the room with brilliant light, which in turn reflected off polished marble. The space seemed to shimmer and glow. Cleverly woven form fields and fountains maintained a comfortable temperature despite the Amarian climate.

"I'm not comfortable being in here with all this glass," Kara muttered. "Not after those explosions on the ships."

"Hmm," Carrick pulled a face. "Not the best choice perhaps in that context. But the hall will have been checked and rechecked and then checked again. Especially if the Empress is going to be at the ceremony." He noted several of the remaining Adepts and other Amar Order members positioned around the room, each deep in concentration. "Have you been checking?" he asked his sister.

"I've done a general sweep. When we sit down, I'll be able to concentrate better."

"I thought they'd have asked us to help," Kara noted. "At the very least they must be aware of how good you are at snooping."

"Is that a compliment?" Merren asked. Kara looked at her blankly.

"Never mind," Merren rolled her eyes. "They're a bit precious about that sort of thing it seems. We've offered and they know we're not going anywhere."

"Now's not the time to be touchy about asking for help," Kara said as they reached their seats. "And what did you mean about a compliment?"

Once seated they had a good view of the vast gathering for the memorial ceremony. Kara watched the doors as a steady stream of people entered until the hall was full. A timepiece struck the hour and a great set of doors opened. Expectation spread silence with each mellow chime. The after-note of the last strike faded to nothing. A single cough broke the hush. At the perfect moment, a fanfare of trumpets split the air and then to the resonant pageantry of a great piped instrument the Empress, resplendent in the ivory soodrey of her state dress, made her entrance.

As one the assembly stood, heads bowing as she processed with solemn dignity. The effect on all was palpable. Great attention had been paid to her robes and gown. They were respectful of the occasion but made it quite clear that here was a monarch of absolute power, the head of a wealthy and powerful nation. There was another fanfare as the Empress ascended the steps to the fabled Jewelled Throne of Amaria. It glistened in the afternoon light, framing the Empress in a radiant glow as she stood before it. She began to address those assembled to mark the loss of life in the powder attacks and Ritesh's failed attempt to capture Varin.

Kara listened for a while and then looked at the faces of the people around her, catching sight of Mia Svara, who sat seemingly unmoved by Essedra's words. The Empress finished and, as convention demanded, bowed to the throne before sitting. In turn, the assembled dignitaries, ladies and gentlemen took their seats. Lord Atma led the rest of the proceedings and speaker followed speaker their voices echoing in the great space.

"Carrick," Merren whispered. "Focus on the middle arch of the blind arcading up from the throne." Her brother quickly did as he was asked, subtly touching the minds in the area. He searched for long seconds. Then shaking his head, whispered back. "I'm not getting anything. What is it?"

"I'm not sure," she said uneasily. "Something nebulous, a slight peak in the field around there. Almost like a… a pre-echo of something." She focused again, tracing the particles of energy along their myriad paths of existence. Searching for a sign, the merest hint and there it was! Something faint, hidden in the background noise of the ambient field. She raced her mind along the path, suddenly recognising it as a lead for a transportation from outside the hall. It had been forming for hours making its detection almost impossible, but it was definitely there and something was coming.

Merren stood, urgency gripping her. Her sudden movement created a stir in those who sat nearby, some heads turned in annoyance at the disturbance. The speaker continued, unaware of anything except the words in front of her. "The Empress!" Merren shouted raising the alarm. This time all heads turned and the speaker broke off.

The Empress's guards moved to surround her, swords drawn, automatically looking for an attacker. "No, no!" Merren was shouting. "Get her out!" She clambered over the people in front of her. "Get her out now!"

Someone nearby screamed. Several people were already out of their seats, confused by the sudden turn of events. Chancellor Nirek had left his seat and was headed for Lord Atma.

"The middle arch!" Carrick shouted and began pointing. "Curse it, the middle arch! The blind arcading!" The Adepts faltered not fully understanding what he meant. "Merren, don't get too close!" he yelled, urgently focusing his will as he scrambled after his sister.

Panic began to break out. People searched for the danger. More stumbled to escape from an unseen threat. Guards rushed into the hall. Carrick shouted again pointing to the arch. There was a blinding flash. Then a boom as the air seemingly tore open. Those who stood in front of the blind archway were instantly vaporised. Seats and bodies were flung across the hall. The room erupted in terror. Merren reached the Empress. Bodily throwing the guards out of her way she grabbed the startled woman and transported. Nirek was steps behind her and, grabbing Lord Atma, transported him to safety too.

Carrick focused his will. He pushed at the transport point trying to collapse it. But the breach was being held open by others. The Fury stepped through, an exotic being of field energy. Kara transformed. The form field pushed at the limit of her abilities and knowledge, the smallest of the Panid's Children, the only thing with a hope of standing against an Elemental. Those in the hall now fled from two apparitions.

At six-foot, the Fury was far smaller than the true Elementals, but its presence electrified the air and turned the floor molten. It swept an arm to its right, shearing through a column. Slagged stone sprayed onto the terrified crowd. People climbed over each other in desperation to escape the vision. Stunned Adepts and Talents struggled to counter the forces caused by the presence of the Fury. Their senses were overwhelmed by the cacophony of noise and light it created. Stonework became molten at its touch. Magnetic arcs pulled and tore at the columns. Glass cracked and shattered. People fell and were trampled. Soldiers and Adepts had to scramble to avoid being crushed. The terror-stricken crowd clawed and fought for the exits.

Mia Svara had managed to climb a granite monument. She fired a discharge rod at the Elemental, showering energy and sparks from its mass like a hammer on an anvil. The Fury shrugged them off, slowly and awkwardly making its way to the throne. Unobserved, an Amarian Talent named Poltack worked his way through the chaos toward Mia Svara. The Fury ripped at the wreckage of the throne and its platform. The stone of the floor fused, cloth became ash and wood became a bonfire. The air around the Fury vibrated and shrieked. The Elemental's original target gone, it should have returned, but the Ildran Summoners controlling it recognised Mia Svara. It turned to meet its attacker. Arcs of energy rippled out from its arms cutting through stone and flesh to get to her.

Carrick struggled to reach a place where he could concentrate, bodies were everywhere. The noise in the hall was deafening. He had to push his fear aside to focus. Nothing had prepared him for this. How could it? He collapsed the distance between himself and a large statue. Reappearing on it, he grabbed at the marble to keep his balance. Yet another commotion caught his attention and he looked to see Kara bounding on four powerful legs through the crowd. People threw themselves bodily out of her way. For a moment he wondered what she was doing. Then he saw an Amarian Adept had attacked Mia Svara. She was pinned to the monument unable to move.

Almost hidden Poltack was rigid with concentration. Uttering the words that directed his use of the field, his eyes flickered fearfully towards Mia Svara and the advancing Fury. He would only have to hold her in place for seconds more and she would be dead. Mia Svara fought to free herself as the Adept struggled to hold her. He only had time to freeze in dumb realisation as Kara leapt, flattening him to the ground. His head struck the paving, knocking him unconscious. Kara spun to face Mia Svara, hackles raised into spines, she roared her challenge. Mia Svara flinched; her arm lifted. Kara closed the gap and then leapt, clearing her and the monument to collide with the Fury. Her momentum only just knocked it to the floor. Her teeth clamped onto its searing shoulder. Neck and shoulder muscles strained as she savaged the Elemental. Its limbs thrashed about it in a ragged storm of light and sound, flaring out across the hall at the last of the fleeing people. The Fury was attempting to gain a hold of her. She knew she couldn't allow it; the creature would crush her to death. Energy peeled off it in ribbons, whipping and lashing at Kara's tough hide.

"The floor!" Carrick shouted at Mia Svara. "Break the bonds, the bonds in the flooring!" He gestured with his hands. "We might be able to trap it!" His words carried across the devastated hall. Mia Svara quickly grasped what Carrick was attempting to do. She focused and directed field energy at the floor beneath the thrashing monsters.

Kara was tiring. She changed her footing, attempting to drag the Fury. It was too heavy. Her only hope had been to keep it disoriented and now its hands found her. The pressure it exerted was immense. A fist of panic began to grip her stomach, but then the ground gave under them. The Fury faltered as the Ildran Summoners controlling it realised what was happening and released its grip on Kara. The Elemental attempted to brace itself as the altered floor began to act like quicksand. Kara leapt onto its chest and sunk her teeth deep into its throat. The pain in her jaws was excruciating. The Fury was forced to divert its efforts and attempt to grapple itself free.

"Jump! Jump!" Carrick was shouting urgently. The words slowly penetrated the pain and exhaustion. Kara released her grip and was immediately thrown back by the Elemental. Carrick pushed, and the Fury sunk deep into the destabilised stone. Mia Svara ceased her disruption of the stone's form field and it became solid. The Fury was fused in place.

Kara had struggled to her feet. Assuming her own form, she was unable to take her eyes off the flailing Elemental. She backed away as it shrieked with anger and thrashed wildly at the ground. The forces surrounding it whipped and cracked at columns and floor. She could hear the stone imprisoning it begin to crack and pop as it gradually became molten.

Carrick was shouting again, the strain in his voice snapping Kara's attention away from the struggling creature. Shocked into movement, she glanced up and then ran. The air was suddenly filled with the grinding of stone. A shower of dust rained down onto the floor as a huge section of masonry shuddered and began to lean. Carrick anchored his will further on the walls behind him and heaved, straining with all his ability. The masonry leaned alarmingly, seeming to teeter on the edge of balance for impossible seconds. The stone floor was now fully molten, the Fury pulled itself free. With a grunt of effort, Carrick finally caused the masonry to over-balance. With a deafening rumble, tons of stone crashed onto the Fury. Its form ruptured, disgorging light and energy. The ground shook and a boiling cloud of dust swallowed everything.

***

"Does the snow ever stop falling up here?" Jai flopped down on one of the large cushions that counted for chairs. Kellim didn't answer but continued pacing the small room given to them.

"No," Bryn replied. "Not at this time of the year."

There was a gentle knock. Glad of even that distraction, Jai answered it and invited Maga in.

"You have news?" Kellim was concerned by Maga's expression.

"The Orders at Naddier and Amar are being attacked." All three looked startled. She held up her hands to block any questions. "The academy at Naddier, the Adepts' Buildings and the Royal Palace in Amar are being attacked simultaneously. May I?" Maga gestured at one of the cushions and Jai nodded. She sat, aware of the questions the men were framing in their thoughts. "I should say first that the people you care about are all safe and well for the time being."

"That at least we can be thankful for," Kellim said.

"So, what's happening?" Jai asked.

"Many powder weapons like those used on the ships in Amar have destroyed a wing of the main academy buildings at Naddier while at the same time The Second of the Three, a member of the wandering Children, has attacked your Adepts' Buildings. Ildra is responsible for the powder attacks, but I am unable to see who directed The Second of the Three."

"Was he after Cali?" Bryn asked.

"Your people there believe so. The Second of the Three is dead." Maga was unable to hide the regret in her voice. "Thankfully, he has failed in his attempt to reach Cali. However, she is now unsure of her safety. And I would be inclined to agree. The rest of the wandering Children who chose not to join us here may attempt to reach her. Their minds are still closed to me and so we must assume that whoever is manipulating them is still in control."

Kellim turned to Bryn and Jai. "I'd feel a lot happier if both of you were with Cali and Aran. The luxury of waiting out the snow is one we can't afford for much longer. It would seem the academies are short-staffed and not as well protected as I'd hoped. If there is a possibility of more attacks we may be forced to reconsider where the best place is for Cali, especially if she's having second thoughts herself. I wouldn't want her to try anything rash on her own."

"Durnin's there, surely he'll keep an eye on her and Aran," Bryn commented.

"Durnin has enough to worry about and young people have minds of their own. With the two of you there we have more options. It may be that another place of safety will have to be sought and she will have a far better chance of getting there with you."

"You're thinking Eth's place, aren't you?" Jai asked.

"Indeed. It's only the journey there that may present a problem. Of course, we may be worrying unnecessarily." Kellim paused, considering this point. "Nonetheless we need to get more information to Durnin, and you would be able to take that to him once the snow allows your departure."

"Then we'll go," Bryn agreed. "But what if we need to contact you?"

"I'll have to head north eventually via Eth's anyway if I'm to intercept Varin. I'll alter my journey so that I'll be in range to contact you, if necessary." Kellim turned back to Maga. "What of Amar?" Kellim asked.

"As we speak the palace is being attacked by a Fury."

"What…that can't be!" Kellim said in disbelief.

"From what I am able to gather it is a lesser and far weaker version and not self-sustaining as the original Elementals were. The Ildran Summoners, who created it, are having to actively maintain its form field and direct it. The Adepts facilitating its transport were aided by a member of the Amar Order." Maga anticipated Kellim's questions. "It would seem that Segat is no longer screened by Varin. The fields he originally set up have run their course. Attempts have been made by the Ildran Order to block my vision and VaCalt is aware of me." She paused briefly as if deciding what she could tell them. "Segat aims to weaken both Amaria and Hallorn's abilities to defend themselves before striking. His particular animosity to Amaria's ruling family will put the country high on his list. He has created yet more powder weapons, and, in its present state, Amaria will be hard pushed to defend itself against them. Soon he will seek to expand his borders further and I believe his mind is set on Sancir."

Kellim started pacing the room. He paused momentarily to look at Maga. She folded her hands in her lap, her unease at his thoughts evident.

"Maga, I need something more," Kellim pressed. "I know prediction is unreliable, but many lives are at risk."

With reluctance, she nodded. "The paths of probability lead me to believe that Sancir will fall no matter what. You can be of no assistance there."

Kellim resumed his pacing. "I need to speak with Carrick and Merren and I must also speak with Durnin and then Eth. Are there others here who could help me accomplish this?"

Maga considered his request. "Yes, there are others," she finally admitted. "Together we may be able to reach that far, but only for the shortest of times. We will help you as much as we are able. I suggest you prioritise what should be said directly and what can be entrusted to Bryn and Jai."

Kellim sighed, "I appreciate the dilemma you face in helping us, Maga. I apologise for my abruptness and thank you for your patience."

***

"What will they do now?" Aran asked.

Ren kicked absently at the charred wood with his foot. "Re-build," he answered simply, looking at the devastation before them.

The fire was finally out, but not before it had reduced the north wing of the main academy to a burnt-out shell. Explosions had torn their way through its cellars and fire had spread quickly while The Second had attempted to complete its task at the nearby Adepts' Buildings. Timbers still smouldered even after the rain had turned to drizzle. The smell of burnt wood marred the air as individuals and groups searched the wreckage, looking for what could be salvaged.

"My sister isn't safe here. Is she?" Aran reluctantly concluded, looking directly at Ren. His feeling of unease had grown to a level he couldn't ignore.

"You know then?"

"I've pieced bits together, the tail ends of conversations and stuff like that. Why are they after her, Ren?"

Ren sighed. "I wish we knew for certain." He thumbed through a blackened book he had picked up only to throw it back. "I do know one thing though," he said earnestly. "This is still the safest place for her, for both of you. This..." he gestured about them. "This was done for another reason, to weaken us. To keep us off Segat's back. It can't happen again now, not here anyway. We'll put things in place so that it can't. As for The Second, it's possible it knew about the powder attack, but it's more likely a coincidence that it entered the Adepts' Buildings at the same time. It seemed like an act of desperation. The transport platforms will be blocked so that can't happen again."

"The Three are all dead now, but there's going to be others, aren't there?"

"That's possible and that's why you're both safer here and the longer you're here the more you'll learn." Ren could see that Aran was not fully convinced. "Think of what you've learnt already. We will teach you how to hide, to subdue your presence and, when all else fails, other ways to protect yourselves. You can't learn that anywhere else."

"I suppose you're right and if we do stay, we need to learn as much as we can, as many lessons as possible."

"Fair enough. You've been pushed as it is, but more lessons can be organised." Ren sympathised with Aran's struggle but knew this was the only place the Order could protect them. "Is it agreed?"

"If Cali's willing to stay, yes."

"I think it's also time that Cali knew," Ren said as he and Aran started to head back to the Adepts' Buildings. "This changes a lot of things and Cali will have her suspicions anyway. The more she knows the less she can wonder about. Knowing, even something bad, is better than guessing." Ren thought for a moment. "Would you like me to tell her?"

Aran shook his head. "No, I'll tell her. But I think she put two and two together a while ago. I know something's playing on her mind. She's probably keeping it to herself to protect me."

***

Captain Vannier watched as Commander Seyres made his way back along the battlements. The Commander returned his salute and looked through the mounted navigation lens, it took some time to sweep the forces amassed against them. The Imperial Ildran army had pushed through Sancir crushing all opposition. Now they had reached the capital, Mel Prin. They'd received advanced warning from the front, but nothing could have prepared them for the sheer size of the military might gathered against them. The city had been evacuated and hordes of refugees were now fleeing to the mountains. Mel Prin was deserted and eerily silent, home only to what remained of the beleaguered Sancir National Army and its Order of Talents. With grim determination, those men and women stood ready to buy the refugees time and prepare themselves for the inevitable.

Division upon division of Ildran soldiers had marched into position, great drums thumping out time, hammering home to every Sanciran ear the numbers involved. Siege towers had been constructed in full view, yet another deliberate demonstration of intent. All of this was beyond the range of Mel Prin's catapults, forcing them to wait, waiting the Commander knew was taking its toll. His men and women couldn't maintain this level of alert indefinitely. Suddenly the drums ended, fading into the wind. The Sancirans braced themselves ready at last to act, to fight. But as time passed the threat faded and tension returned.

"What are they waiting for?" Seyres muttered.

"Sir?" Vannier asked, unable to take his eyes off the Ildran lines.

Seyres looked up from the lens. "What game are they playing now?"

"If only we knew, Sir," Vannier replied.

Seyres felt sorry for the Captain, this was Vannier's first posting. If Seyres had had people to spare, he'd have sent the lad to escort the refugees. But he needed every able officer there was.

"They can't stand there all day, Sir. The waiting will affect them just as much as us."

"It's not waiting for them," Seyres corrected. "They know the agenda, for them each minute that passes is progress…"

He was interrupted as one of his aides pointed. "Sir, movement. Those huge, wheeled boxes we caught site of earlier."

Commander Seyres looked to the lens, focusing on one of the carts now in position behind the lines of Ildran soldiers.

"Bracing the wheel fronts?" Seyres puzzled. "The grounds level, what's that about?" He looked back to one of his aides. "Where's Jauffret? Get me Jauffret."

The soldier rushed off to bring the newly appointed Head of the Sancir Order. The wooden boxing turned out to be no more than a cover. When it was finally removed more carts arrived bearing barrels and crates.

"What are they, Sir?" Vannier asked, puzzling uneasily over the purpose of the long metal cylinders.

Commander Seyres studied the objects and what the teams were unpacking. "Battering rams perhaps, though their configuration would be inefficient. Can't see what they're putting inside? The Ildrans keep getting in my line of sight."

"Commander."

The voice made him turn quickly. "Good, Jauffret. Come and have a look at this. Tell me what you make of it."

Jauffret leaned on her stick and made her way over to the mounted lens. Concerned by what had the Commander puzzled she'd made no fuss over being rushed onto the battlements. Using her good eye, she focused on the activity.

The Commander maintained his patience. He knew the old Adept wouldn't be hurried. He motioned for Vannier to remain quiet.

Jauffret's stance stiffened in recognition. "Commander," she straightened in alarm, "get your people off the walls."

Almost as if on cue one of the cylinders issued a ring of smoke, rocking back violently on its wheels. A latent boom was followed by a startling scream, which cut through the air overhead. All turned as a tower just inside the walls ruptured into dust and rubble. The crack echoed through the empty city. The soldiers and officers faltered, not sure of what had just happened. Seyres began bellowing orders as two more booms reached them and seconds later the walls began to collapse.

***

Merren woke with a start. Her subconscious had made the voice a part of her dream until her mind made sense of what was happening. "Kellim!" she sat up abruptly. The voice faded into the early morning light.

"What's wrong," Kara asked groggily from across the room.

"Shh," Merren hissed, closing her eyes and concentrating. The voice came back faint but familiar.

"I have little time. Bryn, Jai and I are safe in Lont." Merren knew better than to interrupt she could sense how difficult it was for Kellim to reach this far, instead she focused her will and stretched her mind to meet him far to the north of the city. From here she could clearly sense the minds that aided him. "I have much to tell you and questions to ask, but little time to do it."

They maintained the link for as long as they could, but eventually the strain became too much and Merren gladly pulled herself in, exhausted by the effort. She opened her eyes and was not surprised to see Carrick sat on the bed with Kara.

"How much of that did you get?" she asked him.

"Some."

"Nothing here," Kara added impatiently. "So, start talking."

"Kellim and the boys are safe and well. They found The Beholder and will wait the worst of the winter with her before heading on."

"Lewan, Aran and Cali?" Carrick asked.

"Safe and well for now. We were right. Naddier was also attacked, but with fewer fatalities. Most of our people were away serving as support to the forces guarding Hallorn's borders. The last of The Three tried and failed to get to Cali again."

"Safe for now? What did he mean by that?" Carrick pressed.

"The Beholder thinks there may be more attempts to reach Cali but she doesn't know why this group of wandering Children are interested in her. The Beholder is unable to see into their thoughts."

"She doesn't know," Kara said in exasperation. "We get answers and then more questions. Didn't Kellim give you any idea why she can't read them?"

"She believes another mind is at work blocking her sight."

"Not Varin?" Carrick was surprised.

"Not him but beyond that, she had nothing more to offer. Kellim's going to send Bryn and Jai to Naddier with news and information for Durnin. He's going to transport the boys as far as he can at the first signs of a thaw."

"I feel better knowing those two will be there," Carrick said. "It'll give Aran and Cali more options if things get any worse. Was there any other mention of Varin?"

"Briefly that he might be headed north to Dothica. Kellim didn't say why. The next bit's for us. The Beholder is aware that Segat has reached the Sancir capital. He intends to consolidate his position after taking Sancir and then strike at Amaria. He's developed other powder weapons and the Ildran Order is at least double the numbers we thought."

"They're going to need help here then," Kara said soberly. "There's not much left of the Amar Order. Even at full strength…" she didn't want to finish the thought. The war had seemed like such an empty threat, and then at worst a distant one. Now it was coming for them.

"Kellim said that some of the Children in Lont will help." Merren tried to find some good news in what she had been told. "Several are willing to come to Amaria. He seemed adamant that Amaria must not fall."

Carrick frowned. "It is bad. I didn't think anything would convince the Children to come out of hiding."

"Guilt," Kara offered. "They must feel some responsibility for the actions of the others."

"Well," Carrick said, trying to sound positive. "We at least know Varin is out of the way, Bryn and Jai won't be going anywhere until the spring and that for now Segat's forces will pause to secure their progress."

"Time for us to prepare," Merren agreed uneasily.

"Right, I suppose we'd better let them know." Kara stalked off to find Nirek, leaving the two to consider their plans.

"You alright?" Merren asked her brother.

His face was troubled. "How was Kellim able to reach this far, even with help? Fennick's our most powerful Conveyor and he couldn't reach anywhere near that distance, even with several of us supporting."

"There were others supporting Kellim. I'm guessing some of the Children. But we've always thought Kellim, Eth and the others have more access to the field than us and Eth once hinted at Kellim's abilities being exceptional even for a Panid. We've both suspected he can do more than he cracks on." She came over to Carrick and sat next to him. "He's lived a long life, much of it through some of the most turbulent times in our history. There's stuff we've been through that we don't like talking about, some of the things he's experienced must have been far worse. It must be bad enough living with the memories let alone having to breathe new life into them to satisfy the curiosity of others."

Carrick nodded. "I suppose you're right. But every time things get worse we find out it's because of something that happened in the past. An unwanted legacy that seems to be ours to inherit. If we knew more, we might be able to act rather than react. What else hasn't he told us about the Panids and the Great War? What else is lurking out there in the shadows?"

Chapter 18

If Varin listened, he could hear each feathered snowflake come to rest on the thick blanket of snow at his feet. About him, the narrow street was deserted. Weak yellow light filtered its way through the layers of falling flakes. Dothica was the most northerly city in Coth, a city that huddled on the shore of a frozen sea, earning its living from hunting the huge double finned mammals that fed in its cold waters and harvesting the thick hair of its endless moss tundra herds. It had the feel of a place once busy, but now forgotten, a place at the edge of the world.

Thick walls, heavy doors and small widows kept the cold out and the hard-won heat in during six months of winter and so Varin trudged through the streets unnoticed, his coat and boots white with snow. He struggled up the steps of the large dour building and all but exhausted, thumped on its great doors. The echoes rang through the emptiness beyond. With less energy, he thumped them a second time. Again, the echoes receded but this time they faded into footsteps. Unhurried and approaching. Finally, Varin heard the rattle of keys against an inner metal gate. It ground and screeched open. The deep clunk of a key in another lock and the sliding of bolts made him step back before one of the outer doors edged open and a robed figure peered out.

"Refuge," Varin managed, struggling with the unfamiliar language through cracked lips.

The cleric didn't speak but inclined his head and stepped back allowing the stranger to enter, the philosophy of the chapter had always been to offer shelter and food to any who asked. The cleric watched the hooded stranger as he entered to get a better look at the face but saw little. The stranger kept his head turned to the floor and did not make eye contact. Puzzled, the cleric looked out into the blizzard and only when the snow gathered at his feet, did he shut and bolt the great doors. He locked the ornate grill that acted as a second and more protective portal, hooked the keys on his belt and picked up a lantern before leading the stranger into the grey gloom of the abbey.

Outside the wind tugged at any opening as if trying to gain entrance. Inside, its howling was distant, futile, muffled by layers of dust. As they walked the ancient building closed in around them until everywhere was still. Brother Lemeth had joined the order as a boy and been initiated into the Dothican Chapter. To serve the Speaker for Iscca was a privilege and a way for a poor family to educate a son. In his thirty years as a brother of the Speaker he had seen the head of their faith only once; the pilgrimage to the Mammoth Temple in Kemarid had been his life's greatest adventure. His only adventure, but now this visitor. Even beneath the cowl of the stranger's cloak, Lemeth could see the man was not Cothican. He couldn't place him, even someone from the deepest south of Kemarid would not have skin as dark as this man's. It was a rich brown and hinted at hotter climates. Where had he come from? Brother Nimian, the head of the Abbey, would know. The stranger's steps suddenly faltered and Lemeth turned in time to see the man stumble and collapse.

Time passed and for the first time in days, Varin gradually became aware of himself. He had no idea how long he'd been unconscious or where he was. Voices leaked into his consciousness and weak light filtered in as he opened his eyes. The two vague figures stopped talking, the taller was quickly dismissed and the remaining one shuffled out of the deeper shadows to stand at Varin's bedside.

An indistinct face hovered over him, old and pale, peering through thick-lensed spectacles that reflected the candlelight.

"Don't try to get up," the voice was light and reedy but in Koan. "You are still very weak and must rest." The man said more, but Varin drifted away, only experiencing the next few days as a series of sporadic images and sounds.

Brother Nimian had been a widely travelled man and unlike most of the North's population had risked the journey into the south of Koa. He'd seen much and learnt the common language. But had still longed for the wide-open spaces of Coth. So, a stranger from the South was less of an event to him. Over the past four days since the stranger's arrival most of the brothers had found excuses to enter the room for a look at the foreigner whose dark complexion and hair contrasted so in colour with their own. It had been many years since Nimian himself had seen the features of a person from the South and he recognised Varin's features, brown skin and black hair as Amarian.

Nimian was an old man. Frail and watery-eyed, as he would say. His memory of his life was clouded and unclear but his face, etched with deep lines, hinted at adventure and a life lived to the full. He was content, and at peace with the world around him. The stranger was not. Nimian had watched him as he slept and listened to the cries and words of the man's nightmares. Now he watched the same troubled man eat. The weak candles barely lifted his face out of the shadows, a face once sharp now eroded and prematurely aged.

"You eat, but it gives you no pleasure. You sleep, but it gives you no rest, even the calm of this place brings you little peace."

"I eat, I sleep, I rest. They are things I must do and see no reason to make more of them." Varin spoke between mouthfuls. He realised his manner and tone were defensive but had neither the energy nor the patience to play games with this old man. The form field he'd woven to hide his skin colour had failed before he'd even reached Dothica. The brothers here would not be worldly, but they would not be fools either. He couldn't afford to offend them or test their generosity.

"Is that so," Nimian replied untouched by the man's irritation. "What gives you satisfaction? What offers you peace?"

Varin paused. The spoon hovered and then returned to the bowl. "Silence." He pushed the bowl aside. "Why should you be interested?"

"I am interested in all of the travellers who come through our doors, but I am particularly fascinated by you."

"Why?" Varin snapped. It occurred to him he could break this old twig of a man in two and be done with his observations. He expected the cleric to question his appearance, to ask why a southern heretic had ventured into the North, and further still to the very edge of the world. He was surprised by the old man's answer.

Nimian got up unsteadily, but without rushing, gathered himself and then walked to the door, all the time with Varin watching. Taking hold of the handle the old man paused at the edge of the light. "Why, you ask? I will tell you why. You hide so much and closed doors have always interested me." With that the cleric shuffled out of the room, leaving the door ajar. Varin sat for some time looking at it and the weak light it revealed, realising that the old man unnerved him.

It was several days later when he came across Nimian again. Varin had finally been able to get out of bed and explore the ancient abbey. It was a labyrinth of dark muffled corridors barely lit by yellowed candles and smuttering oil lamps. He walked in an amber half-light, almost like a dream and at times he wondered if this was real, or if he still slept. The events on the plain still gave him nightmares and yet, when he was awake, he found it difficult to focus fully on them. They seemed somehow distant and detached as if they'd happened to someone else.

He remembered dismissing the Children, knowing his Order would not be able to pursue him in such numbers again. The whispering had driven him through Coth wanting answers to questions it set in his mind. Winter had closed in quicker than he'd anticipated with deep snow and freezing temperatures. Even though the whispering kept The Beholder out of his mind, the constant effort to mask his appearance and transport himself had been too much. He'd only just reached Dothica at the edge of exhaustion. The rest was fragments. Now rested, he became interested in the long-forgotten library and its books.

Lost in his thoughts he hadn't paid attention to where he was going and so found himself in a part of the abbey he hadn't explored. The corridor behind him was dark and silent, ahead he could just make out a faint flickering glow. He walked on, taking the pool of light his candle offered with him. He reached what he assumed to be one of the abbey's few communal areas and stopped to warm himself by a fire under a large carved mantle. Its light danced on the hearth, seemingly the only life in the space.

"You've closed the door again." Nimian's words brought him up with a start. The cleric was sat on a seat hidden by its high back and the eternal half-light of the crumbling building.

"Come and keep an old man company for a while. The library will wait for you," he added as Varin hesitated.

They sat in silence with only the snap and crackle of the fire, much to his irritation Varin spoke first. "Who are you, old man? Why are you so interested in me and how is it that you knew of my interest in the library here?"

"I am no person of note. But you, you are something we rarely see this far north. I ask myself, what brings a sorcerer to Dothica?"

"I am nothing more than a traveller," Varin said abruptly, irritation was an easy way to hide his surprise.

Nimian merely chuckled, unaffected by Varin's testy denial. "I also ask myself, what are you looking for in my library?"

Varin sat up, turning to face Nimian, this time with open surprise. "Your library?"

Nimian smiled to himself. "My life's work, a store of knowledge matched only, in the North, by the Mammoth Temple. I have travelled the continent and beyond adding to its store. A selfish pursuit perhaps as it is seldom used and little known. The Republic doesn't encourage the spread of knowledge or an interest in the past beyond that of its own writing. Thankfully, the library is all but forgotten."

"On the contrary, I and others in the South have heard many tales of the library in Dothica and its ancient books and stores of knowledge. They are what brought me here, but I had not expected to meet its current custodian."

Nimian seemed heartened by this and didn't correct Varin's' use of the word current. "Then you must let me help you. My knowledge of the library would save you time and allow your departure when winter withdraws."

"That would be useful. If the collection is as huge as I have heard, your help would save me a…" Varin stopped, how had he allowed himself to fall into such easy conversation. The old man knew too much about him as it was. How much had he talked in his restless sleep while the old fool ministered to him? If so, he would have to ensure this information went no further. He was about to ask the cleric where the library was, but the old man had drifted off and was snoring quietly.

In the following days, they spent many hours searching the dusty volumes of the library, lanterns providing islands of warm light in the shafts of cold that reached the floor from the ceiling. Heavy columns held the roof and three arches of glass aloft. The light was filtered by the snow that collected there, despite the monks' daily efforts to remove its weight. Varin was surprised by the old man's energy and knowledge once amongst the collection he clearly loved and cherished. Varin's guarded silence had gradually eased as their joint interest and value in the collected works gave them common ground. Gradually they began to spend just as much time on discussion, philosophy, theory and history as they did searching. As the months passed Varin began to enjoy their time together, despite himself. The old man was extremely knowledgeable and Varin no longer found his insight threatening and his lack of pretence refreshing. He knew no more about the old man's past than he did when he'd first arrived. An inequality that should have troubled him, and yet, it did not.

"Here. Try this one," Nimian shuffled over to the desk they'd set up months earlier. It was now hidden beneath manuscripts scrolls and books. Varin got up to help the old man with the unwieldy volume and took his arm as he lowered himself into a chair with a grunt. "Thank you. My infirmity annoys me at times when it hinders our endeavours. I have never asked the Goddess for personal favours, but now I would ask Iscca to grant me the gift of clear sight."

"Your knowledge far out ways any weakness in your eyes and bones. You have saved me weeks of pointless searching. You and this library would have been prized as a true treasure by my Order." There was some hint of bitterness in Varin's voice.

"Your Order has changed. You said would have been prized," Nimian explained when Varin looked at him questioningly.

"Time brings change, not all of it good. Much gets left behind. You and the brothers here, are custodians of the past and deserve recognition and praise. The preservation of knowledge is a laudable occupation."

Nimian settled himself, putting on the heavy glasses and dragging over his large magnifying glass. "You flatter an old man and it is gratefully received. You have given me a purpose I had not thought I would have again. I had forgotten the joy of these books, as my sight increasingly prevents my accessing them. If I have a regret, then that is it." He shook his head as he turned a dry, yellowed page and peered through the magnifying glass in his tremulous hand.

The days wore on and finally late one afternoon as the winter light faded Varin became aware of the whispering again. It was only then that he realised it had been absent for weeks if not months. He continued reading for a while longer, hoping it would recede. But its insistence grew, filling him with the need to move on. It became impossible to concentrate.

"Have you found anything more?" Nimian asked, gesturing with a gnarled hand at the delicate scroll Varin had thrown aside.

He shook his head and sat back. "Only a confirmation. One of the islands in the seas north of here." He exhaled, rubbing at his forehead in agitation. "I have learnt enough to continue my search but not enough to end it." There was disappointment in his voice.

Nimian nodded regretfully. "I fear my library will not be able to help any further and that you will soon be leaving. Only the Mammoth Temple in Kemarid could house the volumes you now require."

"I doubt that collection will be able to help. The information I seek would be considered heretical there, your tolerance would not be matched."

"Tolerance of a sort. Knowledge brings power. You might be surprised by what is allowed in secret," Nimian responded. "I am not the only one to have ventured south. The Speaker for Iscca hides a past few know about. We travelled the South of Koa together for a time until the aim of our searches diverged. He is not so righteous, or foolish, as to destroy a means to maintain his position. Information, knowledge, books, no matter how sacrilegious, can find a place in the Speaker's library. It will be difficult to find, but the Mammoth Temple hides a great many things you may find useful." He watched Varin, sensing the change within and about him and then looked thoughtfully at the room and at the light peering in from above. "These ancient walls are not impregnable. Some things find a way in eventually." He paused, considering his next words. "You will not want to hear this but nonetheless I will speak."

Varin folded his arms, knowing the old man always spoke his mind whether invited to or not. "I have learnt much in my time here old man and know better than to argue with you."

"Then I must congratulate you on your wisdom." Nimian chuckled, putting down his magnifying glass and removing the spectacles. His actions, as always, were unhurried and Varin waited while the old man organised himself. "I suspect you have become more like the man you once were in your time here."

Varin stirred in his chair uncomfortably, knowing the words held some truth.

"When you return to your search and the world outside, I worry that other influences will take hold again, forces with little care for your welfare. It is almost as if this search is not your own."

"Not my own?" Varin interrupted sharply.

"Despite my age, I have ears more sensitive than most." He nudged the spectacles. "I may need these crude things to help me see, but I am not blind to what is in there." He jerked a crooked finger at Varin's forehead.

"I am quite in control of what is in here," Varin mimicked.

"Be certain this search is truly what you want. Some things are best left behind. All I ask is that you consider what I have said. I say these things in your interest only. You know me well enough by now." With that Nimian made to get up from his chair, shooing away Varin's offer of help and stiffly shuffled towards the endless rows of shelves. He paused there without turning, only just visible in the soft shadows. "I wish you well my friend."

Weak light filtered in through the threadbare curtains that hung across the small window in Nimian's room. Varin looked down at the old man now gently snoring, the sunken eyes, the skin as aged and worn as the pages they had searched and the frail body that hampered a mind still sharp and vigorous. Could he be trusted to keep the nature of their search secret? There was a chance others might follow. He reflected on their time together and on the things he had said. But again, Varin was interrupted and felt the urge to move on, to continue his search...he questioned his thoughts then. His, the word somehow seemed out of place and he lingered over it until the old man stirred. A part of him wanted to stay. He felt at peace here, the study, the discussion and the debate. He had forgotten the pleasures of kindred company, but the pull of the whispering had returned, the sense of urgency that had gnawed now overwhelmed. He had to follow, to see where it led and to what end. He focused his will and drew on the field, reaching his hand across the old man's face he murmured, "Goodbye old man."

Nimian woke with a start as if from a dream. His hand searched for his glasses. But in fumbling across the bedside table, he found only a note. Without thinking he sat up and opened the neatly folded paper. 'A gift'. Nimian puzzled over the inscription's meaning and then it glared back at him.

Chapter 19

Emperor Rasna had spent his reign atoning for the actions of his father, Karna III. But this atonement had continued for too long, the country became too self-absorbed and closed to the world beyond its borders. Empress Essedra's accession to the throne began a new era, a period of slow progress. She had struggled to prove and then assert her authority against a government, powerful houses and an Order all too comfortable with the status quo. But little by little she had replaced, and at times forcibly removed, people who blocked her vision. Now the throne was hers and the great houses, officials and the Order bowed to her rule. Amaria was once again becoming a strong, forward-thinking and ultimately outward-looking country. She was determined to learn from the past and look to the future with the good of the people and Amaria at the heart of everything she did. The powder attacks and the shock of the Fury incursion had strengthened her resolve. Poltack's interrogation quickly led to a hunt that ended with a series of merciless executions.

Work to strengthen Amaria then began in earnest and with an urgency that acknowledged the threat now marching ever closer. The walls that encircled the capital city were being greatly extended in height and thickness, offering an impressive demonstration of Amar's organisation. Each block had been reinforced by skilful adjustments to its form field. Catapults and ballistae crowned newly enlarged towers at regular intervals around and in the city. These weapons had been designed to bring down attacking sky ships, news of the Ildran sky armada and its numbers had reached Amar. The Amarian shipyards had doubled their output as craftspeople worked around the clock in an attempt to bolster the marine and newly formed aerial navy. The Amarian sea and the bay of Amaria had already seen several battles and intelligence had alluded to the extent of Segat's sea navy. Its effectiveness had been alarming, but it was still outnumbered by a nation with a vast coastline and a naval history to match.

At the border with Ildra, the already formidable fortresses that stood guard in the west saw their defences being enhanced as a steady stream of ships flew in resources to prepare them for land and air attack. The Amarian Mountain Ranges had long formed a natural barrier, preventing invasion along most of the country's northern and western borders. The old spice trail had been sealed, only months after its reopening. The fort there was now surrounded by a military camp specialising in ordnance. Enough catapults, trebuchets and ballistae had been positioned to make passage through the narrow trail virtually impossible. The Ugarmas Dip, where the western mountains' lesser heights allowed for a narrow navigable stretch, and the Ugarmas Pass, a dramatic break in the range, each had fortifications unique to the challenges of defending them. These now became the focus of Amaria's preparations.

The mountain forts of the Ugarmas Dip had long been acknowledged as one of the greatest feats of architectural innovation on the continent and were built on the very pinnacles of the mountains that safeguarded the southerly aerial route into Amaria, the only point at which sky ships could cross the natural barrier.

The five interconnected fortresses of The Ugarmas Pass, known interchangeably through the decades as The Emperor's or Empress's Hand was a vast structure, surpassed only by the Ciad Enclosure and the Mammoth Temple of Iscca in Kemarid. The Hand consisted of five forts linked by huge defensive curtain walls that stretched the full width of the pass. Two vast gateways allowed trade entry into Amaria and back into Ildra, while five towers of awe-inspiring height closely controlled air passage. These towers could bombard an altitude beyond the reach of any sky ship and boasted offensive weapons until now, no vessel could hope, or dare to match.

The final development and the one least palatable to the Amar Order had been the Empress's command to build powder weapons, similar to those thought to be in Segat's armoury. Spies had been sent into Ildra to gather as much information about the design and operation as possible. Some information had been brought back along with more disturbing news of direct interest to the Amar Order.

Chancellor Nirek met with Merren in his study. Its furnishings matched the Amarian fashion for low tables, cushioned seating and open archways, made private by light soodrey curtains that allowed any breeze to cool the air. He'd seemed determined to strengthen relations with Naddier and in turn, Merren and Carrick had been asked to extend every courtesy to Chancellor Nirek. Their official orders had been to influence the development of Amar in a way that would benefit all. Now they were there to help out where they could.

Nirek had been surprisingly open with them since their arrival in Amar. He seemed earnest in his cultivation of their trust and

Merren suspected he was ready to consolidate the progress he'd made and further validate his position as Order Head. The Empress had laid no small task upon his shoulders when she'd made him Chancellor of the Amar Order of Talents. The conservative and more fixed elements of the Order had not been happy with his appointment and he'd used many methods to re-structure its Corumn to achieve his and ultimately the Empress's goals.

It was in Naddier's long-term interest to support Nirek and extend its influence further west. King Perin and Durnin were intent on opening an embassy in Amar, as Amaria would ultimately affect the distribution of power in the east of Koa as the country flexed old muscles. Both Merren and Carrick had spent hours working with the Amar Corumn, but this was Merren's first invite to join Nirek in his private study.

She could have filled days in this room searching and reading through the hundreds of volumes that lined its shelves. Some books she recognised only from stories and myths. The collection was easily equal to hers in Naddier.

She smiled as her eye caught sight of one book in particular. The Chancellor watched, taking a certain amount of pride from her interest.

"You have found something?" he asked.

"That's an understatement," Merren turned to look at him. "May I?" The Chancellor nodded, gesturing with an open hand, before coming over to see what was of such significance.

"Ah, The Agant Magica. Alas, its twin is sadly not…" he stopped to look at Merren's expression as she reverently slid the book from its place. "You have it, don't you?"

"Between us, we've got the pair," Merren said shaking her head in disbelief.

"Have you any idea how far I have searched for that book," he laughed. "So many great works were lost in the Great War. Destroyed or hidden away, to protect them, only to be forgotten. It was always my intention to go in search of them. See what remained and could be found intact. But events have conspired to keep me otherwise engaged."

"Life has a habit of doing that," Merren noted dryly and replaced the book. Nirek was already heading back to his desk. She gave the books a final lingering look, before joining him. "I'm guessing you haven't invited me here to talk books?"

"Unfortunately, no. Spies sent to Ildra have returned with information relating to Tebeb of Nebessa."

"Tebeb." Merren was surprised to hear the name. "We weren't even sure he was still alive. He's been missing for decades and not even Kellim has been able to find him."

"We have no solid evidence," he warned, "but it appears that Tebeb is either being held by Segat or willingly helping him."

"I'd doubt both, but nothing surprises me anymore, the world is on its head. Could they give you any idea what he's doing, why he's there, or even where exactly he is?"

"We know very little. The information was stumbled on as we gathered intelligence on Segat's powder weapons. It is unsubstantiated and at best vague but linked to the Fury that attacked Amar."

Merren sat forward. "If there's one person left alive on the continent who could create an Elemental, like the one that attacked Amar, it would be him. Amongst the Panids he was by far the strongest Summoner."

Nirek nodded. "If he is there, willingly or not, he must be removed from Segat's hands. Our spies are currently engaged in locating his exact whereabouts."

"What did you have in mind?" Merren sat back again, her mind racing with the implications of this news and what it would mean to Kellim.

"We are hard-pressed and our numbers are critically diminished. Beyond Mia Svara I have struggled to find anyone with the necessary guile to attempt a… let's call it a rescue. Both you and your brother are needed here in Amaria, so I wondered if Kara would accompany her. An Adept Changer would be ideally suited to the task. I am aware, of course, that the two have a history."

"Like fire and oil," Merren scoffed. However, Kara doesn't like sitting around and I know she's getting restless." She shrugged. "But whether she'd work alongside Mia Svara…"

"Exactly. You will have observed by now, that Mia Svara and I don't always see eye to eye," the Chancellor continued rather dryly. "She will not agree to this because I have asked, but will act out of obligation and will appreciate its success is vital to our Order. I trust you will be able to come up with a way of persuading Kara or even tricking her into an agreement."

"I'll jump straight to tricking."

***

News of Tebeb's whereabouts eventually arrived and, in the end, Kara reluctantly agreed to travel with Mia Svara to Ildra. All too aware of the risks involved, Carrick and Merren had said an emotional goodbye to Kara before she left onboard a newly built sky ship. A sleek design built for speed that would get them across the bay of Amaria with less chance of detection. From there Kara and Mia Svara would make their way west through occupied Urukish and then into Ildra itself.

Sometime after the unlikely partnership's departure, news of the thaw in the far north signalled the start of Merren and Carrick's journey to meet with Kellim and the Panids' Children. Their ship was much bigger, far larger in fact than any other sky ship built since The Field's Cap. Amarian ingenuity had developed a more efficient field engine that allowed something more sizeable to sail the skies. Despite Carrick and Merren's initial misgivings the ship had proved to be safe and not prone to dropping out of the air.

Their journey would be one of superlatives as only a country as large as Amaria could present. At first, it offered a view of the vast plains that surrounded Amar as the ship headed north above the river Am. Then, they headed northwest over the highlands of Amaria, passing over the seemingly endless expanse of lake Myta. This marked their transition into northern Amaria and one of considerable change. The hills to the south and north of lake

Myta caused the rains, which kept southern Amaria green, to shed the last of their water. The ship then followed the course of the river Karna through increasingly arid land. Finally, they struck more sharply northwest and were offered views across the immense regions of the western Ugasi desert to the north of Calk.

A mixture of fascination and alarm had swept through the crew when they first caught sight of the Children, but several threats from the Captain had them quickly refocused on their work. The ship had been navigated as far as possible into the northwest reaches of Amaria and landed in a valley with the North Amarian Mountain range towering above it, a spectacular backdrop for this most unusual of meetings.

The day was bright and clear. A sharp blue sky contrasted with the white of the thawing snow. Carrick and Merren eagerly stepped down the gangplank as the crew worked to secure the ship and prepare for its new passengers. Both waved as they got a clear view of Kellim. Despite the remarkable beings, he stood with, both noted the staff that leaned in the crook of his arm. They recognised The Beholder from her description but had no idea who the others were. One was tall, slim and resembled a man. He wore a long cloak with the hood up against the cold. Two others were similar to The Three, having the same height and heavy build they stood on two legs with strong, muscular arms. Their presence was disconcerting. The sixth member of the group was similar to the feline creature Kara had transformed herself into but was far greater in size. It sat gnawing intently at a huge paw and then lowered it, watching as Carrick and Merren approached. It was clear the Panids had followed a set of common rules for their earlier creations.

"It's good to see you," Kellim greeted, coming forward to hug Merren and Carrick in turn. "You both look well."

"You look tired," Carrick noted with concern.

"The transportation distances we've covered were most taxing. You on the other hand have journeyed here in style. It's been a long time since the skies have seen a ship of that size," he gestured behind them before turning. "But I'm forgetting my manners. Allow me to introduce Maga."

Merren and Carrick both shook her hand.

"It is a pleasure to finally meet you," her gravelly voice hinted at the unease she felt in full view of so many people.

Carrick and Merren did their best not to stare, but their fascination must have shown in some way.

"Of course," Maga noted mildly. "You have not met many of our kind before."

"I'm sorry my brother and I don't mean to stare," Merren explained somewhat embarrassed.

"An apology was not needed. This is new for all of us. This is The Journeyman," Maga introduced the tall, cloaked man-like figure.

"I am glad to meet you," he lowered his hood and they could see a face that was not unlike their own, however, his eyes caught the attention of both. Their intensity and colour were startling. "I identify myself as The Journeyman but am also happy to be called Lors." They shook hands.

"These are The Twins," she continued, gesturing towards the eight-foot figures who stepped forward. Merren and Carrick's hands disappeared in theirs as they shook them.

"It is an honour to help the friends of Kellim," the first Twin said. The voice was deep but articulate, not matching the heavyset frame of its owner. "My sister and I are eager to work with you." The other Twin only nodded in agreement. Despite being identified as a sister Merren and Carrick could discern no characteristics that would support a gender difference. Carrick wondered if the Children chose a gender to identify with or preferred to be identified in different ways.

Maga gestured to the last of the Children who spoke before she did.

"I am The Hunter," the words were a mixture of controlled growl and half yawn. It didn't offer a paw.

"We and Amaria thank you for your help," Carrick said. "I don't wish to rush you but the Captain is in a hurry to be in the air again. The ship is vulnerable on the ground. I think he'd be happy if you would board as soon as possible."

"Is now soon enough for him?" Lors asked.

"Now is good," Carrick replied signalling to the Captain. A second much larger cargo plank was pushed out from the deck and the Children headed for it, taking their leave of Maga and Kellim.

"We'll board and travel with you for a short way if the Captain is eager to be off," Kellim offered. "It would be good to spend a little time together before we have to part again."

Once everyone was on board the Captain wasted no time getting the ship airborne. The Children were made comfortable in cabins or specially prepared areas in the cargo hold and each seemed content with the arrangements. The Twins came up on deck offering their help. At first, the crew weren't quite sure how to respond or even decide what to do with them. But once The Twins effortlessly completed a job, normally needing six crew, barriers quickly broke down and they were soon working together. The Hunter slept, preferring the peace of its quarters and Lors introduced himself to the Captain and his Conveyor. Despite his initial reservations, the Captain was soon engrossed in conversation.

Carrick, Merren, Kellim and Maga, were sat in the Captain's quarters at a large table where he normally held his meetings and ate with his chief officers. Carrick in particular was eager to hear Kellim's news and have his questions answered.

"The crew are coping surprisingly well with their new passengers," Maga noted.

"They were handpicked for this journey. But you'll probably find that many in Koa are open-minded enough to judge people after they get to know them and not before," Carrick replied.

"Even when they aren't people?" Maga questioned.

"A hundred years is a long time. I think we've come a long way in leaving the mistakes of the past behind."

"That is good. Perhaps things have changed for the better."

Carrick smiled, Maga seemed wary of people and had formed her opinions on past experiences. Kellim had, on occasion, hinted of his shame at their treatment. It was clearly an unresolved issue for both sides. Her life would be an interesting story to hear, Carrick thought, but now was not the time to ask about it.

"I've missed you both," Kellim said.

"Same here," Merren smiled.

"Bryn and Jai pass on their greetings."

"How's Jai?" Carrick asked.

"Much improved. There's even a return of, what I assume you could call, his sense of humour."

"Good," Merren laughed. "I've missed that. Are they on their way to Naddier yet?"

"Yes. Lors and I transported them as far as we could and they should have been able to make good progress since then. Spring has returned early to Lont. Thankfully at a time when we most needed it to."

"Have you news of Cali, Aran and Lewan?" Merren continued.

"Only just. The link to Durnin was difficult to make and it took the help of several Adepts for him to maintain it for the shortest of times. Suffice it to say they are well."

"We've missed them," Merren said looking at her brother, an edge of regret in her voice.

"There'll be plenty of time," Carrick soothed, squeezing her shoulder. "What news could you get from Durnin?"

"The academy is slowly rebuilding. The damage was considerable and sadly several lives were lost. However, the

Naddier Order is resolute and heavily involved in Hallorn's defence. The King brought the country quickly and decisively to a war footing. Beyond this, there is little good news. Sancir did not completely fall. Hallorn has been able to push back Segat's forces and liberate a narrow band of the country's western provinces."

"But not the capital?" Carrick asked.

Kellim shook his head. "We fear the King and Queen are both dead and there's no word of Jauffret. She waited a long time to become the Order Head of Sancir and had a chance to enjoy the role for such a small amount of time. Sancir was overwhelmed. Segat's forces are massive and heavily aided by The Ildran Order. For the time being Cian holds, but only because of Perin's support. Hallorn's resources are being taxed."

They spent time relating the events of the past months and as they talked Maga seemed to become more comfortable in their company and contributed more to the conversation. An hour had passed and their conversation was coming to a close. The Captain had allowed the ship to drift along at a slower pace so that Kellim and Maga would not be carried too far south.

"Any news of Varin?" Carrick asked finally.

Maga frowned, slightly irritated at not being able to give a clear answer. "He parted company with the renegade Children and travelled unaccompanied to Dothica in Coth. I say unaccompanied, but cannot shake the feeling that this is somehow inaccurate." She held up her hands in exasperation. "The thought has preoccupied me and nags for an answer."

"Could he have someone with him and could that someone hide themselves completely from you?" Merren asked.

"It is unlikely, but not impossible," Maga mused. "But experience has taught me not to ignore such feelings."

Kellim looked out of the windows at the rear of the cabin. "The sun is beginning to set. It's time we went," he added with some reluctance.

A member of the crew was sent to ask Lors to join them on deck.

Minutes later, Carrick and Kellim arrived on deck. Carrick took this more private moment to pass on word of Tebeb, fearing the Panid would be shocked or even upset by the news. His response was moderate, but Carrick could see the renewed hope in his eyes.

"Forgive my caution," Kellim apologised. "Maga became aware of this possibility but isn't able to sense him. It could be that the Ildran Order is hiding him from Maga's sight. I truly hope Kara and Mia Svara are able to find and rescue him, but I can't let such hopes take hold and distract me from what's ahead of us." He sat down on a crate with a heavy sigh. "Eth, Etefu and I searched for months after the Great War and in the years that followed chased many rumours." He looked up at Carrick. "The Great War didn't have the singular ending that Attrius's epic re-telling suggests. Many of the stories, to use his phrasing, reached their conclusions some years after the Great War. Others, it seems are still unfolding and have yet to be resolved."

"It must be difficult. An uncertain past is a hard place from which to assess the present and speculate about the future," Carrick sympathised.

"Indeed," Kellim agreed. "It makes decisions difficult and there is a temptation to overthink things."

"So, where will you head next?"

"I am certain that by now Varin has, or is very close to discovering the location of The Field's Cap. I want to confirm this and then head back to the Ronce Sea to contact Bryn and Jai. From there I will head north to intercept Varin."

"You don't need me to say take care, but I will, if only for my own peace of mind."

Kellim smiled, "I will my friend."

At this point, Lors and then Maga and Merren came up on deck and hasty goodbyes were said.

Merren kissed Kellim on the cheek. "If you do get the chance to speak with the others, tell them we're thinking about them."

"I will," he promised and, not wanting to draw out the painful process of saying goodbye, turned to Lors. "If you'd be so kind."

The Journeyman closed his eyes, bending his will to the task of transporting. Merren and Carrick felt the clamber of locations crowd in and were surprised how easily he selected a single point from the innumerable possibilities. "I have it," Lors said with some satisfaction. Now they felt the change in his mind, as he collapsed the distance to a pre-set marker. But this was no small transport and both quickly realised the distance involved. His will gathered the field energy to a powerful peek. "Sending," he announced and Kellim and Maga were gone.

***

Kellim, along with the support of Lors, had transported Bryn and Jai several times to a point clear of the most south-easterly mountains of Kersel. After saying their goodbyes, the two men headed west, taking a route that ran parallel to the river Gort's lonely eastern reaches. Their journey crisscrossed the Sancir and Kersel border but kept them under cover of the Kersel forest. The immense canopy of roof trees and green combs stretched from the Western Amarian Mountains, covering the border between Neath and Ildra, spanned Sancir and then dipped south and continued east to follow the great curve of the Ronce Sea, crossing the border into Hallorn only to finish at the Gillern Archipelago and the Bay of Naddier. A total distance of some three thousand miles of uninterrupted forest.

The green combs had kept their needles but everything else in the forest slept. The air was still and trapped the cold. Most of the snow had melted but the main thaw was still some way off. The going would turn out to be cold, dank and gloomy. The first leg of the journey had been a cautious one as they'd spotted Ildran troops scouting and hunting for food in the uninhabited lands of Kersel's southern boundary.

"They've gone," Jai whispered, his breath steaming in the frosty air. He slowly released the tension on his bow and replaced the arrow in the quiver across his back.

"Then why are we whispering?" Bryn asked quietly and blew into his hands to warm them.

"Don't know," Jai whispered back.

Bryn stepped away from the tree he'd been flattened against and walked over to Jai. "I could do without this hiding. It's slowing us down and it's too cold to be stood about."

"We're going to have to get used to it." Jai slung his bow over his shoulder, his eyes still on the trail. "I reckon we've another two weeks of it before we can cross completely into Sancir. Unless King Perin manages to push his armies further east and meet us."

"Let's hope he does. Kellim said he'd sent word for them to watch out for us."

"As long as they can tell the difference between us and spies. I don't want an arrow in me before they realise who it is," Jai said dryly.

"No guarantees there, you always look shifty. It would be an easy mistake to make."

"Shifty. You're calling me shifty. What about that visit to Pidone five years ago?"

"Come on," Bryn groaned. He was never allowed to forget 'Pidone five years ago'. Not by Carrick, not by Merren and not by Jai.

They headed off following the many trappers' paths that crisscrossed the area. This one showed signs that it had not been used for years, so roots and pillow bush had encroached on its edges.

"You know what I'm going to do when we get back?" Jai said thoughtfully as they walked.

Bryn's laugh was a dry one. "I can probably guess."

"A bath," Jai answered pointedly "A proper bath with hot water," he scratched absently at the beard he'd grown since leaving Lont.

"Yep," Bryn laughed. "I remember those things. A long soak and a good meal would be welcome. Though I might keep the beard. Kinda distinguished don't you think?" Jai only looked. "Hmm," Bryn muttered. He looked around at the trees that seemed to have surrounded them for so long. "I miss wide-open spaces and I miss the sea," he added. "It'll be good to walk the cliffs and see the coast again."

"Do you still keep that hut going, the one on the beach?"

"Yep, though I've not been for well over two years. Don't know what state it'll be in now. We should go and check it out sometime. Stay, do some fishing, drink some ale... now that's something I've definitely missed. My own brew's not bad."

"Sounds good to me," Jai agreed, remembering the last stay. "We were with your sister and Merren, weren't we?"

"Err," Bryn thought. "Think so. Didn't you and sis find that wreck a couple of miles up from the hut?"

"That's right," Jai remembered. "It was right up on the beach. I think it'd been washed down from further up the coast by the storms the week before." Jai stopped and turned to look at Bryn. "There's something else I remember too. I thought, for a while back then, you and Merren were getting closer. What happened?"

Bryn exhaled thoughtfully. "Don't know really. Suppose life crowded back in again once we got back. I had to go to Ronce and she had to head off somewhere, I forget now. And the past year we've been on the road, so we never really picked it up again. Too much going on I suppose."

"Is that it then?"

Bryn frowned. "Maybe, I don't know." He struggled as he pieced his thoughts and feelings together for the first time on the subject. "When we got attacked by The Three and she went to find you. I was really worried and when I saw she was safe... it surprised me just how relieved I was."

"Well, maybe you need to think about that some more," Jai encouraged.

"Maybe," Bryn didn't seem too sure. "We'll see when all this is over."

"Don't wait, Bryn. You need to have an honest talk. You never know what's going to happen..."

Bryn was suddenly aware that Jai had stopped. He looked around warily, his hand going straight to his sword. "What is it?" he hissed.

"Something," Jai whispered back, as the two sunk into the undergrowth.

"Which way?" Bryn asked, his voice barely audible. Jai pointed.

They didn't have to wait long before another mounted patrol came down the track towards them. They silently edged their way deeper into the icy gloom of the dense trees. The patrol, like the others, gave the impression that they were not expecting to encounter anyone in this freezing and remote part of the continent. Long minutes passed as the soldiers approached, swathed in furs their breath steaming in the still air. The mounts' tack rattled and clinked in the dead silence, their heavy cloven hooves thudding on the frozen earth. Jai and Bryn heard snatches of conversation, but neither spoke Ildran to any useful degree. When at last the riders had passed and were out of sight, Bryn and Jai cautiously stepped out onto the track.

"The patrols are increasing." Jai looked down the track they had to take. "I wonder if we're getting closer to a camp."

"What would a camp be doing this deep in the forest? I know we're on the border, but there's nothing here," Bryn wondered.

Jai shrugged. "Patrolling the border. They won't want Perin sneaking behind them and cutting them off," Jai offered.

"Seems likely. I'd like to try and find out as much as we can though, so long as it doesn't take us too far out of the way."

"Okay," Jai said evenly. "Let's see what's going on. We can continue along the path, if we meet any more patrols, we'll have to head into the forest."

Bryn nodded and they set off. It was some time before they heard another patrol approaching. When the soldiers dismounted to take a break, Bryn and Jai melted deeper into the forest and decided to work their way parallel to the track. As expected, it was hard going and their progress was slower until they found the remnants of a frost-covered track that headed in pretty much the direction they wanted.

"It's paved," Bryn noted, looking at the uneven surface, which was still in good condition in places, in others the stone had been covered by decades of leaf fall. Still, it made the going much easier. "I'd forgotten about this. I think this might have been the old trade route between Neath and Delak."

"Delak?" Jai asked, shifting his pack on his back.

"A trading town, built in a pass through the mountains to Southern Kersel. During the Great War, the settlement was destroyed. Sometime after the war, the pass was sealed."

"Why?"

"No one seems to know. There are plenty of stories, but that's about it."

"The pass would explain why the Ildrans are up here. Another way into Kersel would help with their plans."

They carried on along the forgotten trail and, as hoped, met no more patrols that day. Several days passed as they followed it through the silent forest. Keeping to the path as best as they could, and without further interruption, they made better time. Occasionally they stepped out into the weak light of a natural clearing where a rooftree had died or fallen. It made a change to see the sky, even if it was grey and leaden. They talked and Bryn was relieved to see more of his friend's normal character had returned. He didn't push Jai to talk, but occasionally he slipped into a conversation about Stran when he felt it would be okay.

The going was cold, showing little progress in the spring thaw and so food was hard to come by. Even this far north the Great War's effects had decimated wildlife. The huge herds only survived in the far north of Kersel and Aylis and with them the predators. Here forest fowl and smaller animals populated the recovering forests; smaller prey that was harder to spot and kill for food. With no time to pause and set traps the two's rations were dwindling as the cold demanded they ate more to keep warm.

As yet another day drew to a close, it became obvious that the trees ahead came to an abrupt halt rather than offering another clearing, the extent of light coming through wasn't from a small area. Edging their way along the loamy ground they could see a large expanse of the forest had been cleared and, in its centre, the felled trees had been used to build a fort. Bryn and Jai peered across the stump strewn stretch, watching the activity beyond. To their left they could see the main gate opening onto the track they'd originally followed. To the north of the fort a new path had been cut into the trees and along this passed a steady stream of traffic heading into the Kersel Mountains. Great mounds of dirty snow had been piled on one side; a lingering reminder of the heavy snowfall that would have brought this traffic to a halt. The fort was rough but substantial and from its appearance expected to be functional for an extended period.

"Well, there we have it," Bryn kept his voice low. "The track we'd been on must turn north just ahead. I wonder if Delak is somewhere up that fresh track they've cut into the forest?"

"You want to head up and see?" Jai asked.

"What do you think?" Bryn was unsure they had the time.

"Even if we found out what they're up to, what could we do?" Jai shrugged. "The Hallorn army can take care of this if they get this far. And Kellim was hot on us getting to Naddier as quick as we could."

Bryn turned on his side to move a branch that was sticking in him. "You're right. We'll wait 'till it's dark enough, cut across the path north of the fort and carry on along this old track. If it still runs parallel to the main trail."

"Sounds like a plan," Jai agreed.

It wasn't long before it started to get dark and they made their way to the freshly cut path and waited for things to become quiet. Finally, the traffic stopped, the fort shut its heavy gates and torches were lit on the stockade. Making sure they were out of sight, Bryn and Jai crossed the path and scrambled over the snow before heading into the forest. They tried to find their way back to the old route, but the light failed and they had to give up. They had no choice but to settle down for the night, taking shelter in the roots of a fallen green comb. Eating cold rations, they prepared for a chilly night with no fire. They'd talked in hushed voices, easing the tension they both felt as they'd made their way deeper into occupied territory. Having squashed up together to conserve heat and keep themselves in the shelter of the roots, they both fell silent.

"We're ok, aren't we?" Bryn asked, unable to let the chance pass.

"What, in here?"

"No, you and me."

"Oh, right," Jai caught up. "I know things have been awkward and I realise that was because I didn't deal with Stran's death very well."

"That's not what I meant. I'm not blaming you. You seem better. I mean more your old self. We drifted, we've been friends, brothers for a long time. I was worried. I mean I…," Bryn stopped trying to find words in an awkward situation.

"We're good," Jai saved him from the struggle. "We've always been good. When something bad happens it kind of takes over and you have to put some things down to get through it. But the good stuff never gets left behind. I knew you were there. You always have been. So yep, we're good."

"I know we've had time to talk lately. But I just wanted to check. That was all. Just in case."

They were silent for a bit longer.

Bryn cleared his throat. "So, if you're okay, will you stop hogging the blanket."

Both awoke with a start, just as the misty dawn was breaking. Voices and the echoing crack of axes on wood echoed through the trees. They'd barely had time to shake off the frost and shoulder their packs when a group of soldiers entered the clearing and stumbled across their silent exit. The Ildran soldiers were equally surprised to see a Hallorn and a Cian in the forest and this gave Bryn and Jai just enough time to make a run for it. The soldiers quickly recovered and with a volley of shouts dumped their axes and chased after them.

"Left," Bryn yelled. They dodged trees and leapt over mounds and ditches as they fought to put some distance between themselves and the soldiers.

Jai was struggling to release his bow from his backpack as it thumped up and down. With one eye on his footing, he grabbed irritably for it and then in one swift movement stopped, turned, aimed and loosed an arrow. It sliced through the air. One of the Ildrans stumbled and crashed to the ground. The other soldiers scattered, shouting at each other and taking cover. Jai quickly sent three other arrows thumping into the trees where they hid, before bounding off to follow Bryn. He released one more arrow after a few seconds to dissuade them from following too quickly.

"Following?" Jai panted as he caught up with Bryn.

"Not yet," Bryn said looking over Jai's shoulder.

"Where now?"

"This way, come on." Bryn sheathed his sword. Jai groaned and followed after a quick glimpse behind.

Bryn was headed for a stream that fed the river Gort. They scrambled down the steep bank, grappling with branches and frosty trunks. The stream was shallow and stony and they splashed into it, finding the going easier despite the icy water. They could hear the shouts of soldiers some way behind and then suddenly off to their left came the sounds of others. Bryn threw himself onto the bank before clambering to the top to peer over.

Jai came up beside him. "It looks like they're all over the place."

I can make out twenty. I don't think they know the stream's here," Bryn said between steaming breaths.

Jai swallowed trying to catch his own. "They probably haven't been this far over. Any sign they're giving up."

Bryn shook his head. "Looks like they've met this new lot and are going to spread out and search."

"That evens the odds."

"Very much in their favour," Bryn said quietly, sinking back down the bank.

They made their way quietly alongside the stream, keeping their heads down and ears sharp. The steep banks began to rise well above them as the stream scored its way deeper into the ground. The shouts had stopped, but they could still hear the odd crack of hidden twigs someway in the distance. They continued further, eyes not only ahead and behind, but also above. It became harder to keep out of the deeper water as tree roots protruded from the banks and ice lined the edges. Suddenly, Jai grabbed Bryn's arm, putting his finger to his lips he pointed upwards. Bryn couldn't see what Jai meant at first but then caught sight of movement. The soldier was close to the edge of the narrow ravine but unaware of their presence at its base. Considering each move, they pressed themselves closer to the bank side.

Jai laid on his back, his bow and arrow ready and his neck craned alarmingly back so he could release a shot into anyone who peered down at them. They kept their breathing shallow and could hear the woman as she moved above them. She was looking about, searching for any signs of the enemy. Each step brought her closer and then she was looking down. It took precious seconds for her to register what she was seeing but in that instant, an arrow met her and she toppled forward almost falling on them. Bryn had his knife in his hand and the woman was silenced, but not before a shout went up from other soldiers close by. Bryn and Jai were forced to pull themselves up ten feet of the bank. Five soldiers had taken cover behind trees and a large fallen trunk and three more were warily edging their way to where the ravine dipped considerably. The soldiers were hastily exchanging hand signals.

Bryn looked at Jai. "This isn't good."

With barely a sound Bryn slid down the bank, drawing his sword when he reached the icy stream. He began edging his way along its side in order to meet the soldiers and give Jai a chance to pick a few off before they were forced to fight.

One of the soldiers shouted, spotting Bryn moving closer to the dip in the ravine bank. The group faltered, but then, thinking Bryn alone, began to advance. One of them shouted something to him in Ildran, it was clearly a command and Bryn could guess its meaning. It was pointless answering back, so he simply shook his head. His meaning was perfectly clear, and the men rushed him. The nearest managed two paces before an arrow hit him in the chest.

The other two closed the distance too quickly. Jai was unable to release a second arrow, Bryn now obscured his view, instead, he scrambled back up the bank and turned his attention to the other five. They were still taking cover, but beginning to edge their way forward, probably assuming the other three had engaged whoever was in the gully. They were obviously intending to come up behind. Jai took his time focusing on his targets, knowing he had to rely on Bryn to take care of himself.

Bryn had his work cut out, the soldiers were skilled and worked to tire him. He held them off. His sword and body moving with speed and precision, identifying the pattern they fought in and as a result their weaknesses. He began to find the rhythm of the fight, forcing the men to work harder, as he increased the pace.

Jai couldn't risk giving away his position and the advantage. The noise of the fight would be audible to the soldiers in the forest and soon pull them out of hiding in an attempt to attack from the rear. He had no idea what they were expecting to find, but the noises of the struggle seemed to have convinced them that now was the time to move. They cautiously edged towards the gully, keeping to the cover of the trees. As they drew steadily closer Jai's chances to pick them off decreased. He held his nerve, and, in the end, this paid off. Two men broke cover to clear the distance to the gully. As Jai's first arrow cut the air his second was introduced and released. The first found its target, then the second. The third narrowly missed. Jai cursed, quickly fitting another arrow and bringing it to bear, but not before the soldier found cover. Jai had to search to relocate the other two. One was closer, but he couldn't see the second. An arrow flashed passed him. He recovered quickly, releasing one of his own and then another two as the closer man attempted to move in. The second arrow stopped him. Jai reloaded and snapped his attention back to his remaining assailants. One was still behind the fallen tree, but the one with the bow had moved. Jai scanned the area, looking for places where ice or pockets of snow had been disturbed. Another arrow twanged into the tree. He rolled around and released his own, it grazed the woman and forced her to move. Jai fired into the ice-covered undergrowth hoping that fortune would favour the shot, but the woman had good cover and eventually made a break for reinforcements. It was time to leave before more soldiers arrived. The fight in the gully continued and Jai was torn between joining Bryn and leaving the other soldier to either run for it or sneak up behind them. He was considering his next move when the Ildran behind the trunk made a scramble for cover further into the woods. Jai released an arrow after him, deliberately aiming to the side. It thunked into a tree trunk, the man ducked through the shower of ice but kept moving. Jai sent another arrow after him to make sure he kept on running.

Bryn made his move. He parried a high blow anticipating the brief break before the next. He used the breath space to duck inside the Ildran's reach and butted him hard with his shoulder. This caught the man off balance forcing him to stumble back and over. The other soldier was thrown, his strike cut through air and his own momentum brought him forward into the reach of Bryn's knife. His shock was cut short as Bryn straightened and followed through with his sword. In his next fluid movement, Bryn stepped back and threw his knife. The other Ildran stumbled and pitched sideways to the ground. Bryn straightened to catch his breath but then spun to face the sound of splashing feet.

Jai skidded to a halt. "It's me, it's me," he shouted. We need to go, now."

Bryn exhaled heavily in an effort to slow his breathing, sheaved his sword and stood for a few seconds, his hands on his hips, catching his breath. He swallowed hard and wearily retrieved his knife.

Jai patted him on the shoulder. "You're out of shape old boy. Come on, we need some distance."

Bryn gave him a withering look, but without speaking began running.

They ran steadily, reckoning they had a reasonable head start, and ignored the pain in their chests and the increasing leaden weight of their legs. Deliberately heading away from any of the paths, they'd previously followed, the two aimed to put as much distance as they could behind themselves and the Ildran soldiers. Only after hours of running, with brief stops to rest and check for the distant sounds of pursuit, did they feel they could slow. Eventually, exhaustion forced them to stop.

"Let's hope they've given up," Bryn managed as his breathing began to slow.

Jai leant against a tree, his eyes closed, willing his heart to slow. The cold air was almost welcome.

"Right," Bryn began as he opened his pack. "We eat and then wrap up to stay warm. We're hot now, but the cold will soon take that away and more."

They ate and put on another layer, all the time listening and looking for any movement in the forest around them. They continued at a forced march, resting when they could, only stopping when it was too dark to continue.

Several days on, the first sign of life they encountered made them both drop to the ground, half expecting Ildran scouts. They watched with relief as an elegant horned animal emerged from the undergrowth, its breath billowing in the chill air. It sniffed and sensing them, suddenly disappeared into the forest with silent bounds.

"We must be closing on the Hallorn front line by now." Jai flopped to the frozen ground with a groan.

"The closer the better. It'll be dark soon. We should find some sort of cover."

Jai eased himself down onto this back. "I'm shattered. This patch of ground and this tree trunk look like a good place to me."

Bryn looked about them and then sat down. It was twilight, the forest was still, and the cold was settling closer to the ground. Only the soft call of a nightwing broke the silence. It was a sound Bryn had always found reassuring. A gentle unassuming call that echoed through the night.

"Okay," Bryan said, too tired to do anything other than agree. "This is as good a place as any. It'll give us some cover." He blew on his hands to warm them and then reached into his bag and pulled out some dried rations, absently chewing on them as he continued his surveillance. He watched as the bare trees faded into the deeper chill of the night.

Jai pulled his coat tighter around him and attempted to make himself more comfortable. He ached from head to foot and would have done anything for a warm bed, it didn't even have to be comfortable. "How much further do you think?"

"I'm not sure. We've been heading roughly west and south. The river Gort must be someway north of us now." Bryn flexed an aching shoulder that was beginning to seize up. "I'll have a better idea in the morning." He chewed on the dried meat a little longer, wishing they could light a fire to keep the harsh chill at bay. Though, he thought to himself, it was still far warmer than the nights they'd spent in Lont. He wondered where Kellim was now and if he'd met with Carrick and Merren.

"I was thinking about what you said before, about Merren. I need to sort out how I feel, for that matter what I feel. Rather than just pushing it aside," he paused. "Maybe when life returns to normal, I'll have time to get my head around things. I'll take first watch. You get some sleep. Jai?" Jai didn't answer and Bryn looked down at him. "And you already are," he muttered, shaking his head and stifling a yawn.

The night passed uneventfully and so did the next few days. The two travelled warily, but eventually found their way back on to one of the main tracks west. This was a welcome change. Their pace had slowed as their energy levels dropped; the path made the going easier. As the frozen track widened it began to show signs of more recent use and so they weren't surprised to hear sounds on the track ahead. They quickly left it and hid. The patrol passed, Hallorn soldiers, the confirmation Bryn and Jai had wanted. They re-joined the empty path and continued. Over the next three hours they hid two more times. Once from another patrol and again from the returning one they'd met first. Sure now, they'd crossed into friendly territory, they decided to greet the next one.

By mid-afternoon, it was clear the forest was rapidly thinning, and the path ahead was heading out into open ground. They suspected that their progress was now being watched and true enough, as they cleared the forest, they were met by four mounted soldiers.

Jai and Bryn approached at a steady walk keeping their hands in plain sight of the archer who had quickly set her crossbow at them.

The lieutenant signalled her people to halt as she continued the short distance to Bryn and Jai.

"I ask myself, what is a Hallorn and a Cian doing this far out?" she asked, reining her mount in.

"Returning home," Bryn began. "I've got papers here for your Commander identifying us and the reason for our journey."

"We've been told to look out for two men answering your description."

"Then you've found us," Jai smiled.

"Maybe we have," the lieutenant responded flatly, moving her mount behind them. "You'll understand my scepticism." She gestured towards her people. "Walk forward and hand your weapons over, we'll escort you in."

Bryn and Jai had no real choice but to do as they were asked. They allowed themselves to be searched and, in the midst of the patrol, headed for the camp. Its placement looked recent, defences were still being hastily set and resources organised. Under guard they were taken to the Captain's tent where he inspected their papers. "Wait here," he ordered and then left, taking the papers with him.

Bryn moved his chair closer to the brazier of hot coals. "Warmth at last." Now the worst of the journey was behind them, his thoughts turned to Cali and Aran, and to reaching Naddier without being held up by bureaucracy. "How long's this going to take? I don't want to be stuck here for days."

Jai looked over at the two guards, checking how easy it would be to escape if they had to. One met his gaze, his face expressionless as he patted the large sword at his side.

"I've seen bigger," Jai said.

Bryn rolled his eyes and settled further into the chair to doze. Time passed. Bored, Jai looked from one thing to another wondering how long they'd be kept waiting and how far he could wind the guards up. He was considering a few questions when the tent flap opened, and the Captain returned with a familiar face.

"Yes, that's them," Ressca said looking at Jai. "As soon as you said one of them looked shifty."

"Shifty?" Jai complained to the grey-haired woman. "She's calling you names again Bryn."

Ressca laughed, despite her fatigue and shook hands as they stood. "It is good to see you both and almost in one piece. This is Captain Berran. He runs things around here."

"Gentlemen," he greeted. "I'd like to talk to you. I'm sure you've seen plenty that will be of interest to us."

"Yep, they're quite busy up there," Bryn replied.

"I imagine you'd like some food and rest before that?" the Captain commented.

"I will sort them out," Ressca said, her manner authoritative as always. "I've my own questions. Come on, follow me," she said, smartly turning to leave.

"Captain," Bryn acknowledged as they left.

Ressca led them through the camp at her usual brisk pace and both men lengthened their stride to keep up with her.

"That's a first-rate scar you're sporting," Bryn noted.

"Hmm," Ressca grumbled. "I've kept it as a reminder never to underestimate VaCalt again and to listen to Kellim with both ears and my mind when he next gives me advice. Months ago, Perin and I met with Segat, a last attempt at peace," she explained. "It didn't go well on so many levels I wouldn't know where to begin explaining."

The camp was busy, but orderly. It was set out in line with the standard military practice of the Hallorn army, being divided into a clearly defined grid, with wide paths to allow for carts and the fast movement of troops. The air was chill and smelt of smoke from campfires and cooking areas, mixed with the tang of pack animals and mounts. The hazy vista of soldiers and tents, supplies and equipment stretched as far as the eye could see.

"They're building up to another push along the Kersel border and then down through Sancir towards Ildra. The idea is to force Segat's forces back into Ildra on two fronts," Ressca explained. "It has been slow progress so far, even with the help of what's left of the Sancir forces."

"Why are you with them?" Bryn asked as they headed deeper into the camp.

"There have been reports that the Ildrans are using their Talents in battle," Ressca answered. "There are thirty of us here just in case we're needed. Though all we've done so far is get muddier and colder." Ressca continued walking, dodging between groups of soldiers and stashes of equipment. Jai was glad she'd not been walking with them since Lont.

"How have things been going?" Jai asked.

"Segat's started moving into Cian. From what we've heard things are not going well there and Hallorn has had to commit more help to prevent them from being overwhelmed. The megalomaniac must have been preparing this for years, his resources seem endless. I don't mind admitting we're pushed to our limits." Ressca reached her tent. "Come on in," she gestured.

The tent was large but warm, having to serve as a meeting place for the Talents. Most of the space was taken up by several folding tables, arranged to make one big one. Ressca had clearly been working, papers and documents were spread across one end. There was a smaller section of the tent that could be closed off and this contained a bed and a couple of chests. Of far greater interest was the end of the table closest to them.

"Hot food," Jai said, dropping his pack and eagerly sitting down. He quickly had warm bread in his mouth and was spooning out a large helping of stew, while his other hand lifted the lid on a second dish to see what was inside.

"It's been a long time," Bryn smiled at Ressca, before quickly sitting and helping himself to the steaming bowls.

Ressca let the two men eat, she shrugged off her heavy cloak and gloves before sitting down.

"You not eating?" Jai enquired between mouthfuls and serving himself a third helping.

"No, I shan't risk getting caught between the two of you. I might be dragged in."

"We've been on cold, dried rations for weeks," Bryn apologised.

"Eat on, it's good to see someone enjoying this stuff."

Ressca watched them. They'd both lost an alarming amount of weight and had injuries that needed attention. Despite their bravado she could tell they were near exhaustion and in serious need of rest. Eventually, their pace slowed and Ressca deemed it appropriate to start questioning them about their journey. As they recounted the events in Lont, she stopped them many times for clarification and to ask further questions about Maga and the Children.

"...and so Kellim intends to accompany us to High Holt and then leave for The Field's Cap," Bryn concluded.

"It's interesting that he thinks Cali will be safer in Aylis with Ethre. That said, I have heard that if the Panid doesn't want her home found it won't be. The academy in Naddier is a mess and with most of us on the front line it's probably best you take her north." Resting her hands on the table she thought back over all she'd been told. "You said the Ildrans were up to something near Delak?"

"We didn't have time to check it out, but assumed they were trying to open up the pass through the mountains," Bryn paused, thinking for a while. "Mind you, at that point they could be navigated by sky ship." Bryn could see Ressca was trying to remember something.

"Oh, that is annoying," she said finally. "There's something else about Delak and the Great War that I cannot remember for the life of me. You should mention it to Kellim when you see him next." It clearly irritated her that she couldn't bring the information to hand. "Something I found in old records, something set down after the war..." Finally, she held up her hands in exasperation. "I must be going senile."

"You said Cian was in trouble," Bryn reminded, pushing his plate aside and stretching in satisfaction.

Ressca nodded grimly. "Segat's moving into Neath, and we know he's trying to push his way above us and along the Kersel mountain edge towards the coast. It appears he's trying to wipe out any possible insurrection inside the mountain ranges. Then he won't need to watch his back while he focuses on Amaria."

"So that's his next move?" Bryn asked.

"That's the general feeling. Amongst other things, he has a family grudge against the Empress and so will most likely follow his emotions in that direction. But that of course is purely conjecture."

There was a call from outside, to which Ressca responded and a soldier entered.

"The Captain would like to talk to the gentlemen ma'am. If they've finished eating."

"Tell your Captain, I'll bring them presently," Ressca responded. The soldier nodded and left.

"Have you both eaten enough?" she asked.

"Stuffed," Jai replied yawning.

"Then we can make our way over in a little while. I don't like to jump when the good Captain commands but given the circumstances."

Chapter 20

Mia Svara and Kara had been flown across the bay of Amaria. Their entry into Ildran-occupied Urukish had been under the cover of darkness. Mia Svara had transported them from the ship and Kara had immediately transformed, allowing Mia Svara to fix a pack to her back. After the constraints of the capital, Kara was now in her element and could follow her nature, regularly switching between forms simply for the exhilaration she felt. Mia Svara on the other hand adopted the only form she could safely maintain for any length of time, this fact she kept to herself.

They had quickly left the east coast behind and descended into fern jungle that obscured them from the regular sky ship patrols. Urukish's sparse population meant they were able to travel quickly and unobserved by locals and the military. Urukish had once been a major power in central and eastern Koa. Its capital had boasted the Lantrium at Lu-Esh, the seat of the Eastern Panids. Its great city-states had dominated the trading world. However, the Great War had laid waste to the country. The population and the land had been decimated, never to recover. Urukish was now a country of jungles and a few self-governed coastal cities.

Their journey through Urukish had been long but uneventful. Their only encounter startled a group picking the highly prized fruit from a grove of giant red ferns. The men and women had frozen, the reddish light filtering through the ferns. Fixed to the spot they could only watch as two predators came loping out of the undergrowth. The group waited to see if the animals would attack as the Adepts passed through at a measured trot. Kara had been unable to resist a half-hearted roar as they'd left, earning herself a look of reproach from Mia Svara. Apart from this, they had no other contact with the Urukish people or any Ildran patrols. They'd made good progress, Mia Svara navigating and Kara hunting for their food, which Mia Svara insisted was cooked and eaten in their true forms. Kara had assumed Mia Svara was uncomfortable with transforming and once aware of this made continued reference to it. After several harsh comments from Mia Svara, the two had travelled on in silence.

Finally, they crossed the border into Ildra and the jungle began to give way to civilization, forcing them to continue as themselves. Kara had darkened her skin and hair so that she looked more Ildran. Mia Svara's already dark hair and Amarian colouring meant she needed to make a smaller provision. Though, on opening their pack, she did raise an eyebrow at the Ildran clothes they'd been given to wear; the female and male dancers of the hinna houses maintained their allure by wearing veils and costumes that only hinted at the delights beneath. Mia Svara changed into them with an air of resignation that accepted the many hazards and hardships this journey and their objective had promised.

Walking for another day they reached a small town and stole mounts. They rode on untroubled because of the respect the hinna dancers commanded and eventually reached Magor, the first of the great southern cities of Ildra. They had passed many patrols and weren't surprised by the conspicuous military presence that protected the city. Magor had been heavily fortified and sky ships patrolled the air. Mia Svara noted the change from the last time she'd been there. She also noted the lack of men and women of serviceable age. Conscription had clearly been effective and possibly the only way to force a people so disinterested in empire-building to enlist. Those citizens left behind seemed to be going about their daily business with only the occasional interruption by the military.

As Mia Svara and Kara entered the city their packs were searched and they were questioned, but the guards upheld the custom of privacy, offered the dancers, and so Kara and Mia Svara were not asked to lift their veils. The city itself was a wonder and both could not help but be affected by its splendour. This was a rich city and it showed it at every opportunity in its architecture, its public buildings and its beautiful squares. Magor and Hass, the capital, were often referred to as The Golden Cities. The amount of the precious metal used to embellish and decorate buildings made it easy to see why. The effect could have been tasteless but had been applied with skill and good taste. Kara had always felt the Hallorn capital to be beautiful but Magor was a jewel. She was both angered and saddened that the focus on art and culture, encouraged by its previous rulers, had now been turned to conquest. She wondered what would become of Magor if the war reached it.

"Do stop gawping. We'll look out of place," Mia Svara said irritably.

Kara didn't reply and was tempted to pull a face, but the thought made her feel childish and she turned her attention back to the city. The atmosphere between herself and Mia Svara had not improved and so any further conversation between them remained strained and functional. Kara saw the irony in having to spend so much time with the person she least liked on the continent. Of all the people she could have been asked to accompany Mia Svara would have been her last choice. Still, the woman was efficient and a powerful Talent, that at least would improve their chances of success.

They made their way through the busy city and its solid buildings. The architectural style favoured was monumental. The buildings were blocky and solid with sloping sides; their upper storeys were relatively unremarkable with small occasional openings providing the only feature. Many had foliage growing in cascades from the flat roofs. Flowers grew in abundance and the people were equally colourful in their choice of dress. The application of gold leaf in intricate designs to the hand and face seemed to be the fashion.

The people gathered around the city's many pools and fountains socialised and conducted business. This didn't feel like a country bent on conquering its neighbours. Though there were guards on civic buildings and mounted patrols were visible in every public space they passed through. Ildra had once been a stabilising influence across central and eastern Koa, respected for its fairness and quiet confidence. But then the old King Ener had died childless, throwing the country into almost thirty years of dynastic wrangling. In itself, this had been no bad thing until House Ivalt's claim to the throne was formally recognised. A mixture of Urukish and Ildran bloodlines the UruIldran dynasty ruled one of the largest city-states in Urukish. Their family was a descendant of the Urukish Queen VaCenet. They were wealthy, though not as wealthy as many of the Ildran dynasties but what they could not match in gold they made up for in ruthless determination. The other houses were caught out and one by one their bloodlines mysteriously ended. Some families went into hiding, but House Ivalt was prepared to go to any length to hunt down those who chose to protect their families through anonymity. Only Prince Immar and his brother of House Havith remained, the needle in House Ivalt's eye, Immar was a direct decedent of King Ener with a greater claim to the throne than any in House Ivalt. It had been a sad day for Ildra and all of Koa had looked on with concern as Segat took the crown and ruthlessly consolidated his position.

Kara stopped and looked at a statue that dominated the avenue, it seemed new and out of place, oversized for its surroundings. Even now, nearly one hundred years later, the Image of Princess DuLek endured. Segat's predecessor was a symbol of Urukish's golden age and was held in great esteem by his family, Segat himself was obsessed with her. Her mother, Queen VaCenet of Urukish had sent her to Amaria in an ill-conceived attempt to stop events from escalating to what would become the Great War. DuLek was assassinated, Amaria's Emperor was wrongly blamed and his country had never been forgiven.

"I wonder what she was like," Kara muttered absently, dabbing at her forehead. The wet heat of Magor was different again from the dry heat of Amar and nothing like the climate in Naddier. "It's so humid."

"You have the persistent ability to point out the obvious," Mia Svara observed.

"You have the ability to be persistently unpleasant. Has anyone made that obvious to you?" Kara snapped.

"Quite..." Mia Svara stopped. "Kara," she said wearily. "We have never liked each other. We *will* never like each other. Up until now, there has been little need for us to communicate and when we have, you either point out the obvious or continue your ridiculous attempts to goad me. Can we exclude the banal and anything childish, communicating only when necessary?"

Kara looked at her but did not speak. Mia Svara raised an eyebrow. "An answer would be appropriate at this point."

"Appropriate yes but not necessary," Kara walked on.

With the atmosphere between them even more strained Mia Svara set about finding their contact. They located the quiet area, which comprised of a mixture of small houses and specialist shops on a relatively narrow paved roadway. Pedestrians ambled along only stepping onto the pavement whenever a cart or carriage clattered past.

They made their way along this road and eventually came to the shop they needed. The contact dealt in antiquities, a popular market with the wealthy of Magor. They entered and waited until the proprietor's two customers had been served and left. At this Kara stopped her pretence of examining goods and stepped over to the counter with Mia Svara. The owner already had a look of expectation on his face, it was unusual for members of the city's hinna houses to patronise his establishment. When Kara introduced herself and Mia Svara in the way that had been previously agreed his suspicions were confirmed. The owner responded appropriately.

"You will have had quite a journey. Please go through," he said, motioning them towards a door that led to his living quarters, before rushing back to attend to another customer.

"He's not what I imagined," Kara whispered as she removed her veil and looked around the room.

"You were expecting someone in black with a mask, perhaps," Mia Svara said curtly.

"No," Kara replied, rolling her eyes as she continued to inspect the room. "I did expect someone younger and well, less *fussy*."

"Then that makes him inconspicuous," Mia Svara replied, sitting calmly on a chair. She removed her veil and unwound the soodrey scarf from around her neck. It ached and she rubbed at it.

"Yes, but does it make him any good at his job?"

"That, we will have to see. Surely you aren't suspicious of him already. I detect no attempt to deceive us."

"Relying on strangers makes me uncomfortable."

"Could you at least sit down and be uncomfortable, instead of pacing?"

Kara sighed and not for the first time wished she had Merren or Carrick with her instead of Spiky Hanny. She purposefully remained standing in petty defiance of her travelling companion. The words to the rhyme dancing through her head, Spiky Hanny ignored her Granny, and into the thorns she fell...

The proprietor returned. "Sorry about that," he apologised, his Ildran accent completely gone. "I have closed the shop so we won't be disturbed. My name is Mesut." Both women nodded. "Can I offer you something to drink?" he asked pleasantly.

"That won't be necessary." Mia Svara sat back in the chair.

"That is most interesting," Mesut pointed at her neck.

Mia Svara looked at him, unaware of what he meant.

"Your pendant; I haven't seen anything like it before. You wouldn't consider selling it?"

"Shall we get to the matter at hand?" Mia Svara said and replaced the scarf.

"I'm sorry, it's a habit."

"What information do you have for us?"

"Of course." The little man sat down in a chair facing them both. When he spoke again his manner was more business-like. Though still fussy, Kara thought. "Your man is being held in one of the larger private houses on the outskirts of the city, having been moved here some time ago from the capital. He is guarded but not heavily. It would appear he has served whatever purpose Segat and VaCalt had in mind for him, for the time being at least."

"VaCalt?" Mia Svara asked.

"Yes, she seems instrumental in Segat's plans around this man. Her orders sent him here."

Mia Svara looked at Kara. Mention of the Adepts name added weight to the theory that the man held here was indeed Tebeb. "VaCalt, is she here?"

"No, but it is through her efforts your man was tracked down and captured," Mesut added.

Kara was instantly relieved to hear VaCalt was not in the city. She had no wish to match skills against an Urulldran Talent of VaCalt's standing. They were in enough danger as it was. "You said our man was not heavily guarded. Do you have any idea of numbers?"

"I am told twenty."

"Not many," Kara was puzzled. "Maybe they are done with him."

"Do you have a way for us to gain access to him?" Mia Svara asked.

"Yes. We have a contact in the house and can get one of you on the staff. You should know that the house is owned by an Adept, from The Ildran Order, his name is Venat."

Mia Svara and Kara exchanged glances again. "That's not good," Kara said flatly.

"What dealings have you had with the Ildran Order?" Mia Svara asked Kara.

"Not enough to be recognised. If that's what you mean. I do know the name, but we've never met. You?"

"We may have met once. I assume Venat is in residence?"

Mesut nodded. "He is often here at this time of year, but arrived much earlier than usual."

"He's the head of their Discipline of Makers. I think," Kara said, after some thought.

"Yes, that's right," Mesut confirmed. "And one of VaCalt's favoured."

"As a maker he is less likely to be sensitive to your presence in the house. You will have to be very careful," Mia Svara said, turning to look at Kara.

"So, *you've* made that decision then," Kara said pointedly. Mia Svara returned her gaze. "When can you get *me* started there?" Kara asked, slowly turning to face Mesut.

The little man chewed on his bottom lip as he thought. "By the end of the week. They are always losing staff, so it should be fairly easy to replace one of them with your good self. We can probably have you assigned as a general serving maid. That should give you reasonable access to most of the residence. Do you have plans for his rescue? I have suggestions that might help. We have watched this house for several years now, along with all of the other Adepts' homes across the country."

Kara and Mia Svara spent the rest of the week getting to know the city and the area surrounding the house. It was a typical Ildran building, slope sided and built from red brick, large and inward-facing onto open courtyards. The residence was surrounded by high walls and gardens, which made surveillance difficult. Access to the grounds was through a large, guarded gate.

They sat on a bench in the shade of a quill tree. Still wearing their hinna clothing.

"At least the house is close to the city walls," Kara said, picking at a stray hair that hung over her eyes. "That could be useful if we need to get to cover quickly."

"I have thought about that and made some preparations. Once you have located Tebeb and assessed the situa…"

"You've made preparations?" Kara bristled, sitting forward and turning to glare at Mia Svara. "*We* will make plans. There are two of us involved in this escapade."

"Don't tell me you are still annoyed about being the servant."

"I have no problem with a little hard work. However, I don't like having decisions made for me by a…"

"It was not a decision," Mia Svara interrupted. "A decision implies a choice. If Venat recognises me, we are lost. I would not be able to maintain an altered appearance over such a period of time…"

"That isn't th…" Kara began to object, but Mia Svara kept on talking.

"I am not as talented as you in that discipline and it is also clear that I am too old to pass for a serving maid."

Mia Svara's honesty completely disarmed Kara, who quickly shut her mouth. The Amarian continued to look straight ahead, calmly assessing the building. Kara stared at her for a moment and then, as best as she could, in one slow but dignified movement, turned to face the house and rested her back against the bench. "Apology accepted," she said primly.

At the end of that week, Kara presented herself at the house for an interview by the housekeeper, who was Mesut's contact there. She was taken on with little fuss and given quarters along with the other female servants. One of the existing maids named Sabiha was charged with showing Kara her duties, the girl clearly wasn't pleased about the extra responsibility. They were short-staffed and she had enough to do. Kara's subtle alterations to her appearance passed Sabiha's scrutiny and relieved some of the initial tension she felt.

Kara quickly fell in with the staff, building a relationship with each over the course of her first week in-service. The closest she came to having any kind of contact with Venat was early one morning as she was opening shutters and preparing rooms for the day. He breezed past, deep in discussion with a man in uniform. She made herself unobtrusive behind a stone column, as all staff were taught, so he paid no attention to her whatsoever, or so she thought.

The first week passed quickly, but despite working through most of the residence she found no sign of Tebeb or even gained an idea of where exactly he was, until a member of the kitchen staff mentioned the closed off west wing. The house itself was an impressive building of fountained courtyards, shady seating areas and open rooms ingeniously cooled by water. It had seen many owners and the use of rooms often changed depending on their needs or whims. Venat had wanted no family and so the west wing had been closed off and fell into disrepair, only recently being opened to house one occupant and the small force that guarded him.

"So how do you get to that bit of the house?" Kara asked as one of the kitchen staff washed and rinsed dishes.

"Oh, you won't ever get to go in there. You can only get to it through the master's study. They keep that wing private and everyone is forbidden to go into his study. Only Sabiha's allowed." She stopped washing and leaned closer to Kara, after glancing around. "We all think there's someone hideously deformed living in there," she confided with a knowing look.

"What makes you think that?" Kara asked slightly bemused.

"Because food goes in and empty dishes come out, but you never see who eats it all. So, it's obvious," she said straightening. "Whoever's in there doesn't want to be seen, so they must be deformed, silly. What else could it be?" The girl stated this assumption with such conviction in her own logic Kara didn't dare disagree. She merely nodded with what she hoped was a convincing expression of shock on her face. The girl was obviously pleased with this and nodded back in a 'told you so' fashion.

At that point, the cook entered the room and the girl hastily busied herself and Kara quickly left.

"That's right girl," the cook said, shaking a wooden spoon after her. "Get yourself gone and start earning some of the money you're being paid. Don't let me catch you skulking around here again."

Mia Svara spent her time learning different routes out of the city and finding places where they might scale the wall, should they need to make a physical escape. After much thought, she decided on two alternative routes if her original plan failed. She sat in one of the city's parks in a quiet area waiting to meet Kara for the first time since she'd entered the house. Mia Svara had set off slightly early, as she wanted to spend a little time looking at the statues and works of art in the park. It was an attempt to ease the tension building in her; the growing military presence in the city and Venat's presence concerned her. A curfew had been introduced at night and there was talk of disappearances, as Mesut put it. He later confirmed that several officials and their families had been escorted away and that other outspoken individuals, who did not support Segat, had also been removed.

On the way to the park, Mia Svara had paused to listen to a public speaker who'd attracted a large crowd of sympathetic listeners. To Mia Svara's ear, his words had made perfect sense and offered an acceptable, though alternative view of the Emperor's rule. But the crowd had been brutally dispersed and the man was made an example right in the middle of the square. The blood had been left, it seemed, as a public reminder. The scene had angered her greatly and stirred feelings she was forced to push aside; they had a task to complete and a part of that was avoiding any unwanted attention. She had resumed her walk to the park, the artwork would be a distraction, a reminder of the real Ildra.

The park and its educational buildings had been set out fifty years ago, its purpose to educate the city's less privileged citizens. Each year an event was organised and the latest acquisitions unveiled. The collection had grown over the decades and Ildra's wealth meant that it was unrivalled. However, the collection had ceased its growth abruptly with Segat's accession to the throne. Relieved the park was still here, Mia Svara had sought out two works in particular. Only to find they'd been removed, a few remained, but many others had been defaced. She had not expected this and it stirred up unwelcome memories of her childhood and the humiliation of the northern Amarians at the hands of their southern compatriots.

Now she sat, her thoughts drawn back to Amar, its politics and the constant manoeuvring of the Discipline heads that wasted so much time and energy. To some extent Varin had been right. His outspoken tirades, on the direction her Order was taking still resonated with her and had taken seed in the minds of others. But he'd left just as his words were beginning to gather momentum. If he'd stayed but another month, the Amar Order might have taken a very different path to its current one. His return and attack on the Corumn had however been a mistake. Violence was not the way to change minds. A lesson Segat would have been wise to learn. She realised she didn't miss Amar and puzzled over the feeling a little longer until she spotted Kara coming along the path. The woman seemed tired, but then changed her stance as she saw Mia Svara.

"Have you missed me?" Kara asked as she approached and sat down. "Hmm, didn't think so," her glib question hadn't been appreciated. She was too exhausted for an argument and then realised that Mia Svara looked equally tired. Kara made an effort. "I've always wanted to come here and see the collection."

"You have?" Mia Svara replied with suspicion, suspecting this was yet another of Kara's attempt to mock her, but as Kara continued to talk it was obvious this wasn't the case.

"I came early to look around," Mia Svara said. She was about to inform her of the wanton destruction she had found, but Kara surprised her further.

"I was going to have a quick look for myself, but knew you would be ticked off if I was late."

Mia Svara sighed. "You don't make it easy."

"What?" Kara asked not understanding.

"To be pleasant."

"You aren't exactly the easiest of people to be pleasant to. You're so superior and judgemental," Kara said wearily.

"And you are tactless and changeable," Mia Svara countered.

The two sat looking in different directions. Kara not wanting to be the first to speak and wishing they could get the task over and return to Amar. The silence between them became awkward as each was forced to consider the truth of the other's observation.

"Oh, for goodness's sake, I'll make an effort if you will," Kara managed, unable to bear the silence any longer.

"Very well." Mia Svara replied a little more subdued than normal and then after another pause. "Have you been able to locate Tebeb?"

"If it is him, he's in the west wing, which is sealed off and only accessible through Venat's study, they must have changed the use of the rooms; it was probably an anti-chamber in times past. The door is guarded on the other side and food is taken in twice a day by one of the serving girls."

"Is there a chance that girl could become you?"

"I've thought about that. She shares a room with me, that's how I know about the guards. Sabiha's quite the gossip, even though she's been threatened not to speak a word about it."

"She is clearly not one to be cowed," Mia Svara observed.

"No, she's quite a handful and the housekeeper's constantly on at her."

"Has the housekeeper been of any further help?"

"No, she's done her part and keeps her distance. I'll try and engineer it so that it's me delivering the food tomorrow morning. I noticed one of the plants in the garden here. A little in Sabiha's dinner tonight should throw her stomach enough to keep her in bed tomorrow." Kara stifled a yawn. "How's our escape route coming along?"

"It progresses and I have identified two as backups. Each should enable us to get clear of the house and city. If all goes well, I should be able to transport us away from Magor, I have placed several markers to aid a safer escape. I would like to put a considerable distance between the city and ourselves. In nine days, Issa and Lissu will be obscured, the night will be dark and provide good cover. The house's proximity to the city walls and its location away from the nearest lookout towers will help us further. The curfew will make things harder, but within acceptable limits. If possible, we should aim to leave then. If you are agreeable?" Mia Svara added.

"It's not much time, but I'll make sure I'm ready. Same time here next week?" Mia Svara nodded in agreement. Kara almost didn't ask. "Would you mind showing me around the collection?"

Mia Svara stood up and for an instant Kara thought she was just going to walk away. "I would be happy to," Mia Svara replied awkwardly. "We can go this way," she gestured.

At the end of their look round the park and its collection Kara bought some sweets, which she laced with the plant sap she'd collected. She left them out on her bed and true to form Sabiha helped herself and was quite sick the next morning. Kara timed her appearance in the kitchen just as the food tray was to be taken through. The cook was furious at Sabiha's absence and snapped at Kara to take it up instead.

"And remember to knock girl, or the guards will have you pinned to the wall and I'm not setting that tray again."

Kara made her way to the study and was about to enter, but instead paused. She was actually feeling nervous and this irritated her. The house seemed to have that effect, the staff were constantly on edge and wary of Venat, even Sabiha preferred not to talk about him.

"Where are you going?" an imperious voice demanded.

Kara was startled and turned quickly. Venat was stood uncomfortably close. Would he detect her minute use of the field to alter her features? If she messed this up it would be impossible to get to Tebeb. Focus she scolded herself, you didn't even sense him coming. Her natural instinct was to meet his gaze directly, but she thought better of it and tried to appear flustered. The effect, as anticipated, was not lost. "I'm to take the food through," she said dipping her head and trying to sound timid.

Venat stepped even closer, a smug smile on his lips. "You're new here, aren't you?"

"Yes sir."

"I've noticed you," this was clearly meant as a compliment.

"Thank you, sir," she said, thinking she might drop the tray down his front if he took another step closer.

He reached out and slowly inspected the items on the tray, every now and then looking directly at her, testing her reaction. Kara avoided eye contact. "You're different to the other girls. Something I can't quite pinpoint, but it intrigues me," he said at last, trying to look into her eyes.

Kara corrected herself. It wasn't the house that had an atmosphere, it was his presence in it. She didn't like playing a role, pretending to be something she wasn't and so had never found herself in a situation like this before. She felt distinctly uncomfortable and Venat sensed this. "Yes," he mused, taking a step closer so that he pressed lightly against the tray. "Quite different."

"I must go," Kara said, making to open the door without dropping the tray. "The cook is expecting me and I'll get into trouble if I'm any longer."

"We can't have that, can we," he purred, but didn't hurry to move "Very well, you may go. Tell the cook you are to bring the meals through from now on." He smiled in a self-satisfied way, which made Kara want to punch him.

"Yes sir, thank you sir," she managed, pushing the door open and stepping quickly into the study. Venat mistook this sudden departure for coyness, enjoying the effect he'd accomplished.

As she carried the tray through the study and tapped on the room's other door, she could feel his eyes boring into her back. A glance over her shoulder confirmed this, he was still there returning her gaze, unblinking. Scale belly, she thought to herself, an involuntary shiver passing through her. At that moment, the connecting door swung open. A guard on the other side blocked her way, but after a tepid inspection of the tray allowed her to pass. Kara took one last look over her shoulder as the door closed, Venat was still there watching.

The door clicked shut behind her. She felt instantly relieved by the barrier between herself and the Urulldran Adept. Convincing herself it was tiredness that was getting to her, she focused her mind back on the job at hand. She now found herself in a gloomy stone corridor with many closed openings leading from it.

"Fourth opening down," the guard grunted before returning to a table and chairs placed against the wall. She noticed a set of cards set out for two players and heard a water closet flush some way ahead of her. As she passed, the other guard appeared, wiping his hands on his trousers.

Above her head, small openings provided the corridor with murky shafts of light, the stone had once been painted with intricate designs but they were now faded and the whole place had a dusty forgotten feel, it clearly hadn't been used for a long time. She reached the opening indicated, now blocked with a rudimentary door that looked completely out of place. Two more guards were sat either side, both looked bored and didn't bother to stop her. She wondered where the other guards were and decided that the number Mesut had quoted allowed for shift changes. She quickly balanced the tray on one hand and knocked, there was no answer so she cautiously opened the door and went to go in.

"Hey, you," one of the guards grabbed her arm. "Empty that onto the food before you give it to him." The guard dropped a small vial onto the tray. "And make sure you give it me back, empty. No funny business, or else," she threatened. Kara nodded and entered.

The room was scruffy and stank. There was an unmade bed in the corner, a table and a chair, but apart from these the room was bare. The window shutters were closed and after putting down the tray she went over and attempted to open them. The air needed clearing and a breeze would cool the unbearable heat. They had been nailed shut. She peered through a small gap in them, taking note of the grounds some distance below, before giving them another shake.

"Y-you're, wast-ing your time," a voice mumbled groggily.

She spun round to confront the speaker. The door had been knocked closed revealing a man sat on the floor; his knees pulled up to his chest so his forehead could rest on them. He didn't look up. He was painfully thin and dirty. His clothing was poor and his black hair looked like it was growing back after being roughly shaved. There were the remains of manacles on his wrists. The scarred skin told her they'd been in place for some time. She couldn't see his face, but the voice sounded young, which surprised her, as she assumed Tebeb would be of a similar age to Kellim. Her heart sank, could it be that after all this time they'd got the wrong man.

"I've brought you some food," she said, hastily opening the vial and pouring the liquid into the bed pot.

The man didn't speak.

"Is there anything else you need?"

His head lolled back against the wall. "Y-you... sound... different," he slurred.

He was clearly having difficulty concentrating. His beard covered a lot of his face, but she could tell he was about Jai's age, maybe a bit older and had the deep black skin of a Nebessan. At least the man was from the right country. Kara quickly stepped over to him, mindful that she shouldn't linger.

"What's your name?" she asked urgently bending down to look at him.

"What?"

"Your name?" she hissed a little louder.

"Name... my n-name... Tebe..."

The door swung open nearly knocking Kara aside and a guard stepped in.

"What's taking so long?" she snapped.

"He'd fallen over," Kara lied and got up.

"He's always falling over. Leave him and get going," the guard ordered irritably.

Kara knew it was pointless to argue or to make a fuss. She did as she was told and left, making her way back down the corridor and returning to the study. Venat had gone, which was a relief, so she swiftly made her way through and got on with her never-ending tasks and she didn't want to be late for the evening tray. Back on the servant's stairs she paused, suddenly feeling very weary. The early starts and long days were catching up with her. She was more tired now than she had ever been and wondered how Sabiha managed so well. With a sigh and an effort, she straightened herself and hurried down. She began to think through the problem of getting a heavily drugged man out of the house. They'd brought some antidotes, assuming that Tebeb would have to be drugged to contain him, but which would be the right one? She wasn't a healer and hoped Mia Svara would be more knowledgeable about such things.

Even though she was tired Kara made good use of the next few day's tray duties, steeling herself against Venat's leering gaze as she passed through the study. She was finding his attention very unsettling, feeling more and more uneasy at having to tolerate his behaviour. His tray inspections were humiliating and though she would have happily kicked him in the groin, as he pressed against the tray, she knew she couldn't, or all would be lost. She made herself focus on the task, noting the guard changes, the view and layout of the grounds beyond the openings she passed. She also did her best to assess Tebeb's condition.

Two days before her afternoon off, Kara and Sabiha were cleaning one of the downstairs withdrawing rooms when Venat entered. They both stood and made to go, but he remained in the entrance forcing them to ask to be excused.

"You may go," he said gesturing for them to pass, barely moving so they had to squeeze themselves past him in order to leave. He smiled to himself at their evident discomfort.

When they were well out of earshot and back in one of the servant's corridors. Sabiha stopped, shuddering involuntarily and put her pale of water down. "The letch, I'd like to chop off his todger. That'd cure him."

"He's everywhere lately," Kara looked back the way they'd come. "Are you sure you're alright?" She had grown to like Sabiha, and they'd started to get on after their shaky start. Kara even felt guilty about drugging her.

"Oh, I'm fine," Sabiha sighed. "I suppose it's part of the job."

"No, it isn't and don't you forget that. Have you thought about looking somewhere else?"

"I might end up somewhere worse," she scoffed. "He only notices me when you're around anyway. It's you who needs to be careful," Sabiha warned before picking up the pail again and setting off back to the washroom. "He's got his eye on you."

Kara didn't see Venat at all over the next two days. Sabiha informed her he was away on business and so, on her afternoon off, she headed for the park feeling less uptight and at least relieved to be out of the house. She made her way through the city, unpleasantly surprised by the changes that had happened in the last eight days. As a servant, she had been too busy to leave the house. There had of course been gossip, but seeing all of the changes in one go was unsettling. Streets were emptier, the public markets were gone. Huge murals of Segat had been placed in prominent positions in most of the main squares. More sky ships patrolled the air space over the city and all the faces she saw were Ildran or Urukish. No foreign nationals, they'd all gone. Unwilling to linger she made her way quickly to the park; not even sure it would be open. She was desperate for a few moments to herself, some time to sit in the heat of the day and let it sink into her tired bones.

She arrived at the meeting point and sat in the sun, there were other people about, but not many. Birds chirped in the trees about her, they were a constant feature of the city and the only thing that hadn't changed. The little blue creatures were everywhere and the sound of their calls was a part of the atmosphere of its quieter parts. They now seemed even more conspicuous in the eerie silence. She watched them flutter and squabble over crumbs, bouncing about on their little red legs, heads cocking to one side as they looked for the next scrap. She almost wished she could fly away with them. Lost in her thoughts it was only when the birds suddenly scattered that she was aware of Mia Svara's arrival.

"I didn't mean to startle you. You look tired," Mia Svara observed not unkindly.

"It's been a long week," she said by way of a reply as the other woman sat.

"Everything's ready," Mia Svara began, sensing the fatigue in Kara and allowing her to sit and rest. "I have placed supplies at some of the closer markers. I should be able to transport the three of us a reasonable distance away from the city and make it difficult for anyone to pursue. It's been quite exhausting. Have you been able to locate and communicate with Tebeb?"

Kara stretched and sat up slowly. "Yes, but he's heavily drugged and in a poor state."

"Have you any idea what they're using?" Mia Svara asked, a note of concern in her voice.

"Not really. They give it to me to do, I pour it into a bed pot and they check the vial's empty," she shrugged. "He's lethargic, can't focus, mumbles, can barely concentrate and his breath smells!" She grimaced. "Actually, *he* smells, his breath stinks, but there's a definite smell of… you're going to think this stupid," Kara warned. "It smells of dirty socks."

"Not at all. Your observations are very concise," Mia Svara complimented. "Dirty socks would suggest the use of leriun. The Ildran Order is now well known for its use of poisons and drugs.

I had thought they would be using something more sophisticated. But at least we have an antidote for that," she said reaching into the bag she had brought.

"I should be able to put it into his food after the guards have inspected it. They aren't that interested."

"Good. If you're able, begin adding some of the antidote to his food from tonight. A few drops should do it. It will take some time to build up in his blood's stream, but it will begin to make a difference in time for our departure."

"Okay."

"At the risk of insulting you," Mia Svara began carefully. "Are you quite sure the man you speak of is Tebeb."

Kara rolled her eyes. "I'm as sure as I can be about a man no one has seen for almost a century." Kara relented, aware that Mia Svara was making a concerted effort to be pleasant. "He's been able to answer the questions we agreed on, though it's taken some time and he matches the vague description we've been given, apart from his age."

"His age?"

"He's very young for a Panid."

Mia Svara nodded slowly. "Remember we were told about that. It was thought he hadn't aged as the others have."

"That's, right. I'd forgotten." Kara exhaled heavily. "I'm tired, ignore me. Things are getting to me that normally don't."

Mia Svara waited, trying to read Kara's expression. "It must be very hard," she said finally. "I don't envy your position in the house with Venat. But you are coping admirably."

Kara was surprised by the compliment, but grateful enough to thank Mia Svara for it.

"Your escape plan?" Mia Svara asked, the brief interval of pleasantness needfully pushed aside.

Kara yawned. "Do we have to do this now? I'm shattered."

"We're taking a considerable risk as it is, Kara. If we are unclear about any aspect of our arrangements, we will fail. Venat is a powerful Adept and will have directed energy weapons in the house, if not on his person. Our actions must be rehearsed."

Kara knew the sense in Mia Svara's words so didn't argue further. She stifled a yawn and pulled herself together. "There are four guards on duty at any one time, but none are in his room. I think the other guards sleep in rooms on the floor directly below. I've seen one or two of them on the lawn there." She closed her eyes and rubbed absently at a temple. "I've been able to get some food down Tebeb each day, which has made a surprising difference. The guards made a fuss at first and then just gave up and let me get on with it." She yawned again. "Erm, the two outside the door aren't always there. Sometimes they talk to the two up at the study door. I'll find a way of making sure they do that when we make our break. There's a fair distance between them and Tebeb's room so I should have enough time to get him, get through the shutters and meet you on the lawn below." Kara shifted her position and turned towards Mia Svara. "The shutters are locked so I'll have to smash them to get out. This will alert the guards on the ground floor. You might have to delay them."

Mia Svara thought for a while. "Then I'll hope they are sound sleepers. The first of the markers is some way off, making it difficult for anyone else to reach it. Dealing with the guards will mean I'll have to draw on the field even deeper to make the transport, and that will add time to our departure. If Venat gets to us, we will have to defend ourselves and I may be unable to effect a transport."

Kara was surprised by this. She'd expected more of Mia Svara's ability. She was known for her sparing use of the field, but surely now was the time to abandon that. She was about to raise this point, but decided better of it. Mia Svara had shown trust in her, she would try to do the same. "I forgot to say," Kara suddenly remembered. "Venat's left and isn't expected back any time soon, so that's one thing we won't have to worry about," Kara stretched. "Simple really."

Mia Svara raised an eyebrow. "I don't need to remind you to be careful…"

But you will, Kara thought wearily.

"…and in my experience, things are never simple."

The last of her time at the house trudged by and on the final day Kara was about her morning tasks when one of the other serving girls came running through the room.

"He's back," she hissed. "Get this mess cleaned up quickly and get yourself out of his way. He's in a stinking mood."

Venat hadn't been expected back for several days. More than enough time for Kara, Mia Svara and Tebeb to be miles away. Her growing ease was now shattered. The careful plans she'd made had not included the Adept. She straightened and stretched her back. This was the last thing she needed. Now she'd have to alter her plans to include him. She clumped out of the room and wearily headed for the kitchen. She collected the morning tray, with a yawn and wondered if Venat would be in his study yet. With fortune's favour, he'd still be busy in another part of the house. Climbing the servant's steps, she heard his voice downstairs in the reception room and increased her pace in the hope of getting upstairs before him. On entering his study, she noticed one of his desk drawers was opened. She looked at the door to the west wing and then at the draw. Her nagging curiosity made her falter. Carefully she put the tray down on the dresser and checked the landing. She could just to say hear him below. He must have left the reception room and was in the corridor that led to the stairs. From what she could make out he was in conversation with the Captain of the guards. She had minutes. She sprang back into the study and quickly stepped across the floor to the desk and the open drawer. So, this is where he keeps them. Several, foot-long rods were placed in a specially padded tray. Kara recognised them as directed energy weapons, beautifully crafted rods that held a relatively large charge of field energy. The energy could be released, producing several bolts capable of killing. Voices suddenly sounded at the bottom of the stairs. He must have moved closer, but he was still talking irritably with the Captain. What had got Venat so riled?

Without another thought, she carefully pushed the drawer closed and locked it. Where to put the key! She couldn't keep it. Maybe outside? No, someone would see. Bookshelves! She scattered papers with a careless turn and dashed over to drop the key behind a row of books. She paused and listened. The conversation had stopped and she could hear Venat's heavy footfalls on the main stairs! The papers or the tray? She was about to dash for the tray but caught sight of another rod on the desk. It was the one Venat always carried with him. For a second, she hesitated. Venat was nearly at the top of the stairs. She grabbed the rod, stuffing it in the folds of her dress. He was at the door, but she wasn't near the tray. There was a call from below and Venat stopped to respond. His temper flared. Kara almost threw herself at the tray, lifted it shakily and moved as quickly as she dared. She tapped on the connecting door. "Come on, come on," she said through clenched teeth, listening to Venat rant. There were footsteps, the door clicked open and for the first time, she was relieved to see the guard's face.

"You're late," he accused.

"Then get out of my way or I'll be later," she pushed past him with a glance backwards. Hurrying on, she dumped a large handful of biscuits on the table. "There'll be more of those next time," she said and swept down the corridor, heart thumping.

Mia Svara was furious with herself. He'd seen her! She'd been carrying out a final check. Kara had said Venat was away so she'd removed the veil only for a moment to cool her face with water from a fountain. She'd straightened, ready to replace the veil, when the carriage had pulled up. Her sudden awareness of his proximity made her look at the exact moment he'd passed, and for a fraction of a second her eyes had met Venat's. She was sure in that fleeting moment he'd recognised her. Thankfully, she had been steps away from a corner and once round it had quickly turned down several others. Now she calmed her breathing, hiding in the shadows and assessing the situation. Was it possible he hadn't recognised her? It had been ten years since they'd met and only then by way of introduction. He had moved on to meet others and had been quickly distracted. They had met for seconds, a bland and unremarkable encounter, but she knew, curse it, he had recognised her.

The hours dragged with everyone on a wire. The more Kara willed time to pass the slower it went and to make things worse, the temperature was hotter than ever, making everyone irritable and every job a monumental effort. She'd always loved the heat, but now it just made everything harder. At least she'd kept herself out of sight and managed to get rid of the rod. It was no good to her, like the others it would be designed only to operate at Venat's touch.

The morning passed slowly as she worked and the afternoon crawled through the heat of the day until finally, evening came. She entered the kitchen silently and pocketed several handfuls of biscuits. A promise made to draw all four guards together at the connecting door to the study. She hoped they would be expecting the treats and so would be there waiting. She collected the tray with a sense of tension that even the cook picked up on.

"What's got you in such a mood? You be careful with that."

Kara didn't answer, but took the tray, belligerently banging the door open with it as she left.

Sabiha met her on the servant's stairs.

"Be careful up there," she said, gently squeezing Kara's arm. "He's still in a right mood with himself. Something's happened to bother him and it'll be us who get it. He's had someone in there with him and they've only just gone. There's been comings and goings all day long. There are even extra guards in the streets outside and everything."

"Don't worry about me. I'll be fine. You just think about what I told you,"

Sabiha giggled. "You sound like my mother. And one of those is enough. Hurry up or we'll be starting supper without you."

Before Kara could ask her about the extra guards, Sabiha headed off down the stairs. I'll miss you, she thought and then turned. Come on, she said to herself, get yourself sorted and this started.

With tired legs, she climbed the rest of the way and using her shoulder, carefully opened the door that marked the boundary between the hot utilitarian staff corridors and the cooler comfort of the main house. Her sandals had echoed and crunched on the stone steps and now they were hushed by wooden floorboards. Another servant was lighting lanterns as dusk drew quickly on towards night. She reached the study door and with what now amounted to practised ease, balanced the tray while she knocked. The usual pause lasted longer, Venat liked to make her wait before he allowed her to enter. She could hear sounds as if he was searching for something. Would he have had time to miss the rod or his key?

She knocked again.

"Come in," he said tetchily.

"This is the last time," she muttered, steeling herself before pushing the door open with her knee.

Venat threw the papers he had in both hands down on the desk. The rest of the room was in some disarray. He'd been looking for something. She could only guess it was the rod or perhaps the drawer key. On seeing her, he stopped what he was doing and got up from his desk, slowly walking over. Kara paused in the doorway as he now blocked the way through the room. He stood, looking her up and down before closing the distance between them. He seemed to find something amusing and taking hold of the other side of the tray went to lift it from her hands. Kara tightened her grip unwilling to let go.

"Release the tray," there was an edge to his voice, the smile was frozen on his lips.

Not wanting to create a scene, or attract attention from the rest of the house, she eased her grip. He jerked the tray free of her hands and set it heavily on the dresser to his left. Reaching passed, he pushed the door shut with a deliberate flourish, never taking his eyes off her and stepped forwards. Kara moved back, coming up abruptly against the wall. Venat hovered for an instant, looking down at her, enjoying the moment before pressing himself against her. Kara looked away and would have slid into the wall if she could. Venat's breath was heavy. He stroked a hand down her neck and then slowly down her arm to her hips. His brow knitted and he went to reach into the folds of her dress. Kara tried to pull away, but he grabbed her roughly and ripped the pocket open spilling biscuits on the floor.

"Sweets for the sweet," he leered and went to kiss her, grabbing clumsily at her breast.

The sudden pain jolted Kara some way back to her senses. Adrenalin swept away fatigue. "Bollocks to this!" Suddenly angry, she shoved him back.

Venat's expression changed and he lunged forward, striking the back of his hand across her face. Kara reacted immediately, pushing him back again, this time far enough to bring her fist into action. Her blow split his lip. Venat looked at her, flushed with anger and shock, his face contorting in scorn.

"You little bi…"

Kara's second blow smashed straight into his jaw, knocking him cold. He fell back over. She only just managed to grab him, but his arm flopped out and upset the tray.

The door to the west wing swung open and a guard entered the room, her eyes searching out the source of the noise. In the time it took the woman to appraise the situation Kara focused her will, drew on the field and transformed, her careful plans in tatters. Unable to process this startling event the guard had just enough presence of mind to shriek at the terror headed for her. It leapt, the force sending her sprawling to the floor. Kara bounded through the doorway, knocking the feet from under the next guard as he fumbled for his sword.

The other two guards rushed her: weapons drawn. She increased her pace. The corridor wasn't wide enough for both of them. The first guard slashed at her hide, blunting the blade as she slammed into him. He fell back onto the second and the two were caught up in a tangle of claws and teeth. The panicked shouts grew until she managed to untangle herself and leapt clear.

She knew the commotion would be heard downstairs and so wasted no time in bounding the length of the corridor. Erupting into the room she spotted Tebeb as he got up. At least he now had enough of his wits about him to scramble for cover. Kara transformed and turning her attention to the shutters, focused her will and broke them like twigs. Grabbing Tebeb, she half dragged him to the opening. Distant noises informed her that the guards were approaching with due caution. She could also make out Venat screaming orders. She got Tebeb to the ledge as the guards reached the door. She leapt, dragging the Panid with her. The instant they hit the lawn Mia Svara appeared out of the shadows and hurried over to haul Tebeb to his feet.

"Ready?" she asked hastily, eyes darting to new lights in the rooms facing the garden.

Out of breath, Kara could only nod. Mia Svara focused and the field rushed to respond as she collapsed the distance between them and the first marker. Seconds later, the remaining guards, amidst angry shouts and orders, burst out onto an empty lawn.

Chapter 21

"So, this was once a city," Kara marvelled, carefully picking her way around the ruins that still managed to hold themselves above the tide of the forest undergrowth.

"Yes. This was once the Urukish capital. The Lantrium of Lu-Esh shone here," Mia Svara replied.

"It must have been quite a sight," Kara said.

"Quite," Mia Svara agreed as she pulled away at ferns to get at the packs she had hidden there. "This hasn't been a city since the Great War."

"What happened?"

"It, like the country, was laid waste," Mia Svara responded.

"And so, the jungle took it all back," Kara said thoughtfully. She didn't want to think about the forces that could destroy a country. She was about to ask Mia Svara if she was alright. The woman looked tired, she'd transported them a long way and often, but this didn't seem to fully explain her fatigue. She looked drawn, but was now engrossed in her weeding and so Kara decided to leave the matter alone and leapt to the top of a broken column. She stood there, hands on hips, listening to the ever-present noise of the jungle. The canopy of giant red ferns spread above her and through that, a stilt tree pushed its way into the unbroken light beyond. Below her, sections of moss-stained masonry emerged defiantly from the vegetation. It was difficult to picture the city that had once stood here. A city and a Lantrium that had been so much a part of history. All gone, except for a few bits of stone. She could just make out the Uru river. It would have accommodated a port of considerable size that suddenly made her wonder where the port towers had been. She looked around, surely such massive things would have remained visible above the tree line. But there was nothing. Again, she was forced to wonder at the forces arrayed against the capital in the Great War.

"We should leave soon," Mia Svara said, her brief inspection of their supplies completed. "That was the last of my transport markers, but I'm not convinced we are in the clear. The Panid seems recovered enough, so we should press on."

"He's still weak," Kara knew she was stating the obvious and readied herself for the usual arch retort.

"He will have to cope," Mia Svara said simply, there was a vague hint of understanding in her tone. "The ship is set to return at regular intervals. If we miss the last one, they will give us up for lost and we will have to head north along the coast and hope to find transport not overrun by the Ildrans."

Kara turned to look back at where Tebeb was still sleeping. He didn't look like he'd be able to walk far, but sitting around here, at the end of a series of transports, still traceable from Magor, was a risk. "I could try something," she said.

"Try something," Mia Svara repeated with suspicion.

"He's not going to get far walking and neither of us can carry him with the forms we've used so far. I could try something bigger."

"That would involve an addition to your body's mass."

"I've done it once before, it's a bit tricky, to begin with, but once it's done."

"Tricky would be an understatement, but if you are willing to take the risk." Mia Svara didn't finish the sentence, there would be no point arguing. Questioning Kara's ability would be taken as an insult and they'd spent enough time here without extending it further with an argument.

"Okay," Kara shrugged. "I'll give it a try. Probably best if you stand back a bit. I don't want to pull you in by accident."

Mia Svara made no further comment and stepped over to where Tebeb still slept. She was forced to acknowledge Kara's commitment to their undertaking and even an element of respect for her daring, or foolhardiness. She stood for a while and then felt Kara draw on the field, detecting the formation of a second larger form field about her. Normally a Changer would surrender their form field and flow into the new one, the two fields being approximately equal in mass. Transforming into a larger form required extra substance, which could be drawn from the field. The addition required skill and ability few could now equal. Before the restrictions placed on the field by The Field's Cap such additions had been easier. Mia Svara knew of few Adepts who would even consider attempting this but still found herself open to the possibility that Kara might succeed where others had not even dared to try. She could sense Kara was readying herself and the field responded. No witness to a transformation had yet come up with the words to describe the change, many found it unnerving and even disturbing on a primal level. Mia Svara watched now with fascination. For the briefest of moments, field energy became visible, faint traces flooding into the form. Mia Svara could feel it, hear it, her skin tingled, the sensation was exhilarating and then it was done, the feeling gone, the humidity closed in, the jungle noise returned and the mount took a hesitant step forward.

"Well done," the words escaped before she could stop herself, spontaneity fuelled by what she had witnessed, and then it passed and her control returned. "I am assuming you can manage the packs as well."

The mount flicked its head in an attempt at a nod.

"Then if you allow me, I will wake the Panid and help him onto your back."

Over the next few days, Tebeb went from being tied to Kara to holding onto her. He steadily became more communicative and less confused, but still couldn't remember anything of what had happened before he arrived in Magor. They had spent time explaining these events to him and occasionally some of their words seemed to light a memory, but most of it remained a mystery.

Now, they set camp early by the side of the river. It had been another long humid day and all were tired. Their progress was slow despite retracing their tracks. Mia Svara looked at the exhausted Panid and then about them, trying to figure out how far they had left to go, it couldn't be far. "See if you can explain the art of bathing to him. I will collect firewood."

"Well, you heard her," Kara said wearily. "Mia Svara thinks you smell and should take a bath."

Tebeb sniffed at himself and pulled a face. "How long have I smelt this bad?"

"Weeks." Kara rummaged in one of their packs. "Here," she said, handing fresh clothes to him.

"Thank you," he examined them and then stopped as he remembered something. "It was you who used to come and see me in the room and make me eat. Was it always you who came?"

"No, that would have been Sabiha. It was me for the last couple of weeks," Kara explained.

"I can't remember her much at all," Tebeb said struggling to piece images together.

"I'm not surprised. You were drugged to the eyeballs. Don't rush things. It'll all come back eventually," she encouraged as her thoughts lingered on Sabiha. She hoped the girl was safe and had even moved on to another place of work. Somewhere away from Venat.

Tebeb got up with a grunt. He was still weak and unsteady on his feet and took a moment to get his balance.

"Can you manage?" Kara asked.

"Think so, it's just one foot in front of the other."

Kara watched him and the show of determination he put into every step. He paused and her resolve to let him do it on his own evaporated. She walked up to him. "Let me help, I feel cruel just standing there."

Tebeb looked at her, "Might be a good idea."

"I'll even scrub your back."

Tebeb laughed which quickly broke down into a cough. Kara grabbed hold of his arm before he fell. Eventually, the coughing stopped and his breathing returned to normal. She helped him down the small sandy bank and to get his shirt off. She winced at the sight of the bruises and burns on his sides and the long welts on his back. She was glad he hadn't seen her reaction. Whether it was sympathy, exhaustion or what, she couldn't say, but at that moment she felt something for this man she hardly knew.

"I'll wait over here and give you some privacy. Shout if you need anything. I don't embarrass easily; I have two brothers."

"Thanks," he said, awkwardly removing the rest of his clothes and lowering himself into the water.

Kara sat with her back to him and the two chatted as Tebeb washed. He asked her about their time in Magor and then about her family and how she had come to Naddier.

"Pretty straightforward forward really. Like I said I come from a big extended family, nothing special. We all got on, most of the time. Everyone worked hard, we were always well fed and lived in a nice house in a village near Oren. I was identified at an early age and so my parents got regular visits from the academy, which helped when I started to explore what I could do."

"How old were you?" Tebeb attempted to clean his back.

"About ten, but I'd been well prepared and so when I started using my talent it wasn't a problem. Though I think I gave my parents a scare or two when I learnt to change fully. That's it really. All very average."

She waited until he had finished scooping water over his head, before asking her questions.

There was a pause behind her. "Everything okay back there?"

"Err, fine," Tebeb said, sounding a little distracted. "The manacles have come off; I must have lost a lot of weight. I remember they cut into my skin the first time they…"

Again, there was a pause, but this time Kara sensed Tebeb was struggling with emotion. "Are you alright?"

He cleared his throat. "Sorry, that came at me from nowhere."

"Don't apologise. I can't begin to imagine what you've been through." He didn't answer and Kara waited until he'd finished washing. "What about you, when did you realise you had talent?"

"You're talking a long time ago."

"Are you really the same age as Kellim?" Kara interrupted.

"More or less," he replied. "What makes you ask?"

"When was the last time you saw Kellim?"

"I don't know," his voice became subdued. "I remember events up to the later stages of the war, as clearly as if they were yesterday, but everything starts to break up after that. I was injured badly in Cian. From then on, my memory started to let me down. I don't remember the end of the war. And only snatches of the decades since its end. It's hard, frightening even. Can you imagine whole sections of your life just disappearing? I would wake up somewhere strange and over time realise that I'd no recollection of the past ten years or the past five and so on."

Kara thought it best not to mention that Kellim had grown old, albeit unnaturally slowly, while he had apparently not aged a day since the end of the Great War. She wasn't sure just how much he knew and if it would be a good idea to tell him at this point. He called it the war, obviously unaware that history had re-named it the Great War. She thought it better for now to avoid the subject, offering to give him a shave and a tidier haircut. He agreed and they continued to chat about more mundane things.

"There," Kara said, standing back to admire her handy work. "Beard gone, hair, well it's a bit neater than it was. You look quite presentable. Now, all we have to do is get some food inside you and you might look like your old self."

"Thanks, Kara. I appreciate all you've done. All you've both done. I feel like a person again."

"Good," Kara said genuinely pleased. "What do you think Mia Svara?" she turned to give her a clear view.

"Well. I can't smell him from here so that in itself is an improvement. The fact that he still has his nose and both his ears must also be a relief," Mia Svara put her bundle of wood down and altered what she was about to say, managing. "He looks quite presentable."

"There," Kara said, turning back to Tebeb, satisfied with Mia Svara's response. "It's official. You're gorgeous."

***

If the first part of their journey had been slow, but eventful the second part was, by contrast, fast and dull. After an overnight stay at the army camp, Bryn and Jai were given all the papers they would need to get to Naddier. They wished Ressca goodbye and continued on their way. At first, they rode back with a small escort and then continued by sky ship across the Sancir border and onwards, skimming the coast to Naddier. They landed late one afternoon, after finally gaining permission to fly over the city's enhanced defences. The port towers now had a strong military presence and soldiers, Talents and officials inspected everything that came into and left the city. It took them a long time, even with their papers, to gain entrance. Once on the ground, they decided to walk to the Adepts' Buildings not knowing what to expect when they got there.

They passed the main academy entrance, watching as a steady stream of strictly monitored carts entered and left the gates. They could see a large amount of damage had been cleared and building work was well underway.

"Guards here too," Bryn noted as they approached the gateway to the smaller Adepts' Buildings.

"So long as that's the only change," Jai added.

They were stopped by the guards but then hailed by one of the Talents assigned to check all those who entered.

"Bryn, Jai," the Master Speaker greeted. "I hardly recognised you. You both look like you could do with a rest."

"Pellin, it's good to see a familiar face," Bryn shook hands with the young man. "Are we okay to go in?"

"I'm afraid only after you've been checked. We've had some problems. So, if you wouldn't mind," he gestured to the guards, his own subtle probing satisfied.

They made their way to their rooms, noticing the repair work and the guards posted at the doors and entrances. They just reached the corridor when, Cali, Aran and Lewan came charging along.

"You're really here!" Cali called, throwing her arms around Bryn and then Jai. Bryn couldn't help noticing she'd lost weight and despite her warm welcome looked tired.

"It's good to have you here," Aran followed, hugging them both. "You look like you've been in the wars."

"Not yet," Bryn winced involuntarily as he lowered his pack. "But near enough."

"We only just found out you were back," Lewan explained, greeting his friends warmly.

"I'm so glad you're here," Cali enthused. "I need to hear about everything you've done and seen. Durnin told us what he knew, but there must be so much more." She said beaming, her arm still around Jai's waist. "Is Kellim okay?"

"He was well when we left him," Bryn answered, thinking to himself he hoped that was still the case.

Jai smiled and stifled a yawn. "We've missed the questions," he said, squeezing Cali. "It's good to be home. But right now, I need a bath."

"And a sleep," Bryn added.

"Too right," Jai agreed with obvious relief at the thought of a comfortable bed. "A bath and rest before we have to sit in Cali's interrogation chair."

"Well, we'll let you get sorted and see you at dinner," Aran said, seeing the two men were shattered.

"Sounds good," Bryn said thankfully. "Come back up here and we'll eat. I'll ask for some food to be brought up."

A mixture of more welcome backs and quick goodbyes were said and then the corridor was quiet.

"Did a hurricane just pass through here?" Jai said, opening his door.

"Certainly, a breath of fresh air. I'm glad they're in one piece," Bryn replied a little distracted. For now, their journey was over. They were safe. Kellim, however, was on his own and looking for a man whose actions threatened the whole of Koa. Carrick, Merren and Kara were a long way from Naddier and possibly facing the approach of another man whose actions also threatened the whole of Kao. He entered his room and closed the door, his thoughts lingering on Merren.

The next day, they met with Durnin in his office. He welcomed them back, taking Kellim's letter as Bryn handed it to him. He'd set it to one side, eager for first-hand news of their journey. Jai noticed, however, that his eyes occasionally strayed to the battered parchment.

"I spend my time divided between here and Oren and the front in Cian." Durnin was saying. "They wouldn't accept our help at first, but Segat's forces are packing a punch. If he committed his forces entirely on Hallorn we'd struggle," he was picking his words carefully. "Those powder weapons give him an advantage." He tapped at the pad on his desk with a pencil, before putting it down as if reluctant to admit to the severity of current events. "We've started to develop our own you know," he admitted. "Just as a backup in case our Talents can't hold him at bay."

"A sensible precaution," Bryn replied. "Are you getting any news from Amaria?"

"We've managed to get a reasonable system working. Conveyors are working in groups relaying information from Oren across Hallorn to the Ossig Isles. The information is then conveyed to Jedesyut. They send it across country and onto Tirasa. From there it's conveyed to Amaria.

"Impressive," Jai commented.

"It's taken some setting up, but if we lose the Ossig Isles we'll have to find another way of spanning the gap between us and Jedesyut."

"Ressca said Segat was using a lot of his Talents on the frontlines," Bryn said.

"He's using everything at his disposal. The Fury attack on Amar was, to say the least, a surprise; a creation no one has attempted since the Great War. We can only guess at what else the Ildran Order is capable of. Since the attack we've taken no chances and placed our strongest Summoners on all the front lines," Durnin paused. "That said, they have met with little in the way of success in creating Elementals of their own. It is an ongoing process and one I had hoped to leave forgotten in the past."

"So how come the Ildrans managed it?" Jai asked.

"We're not sure. One possibility is the Panid Tebeb. He's reputed to have created the Guardians and certainly would have understood how the Fury could be created."

"Why has no one gone looking for this Panid earlier?" Jai asked. "Even Kellim hasn't seen him since the Great War."

"No one's seen Tebeb since the war," Durnin corrected. "He disappeared shortly after and has managed to keep himself away from the world since then. How or why, I haven't the foggiest. I know Kellim, Ethre and Etefu searched endlessly for him. But now Nirek thinks he's in Ildra and has sent Kara and Mia Svara to bring him back."

"Kara and Mia Svara!" Jai exclaimed sitting forward in his chair. "They hate each other. Wow, I wish I was there."

Durnin chuckled. "Strange times call for strange alliances."

***

"Go, go now!" Mia Svara yelled, barely audible above the noise of the Fury's presence.

Kara faltered, torn between helping Mia Svara and doing what she knew she had to.

"I'll come back for you. I promise,"

"Leave!" Mia Svara shouted.

Hating herself, and with no time to transform, Kara half carried, half dragged Tebeb into the undergrowth.

Mia Svara turned; the surrounding jungle writhed about her. The clearing was chaotic, ripped and tossed as if by a storm. She struggled to keep her footing. Energy ribbons lashed randomly at trees and ruined masonry, sending fern and dirt into the maelstrom as the Fury cleared the portal. Weaker than the one at Amar it was still more than a match for her. She could sense the distant minds controlling it. How had they found them? She tested the ground below the Fury, but there was no rock; the same simple trick wouldn't work again. She needed another way to delay it, long enough to allow Kara and Tebeb to escape, but even now, in the path of a creation of chaotic energy, she had to keep her own inner chaos at bay. She unclipped both discharge rods and moved to their most effective range. Several bolts of focused energy erupted from the slender rods. The air rippled and cracked like thunder, disrupting the Fury's form field. Pressing her attack, she stepped closer still, firing bolt after bolt. It was blown back into the trees and still she fired, closing in until the rods were exhausted. The Elemental's form field destabilized with a searing flare of energy, it hit her full on and swept her back into the undergrowth.

Mia Svara awoke with a start and ignoring the pain, searched inside. The chaos was contained. The pain increased as she tried to sit up. It was a while before she gained control of it and was able to look at her hand and arm. She was burnt, the flare had caught her right side. Her vision was clouded in one eye and there was sudden warmth on her neck. She touched one ear and then the other, more blood, the flare had damaged her hearing too. Trying to focus, she eased the pain and carefully got to her feet. She took a few faltering steps, unaware of a disturbance in the jungle. She needed to leave, but walking was an effort, she stumbled again, sense telling her she was going nowhere. She lowered herself to the ground. She would rest a while longer.

Behind her, the forest was moving. Energy bent and pulled at the tree's leaves as they came spinning angrily after her.

Chapter 22

Carrick rubbed at his eyes; he'd slept properly for the first time in weeks. His body still ached but his head felt clear. He reached for the hot drink Natesh had set before him, but his hand still shook, so he let it rest on the table.

"No more today," Natesh said firmly. "Or tomorrow. You've pushed hard enough the last few days."

"Ok," Carrick agreed reluctantly.

Natesh sighed, relieved that Carrick was now listening to him and stepped through the doorway into what passed as a small garden. He took a deep breath of the morning air and let the wind blast him as waves boomed on the pebble shore. He was glad that the worst was now behind them.

Weeks ago, back in Amar, Carrick had continued to be troubled by Varin's use of a staff, seeing it as a threat they were unable to counter. Merren had suspected the source of his preoccupation and, not for the first time, attempted to convince him the problem wasn't his to put right. Then, news had arrived that Talents in the Ildran Order were attempting a similar project. With this development in mind, Carrick had secretly talked to Jeeva, Amar's Adept Maker, and she had agreed to fashion a staff for him. Having never done this before she was excited by the project and after considerable research had begun her task, crafting a staff and weaving in the form fields that would allow it to work. The first attempt had exploded, rather spectacularly. Undeterred she had tried again and had watched with anticipation as Carrick's fingers closed around the second attempt. There had been smiles and satisfied nods as staff and user connected.

Carrick's first attempts to direct his will through the staff had been a source of much joking between them. With practise he'd managed to charge the staff and, to the surprise of both, directed a small amount of energy a short distance at a half-buried iron rod. The flash had popped in the air making them both jump and then fall about laughing. Carrick had practised for weeks only improving to a bolt of energy that struck the rod from a greater distance. In the time that followed, he made no further progress. His frustration had become evident, and Merren had attempted to dissuade him from pushing further. Carrick wouldn't be deterred, the two had argued and parted in anger.

Merren had left for the Ugamas Dip but not before asking a mutual friend, called Natesh, to keep an eye on her brother. Days later, rather than let Carrick continue alone, Natesh had agreed to monitor him as he attempted to develop his ability with the staff. Not wanting to alert Chancellor Nirek to this questionable pursuit, Natesh and Carrick had left Amar and headed for the small house Natesh maintained when he needed a break from the politics of the Amar Order.

Time had passed, and at first, Carrick had been reasonable about the process, minutely pushing against the limitations of The Field's Cap. Natesh had watched him battle against the pain of this process, using his skills as an Adept Healer, to ease Carrick's pain and repair the minor damage incurred. But as time had passed Carrick had pushed himself more and more and Natesh had become concerned. Carrick's abilities had increased, but so had the injuries and Natesh found he was repairing deeper, more alarming damage. Carrick began living with headaches that had plagued him unceasingly, his stomach was unable to cope with food and he wasn't sleeping. Natesh would often wake to find Carrick talking to himself as if someone else was in the room, or in his head. By day Carrick had been at best irritable and at worst paranoid, blaming Natesh for the whispering that had dogged his waking hours and invaded his dreams.

Natesh had tried to persuade him that enough was enough, but after many arguments he had given up and watched the torture on a daily basis. Natesh had even tried to drug him, but Carrick had become aware of this and exploded in rage. At that point Natesh had decided he needed to leave. He'd packed and even begun riding down the beach, only to turn back, knowing Carrick needed his help and that he'd made a promise to Merren.

Natesh had returned to find Carrick unconscious and had taken the opportunity to send him into a deep sleep, extending the rest for days before allowing Carrick to wake naturally. One morning, Natesh had woken to find Carrick gone. He'd hurried to the windows and with relief spotted him down on the beach, staff in hand. Natesh had dressed and gone to see how Carrick was, ready to defend the enforced rest he'd placed on him. As Natesh had approached, Carrick had greeted him with an apology that sounded more like his old self. He'd then asked Natesh to watch. Natesh had agreed and waited patiently as Carrick had turned towards the distant iron rod part buried in the sand. Raising his staff, he'd concentrated. Natesh had instantly sensed Carrick's connection to the field had changed. The air had begun to prickle and still Carrick had drawn further on the field. The staff had hummed suddenly, and a ragged strike of energy had erupted from its tip and struck the rod, the ground around it had exploded leaving a large crater. Both men had watched as the sand and fused silicon patted back down onto the beach, the noise of the sea filling the air again.

"I'll do it your way from now on," Carrick had promised, adding another heartfelt apology.

"Your sister needs to hear that too," had been Natesh's only response.

Carrick had winced. "Hmm, when you're right you're right."

Since then, Carrick had kept his word and although the going had been painfully slow, they had made progress.

Now, Natesh waited outside listening to the sound of the waves. He'd noted the shaking hand and knew Carrick was exhausted.

Carrick watched Natesh step outside and tried again for the hot drink. This time the shaking had eased enough for him to pick it up and take a few sips. It was slightly bitter, but everything tasted bitter lately, he wished he could get the taste out of his mouth. Eventually the drink began to take effect and Carrick decided to get up and join Natesh. He was a little unsteady on his feet and waited a while so that Natesh wouldn't see this and force him to rest for even longer. He perched on the edge of the table and drank more, taking careful sips so he didn't burn his mouth. Finally feeling steady he went out to join Natesh.

"An ear for them," Carrick asked seeing Natesh sat on the stone wall.

"Sat here, looking at this, you wouldn't know we were at war," Natesh said thoughtfully. "There must be people all over the continent oblivious to the fact. Just getting on with their lives."

"I hadn't really thought about that, but yes there must be," Carrick wondered at his friend's thoughts. He didn't seem to fit in at the Amar Order. He wasn't struck with the same need to gain rank. The drive that appeared inherent in every Amarian Talent, to climb to a position of authority, to manipulate and use every conversation to their advantage, wasn't present in Natesh. He was the voice of reason and a point of stability. "Do you ever regret joining your Order?"

Natesh thought for a while. "No, but there are times when I get sick of all the 'in house wrangling'. There are too many egos that need stroking and perhaps too many people gullible or ambitious enough to do it. Is it the same at Naddier?"

"Some, but not on the scale here. We have a few egos, but they're quickly slapped down. Durnin comes across as the affable uncle, but get above yourself and you'll regret it."

They sat for a while, watching sea birds swoop and hover on the air currents forced upwards by the rolling waves. It was peaceful and Natesh felt calm for the first time since they'd arrived. "Have you thought any more about going back and sorting things out with your sister?" Natesh sensed now was a good time to broach the subject.

Carrick leaned against the wall. He could feel his legs starting to tire. "Yes. I know I should. I keep thinking I'm going to see her coming down the beach one morning. She's not one to hold onto things."

"She was only worried about you."

"True, but I felt this was important. You're pretty shorthanded at this end. If I'd been able to do what I can now, more people would have survived the Fury attack. If Segat's got more of those things we won't stand a chance, unless we push the limitations placed on us."

"That's what Varin wanted us to do in the first place," Natesh said pointedly.

"And before all of this I would have said he was wrong but..."

"Varin's dream seems to have become a reality, in a roundabout way," Natesh said dryly.

"Perhaps it has. How ironic."

They watched the skimming sea birds a while longer. The constant noise of the waves was somehow comforting. Natesh finally spoke. "Have you tested your abilities this morning?"

"I thought I'd better wait until you got up. I didn't want another telling off," Carrick smiled.

"Who said nagging never works," Natesh replied.

"To be honest," Carrick admitted. "I've been holding off. I felt different this morning."

"In what way?" Natesh asked a note of concern in his voice.

"Don't worry," Carrick managed a half-hearted smile. "Not in a bad way." He paused, trying to find the words to explain something he didn't fully understand. "For a start, the whispering has gone. It's taken me a while to realise it. Thinking back, it went after you put me in that deep sleep. Maybe you should have done that earlier."

"I tried. You weren't exactly pleased."

"That's true, and somehow it seems distant as if I was watching myself be angry," Carrick puzzled.

Natesh nodded slowly.

"I'm sorry. I still don't know what the whispering was. What it was a sign of..." he gave up and rubbed at his forehead. "I can't put it into words. It made me want to continue even when I knew I should stop and I felt angry for no reason when you tried to stop me. Do you think I was going mad?"

Natesh laughed. "A few weeks ago, before you collapsed, I'd have said yes. But now, I don't know, you're back to normal. It was like your whole personality had changed. Anyway, what else feels different?"

"I still feel exhausted but now just physically. Before my mind felt drained too. This morning my head's clear."

The afternoon found them on the beach. The wind had dropped and the sea was calm. Natesh had set an iron rod some way off, having walked back past several craters now partly filled in by the daily movement of sand and pebbles.

"Ready?" Natesh asked as he approached, his boots digging into soft grit.

Carrick nodded apprehensively. "I think you should stand away a bit."

"I always do. This time I'm going to stand a long way back," Natesh joked, trying to ease the tension.

Natesh watched as Carrick prepared himself and began to focus his will. From the second he started Natesh could feel the difference. The energy field was more responsive. When Natesh drew on the energy to heal it always had the feel of treacle. This seemed to flow more like water. He could feel it building much quicker and the air already had the static feel associated with a concentration of field energy.

In less time than before, Carrick raised the staff and willed it to discharge. No short-lived bolt this time. The staff's hum sank to a deeper pitch, there was a flare of light and a beam of brilliant energy sliced through the air. The iron rod disintegrated in a flash of molten sparks and the ground around it bulged and then erupted in a large detonation, spraying sand and silicon halfway back to where they stood. Natesh had flinched involuntarily and Carrick stood frozen, looking at the crater. Above them, sea birds screeched and wheeled in outrage.

"Are you alright?" Natesh asked as he walked cautiously over.

Carrick seemed to be checking himself before answering. "Yes, I think I am. Nothing's dropped off and my head's still here."

Natesh slapped him on the back, the tension lifting. "Good work."

Carrick let out a whoop of delight and shook Natesh's hand. "Thanks to you."

Several days later, after making Carrick rest, Natesh locked the door to his house and climbed onto his mount.

"We should make Amar by tomorrow. You sure you're up to the journey?"

"I'm ok. I'm eager to get back." They started off along the beach at a steady trot leaving the small house behind. Carrick wasn't sorry to leave, his memories of the past weeks already seemed distant, even a little unreal and weren't ones he wanted to take with him. He took a last look back at the small cottage and the sea beyond, before coaxing his mount on to catch up with Natesh's. Now that they were on their way, his thoughts turned to what was happening in the wider world. He was eager to see his sister and perhaps make amends. He was also impatient for news of their friends.

The sky ship journey was short and upon their return to the Amar Order buildings Carrick thought it appropriate to speak with Chancellor Nirek first. It wouldn't take long and then he could find Merren.

Nirek noticed the change in Carrick's appearance immediately. The weight loss and the dark circles under his eyes gave some impression of what the Hallorn Talent had put himself through. The Chancellor listened thoughtfully as Carrick related the events of his time at Natesh's.

"You took a terrible risk," Nirek said finally. "And one I could not have encouraged, but the war is coming and I fear we will need all the help we can get."

"So Segat has made further moves?" Carrick asked, aware that events in the world beyond the beach house would have moved on a pace.

"Yes," Nirek nodded gravely. "He seems to be clearing away the pockets of resistance in the North. Neath and most of Sancir are under his control. His forces are preparing to push into Kersel and westwards along the northern coast of Sancir towards Hallorn. He has consolidated his hold on Urukish, Selarsh, Hon and much of Cian." He pointed to a map and its covering of flags and markers now set up by his desk. "Your people are only just holding his forces back along a narrow stretch of the Cian coast and so the capital still stands. His powder weapons and The Ildran Order under VaCalt are proving a powerful component of his armies."

The Chancellor continued to bring Carrick up to date until he could see the man was becoming tired. "It would seem now is the time for you to get some rest. But before you go, I have news from your sister."

"Oh," Carrick said a little surprised.

"Segat has been testing our defences at the Ugarmas Dip. She volunteered to go there and spearhead a counter strike shortly after you left, and so isn't here to greet you." The Chancellor noted Carrick's sudden concern. "She anticipated your reaction and left you this note. Oh, and this," Nirek passed him a hat.

Carrick took hold of it not knowing what to say, but quickly opened the note. He read the short message and then chuckled. "The note," Carrick began, "reads as follows. Dear brother, I sincerely trust this finds you well and in full control of your faculties! However, should that not be the case, please find attached this hat, which may be used to cover any large holes in the top of your head. Love Merren."

***

"Get us in closer!" Merren shouted above the icy wind buffeting the barge.

In response, the Amarian Captain expertly swung his craft closer to the much larger Ildran vessel. Even though it was unencumbered by sails, its three Conveyors still had to work hard to propel the small barge and out manoeuvre their adversary. The field was diffuse at this altitude. Talents had to supplement field engines to keep craft in the air.

The Ildran Captain had positioned his ship to fire on the nearest fort of the Ugamas Dip and wasn't prepared for the speed of the Amarian barge. It had come from below, partly hidden by the blizzard. Bellowing orders, he tried to reposition, his ship was weighed down by ice and this part of the pass was narrow. Air starved peaks towered over them and just out of range ballistae and catapults waited on the lower crags.

Merren focused, drew in as much of the weak field as she could and transported herself and fifteen soldiers onto the Ildran main deck. The men and women quickly deployed to dispatch the Ildrans loading the powder weapons. The ship's complement of soldiers moved to engage. Driving wind whipped the snow and a thousand little blades of ice attacked both sides.

With effort, Merren now transported herself to the wheel deck, directed the field and sent the Ildran Captain and two men crashing onto the icy main deck below. Turning quickly, she locked minds with the two Ildran Conveyors. Both were strong, but no match for an Adept as powerful as her. It was only seconds before both pitched forward, clutching at their heads. Merren took a chance, grabbed a navigation lens and sent both sprawling to the deck. The ship lurched alarmingly as their focus was lost and the ship's field engine struggled to keep the craft in the air. Merren had to focus and support its efforts before they crashed into the mountain peaks. Yet again she was reminded just how weak the field was at this altitude.

Seeing she was distracted, the two men, swords drawn, started climbing the steps back towards her but she gained control of the craft in time to shatter the wood beneath their feet. Both screamed, falling back onto the frozen deck below. She grabbed the wheel and began turning it quickly in order to bring the Ildran ship closer to the first of the mountain forts. The fighting was close and bloody. The fifteen soldiers she'd transported were hard-pressed. Merren was all too aware they needed to reach reinforcements and that she couldn't keep the ship in the air for much longer. The blasting wind was in her favour, but they weren't gaining enough speed. She looked at the half-frozen sails and then about her. Her people were being pushed back. She focused her will and began forcing the ship forward. Its weight was huge and she strained to draw on enough of the field. The bulky craft lurched, its bow lifting as it picked up momentum. She gripped the wheel, glancing again at the soldiers on the deck and pushed with all of her talent, hoping the field engine and lift mechanisms were located aft.

The soldiers on the fort's jetties watched suspiciously as the large vessel emerged from the swirling snow. When it showed no sign of slowing, they scattered as it bore down on them and then smashed into the metal structures. The bow shattered and the ship's timbers groaned in protest. Merren was flung against the wheel and many of the people on the icy deck lost their footing. Now the Amarian soldiers could board and came scrambling over the distorted metal jetty. From then on, the battle was a foregone conclusion and those Ildrans with enough presence of mind surrendered and were taken captive.

The fighting over, Merren stood behind the wheel watching the last of the enemy soldiers being escorted off the ship. She patted her gloves to get rid of the snow that covered them. As the adrenalin left her body the cold slipped in to replace it. She looked at the fort clinging to the ridge, you'd think in something that big they'd manage to build one room that was warm. Terrace after fortified terrace climbed the ridge from the frozen lake below to the edge of the breathable air hundreds of feet above her. Up there the blizzard was closing in and the highest reaches of the fort disappeared in the grey mass. She looked down as two Talents came on board, along with an Amarian crew to try and dislodge the ship and make it stable. On what was left of the jetty, she could see the fort's Commander dishing out orders. He gave her a disapproving look as he stepped on board. Along with two women he climbed what was left of the wooden steps. Merren stood aside from the wheel and the women quickly got on with their task.

"When I said to capture the powder weapons at all costs, I didn't actually mean you should take out the fort as well." The Commander's breath steamed in the freezing mountain air. "That said," he continued before she could object. "You saved a lot of my people's lives and for that, I'll overlook the damage to the main jetty. Well done ma'am," he congratulated with a wry smile.

"Thanks Commander. Perhaps you'd like me to pilot the ship that takes you home after all of this."

The Commander gave her a meaningful look that spoke volumes.

"Careful Commander, I can read strong emotions."

"Yes, I should imagine abject terror is easy to sense. How did you know the field engines were aft and not in the prow?"

"I didn't."

With that they headed for the powder weapons on the lower deck.

"Getting our hands on these will help us no end," the Commander said with satisfaction as he and Merren examined them. "We'll have them on their way to Amar within the hour. They are considerably bigger and more efficient than anything we have so far."

"Anything that doesn't blow itself up would be an improvement on the current state of progress in both Hallorn and Amaria," Merren noted.

"I'm afraid you're right. That's why this day will be remembered when the history books are written. Your work here is done. Where will you go next?" the Commander asked.

"I'll join the Eland when it sets course for the third rendezvous with Mia Svara and Kara at Urukish. The Ildrans have a greater presence in the skies along the coast and I might be able to lend a hand if the two women show with the Panid Tebeb."

"Of course, the Panid. I would be very interested to meet him."

"You, me and most of the Naddier and Amar Order," Merren replied. "But until then I'd like to get in and find a fire to thaw in front of."

A day later, the Eland left from the repaired jetty and headed south to wait for Mia Svara and Kara's return. Merren had been fine while she was busy, but now, despite the threat of discovery, things were quiet enough for her to feel anxious. The women had missed the first two rendezvous and now she was concerned that they wouldn't show again. Merren couldn't help but wish the ship faster or the distance shorter.

They arrived above the Urukish rendezvous point near the estuary of the river Uru. Now that they were stationary, the Master Speaker began weaving more substantial form fields of concealment around the ship and a pattern of patrols was organised to search the surrounding jungle.

The days passed and they saw several Ildran ships monitoring the area, those that did were on set patrol patterns that conveniently kept them a safe distance from the Eland.

***

Kara had run all day, the form she'd assumed didn't tire easily, but at this pace even she was beginning to struggle. Tebeb had not complained, but was suffering greatly from the endless motion and the effort of hanging on as Kara made her way through the jungle. She stopped often to allow Tebeb to rest, but could see he was gradually becoming weaker. She came to a halt by a small stream that fed into the Uru and waited while Tebeb eased himself down. He sank to the ground with a faint grunt of relief.

"Just rest," she urged. "I'm going to find us food."

When she returned Tebeb was still and for a brief moment, she couldn't see his chest moving. But he stirred and, after checking on him, she expertly skinned and gutted her catch. She risked a small fire and while the meat roasted, she split open a fruit and scraped out its soft innards.

Tebeb slept for several hours, the sounds of the night jungle gradually taking over from the constant chorus of the day. The insects and birds had returned to the jungles of Urukish, but like so much of the central and southern continent the larger animals had been wiped out in the Great War. The thought made her think of the ruins and of Mia Svara, she still expected the woman to come marching out of the undergrowth, but as each day passed the hope of this happening grew weaker. She looked at Tebeb. "You better be worth it," she muttered and then felt guilty. He stirred and she went over to help him sit up.

"Here, drink this and try some fruit. It'll settle your stomach."

He drank slowly and ate with little appetite, but eventually, the water and the fruit made a difference.

"How much further do you think we have to go?" Tebeb asked.

"Some time just after first light tomorrow, give or take. The ship should be there now, waiting. I just hope they're able to hang on. I noticed an Ildran sky ship in the air above us earlier today."

"Do you think they saw us?"

"No, I took cover as soon as I saw them and they carried on without hesitation. So, I think we're ok. How's your memory doing?"

"The leriun's out of my system and it's just the withdrawal symptoms I'm struggling with now. Bits of recent memories have been coming back, faces, names, all Ildran and Urukish. Some events..." Tebeb broke off sharply.

"Do you mean Hass? Do you need... do you want to talk about that?" Kara asked awkwardly.

"No," he replied bluntly, shaking his head. "I'm sorry, can we change the subject?"

Kara nodded. "How about food? I think this is ready." She moved closer to the fire and removed the meat from the flames.

Tebeb got up, wincing at aching muscles as Kara split the meat between the two of them. He stretched and then came to sit with her. They both ate, Tebeb trying to think of a way to start a conversation.

"You spoke of your friends Merren and Carrick?" Tebeb said at last.

Kara smiled at the mention of their names. "It seems ages. I can't tell you the number of times I wished they were with me in Hass. We've a lot of history. They were the first people I got to know when I joined the Order," Kara said between mouthfuls. "They're brother and sister and probably the people I'm closest to outside of my own family. You'll meet them when we get back to Amar." She licked at juice running down her hand. "Then there's Bryn and Jai, I've no idea where they'll be now. They're good fun to be around." Kara hadn't had time to think of her friends and now she had, the ache of missing them returned. She took a drink and cleared her throat. "I can't imagine trusting anyone more than I do those four."

"Good friends." Tebeb smiled gently, seeing the emotion the memories brought her. He finished eating, putting off his next question. "You know Kellim, right?"

"Yes, absolutely. Not as well as Merren and the others, but yes."

"We were good friends. I've a lot of memories of him. Good memories. He could be hot-headed, was always a bit of a joker and constantly getting into scrapes."

"Really," Kara was surprised, the quiet, reserved man she knew was a long way from the description Tebeb had just given her. She wondered just how much Tebeb was aware of the passage of time and its differing effects on his friend. Uncharacteristically she considered erring on the side of caution. But that lasted a full minute. "Oh bollocks." She dismissed restraint, it was a lot of energy spent getting nowhere. "You know you still look like you're about thirty?" Kara decided to tackle the issue head-on.

"Well, I've not had time to look in a mirror lately, but I suppose so."

"Kellim's an old man. He hasn't stopped ageing like you. He's done it slower, but he looks seventy even though he must be hundreds of years old." Kara waited for a reaction and studied Tebeb's troubled face as this news sunk in.

"I don't understand. We don't age," he said incredulously. "I mean how old are you? You look like you're in your mid-twenties?"

"Tebeb, I look like I'm in my twenties because I am in my twenties."

"What's happened? Kellim looked a little older than me, we were both very old even then and hadn't aged. Why..."

"You have been out of it!" Kara was surprised by just how much Tebeb didn't know. "Haven't you been around *any* Talents in the past hundred years?"

"Well, no, I mean, I don't know." Tebeb's brow knotted as he tried to piece together fragmented memories. "I don't remember anything towards the end of the war and the decades that followed are patchy at best. I had no real sense of who I was or where I was in those years. And then when the Ildrans captured me I was drugged most of the time. They only brought me around when they wanted to..." he broke off and pushing those memories away looked at Kara. "You've told me bits, but now I need to know it all. Tell me all you can about the last hundred years, Kara."

"I'm sorry Tebeb. I knew your memory was patchy, but I had no idea."

"It's ok. Tell me."

Kara related the series of events following the Great War, putting in as much detail as she could. She continued until Tebeb couldn't keep his eyes open. At that she thought it best to stop, promising to continue at another time, she was tired too and had talked for longer than she'd intended. They would be up well before first light and she needed to rest if they were to continue at the pace she'd set.

The time to wake came all too soon, they ate quickly and resumed the punishing journey through the jungle. Kara knew they didn't have far to go, but she didn't dare let up in case they missed the ship. It was just getting light when her senses caught the smell of people and the unmistakable scent of Merren. She stopped and let Tebeb climb down.

He sat willing his stomach to settle, glad of the break. "Not that I'm complaining but why have we stopped?"

Kara transformed. "I could smell Merren," she said excitedly. "They're close. Can you walk?"

Tebeb heaved himself to his feet and they began to make their way through the jungle. After a short distance Kara halted, looking about her. The clearing was silent, but then Merren stepped out of cover.

"It's them," Merren called back into the undergrowth. "Hold your fire."

Merren ran over and embraced Kara tightly. It was a while before they broke to look at each other. "You look exhausted," they chorused and then laughed with relief.

"This is Tebeb," Kara introduced.

Merren managed to cover her surprise and greeted the man she'd expected to be older. She looked questioningly over his shoulder and then more urgently at Kara. "Where's Mia Svara?"

Kara slowly shook her head. Tears welled in her eyes and although she fought it, her face crumpled as she began to sob, the relief and the strain finally catching up with her. Merren took her in her arms, rocking her gently as the soldiers emerged from cover and came to escort them to the safety of the Eland.

Chapter 23

The Panids' Children entered Naddier through its sewers, like them, old, abandoned and long since forgotten. The renegade Children, now released from Varin's will, had joined those labelled as the wanderers, and all now sought The Purpose. Driven on by the whispering, ten now worked together with one aim, the promise of their continued existence. A ship waited for them and many dared to anticipate the journey to their final destination.

As night fell The Fire of the Sea entered the shallower water of Naddier's port. She too was eager to be on her way north once this part of her task had been completed. She was to create a diversion and draw attention away from the city. She swam with ease, keen to fulfil her task. After decades in the deep oceans the whispering had reawakened a need to revert to her original purpose, seek out enemy ships and burn them.

There was a commotion in the corridor as Bryn headed to join the others for their evening meal. It was odd to hear any noise. The Adepts' Buildings were almost deserted, as most of the Adepts and Talents had left to support the fighting in Sancir and Cian.

"What's going on?" he asked the nervous apprentice, who came running in his direction.

"The port." He didn't stop. "It's under attack!"

"Does Durnin know?" Bryn shouted after him.

"I'm going there now."

Bryn quickened his pace and found the others in the communal area. They were stood at its large windows and he went over to join them. His eyes quickly skimmed across the city to the low cloud over the harbour. It flickered from the reflected light of several raging fires. He could just make out two ships aflame and what would be a section of the harbour jetties.

"What caused this?" he asked, coming to stand beside Aran.

"Someone said Segat's started his invasion, but we've also heard it's an accident, another rumour is one of the Children caused it," Aran said uneasily.

"There's nothing confirmed yet," Jai added. "Lewan's gone to find out what he can."

They were startled as an explosion lit up the area. Even in the dark, debris could clearly be seen arching across the sky and into the other harbour buildings.

"What was that?" Cali asked, unable to look away. She seemed uncharacteristically anxious and Bryn was concerned that the strain of the past year would be added to.

"It's reached the warehouses, must be an oil store," Bryn replied trying to see if the fragments had started any secondary fires. "We're safe here though. The fire won't be allowed to spread far."

They heard Lewan's approach and turned to see him round the corner, now wearing his sword and a worried look on his face. Instinctively his eyes searched out Cali. Bryn saw this and guessed at his news.

"It's one of the Children," he said, moving to Cali and taking her hand.

She moved towards him. "Is it still there?"

"It's heading back out to sea."

"So did it cause the fires?" Aran asked.

"Yes, but I couldn't get any answers why."

Jai flashed a quick look at Bryn and then headed off to get their weapons. "I won't be long."

"Bryn, what do you think it wanted?" Cali asked nervously.

"It could be any number of things. Try not to worry. Come and sit down."

Bryn kept them talking as they waited for further news. Jai returned, handing over Bryn's sword and a pack. Durnin followed closely behind.

"Here you are," he said with some relief. "Has someone told you what's happened?"

"We know about the attack," Jai replied.

"Right, then you know as mu…"

Durnin was interrupted by a loud reverberating crash and startled calls. They got to their feet as more crashes and shouting came down the corridor from the main entrance. For long seconds everything went silent and then a frightening mixture of explosions, roars and screams echoed towards them. Jai, Bryn and Lewan instinctively stepped in front of Aran and Cali; weapons drawn.

Durnin had started to move forwards, motioning for the others to stay where they were. There was a sudden rending sound and the wooden floor bulged and then imploded. He didn't have time to react and fell into the cellars below. A sudden flare of light erupted from out of the gaping hole and an impact reverberated through its depths. There were several more explosions, followed by shrill screams. A thick cloud of dust billowed up into the room marking an abrupt silence.

Bryn made his way across the floor to the jagged edge and attempted to look down. In the dusty flickering lights of the cellar, he could see a fur-covered body half-buried in the rubble.

"Durnin!" Bryn shouted, searching the gloom. "Durnin!"

"Anything?" Jai said, coming forward.

"Careful, the floor's unstable," Bryn warned.

There was movement below and the sound of disturbed bricks. A cough gave away the cause and Durnin stepped into view, brushing himself down, he looked up.

"Can you pull me up?" he said, making out Bryn and Jai.

Without hesitation Bryn lay down and stretched over the edge of the hole. "A little further," Bryn strained trying to reach Durnin. But the gap was too big.

Jai rushed to the window and yanked down a curtain. "Here use this."

Bryn fed the curtain down into the space below, his eyes returning to the doorway and corridor beyond, the noises had stopped. Durnin scrambled over the debris and wrapping the end of the curtain around his arm, gripped the thick cloth tightly.

Bryn moved back from the edge and along with Jai pulled Durnin up. They were about to speak when a series of much closer crashes echoed out of the corridor. There were shouts and sword fighting. Two soldiers backed into the room, trying to hold off one of the Children. Heavily built, it fought with two curved blades held in armoured hands. It was distracted momentarily as it spotted Cali. Seeing his chance, one of the soldiers slashed at its unprotected side. The Child answered with a swing of its spiked tail. The soldier was knocked off his feet and then stamped on. At the same time, it struck out at the other soldier. She couldn't hope to deflect the blow and was knocked into the hole. Her startled scream ended abruptly.

Durnin pulled a short metal rod out of his pocket and discharged it at the Child. A bolt of intense energy struck it with little effect. Three more followed in quick succession, knocking it back. The creature righted itself and roared angrily. Durnin saw it assess the width of the hole and quickly aimed at the exposed beams. They shattered and the Child lost its footing before pitching headfirst into the cellar. Durnin discharged the rest of the weapon's store of energy after it and then risked a look down. "It's unconscious. To the door, quickly."

"Come on!" Bryn urged.

They all edged their way around the hole.

In the corridor, Durnin lead the way, closely followed by Bryn with Jai bringing up the rear. Lewan stayed close to Cali and Aran, offering as much reassurance as he could. Their eyes scanned everywhere; weapons poised against the unexpected. The corridor, once cosy and welcoming, now felt unfamiliar and threatening. The silence was disconcerting.

"We need to get them out of here," Durnin spoke quietly to Bryn as they made their way down the corridor. "They aren't safe."

"Then we'll leave tonight," Bryn replied. "My ship's ready and the weather's settled enough for us to attempt the crossing."

They slowed, hanging back in the cover of the corridor, listening for any sounds. The main entrance hall was just in sight. Durnin edged his way out, looking sharply from side to side, another discharge rod in his hand. He looked back at Bryn, motioning for them to wait, and in that moment a shape swept him off his feet. Durnin screamed as the creature mauled him. Bryn darted forward and Jai immediately pushed his way through the others, ordering Lewan to stay.

Jai released two arrows at the creature's hind. It spun around on all fours, talons scratching on the floor. Baring its bloody teeth, it roared defiantly, its eyes seeking out Cali.

Bryn moved quickly, slashing at the creature, driving it away from Durnin. Jai kept his aim focused on one of the creature's eyes as it slowly backed away, a low growl rumbling in its chest. Its gaze moved steadily from Bryn to Jai, assessing the threat and looking for a sign of weakness in either. Both glared resolutely back never wavering. The creature sensed it had lost the advantage and suddenly turned and ran, but not before Jai released another arrow. It found its target, but his next was swallowed by shadows.

Bryn sheathed his sword and went to Durnin. Jai moved to the entrance, clambering onto one of the broken doors and cautiously looked out. Ashen faced, Aran guided Cali across the hall to where Jai waited. She was visibly shaking but forced herself to keep moving. Lewan looked nervously back down the corridor for any sign of the other Child before following. They all watched in silence as Bryn covered Durnin's body and returned grim-faced. Cali fought back tears as they were hurried on. Bryn pushed aside his own emotions, knowing he had to keep them all moving.

Outside Talents had now engaged two more of the Children and several contingents of guards were fighting others. The Children were outnumbered, but not outmatched.

Jai led them from the cover of the columns. The sounds of fighting swept over them in waves, punctuated by shouts and screams and the chilling cries of creatures they didn't recognise. Explosions and impacts lit the walls of the inner square. On the green, the ancient gnarlwoods burnt like torches and smoke choked the night air. The fires cast flickering shadows that stretched beneath their feet, making the familiar suddenly seem unreal and distorted. Jai moved ahead, checking doorways and any possible hiding places as they hurried away from the fighting. They moved in stages, from one point of safety to the next. The gatehouse was just in sight, its covered arch leading to the city streets. There was movement in the shadows and Jai faltered only to feel some relief when soldiers emerged. Several headed toward them, but the majority ran to bolster those already fighting. A window to their left erupted and Durnin's killer leapt desperately into the air. Out of control, its landing knocked Lewan and Aran over and they skidded some distance on the slippery paving. The Child struggled to regain its footing and seeing Cali managed to lunge at her. Bryn was there to block it, forcing the creature to halt abruptly or be impaled. For a second, the two-faced each other again, Bryn stepping to keep himself between Cali and the Child. Lewan and Jai silently closed in behind the beast.

Cali was fixed to the spot unable to move. She tried to stay calm, attempting to focus enough to start drawing on the field, but she struggled, her own growing terror and the images of Durnin's death still a vivid memory. Her eyes met the Child's. They burned into her and she read the determination there. I'm the reason for all of this, all this is because of me.

She was suddenly angry. "What do you want with me!" she shouted. "If its help, I'll never give it. Look at what you've done!" she spread her arms angrily.

The sudden movement startled the creature and it leapt.

Cali swept her arm instinctively. Her will joined the motion and the Child was sent reeling back over. It smashed onto the ground.

One of Jai's arrows found its exposed belly. Lewan saw his chance and lunged. The creature screeched in pain and scrambled to its feet, trying to spin round, but Bryn seized the opportunity and stabbed into its neck. Soldiers joined them and finally overwhelmed, the thing fell, hitting the ground heavily. Behind them another Child had broken free and was advancing, the soldiers ran to meet it.

Jai rushed on and Bryn shouted above the noise of the fighting, his eyes scanning the way ahead. Lewan reached Cali, she took his hand, still trembling with the sudden anger. She looked at the fallen Child and then at the other now engaging the soldiers. Bryn grabbed Aran and moved them all on to where Jai waited in the flickering shadows of the gatehouse. They checked the roadway and satisfied it was clear, continued into the city.

In the confusion, more soldiers hurried past them, now realising the true centre of the attack. One of the commanders recognised Bryn and ten of his people were ordered to accompany them to the city's port towers.

The journey to the towers was not an easy one. They progressed slowly, acutely aware of the possibility of more attacks and hindered by the growing panic in the streets. More soldiers appeared, having been dispatched to maintain order.

Working their way through the crowds, the group finally reached the towers. If it hadn't been for the guards, Bryn doubted they would have made it. After being checked through security, they made the ascent to the top in silence, only the hum of the winch marking their progress. The noise of the confusion fell away as they climbed. Cali stood, her senses numb to everything around her, the night's events playing over and over in her mind. Lewan held onto her, catching his own breath, he kept a hand on the railing as the lift swayed and shuddered its way to the top. Aran absently moved in time to the motion, his eyes fixed on some distant point in his own thoughts, ignoring the rhythmic flash of lights as they passed level after level. The urgent hum of their progress became the only sound he heard. Jai and Bryn remained alert, thinking through their next move. Just as it seemed they would climb forever, the drone of the winching mechanism altered and the lift slowed to a jarring halt.

At the top, they were stopped at various points to have papers checked until they reached Bryn's own jetties where several ships were moored. The guards instantly recognised him and let the small group board the Talern. The crew quickly geared up to depart and shortly after, they cleared their moorings.

The Talern slipped through the air. Below it, fires burned and explosions reached into the sky. The smoke rose on thermals, carrying sparks that danced and billowed like swarms of bright insects. Aran stood numbly watching it all as they slipped away. The sails caught the wind, making him look up suddenly, as the ship picked up speed.

The sense of relief was brief. They now had time to take in the full implications of what had happened, the memories of Durnin's death and the terror of the Children etched in each of their minds. They flew over the Bay of Naddier and out across the open sea. Most ships made the journey in a series of stops along the coast of the Ronce Sea, but Bryn had decided they would cross the large expanse in as straight a line as possible, heading for Per and then inland and across Kersel. They would attempt to contact Kellim through the ship's Conveyor, hoping the Panid had been able to keep to his earlier plans of skirting the Ronce Sea. The route over the Ronce sea engendered some risk, as sky ships were not as robust as their sea-going cousins and the area was prone to storms. However, Bryn and the Captain both felt the season was now far enough on to minimize this threat. They sailed on through the long night, guards keeping a watch on the skies around them. Fear of yet further attacks keeping their senses keen.

Finally, the morning began to light the horizon and the group assembled after a restless night. Breakfast was a subdued affair; Cali didn't eat at all. She was withdrawn and Bryn wanted to give her time to make sense of her thoughts and feelings. She spent much of the day with Lewan. Heeding Bryn's advice, he was careful not to press her on the subject of their escape, listening when she wanted to talk and distracting her when she needed to be. When Lewan sensed she needed a little space, Bryn suggested he joined Jai sparring, it would keep them both occupied.

The noise of swords rang out from the fore deck and some of the crew stopped on occasion to watch as the two men parried and thrust, practised a feint, countered or lunged with increasing speed. Bryn asked his Captain to keep Aran occupied and so he spent time talking to the Master Conveyor, Aln. With the Captain's consent, Aln showed Aran how to push the Talern with his will and the two worked in tandem, combining to manoeuvre the ship as it continued its journey. All the time Bryn kept a discrete eye on them all, but for the most part, he watched the skies.

On the second day out, the sky cleared and the sea could be seen stretching out below them in all directions, a perfect disc from horizon to horizon. Cali stood, at times watching the activity on deck or the glistening waves passing far below. She saw Bryn approach and attempted a smile.

"It's so strange, there's no land anywhere just endless waves," she said.

"There's always been tales of islands far to the west beyond Ronce. Mennen, the first of the Panids, is supposed to have sailed in search of them at some point in his long life. We don't know if he found them and certainly no one's found them since. Most people think you could leave the west coast of Hallorn, circle the Ocean of Koa and not see land until you arrived at the east coast of Kemarid of Lagash."

They were quiet for a while, Bryn waiting to see if Cali wanted to talk.

"I know they're after me," she said quietly.

Bryn briefly considered dismissing the idea as nonsense but thought better of it. "How long have you known?"

"Suspected since the attack in the woods, but known for sure?" she shrugged, thinking about it. "After the last attack from The Second of the Three. You all knew, didn't you?"

There was no hint of accusation in her voice, but Bryn still felt the need to explain. "We weren't sure to begin with and when we finally were, we thought it best not to burden you with it. Especially when we couldn't explain why."

"And does anyone know why?" she'd hoped for something more than that.

"Only that in some way you are special to them."

"Special, me? There's nothing special about me," she became angry. "I thought The Beholder was supposed to know everything, hasn't she told Kellim what the Children want!"

"She thinks someone is blocking her," Bryn let her anger flow. It was better out than in.

"Someone!"

Bryn shrugged, equally frustrated. "Kellim should have some answers by now and when we get to Eth's, she might be able to help."

Cali was about to say more, but she caught sight of the others looking at her. She stopped herself and took a long, slow breath. Rubbing her forehead, she calmed herself. "Sorry, Bryn. It's not your fault."

"No apology needed."

"Enough's happened because of me. I need some real answers to stop my imagination from inventing them. Will it be safer at Eth's?"

"Yes, you'll be safe," Bryn reassured.

"I'm not worried about me," she corrected. "It's all of you. I don't want anyone else to be at risk, to die because of me." The feeling of guilt was awful and the images of Durnin's death were horrible.

"Let us make that choice Cali. That's not your burden. As your friends we must be allowed to choose, to share that risk." He turned to look directly at her to emphasise his point.

She agreed reluctantly. "It's just that I feel so helpless. I'm afraid for the people around me and I'm... I'm angry. Angry at what the Children have done. Angry because I have no say in this."

"Then use that anger."

"How? I don't understand."

"Use it to push away the fear, to focus. Use it to plan your defence, to stay alert. The fear and the anger can become your allies. You've defended yourself before, back in the woods in Sancir and at the Adepts' Buildings. You knocked the Child out of the air like it was an insect."

"But both times it wasn't controlled, I just reacted."

"That may be so, but you did use the fear, even if it wasn't a conscious decision, you still did it. You're not helpless. Instinct can become an act of will."

Cali leant on the bulwark and looked back along the side of the ship. Naddier was a long way behind, she wished she could have left her worries there. She wished her actions there had been deliberate. A sense of control was what she lacked. She felt the events in her life were purely in the hands of others. Their intentions unknown and all the more frightening because of the unwanted mystery.

Bryn watched Cali, she was distracted by her thoughts and he hoped his words would not be lost amongst them. He looked at the others on deck. Durnin's death was still an open wound, for all of them, and he couldn't help thinking back over current events. He'd tried himself, over and over, to make sense of them and got nowhere. So far, they were all safe, but events had scattered them and broken the group. Spread them so very far apart, yet again his thoughts lingered on Merren until Cali's voice brought him back to the ship.

"Bryn," she said with an edge to her voice.

He turned to see her pointing at some point beyond the ship's aft. "What's that?"

Bryn leant over the bulwark and narrowed his eyes in an attempt to get a clear view of the small dot in the distance. "It's another ship," he said warily. "I didn't expect to meet anyone out here. Let's go and check with the Captain. He knows this area well."

Cali's stomach tightened and the tension began building in her again. They stepped up onto the wheel deck and while Bryn talked with the Captain, Cali pointed the dot of a ship out to Lewan. It was difficult to see how big it was, which direction it was headed or actually, if it was moving at all.

"The Captain says he meets very little out here even in summer," Bryn said, coming over to join them and waited to hear what Lewan could make out.

"It's definitely a ship, large, three masts." Lewan peered through the navigation lens a while longer. "It is headed in the same direction as us."

Cali looked at Bryn.

"It could be anything. It's not impossible to come across other ships out here," he said, reading the concern on her face.

"We'll alter our course and quicken our pace," the Captain said, "and see how they respond." He nodded at the Master Conveyor. Aln began to focus his will, to draw from the field, adding to the push of the wind in the Talern's sails. Their speed increased and as the minutes passed all watched, hoping the other ship would continue to fall away.

"They're altering course to match us and the distance is closing, Captain." The crewman raised his navigation lens again.

"What can you see?"

"It's slavers!" he said in surprise. "They're flying the flags."

The others looked at him in equal surprise.

"Slavers!" the Captain snapped, grabbing the lens. "This far out, don't be..." The Captain broke off, double-checking what he could now clearly see. "Don't just stand there," he shouted. "Ready the ship, prepare for attack!"

A bell began to ring and the crew took their posts. Bryn had anticipated the possibility of trouble and had brought some of his company's private soldiers with them from Naddier. Both Jai and Aran appeared on the wheel deck, wanting to know what was going on.

"This still doesn't sit right," the Captain was saying. "There's nothing out here for slavers. And if they risk an attack, they're in for a nasty surprise." There was a certain amount of satisfaction in his voice.

"Do you want me to continue pushing?" the Master Conveyor asked.

"It looks like they're going to catch us even if you do. They're bigger and faster than us. Rest up, we may need you later."

Aln nodded and the Talern slowed. The Captain turned to Bryn.

"Any help you can lend would be appreciated, Sir."

"You have that," Bryn replied. "Cali, I want you and Aran down below.

"But I can help," Aran objected. "I've been working with Aln and I could support him if he needs it. We both could," he added pointing at Cali and himself. "We've done the work back at Naddier," he looked from Bryn to the Captain and then at Aln.

"It could help," Aln ventured, seeing Aran's look of frustration.

"Who's going to defend you if they get on board?" Bryn asked.

"If we help Aln," Cali added, "they might not get on board. I'm sick of running, Bryn."

Bryn looked at them both, not entirely happy with the idea, but he'd told her to use the fear, and she was. "I'll compromise, you stay here, right here." He pointed at the deck. "Help Aln, but if they board, you're straight down that hatch. Is that clear? And you're to keep out of sight and focus on a way to defend yourselves."

The slaver's ship gradually drew closer, every minute of its progress watched and with each of those minutes the tension grew. The crew began to shuffle uneasily, eager for the fight to begin and be over. Gradually its shape and outline became clear to the naked eye, but at this point, it altered direction and began to run parallel with the Talern.

"What are they up to now?" the Captain grumbled, lowering his navigation lens from his eye.

"They're out of weapons range," Bryn noted. A quick look at Jai confirmed this. "Even Jai and his longbow couldn't reach that far."

"Maybe they've changed their minds," Lewan offered. "They're close enough to see we're heavily defended and there doesn't seem to be many on board."

"They'll have more hiding below decks," the Captain said, scratching his chin. "They wouldn't have got this close if they didn't intend to do something." His expression suddenly changed. "Powder weapons! Look for anything unusual on deck, any vents in the side!"

Navigation lenses scanned the ship in a sudden flurry of concern but found nothing. Jai edged closer to where Cali and Aran were sat, bow in hand, judging how much closer the ship would need to be. The minutes passed in mock peace as the Captain discussed options with Bryn and Aln. Cali suddenly started, jumping to her feet, she frantically searched the deck. All eyes turned to her.

"What is it?" Jai asked scanning the deck, an arrow ready on the huge bow.

"The air..." was all she had time to say as a hooded figure and twenty mercenaries appeared on deck. The intruders quickly spread out as the figure looked about it. The crew and soldiers responded and quickly engaged them. Jai's bow creaked and an arrow hit one of their assailants with such force she was knocked off her feet. He already had another ready and was about to fire.

"Go for the one in the cloak!" Bryn shouted.

Jai didn't falter and released the arrow. It sliced through the air where the figure had been. The air on the wheel deck prickled and the hooded figure was right beside Cali. No one had time to react. It grabbed her and made to leave, but something happened in that second and it was thrown back. Terrified, Cali had reacted out of instinct. She refocused her will and disappeared. The figure stumbled and was gone. Aran raced to the railings scanning the deck below.

"I think she's down here," Aran pointed desperately, somehow knowing her actions.

Bryn followed his finger and leapt down the steps in one bound, closely followed by Lewan. Jai joined Aran and hunted for any signs of the figure. Cali appeared and a second later Aran yelled and pointed. Bryn and Lewan began to fight their way towards her, while Jai aimed. The intruders had pushed their way from the fore deck and along the starboard side. The fighting was ferocious.

Cali kept to the cover of some crates, looking around, she tried to calm her breathing, to think. The hooded figure appeared a short distance away, urgently looking about it. Jai saw it and sent an arrow skimming. The figure transported. Cali saw it reappear on the other side of the deck; she didn't duck in time.

Bryn caught sight of her and fought his way forwards. Lewan dodged around, attempting another route. The figure spotted her and transported. From the wheel-deck, Aran had focused his will. Jai reloaded and waited. Then the figure was there. Cali threw herself back as it made a grab for her. Aran reached out and Jai's arrow was released. Somehow the figure became aware of it and made to transport, but Aran had it and pulled back. The sudden reaction yanked Aran onto the railings nearly pulling him over. The arrow only grazed its mark.

Cali panicked, but then used the emotion and transported to the clearest spot she could see. Taking cover, she looked back, the figure was gone. She instantly looked about her but could see no sign of it. Bryn reached her last position, looking up as Aran pointed urgently to where he could now see her. Lewan also followed his directions, fighting his way through the confusion.

Aran began to re-focus as Jai scanned the deck with another arrow. There was a commotion behind them as the figure appeared. It lunged for both. There was a blur and then air blasted them as they plummeted to the sea.

The figure was gone before Aln and the Captain could react. Aln dashed to the railings looking down.

Bryn finally reached Cali. He took her hand and began leading her around the fighting as Lewan watched their backs. The soldiers and crew had pushed the mercenaries back to the fore deck, but the intruders refused to surrender.

The hooded figure transported herself to a place of cover. She paused briefly to gather her strength, removing the boy and the bowman had been a risk. She hadn't expected as many complications, the girl and the boy were reportedly easy targets but both had proved to be otherwise. The mercenaries she'd brought had been intended as nothing more than a distraction while she recovered the girl, The Purpose. The Traveller lowered her hood, searched the deck and then transported to another point of cover, knowing time was not on her side. From here she had a better view and saw the girl. The two swordsmen were with her. She would have to take all three. The people on board her ship would have to deal with them. The Traveller replaced her hood and focused, preparing for the transport.

Jai tumbled, his senses reeling as air rushed past him. He struggled to control the fall in a desperate attempt to slow it, to give himself a chance of hitting the water and surviving. For seconds he fought the air and then suddenly, Aran crashed into him, grabbing at him desperately, trying to get a hold. Jai realised what he was attempting and reached out. They bounced against one another in the roaring air, clutching and grasping at flailing limbs. Fingers hooked and slipped free, hands snatched air, and then clothing, until finally, they managed to grapple hold. Aran focused. There was a heartbeat's stillness before they crashed back onto the deck. Aran was knocked unconscious and Jai landed only slightly better.

The Traveller waited for the right moment. The two swordsmen had to be looking in different directions and when they did, she transported. With calculated skill she appeared just short of the girl, pushing air before her in an attempt to knock the men over. But the force was partially blocked, the younger one was knocked clear, but the man maintained his footing. The Traveller hesitated and, in that moment, she was trapped.

Seeing Lewan hurt ignited Cali's anger. She fixed two points inside the hooded figure and collapsed the space, it imploded. Bryn threw himself to the floor, clutching at anything to resist the pull. Somehow Cali braced herself until the last particle of the figure had been obliterated. As the air stilled, she moved away and drew in more from the field. The remaining mercenaries were swept off the deck as she walked to the edge. Gripping the bulwark, she focused. The railing cracked, as did the timbers of the distant ship, snapping and shattering as she ripped it apart chunk by jagged chunk. Its crew screamed as the planks beneath their feet erupted, the masts broke and sails billowed and flailed as if trying to flee. Cali lifted her hands and grasped violently at the air before her. The slaver's ship jerked with a great shudder that sent its people tumbling. The air was filled with a wrenching sound as the ship broke in two. Bodies, timbers and equipment fell from the broken hull. She drew back her hands and for a second the jagged mass seemed to hang in the air. Shaking, she watched the debris fall almost as if time had been slowed. In that silent space, for the briefest moment, she was conscious of a presence, a whispering. She shuddered, and as her will relaxed. The connection ebbed and was gone.

Cali let out a sob and looked at her cut and bloodied hands. Lewan came to stand beside her, gently cupping her hands in his.

The fighting was over, and all on board stood in silence, struggling to comprehend what they'd just witnessed.

Chapter 24

Tebeb sat on a low wall seemingly heedless of the sheer drop below, the private gardens of the Amar Order behind him, the sprawling city before him; its domes shimmering in the afternoon haze. He looked isolated; neither part of one place nor the other.

A breeze had sprung up, bringing with it dust from the plains beyond the city walls. In the distance, he could see the River Am and its famous red sailed boats tacking their way up its dark waters. He had not seen this city since its destruction in the war. How different it looked now, alive with noise and activity. The world had changed while he had wandered through it and now it was a stranger to him.

Merren and Kara sat watching him in the peace of the gardens, the noise of the city a distant background note.

"He must feel so out of place," Merren worried. "The world he knew is gone and all of this is unfamiliar. He looks healthier, but what's going on in his head?"

"Food, a wash and rest make a surprising difference. The other stuff, well that's going to take time."

"Did Natesh have anything new to say after he'd examined him this morning?"

"Nothing," Kara replied, still looking at Tebeb. "No one's got a clue why he hasn't aged, it's not his link to the field. It's strong, like all of the Panids, but not strong enough to explain his complete lack of wrinkles. But I think the Ildrans were looking for a lot more than just that. Natesh did find traces of other drugs in his system and thinks the Ildrans were trying to restore his memory. They probably managed to get him to remember what they needed, put him out of the way until he was useful again and then drugged him again to keep him quiet."

"His memory hasn't returned fully?" Merren asked.

"No. Recent memories only and they're still very patchy. Three names keep surfacing though." Kara's tone hardened.

"Who?"

"VaCalt, Imalt and Ducat. Especially VaCalt."

"VaCalt, the UruIldran Butcher…" The woman's name made Merren shudder. "I can't think about that creature." She pushed the thoughts aside. "Has Tebeb used his talent yet?"

"Still refuses to."

"Has he said why?"

"No, but I think it's linked to what VaCalt forced him to do." Kara thought of the conversations she'd had with him.

"He can't blame himself for that."

"The Fury the Ildrans used were created through his knowledge. He blames himself for somehow not completely resisting the things they did to him."

"That's a lot of guilt he doesn't need to feel." Merren paused, looking at Kara "And you?"

Kara was jolted out of her thoughts by the question and finally looked away from Tebeb. "Oh, me. Fine," she dismissed with a lazy wave of her hand.

"Really?" Merren asked, looking sceptical. "And who do you think you're kidding miss?"

Kara let out a long sigh and drummed her fingers on the tabletop. "We thought we'd got away. Our careful plans didn't include his tag."

"So, he was marked?"

"Yep, either something was stitched into his clothes, or more likely the manacles he was wearing were used as the tag. Such an obvious mistake on our part." She lifted her hands in frustration. "And now they won't let me on the ship they're sending to find her. I could search the area far better. I know our route, they don't!"

"Mia Svara knew the risks, Kara. I know it's hard to accept the loss and look to yourself for the blame."

"You're right, I've told myself this a thousand times, but it still doesn't make it any easier. She died and we lived. I can't help feeling I owe her. Going on the search would at least make me feel... Oh, I don't know. Like I hadn't just deserted her."

"If things were different. They'd let you go, but you know where we're headed. They need all of us. Letting you go on that ship would lessen our chances of holding Segat at bay. There are a lot more lives at stake in Amaria."

"I know, I know," Kara said irritably and then sighed again. "I just feel like I'm giving up on her."

Merren took her hand gently. "You argued more than any of us to wait longer and searched until the last possible minute. No one would think that."

"I just need some time." Her voice was subdued.

"It'll get easier."

A shadow fell across the table and both women looked up. "Am I interrupting?" Tebeb asked.

"No, just sorting out my addled brain," Kara grumbled.

"Maybe you could have a go at mine next," Tebeb suggested.

Merren smiled. "Come and sit. I've been trying to place your accent. It's been niggling me for ages," Merren said conversationally as Tebeb took a seat.

"It's Nebessan, or Firrican as it's now called. I don't know if anyone from there still speaks with this accent."

"They don't, that's why I couldn't place it. And it's Nebessa once again. They took back their proper name as soon as the Great War ended," Merren said.

"More change, the catching up continues." Tebeb was quiet for a while, distracted. "I'm speaking in front of the Corumn again," he said as if suddenly remembering the unpleasant thought. "I don't think it's because they like my accent."

"This afternoon?" Merren asked.

"Hmm," Tebeb pulled a face. "It's almost as if they don't believe me. Like I went willingly to help Segat."

"They're just desperate for answers," Kara said, hoping to reassure him. "They've been hit and hit hard. I don't think they're used to it."

"They just want to be clear about what we might be facing," Merren explained. "If Ildran Summoners can create Elementals they've got to think of a defence."

"All of that will depend on the field strength. The size of anything they can realise will be limited as well as the number. They'll not be able to create a self-sustaining form field like the Children and that will limit them further. Their Summoners still have to continually focus the field to maintain, animate and control whatever they manage. So, we at least have some things in our favour."

"That makes sense," Kara agreed. "I'm restricted by the field strength. I can only sustain a form field up to a certain size and then for far less time than the Panids were able. If there's a lot of field use in the vicinity I'm limited even more."

"We had a lot more freedom in what we could create and maintain before The Field's Cap was put in place," Tebeb said nodding. "You know, my memory of then is clear, but the very last part of the war and beyond is just fragments."

"Didn't Natesh have some suspicions about all of that?' Kara remembered an earlier conversation.

"Yes, he thinks my memory may have been tampered with."

"By the Ildrans?" Merren asked.

"From the time of the war. He's not exactly sure," Tebeb explained. "He said he wasn't skilled enough to go as deep as he needs to, so I'm left to wonder about what was done, why and by who."

Kellim waited patiently, humming a tune from an old song, a song very few people would remember. Behind him, a building that had once been something, other than a ruin, looked out over the landscape with him. Kellim had watched the building slowly crumble into the ground over the decades he'd been visiting Eth. Like him, it had seen a time before the Great War and witnessed the changes it had brought about. He had once been a Panid, it had once been part of a fortress. They'd both outlived their former occupation. How things had changed, and how quickly the past was forgotten with the passing of generations. He looked up as the wind blew, stirring the branches of the giants behind him. He noted the subtle change in the air, another sign of the passage of time. The season was turning. The mornings were still cold, there had been a light frost, which had yet to lift, but spring now had a firm hold. Kellim looked at the countryside around him. Kersel was a wild place of limestone crags, green comb forests and great expanses of pillow bush. He liked its bleak beauty. He liked the fact that it had changed less than most places. It was here and in Aylis, that Kellim had held onto some hope of seeing Tebeb again. That somehow, if he were still alive, the fourth of the remaining Panids, would find his way back here to a place of familiarity. A place that had changed little since the time of the Panids. It was difficult for Kellim not to dwell on Carrick's news about Tebeb, that his friend had perhaps been located and that there was a real chance they would be reunited.

Again, he pushed the feelings down, the sense of anticipation and hope was distracting. His journey wasn't over yet. Soon he would travel over and through Aylis. Despite the responsibility of protecting Cali, and his possible confrontation with Varin, Kellim couldn't help but look forward to it. If Kersel had resisted change then Aylis had remained suspended in time. Being remote, the progress of Koa's other countries had failed to reach it. Entering Aylis always felt like a return to a way of life he remembered from his distant youth. An untroubled and simpler time and one of the reasons why Eth had chosen Aylis as her retreat and why Etefu spent more time there than any other place. The last of the Panids found something there the rest of Koa couldn't offer. Kellim suspected it was a sense of belonging, the land and its ways were as ancient as them.

The City of Per was only just visible, a bright patch on the edge of the Ronce sea. As he watched a speck appeared above the horizon and steadily grew as the morning drew on. He let the ship draw nearer before communicating with its Master Conveyor.

When the Talern was still a distance off, he focused his will and transported to the deck. He sensed the difference in Cali the instant he arrived but decided to make no comment before speaking with Bryn and Jai. They all looked tired and troubled, Cali, in particular, seemed distant and not at all her usual self. She would have questions and he feared he had no real answers to give her. But he was glad to set all of that aside for a time as they came to greet him. It was a happier moment in weeks of travel and worry.

That night, Aran found Kellim up on deck looking at a star-filled sky. "The northern skies offer a wondrous display, don't you think?"

"It's amazing," Aran came to stand with him and looked up.

"Your sister has suffered no ill effects from her field use. We had a long talk and she seems a little more at ease."

"She's eaten something tonight, which is a good sign, Thanks Kellim. I was worried."

"I don't think I said much that you or Bryn and the others haven't already told her. Perhaps just a bit of underlining. Sometimes you need to hear things more than once to make them take hold."

"Whatever it was, it helped."

"Then I'm glad. And what of you my young friend? How are you holding up?"

"I don't know really. I want to protect her, but I don't know-how. And then there's Carrick and Merren and Kara and Lewan and Bryn and Jai and I... I..."

"That's a very long list," Kellim smiled gently. "It's difficult not to worry about the people you care for. And I shall risk telling you the obvious, they can look after themselves."

"I know, but...It's just hard, that's all. I worry."

"And they will be pleased to know you care and are glad of all you've done to help."

"I'm not sure I've done anything."

"Cali told me about your bravery back at Rel. That helped a lot of people. Leading the slavers away from your village gave others time to escape."

"And got me caught. At least I felt I could do something then, but I haven't done anything now."

"I think Jai would disagree. You saved his life on the Talern."

"I'm not sure I had much of a choice."

"It would have been easier to save yourself and leave him to the waves."

"I couldn't have; my first thought was to get to him." Voicing the thoughts made Aran realise just how important that had been to him.

"Remember what I said about being part of something?"

"Back at Leet?"

"Yes, being part of something means that you are not responsible for all of it. We all contribute, share the work, the risk. Sometimes we step forward and act, other times we allow ourselves to be helped." Kellim looked at Aran and the young man nodded. "These old bones need a seat. Come and rest your much younger ones with me for a while."

They found a convenient spot on the deck and sat. Kellim rested his staff in the crook of his arm and then looked at it irritably. "Used to be able to collapse it down to the size of a pin, shame. I'm not sure I'll get used to carrying it about." He laid it down on the deck. "I seem to be adept at putting it in my way."

Aran had been longing to ask him about it. But it had seemed a petty interest, with all that had happened. But now Kellim had mentioned it, it seemed like he'd been given the chance to talk about something else. If Kellim's aim was to offer him a distraction, he would take it. "Bryn said, he'd never seen you with a staff. Is it new?"

Kellim chuckled. "No, not by any stretch, it's almost as old as me. It was given to me by my master, Mennem. Mennem asked Maig to make it for me. It and I went everywhere. After the Great War I left it with The Beholder, it had too many memories attached to it. And then time passed and I, well, not quite forgot it, but got used to getting by without it."

"Did all of the Panids have a staff?"

"No, very few actually. Each found their way of directing the energised field."

Aran looked at him, wishing to hear more, and for a change, Kellim was glad to continue the distraction.

"Some used wands, as they were sometimes called back then. They were a little like the discharge rods still in use now, though they could continually self-charge. Some used spheres," Kellim paused for a moment. "They were quite clever really."

"Like the ones you've used?"

"No, these were far more sophisticated. Form fields allowed them to float, hide their presence and direct energy. They used to hover over Tsu-Sek's shoulder like Goody Wise's companion, Skrett."

New names, Aran thought. People Kellim hadn't mentioned before. "Goody Wise had a friend who sat on her shoulder?" he asked, sure he'd misheard.

"Strange as it sounds, yes. He was a talking bird."

Aran had another question. An obvious one that begged answering but Kellim had moved on, clearly a talking bird was such a mundane thing back then he didn't feel the need to explain it.

"A surprisingly shrewd bird. He was Goody's constant companion. The spheres were always there hovering over Tsu-Sek's shoulder, looked like they were watching you. She learnt her craft from Maig, the first Maker. Now, she was an interesting woman with a complex past. Maig also made several other things for our group. A gauntlet for Aigner, which was a particular work of art. A metal glove that fitted over his hand. He had a certain charismatic flair about him, though he nearly blew his hand off when he first used the thing."

"Would they work now?"

"The ambient field is not strong enough."

"Why do you carry your staff if the field isn't strong enough? Is it for something else?"

"Well," Kellim began evasively, "let's just say I am able to sidestep some of the restrictions of The Field's Cap, or rather, it can't limit me to the same extent as others." He gave Aran a conspiratorial wink.

The ship continued its journey north-east, eventually reaching the low mountains at the far easterly reaches of Aylis. Winter was still more in evidence here with patches of snow hiding in hollows and valleys untouched by the early spring sun. Kellim spoke to the Captain and the Master Conveyor, directing them to the forest that brushed the feet of the range. At its edges, goodbyes were said and thanks given, before the small party assembled to leave.

"Aran, Cali," Kellim drew them to the bulwark. "I think it's a good time for you to practise transporting yourselves. What do you say? I'm sure you are up to it." The suggestion was more of a ruse, allowing Kellim to assess Cali's link to the field and, he hoped, allay her fears about using it. There was still a possibility she would need to defend herself and any lack of confidence or hesitation at using the field could only put her safety in jeopardy.

They'd done a lot of work on transporting at Naddier and Aran was eager to show Kellim what they'd learnt, if nothing more it was a distraction. Cali was nervous about accessing the field again, but Kellim calmly reassured her. "The field is only potential. I'll keep an eye on things. Try not to worry and give it your best. Aran, you go first."

Aran walked to the railing and fixed a spot on the ground below. Focusing his will, he collapsed the distance, instantly reappearing below. He waved back to the ship. Kellim was pleased at how competently he performed the task, confirming his belief that the boy was a natural. Aran swelled with pride at Kellim's evident satisfaction.

Cali looked at Kellim. He gave her an encouraging wink. She stepped forward nervously, took a deep breath and tried to push aside her fears. The field responded and to her relief nothing was amiss, no whispering, everything was as she needed it to be. She signalled her readiness, sought the point she wanted, collapsed the distance between and was gone, reappearing beside her brother. Her ease with the task wasn't quite equal to Aran's, but the difference came in the way the field responded. When Aran had transported Kellim recognised the same sluggish movement of the field most Talents had to contend with, but for Cali it was more receptive. Kellim was fascinated by this and began to conjecture why this had not been apparent earlier, and how recent events might have uncovered the latent connection.

With everyone safely transported the ship began to turn, ready for the return journey to Per. They watched for a while as it sailed into the distance and then Kellim led them off into the forest. Cali suspected he had been up to something and so quickly fell in at his side. Kellim just as quickly gave up his small ruse, deciding it was indeed best to be honest with her. If nothing more this could be an opportunity to reassure her. Their feet fell on soft needle strewn ground between green combs and resin barks. They discussed Cali's link to the field and how it had changed until Cali brought their conversation back to the Children.

"It is clear they see you as a solution to a problem," he began after some thought. "What that problem might have been we can only guess at. Perhaps they had sensed your link to the field, and hoped to learn that secret."

"If I knew what the secret was."

"That taken into account, their attempts were misguided and are now at an end," Kellim reassured.

"How do you know?" Cali asked, hoping his assumption would be based on certainty.

"The Children you've described match the ones known as wanderers and the renegades. Maga was sure of numbers, despite not being able to access their memories and thoughts. From what you've told me all are accounted for. Only The Fire of the Sea survives and she cannot reach us here." Though privately, he speculated on its route north and a possible reason for this.

"I hope so," Cali said, not fully convinced. There was a pause and Kellim waited patiently while she considered her next words. "The ship," she said finally. Kellim nodded. "I've never…it was like I…"

"Take your time," he eased.

Cali smiled apologetically and calmed herself. "It was like another part of me was released and the field answered in a way it never has before," Cali struggled to express her thoughts. "Once I started, I couldn't stop. I felt so angry. Angry about Durnin. Angry about all those people at Naddier. And I…I did a terrible thing," she said, finally admitting her deep sense of guilt.

"Your natural instincts cut in, nothing more." Kellim wanted to allay any worries she might have about her actions. "You've been pushed a great deal and finally you snapped and released all the tension and fear you've been suppressing. It has happened to Talents in the past and will continue to do so in the future. Strong feelings, emotions and stress seem to affect the field and our subconscious ability to push The Field's Cap."

"But all of those men and women…"

"Slavers," Jai broke in. "They know the risks they take living that kind of life and will have been responsible for ending and ruining many others. They attacked us and you acted in self-defence."

"But I shouldn't have been able to do all that. Should I?" Cali asked.

"Clearly you can," Kellim replied mildly. "How you are able to, and to such an extent is the question, and a very interesting one at that. It's certainly nothing to worry about. A few of us are less restricted by The Field's Cap. That list now includes you and quite possibly others we are unaware of. It's just as well we are headed to Eth's. She and Etefu may be able to throw a little light on the situation."

Cali seemed reassured by this. The discussion had come at the right time.

"Now Jai," Kellim said as they walked on, "What's the possibility of you bagging us a couple of forest fowl for dinner tonight?"

"Pretty good. I've heard them and there's plenty of predator tracks, which means the wild stock should be good. You should set wards tonight; we don't want our supplies ending up on their menu."

"Predators? Cali asked.

"Yep, this far north the wildlife survived the Great War. There are some big animals up here. If we're fortunate and reasonably quiet, we should see a few."

"Fortunate?"

In the following days, the path rose and dipped along and over the wild and dramatic landscape. Their conversations continued, weaving from subject to subject until finally, they reached the top of a steep rise that presented yet another tree-filled valley. Kellim stopped, a look of contentment on his face.

Aran wasn't sure why he'd chosen to stop and admire this particular view. There'd been so many.

"More trees," Cali came to stand with them.

"How much further?" Aran asked.

"We're here," Kellim gestured at the valley and was greeted with puzzlement. "You might recall a mention that if Eth didn't want you to find her home, you would not."

"So is her farm there?" Cali asked, squinting to make out any trace of a settlement. Seeing none she turned back to Kellim. "Doesn't she want us here?"

"Well of course I do," a voice behind them made everyone, except Kellim spin round. The accent, like Kellim's, hinted at an older era. "It's so good to see you," Eth laughed, a rich full sound.

Cali watched Eth greet Kellim and Bryn, handing out good-natured comments to each. She was a large woman who appeared to be in her late sixties, clearly Aylisian with her light freckled skin and auburn hair. She dressed in sensible farming clothes, swamped by a huge overcoat and a long scarf that was wrapped around her neck and over her head. She turned to Jai, opening out her arms. He grabbed her around the waist in a great hug, lifting her off the floor and spinning her around, which made her shriek even more with laughter.

"You still know how to make a heart flutter," she said, comically fanning her face with a hand. Back on her feet she turned to look at Lewan, giving Jai's hand a last squeeze, a simple gesture he understood.

"You've changed so much in the last two years. Come here and give me a hug. Oh, come on," she chuckled. Lewan went slightly red as he stepped over.

"And you must be Aran and you Cali," she said, finally catching her breath. She smiled at the two newest members of the group. Holding out both of her hands she led them back to the edge of the rise.

"Now, you know you're welcome," she said.

They couldn't help but be surprised by the view that now greeted them. Instead of the endless treetops that had appeared to fill the valley, they could now see the substantial grey stoned farm and its many outbuildings. Several other cottages nestled amongst twenty or so fields of varying sizes, some set with over-winter crops and others with livestock. Smoke drifted up from several chimneys and the sounds of Eth's flocks could be heard drifting up from the fields.

"Welcome to High Holt," Eth said proudly and then led them both down a clear path.

They chatted as they walked down to the farm, its peace and tranquillity enveloping them. The air was still and damp and filled with the smells of animals and hay. Several farm hands acknowledge Eth as she passed and she greeted them in turn, handing out instructions in Aylish. As they walked, she pointed out various features of the farm and its land, explaining their purpose and the plans she had for the year ahead. Kellim asked many questions, interested in all Eth had to say. Finally, she led them across an open area in front of the main house and in through its gate and small garden. Opening up the door they stepped into a large kitchen dominated by a range and an enormous table and dressers. The atmosphere was warm, welcoming and smelled of fresh baking. Eth went over to a young woman, who on their arrival had lifted a large kettle from the range and was pouring piping hot water into a pot. She greeted her and they chatted briefly while Eth unwrapped her scarf and took off her coat. "This is Aenbecan, she's the nearest I've got to a daughter."

Aenbecan smiled at them, a little shyly. "You all look tired. I hope you're able to stay." At that she excused herself and taking her coat from the stand, turned to Eth. "I'll be over later to help you with the cooking."

"I can manage," Eth replied. "You've a household of your own to keep."

"If you're sure. Then I'll pop in tomorrow, bye menna."

"Not too early dear," Eth came over and kissed her on the cheek.

Wrapped deep in her coat, Aenbecan left. Kellim waited till the door was shut. "So, you adopted her after all."

"She's married and is expecting, it was right that the child should have an extended family," Eth explained.

"A good thing," Kellim smiled. "She's always called you menna."

"Put your stuff over there and sit yourselves down." Eth put on an apron. "I thought you'd be glad of something hot to drink and a bit of something to eat."

As they settled themselves, she disappeared into her larder and began to bring out various plates and bowls of food, it was hardly 'a bit of something'. Setting them on the table, she asked Jai to get plates from the dresser and Kellim to pour everyone a hot drink. Finally, she placed a freshly baked loaf in the centre. Taking a step back she checked everything and satisfied, wiped her hands on her apron.

"Come on then, tuck in. You must be hungry."

They didn't need asking a second time and began helping themselves to the food set before them. They chatted as they ate and Eth listened, commenting on various pieces of news Kellim had been unable to pass on from Lont.

The very next morning and afternoon, Eth had them working on the farm and later at Kellim's request she took Cali up into the woods foraging for additions to their evening meal. Eth subtly probed her mind, asked her questions and generally helped Cali to understand why her affinity with the field had developed. Cali seemed happier having this unknown answered.

"As for the Children's interest in you, I can offer a strong possibility, but not a definitive answer, and not an easy answer to hear."

"Anything would be a start."

"Let's head this way while I explain. A Talent's connection to the field affects their ageing process. The stronger the connection the slower they age. The field repairs their form field more effectively. The Children were created with a time-limited link to the field, to be blunt, they would cease to be once their usefulness had passed, stopping them from becoming a danger once the peace had been won."

"But some of them are still alive. What happened there?" Cali asked.

"Sometimes their creation was done under pressure, things were left out in order to complete the task. When you're losing a war, you want troops on the ground quickly. A few of the Panids purposefully left that element out of the form fields, allowing their creations to live on naturally. But even they must age and die eventually, as we all will. There have been Panids who expected and intended to live forever, they looked for ways to extend their lives, so it's not a great jump to think that someone has promised the Children a way to achieve it, in return for their services. Maga had some notion that someone else was involved, someone directing or influencing the Children."

"Were the children being used?" Cali concluded.

"Possibly. Acting alone, this person wouldn't stand a chance of getting to you, but with the Children's help they would all get what they wanted."

"Then why don't they just ask?" she said.

"You might say no."

"So, they'd rather force me to help them."

"Individuals can have reasons for their actions, reasons that to us seem ridiculous, but to them appear reasonable and justified. Varin for instance, and there will be others out there like him."

"Talents in other Orders."

"I said it wasn't an easy answer, but I think it has the strongest possibility of being an answer, or at least part of it. The Children who posed a threat to you are gone and now you are here. Nothing finds this valley unless I want it to. Only the field, the air and the rain get in here and they are too busy to do anything other than exist."

"It's a start," Cali said, feeling she had gained some control of the events surrounding her. Knowing the Children were no longer a danger made an enormous difference. The idea that any remaining threat may be another Talent was somehow okay. She could put a face to that threat, he or she wouldn't be some unknown entity. She could defend herself against a person and for now that problem felt like a distant one. As they gathered flattops, shrooms and the smaller brown-caps the task gradually stole Cali's focus and by the time the last one was put in the basket the conversation had moved on.

"The woodland feels ancient," Cali stood looking about her, breathing in the still air.

"That's an interesting observation," Eth said.

"I'm not sure why I said that, but there is a, well a feeling of age and power." She struggled for the word. "A sense of the past and something that belongs here. I'm not sure how to put it. Am I being silly?"

"Not at all," Eth hooked the basket over her arm and came over to stand by Cali. I can sense the age of the place too. Today and in times gone by, folks in this part of the world revered trees and buried their dead at their roots, believing the trees would take up their memories and be witness to the passing of the generations. They believed it was possible to access those memories in the rings of the tree's growth and so knowledge would never be lost. Some of these trees were used in that way, the woodland here is ancient and undisturbed. That roof tree over there, it's been here for over two thousand years, there have been many burials between its roots. So, you're quite right, this forest is old and has a strong connection with the past."

"It's interesting how peoples' beliefs vary from place to place." Cali looked at the tree, thinking about all the things that had happened during its long life. "It would have been here when the Lantriums were built."

"And for longer before then. It predates and has outlived the time of the Panids."

"Was it very different, I mean when you were a Panid?" Cali asked.

Eth lowered herself onto a fallen tree trunk. "Different and the same," she added wryly. "Different in that many of the old ways and traditions still lived on. The countryside, the jungles and forests were wilder and stretched endlessly. The same in that people lived their lives, working, resting and caring for their families. As for the Panids, well, we led and others followed. Deferring to us, seeking our advice even fearing us." She shook her head. "Too many enjoyed that. There were only fifty Panids, a very small number compared to the numbers of Talents now, but our powers and our abilities were far greater. We were treated like royalty and afforded the same privileges. It was a golden age in many ways, a prosperous, grand time, full of marvels. But looking back now it seems so unequal, it couldn't have lasted forever. The cracks were already forming when Mennem and the original Panids left. Looking back now, war or some other confrontation was inevitable. The war, the Great War, took a terrible toll on Koa and its people. The continent was not the same afterwards, the rich and exuberant attitude became sober and restrained. The order of things changed and in some ways for the better. All Talents were trained, not just the powerful few. The responsibility, the risk, was shared between many hands."

"Risk?" Cali asked.

She got up. "The Panids, we made mistakes. A lot of power was wielded by only a few individuals. An obsession, a whim, a grudge wasn't opposed or diffused by the collective tolerance of others. Now the Orders govern themselves and prevent the field's misuse. Just like some of the beliefs of the Aylish and their trees, the time of the Panids has passed, their purpose has been lost."

"Is that why you left and came here?"

Eth sighed. "You could say that. It all amounted to the same thing; I'd had enough. So, I came back to the country of my birth and then headed as far north as I could, far enough to forget and be forgotten."

"Sometimes I'd like to be forgotten and run away." Cali's hand went reflexively to her mouth. "I'm sorry," she quickly added, realising the implication. "I didn't mean it like that."

Eth laughed. "You are right, I was running away."

They walked on a little way. "So was the farm already here. Is that why you came to this area?"

"There was nothing here when I first came. I started building myself a small house up on the ridge there." She pointed. "A young man, by the name of Eógan, arrived in the valley and gave me a hand that summer. He was from a fortified village called Talorgen, some way from here, and was hunting in the area.

Summer came to an end but he stayed and eventually built himself a home a little way into the valley. If you look through that gap in the trees, you can just to say see it." Eth pointed again and Cali followed her direction.

"It's big for a house meant for one," Cali said expecting a small hut.

"It was added to over the years, first by him when he married and started a family and then by his children and their children. They each built their own homes and helped build me a new house in the valley. Over the years we've become our own community. Eógan was a good man. He would be proud of the generations that followed him."

They continued to collect more of the brown-caps, shrooms and flattops. Eth pointing out others of varying shapes and colours, carefully advising which were edible and which should be left untouched. They walked deeper into the ancient woodland.

"Oh no, not those," Eth chortled as Cali asked about a brightly coloured cluster huddled on a rotting log. "Not if we want to remember dinner and the rest of the next day. Now these over here…" Eth turned back to the ones she had been about to pick and then stopped aware that Cali hadn't moved. She looked round to find the girl staring to the north. Eth listened for any sounds in the woods, looking through the trees, her own senses looking for a predator.

"What do you sense Cali?" Eth asked eventually and stepped over to her.

"I, I thought we were being watched and I heard something," Cali answered distractedly, still staring at the same spot.

"What was it like?" Eth asked quietly, not wanting to break the link.

"Whispering," she said, finally looking at Eth. "Almost like before, when I destroyed the slavers ship and back in the woods in Sancir, but this time outside, not in my mind. I can't quite explain it."

Eth pushed her mind out further and for a fleeting moment caught the edge of something before it retreated. It unnerved her. There was a familiarity to it that she couldn't place. Aware that Cali was now staring at her, she altered her expression.

"Could that someone, the one using the Children and making promises to them. Could they have followed us here?" Cali asked.

"I would be aware of anyone near this valley and as I said, they would not be able to enter. Even Kellim couldn't get in here if I didn't want him to. There are a lot of voices out there," Eth said, gesturing about them. "Similar to what we were talking about before, distant things, whispers of the past. This far north, close to The Field's Cap the ambient field traps the shadows of form fields and replays them over and over again when the conditions are right. It can be sounds, voices, whispers if you like, and the shapes of things that were once alive. The high concentrations of field energy can trap the shadows of form fields, you said there was a sense of power here. I suppose those echoes could explain how the belief in trees' ability to store memories began."

"What do you mean by echoes?"

"If you know how to, you can learn much, seemingly from the very air around you," she said, sensing Cali was still apprehensive about what had just happened. "Come this way, we're not far off a good spot, I'll show you something of what I mean." Eth headed off and Cali followed, with a last uneasy glance north. They reached a clearing and Eth stopped and put down her basket. "You remember I mentioned the ambient field strength this far north, it tends to pool in this particular spot, let's see if this still works." Closing her eyes again, Eth focused her will.

Cali waited, a strange sensation settling on her as the woodland fell still. It seemed to close in around them. The air prickled and became chill. Then a magnificent horned animal stepped out of the undergrowth, walking through a massive green comb as if it wasn't there. She could see every detail of its thick coat. Its body was ethereal, glowing a faint blue, stirred by some unfelt breeze, every tree behind it could still be seen. It moved forward on feet deep in the soil, but this didn't seem to affect it, as if it were treading on some older, lower level of the ground. It paused briefly to sniff the air and seemed to stare at something in the trees. Long seconds passed, before eventually, with a jerk of its head, it moved on, trotting back into the woods. Cali held her breath, watching as it slipped through trees that hadn't been there when it was alive. The air settled and the woods opened up again, almost as if coming back to life.

"What was that?" Cali asked in awe, her voice a whisper.

"An echo of the past," Eth said, watching her closely. "He used to pass through here some eighty years ago. We met many times. He would stare at me and I'd watch back. Then one season he didn't come. I assume old age finally got him." She sighed and gestured to where the animal had stood. "That was a field image, to give it its proper term. We only get them this close to The Field's Cap now. But there was a time when they could be seen all over Koa and could be summoned to offer glimpses of the past. The Cap put an end to that, the ambient field became too weak to store them." Eth looked up at the sky. "Come on, we should head back, it'll be getting dark soon. The days are still short this far north."

They returned via Kellim who was still out checking Eth's livestock and tending to minor injuries and ailments.

"You should do well for young this year," he called by way of a greeting, as they came down the path.

"Yes, it was a good summer and the winter's been mild here," Eth replied.

"And how are you feeling?" Kellim turned to Cali.

"Good thanks. Having things explained helps put them in their place, makes them less worrying somehow."

"We might have some more answers for you," Kellim said cautiously. "Now don't build your hopes up," he warned.

"You'll have heard Kellim mention Etefu?" Eth asked. Cali nodded in reply. "Well, he spends some time here in the spring, to help with birthing. Kellim has managed to reach him and he is going to come early. He, along with Tebeb created some of the Children."

Cali brightened at this. "So, if anyone will have more answers it should be him."

"Possibly," Kellim said again with care, not wanting to build her hopes.

"But there is a chance?" Cali said, wanting to hold on to the possibility of further understanding. "Even if they aren't a threat anymore, I still want to know."

"A chance," Eth said. "Now, be a love and take this basket up to the house for me. I'll follow you up in a moment."

Cali took the basket, suspecting that Eth and Kellim would want to talk about her. She didn't mind, she knew they had her best interests at heart.

"She's more like us," Eth said, watching Cali head up the path. "You didn't pick up on anything before now?"

Kellim seemed a little offended by this. "We have been a little busy of late," he said tetchily. "And it would appear her affinity has only just surfaced because of pressure and stress. Under normal circumstances it may not have revealed itself for years, if at all."

"The natural cycle is a marvellous thing," Eth mused. "She could be the first of many. It could be that Talents will naturally evolve a way of bypassing The Field's Cap, given enough generations."

Kellim stroked his beard, pondering on Eth's words. "Perhaps so. Either way I hope Etefu arrives before I have to leave. It would be good to see him."

"He should arrive soon and the three of us need to talk. Something happened in the woods up there," she gestured. "How long have you got before you have to leave?"

"Three more days will still allow me to intercept Varin before he reaches The Field's Cap. I'll attempt to confirm his intentions and stop him if necessary."

"Attempt? Do you really think he's that strong?"

"Yes."

"So, it had crossed your mind that he might actually try to break The Field's Cap."

"We must consider all things. No matter how absurd. It would be foolish not to. Though I still can't bring myself to believe such a thing. It would mean his destruction. There is no way he could survive the release of field energy that would ensue. There has to be something else."

"Then we need to know what that something else is before it turns our world upside down," With that she bustled off to the farmhouse. "Dinner in an hour," she shouted, not looking back.

They had just sat down when the farmhouse door swung open and a large, black-skinned man burst into the kitchen, throwing his pack aside dramatically. Cali couldn't pinpoint his accent until Jai leaned over to her. "Nebessan."

"Where is she?" his deep voice boomed as he looked around the room. "Where is that temptress of the North?"

He caught sight of Eth and headed for her; arms outstretched. She shrieked with laughter and dropped her spoon, running for the door that led to the rest of the house. Etefu charged after her, making all kinds of over-the-top lusty noises. Kellim rolled his eyes. Jai and Bryn laughed, the others didn't quite know how to react as they listened to the thumps and giddy laughter that echoed around the house from various rooms. After a short while, Eth reappeared in the kitchen pausing only to catch her breath.

"I must be running too fast," she gulped, red-faced and dishevelled. "He hasn't caught me yet." With a look over her shoulder, she catapulted for the door, a mass of skirts and apron, just as Etefu entered and roared with comic delight. Eth shrieked again as she ran outside, Etefu in hot pursuit.

"I believe they do that every year," Kellim observed.

The chase soon came to an end, it was dark and both parties had ran out of breath, so it was minutes later when they returned and Etefu settled his big frame into a chair. As they ate, introductions were made and the conversation flowed until full stomachs and the busy day began to catch up with them. One by one the others retired to bed.

"That was a fine meal Eth, a fine meal," Etefu's rich voice rolled out the words in Koan with a thick accent that hinted at both the country and distant time of his birth.

The three Panids sat alone and Kellim decided now was the time to talk of the fourth. He related Carrick's words that Tebeb was in Ildra and being held, perhaps, against his will.

"That was some time ago now," Kellim concluded. "There has not been the opportunity or the time to seek an update. I can only hope they have found him and that, at some point, we will all be reunited."

Eth and Etefu accepted the news with the same guarded hope Kellim had but before discussion could linger on the possibilities Kellim began to relate all that had happened in relation to Varin, the Children and Cali. "There is only one word that comes up again and again in all of this," he said at the end of his tale.

"A word?" Etefu puzzled.

"Whispering," Kellim replied.

"Talk some more," Eth said, thinking back to the incident in the woods with Cali.

"Bits of this and that," Kellim thought as he spoke. "Fragments from many conversations that on their own explain nothing. At Aurt I sensed two strange things that puzzled me. One of which was focused around Varin, a whispering would adequately describe it. In Sancir, The First of the Three spoke of the whispering to Merren. Maga talked of being blocked, of another mind at work, she spoke of whispering and Cali spoke of hearing the same nebulous whispering on two separate occasions."

"In the woods today, she was distracted," Eth said. "She described it as whispering. I explained it away until I could consider what I'd sensed. The direction at least was clear. Northwest of here."

"Manifland?" Etefu looked at her.

Eth nodded. "With the whispering I sensed the field and a consciousness directing it," Eth explained. "If the whispering is the link between Maga, Varin, the Children and Cali then

Manifland is its current location. It can not be a coincidence that Varin is headed there."

"This complicates matters further. Did you get any sense of the identity directing the field?" Kellim asked.

Eth didn't have time to reply, instead Aran burst in through the door. "Cali's not in her room. I can't find her!"

Kellim leapt to his feet and was gone.

"Wake everyone," Eth said. "I'll search the farm."

***

Carrick stood atop the immense walls of the Empress's Hand. Beneath him the featureless stone curved to the desert floor. To his right the wall ran to the nearest of the five forts, to his left it stretched into the distance. The sheer scale of the five fortresses and their cliff-like walls defied further description. Now he looked out over the Ugarmas Pass, an empty, featureless expanse shimmering in the haze. Behind him stretched the Amarian military. Ships moved across the sky, docking and unloading cargo, a steady train of carts brought in further supplies, soldiers were drilled, orders echoing off the walls, tents were pitched and cooking fires burned. The extent of the industry and activity matched the enormity of the walls that towered over it.

Tension pervaded the air. Segat's focus was now fixed on Amaria. Everyone on the front line felt it. Stories of the weapons Segat had used to finally take Cian were rife and added a keen edge to the anticipation and uncertainty. The lookouts, the battlement guards and the Talents' senses focused on the pass and what they could only imagine was heading their way. Soldiers were not allowed time to think, but it was up to the Adepts and Talents to control their own imaginations. A hundred years of peace had not prepared them for war and so they found their way day by day. Inevitably arguments had broken out as nerves were stretched and the Adepts had been forced to restore calm in their own Order.

Merren stepped up onto the top of the battlements. The air was dry and dusty, clinging to lips and exposed skin. Above her, the Amarian flag snapped in the brisk hot wind. She combed hair out of her eyes and then shaded them as she looked for her brother. She'd been up since dawn transporting the largest of the wooden beams used to construct the trebuchets. She was exhausted and both were feeling the strain of maintaining order amongst the Talents in their charge. As she approached, her brother turned to look. She could still see traces of his ordeal and his constant struggle to manage a greater link to the field.

"Has Tebeb changed his mind?" Carrick asked impatiently.

"He needs time. He won't use his skills unless he's sure he can control what he creates," Merren caught the irritation in his voice and attempted to explain. "The Great War is still a recent event in his mind. He's no real concept of the time that's passed since then."

"Time is one thing we don't have. Can't he see how much we need his help?"

"I'm sure he's only too aware of that," Merren replied, trying to keep the irritation out of her voice.

"Then I don't see what the problem is. We've all got things to deal with. It's about time he stopped wallowing in his…"

"That's hardly fair," Kara snapped. They both turned sharply to find her, hands on hips and jaw set.

"I do wish you wouldn't do that sneaking up thing," Merren complained. "We're all on edge as it is."

"Maybe you should check who's about before you start a conversation," Kara said sharply, before turning to Carrick. "Have you any idea what VaCalt and her cronies put him through? What they did to get the information out of him? There probably isn't an inch of him that's not been cut, burnt or sliced. His mind's been peeled and tortured in ways that make me sick to my stomach. They took what little he had of himself and squeezed it until they got what they wanted and then threw away what was left." She took a breath to calm her anger before any tears started. She hated that they came so easily. She turned to look out across the pass, not wanting to look at Carrick. "Your newfound ability doesn't seem to have made you any more sensitive to the people around you," she added, once she could trust herself to speak.

Carrick was taken aback by Kara's sudden outburst and was embarrassed by his insensitivity, especially when he saw Tebeb was now standing at the top of the steps. "You heard all of that?" he groaned.

"Near enough," Tebeb replied flatly.

"Oh bollocks," Kara rolled her eyes, wishing she could slide right into the wall and stay there.

"Maybe," Merren gave her a gentle nudge, "you should check who's about before you start a conversation."

"Just push me over the edge," Kara muttered. Merren laughed despite herself.

Tebeb walked over and hoisted himself up onto the wall, sitting in between two of the crenelations. "What you both said is true," he said finally after the silence had just started to become uncomfortable. "Though I'd rather you hadn't announced it to the world in general."

"I wouldn't worry too much," Carrick gestured about them. "News has got around about my pushing against The Field's Cap and everyone generally gives me a wide birth. They think I'm going to explode."

"And I've had to snap so many Talents back into line," Merren admitted. "They flinch each time I open my mouth. So, as you can see, it's deserted wherever we are. No one wants to be near us."

"Would an apology be a good idea right now?" Carrick asked.

"Who from?" Tebeb replied. "Me, you, Kara? I'm not sure what good it would do. When you're right you're right," he shrugged. "Did you notice that wide berth just got wider? They all think I'm an Ildran spy. Their eyes narrow if I move my hand too fast to scratch my nose. Then there's you skulking around..." Kara gave him an outraged look, pointing at herself and mouthing me? Tebeb continued. "The people here are more comfortable with the Children than any of us. You'd think they'd been here for decades. No one bats an eyelid when an eight-foot giant walks by, or a predator big enough to swallow them whole turns a corner, but one of us comes along and they fall over themselves to be elsewhere."

"My advice would be that we all need a holiday," Merren said with an amount of irony. "But that isn't going to happen any time soon, so I suppose we'd best get over it."

"Easy," Carrick said with a wry smile.

"Yes," Tebeb sighed. "Easy as falling off a cliff." He indicated the drop behind. "That aside, there's a reason why I came up here. I want one of you to take me a way off from here, so I can try and sort out my talent." Carrick was about to speak, but Tebeb held up his hand. "You were right. I need to get this sorted and the longer I leave it the harder it's going to be. I think I'm scared I might not be able to do anything. That it's gone."

"Do you want one of us to stay with you?" Merren offered.

"No, you're needed here and if I get this wrong... It's best I'm on my own."

"When do you want to go?" Carrick asked.

"Now, before I lose my nerve. I'm packed." He turned so they could see the bag on his back.

***

Kellim returned after searching through the night for Cali. He was now convinced she was headed for Russon. They had all gathered in Eth's kitchen. It was early and only chill morning light crept in through the windows.

"I thought I was bringing Cali here to safety," Kellim shook his head. "Instead, I have done what the Children failed to do and brought her to a point where the whispering could influence her directly."

"We could do with Maga right now," Jai noted.

"I've tried reaching her but to no avail," Kellim said, setting a pack down on the table. "And now I must go."

"Then we'll come with you," Bryn said.

"I'm coming as well," Lewan said firmly.

"As much as I appreciate that," Kellim replied. "You'll only slow me down. I'm sorry, but I can cover far more distance on my own and stand a better chance of getting to Cali before she reaches Manifland. She'll have to find a way of crossing the Sibura Channel and that'll slow her down. When I know Cali is safe, I will deal with the source of the whispering and Varin."

Lewan couldn't hide his frustration and anxiety. He left the room, making some excuse of unfinished work from the previous day.

"Is that where it is?" Aran asked. "Northwest of here?"

"Yes," Kellim replied vaguely as he checked his bag. "Manifland is a small island. Russon lies on its southern coast."

Eth came out of the larder. "Right, there's enough in there to last you. Make sure you eat," she warned, handing him the pack. "And for all our sakes be careful." She hugged him tightly.

Kellim said hurried goodbyes, not wanting to linger or think about the probabilities of his return. The uncertainty and abruptness of the night's events added an intensity to his departure that left them all subdued and quiet. It was some time before they stirred and occupied their hands and their minds with work on the farm. It wasn't until lunchtime that Jai's vague suspicions were confirmed when Aran and Lewan failed to show.

"They've taken supplies and a map from my study," Eth said upon her return to the kitchen. "I've searched the surrounding forest and they're nowhere near."

"They've also been through Kellim's old pack," Jai added. "I don't know what they found there or even if they've taken anything. But they were looking for something."

"Curse it," Bryn said angrily. "Do they have any idea of how dangerous it will be up there?"

"There's no way either of you can get us further north?" Jai asked Eth and Etefu.

"Aran will have transported them well away by now," Eth replied. "And in what exact direction I can only guess. Etefu and I will search some more, but I think the chances of our stumbling on them are small."

"We'll search until nightfall," Etefu got up. "After that, you'll just have to stay here with us. We'll find ways to keep ourselves occupied. The time will pass soon enough and then we'll have them all back and safe," he said with a worried glance at Eth.

Chapter 25

Varin appeared on the beach, icy waves crashing behind him. He looked towards the remains of the village, toying with the small copper sphere in his hand, they'd failed him in Amar but got him here days early. Letting it fall from his fingers, it rolled and was claimed by the sea. He began walking. The whispering blocked the island's protective wards and so he climbed the worn steps of a harbour wall and continued along its pitted and uneven surface.

This was Russon, the only settlement on Manifland, abandoned after the building of The Field's Cap. The grey stone of the buildings matched the low sky. Everything appeared drained of colour, bleak and desolate. The buildings were now only shells, the roofs and other wooden structures had rotted or been blown away by the frequent storms that buffeted the island. The men and women who'd lived here then were long gone. He stopped briefly to look at an ancient, paved platform and the strange stone spheres arranged on its surface. The largest was easily taller than him and all were incised deeply with symbols he didn't recognise. He wondered vaguely at their use until the whispering moved him on.

The main path took him up through the village and as the ruins thinned, he reached the top of the rise and paused, turning to look back out to sea. The churning surface stretched to the far shore of the mainland, a grey mass on the horizon. He was the only person in this grey world. He stood for a while longer until once again, the whispering moved him on. There was a sense of anticipation that wasn't his. He questioned it no more than he had any of his actions in recent months. The path ran down into the lee of the hills. His would be the first feet to set foot on it in a hundred years.

He followed the path until he found what he was looking for. Sheltered from the constant pull and tug of the wind. The entrance, if it could be called that, was a solid stone block fused into the rock of the hillside. He stepped forward and touched it, sensing the form fields woven into the structure. They had eroded with time and he found signs that they had been weakened from inside. He resisted the urge to start work on the entrance and instead returned to the village. He would shelter in the most complete of the ruins, rest and eat, renew his strength and then attempt to crack open the block.

It was dark when he woke and unwrapping his cloak, he found the wool damp and the air chill. The small fire he'd built barely glowed. Focusing, he encouraged the flames and added more wood. It crackled and spluttered and eventually came to life. As he sat warming himself, he became aware of ripples in the field. He got up and walked to an empty window looking out across the village, the cold light of the twin moons barely lit the ground. Here and there Varin caught glimpses of movement, insubstantial glowing figures, some appearing for seconds others walking and going about, what had been their daily lives, their motion was slow and strangely graceful. He watched as a faint shape slowly made its way up the path, only just discernible as a figure. It faded further as it approached and then was gone, reappearing back down the path to walk the same steps. He returned to the fire, making a hot drink to warm the deep chill in his bones and ate a functional meal. This done he left the building and ignoring the figures headed back to the entrance.

There was a faint trace of light on the horizon, an indicator of the coming dawn. He finished his study of the block and the complex work designed to keep it sealed. Its original design had included self-renewing elements, but these had been broken perhaps five years ago, so the seal was greatly weakened. Again, there were signs this had been done from the inside. He spent much of the day destroying elements of the block's structure and bit by bit the stone lost its protection. Finally, he found the point he needed, a weak spot. Focusing his will, he drew on the field and began to stress the block's structure. With each second, he pushed harder. The stone began to vibrate, sending tremors through the ground. He pushed harder still. Small stones broke free and tumbled down the hillside. Varin stepped back to avoid the debris, committing himself to the task, knowing either he or the block would be broken. The figures in the village flickered out of existence, the local field unable to support them as Varin drained it. He focused his will to its fullest extent. The whole hillside rumbled now. Varin's shaking hands lifted, almost pleading with the block to give up. His face was gripped by pain as he was compelled to continue, compelled to push yet harder. The block was beginning to distort as its form field buckled under the huge force he exerted. Large sections of the hillside began to slip and collapse. Cracks opened in the ground. Varin began to shake violently, his will overwhelmed by the torrent of field energy. Finally, with a deafening crack, the block split. The detonation echoed across the island as the defeated hillside slumped on itself. The rumbling faded like distant thunder and in the silence that followed the pale figures flickered back into existence and continued their endless echoes of the past.

Varin came to, aware that it was light before he opened his eyes. It was some time before he was able to stand and when he could, it took him much longer to make his way back to the village and his shelter. With an effort, he restarted the fire and searched his pack for food. When he'd eaten, he added more wood to the fire and pulling his cloak around him slept.

When he woke again the sun had passed overhead and was sinking behind the hills, trailing dusk behind it. Stiffly he forced himself to move and eat. This chore complete, he packed his things and left the crumbling shell. He walked to the entrance, the sense of anticipation growing. On reaching it he didn't pause. Focusing his will, he reached forward grasping at the air with his hands and pulled violently back. The field responded and the split halves of the block were torn from the hill and flung aside. Detaching his staff from his pack he walked into the gaping hole and began his descent of the wide steps that led underground. He knew the source of the whispering was waiting for him and that the way ahead had been cleared.

***

Cali awoke; her legs numb from the icy water of the approaching tide. Falteringly she got to her feet. Her mind was leaden, the cuts and bruises on her face and arms didn't seem to bother her. Weak thoughts tried to surface, her own voice desperately shouting from a long way off. It didn't matter where she was. She didn't even know why she was here, the whispering only told her how to move and in which direction. She walked for a long time, staying on the beach knowing only that she was getting closer.

It was dusk when she reached the ruined village of Russon, vaguely aware of its shapes and of movement. The change in the ground beneath her feet registered only as she moved from black sand to stone and then cobble. Her legs kept moving, all the time bringing her closer.

***

The small boat rose and dipped alarmingly on the waves as Lewan struggled to steer it. The shore of Manifland was only just discernible in the fading light of dusk. Aran lay shivering uncontrollably in the prow, occasionally racked by spasms. Lewan's face was awash with anxiety, desperate to land the ship and get Aran near a fire.

Aran had transported them repeatedly, continuing even when Lewan had asked, and then all but begged him to rest. He'd refused, threatening to leave him behind. With no choice, Lewan could only watch the toll Aran's efforts took with each transport. He'd used the copper devices stolen from Kellim's pack to get their boat halfway across the Sibura Channel. These spent, he'd resorted to his own will again, each time forcing himself to move them further and each time emptying his stomach until only bile burnt his throat and his body succumbed to increasingly violent tremors. The final transport had brought them in sight of the coast. Now his face was ashen, his eyes had glazed over and he was contorted by convulsions, mumbling and wailing incoherently. Lewan feared for Aran's life and fighting the waves and tide, rowed with all his strength.

The swell of a wave brought them careering onto the beach. Lewan gripped the sides of the boat to stop himself from being thrown out. The oars slammed forward and then broke free, spinning into the foam. Soaked, he managed to scramble out of the boat and grabbing hold of the prow, willed his shaking arms into effort. The icy waves crashed over him, nearly sweeping him off his feet, but somehow, he managed to drag the small craft onto the beach. He hung over its side, exhausted and dripping until he caught his breath and then looked to Aran, but he couldn't see any signs of movement. Panicking he scrambled into the boat.

"Aran, Aran!" He shook him gently at first and then harshly, lifting him so that he could see his face properly. Aran's lips were blue. Lewan felt at his neck, but couldn't find a pulse. Clutching hold of Aran's shirt and coat he dragged him out of the little boat and laid him on the beach trying to force any water out of his lungs and then turned him over. He listened for a heartbeat. There was nothing, he desperately pumped at the centre of Aran's chest and then pinched his nose and angled his head back, before forcing air into his lungs. He continued, over and over, fear gripping him more as he worked without effect. Again, Lewan paused to check for some sign of life. Nothing. Again. Nothing. Again and again, he tried but it wasn't working. Desperation overtook him and tears streamed down his face. Finally, realising his efforts were futile, he broke down.

"I'm sorry, I'm sorry," he sobbed, clutching at his friend as if somehow, he could pull him back. Finally, he lifted him, hugging him in his arms, rocking him as he wept. Then there was a hand on his shoulder. With sudden fear, he wrenched free and scrambled to the side.

"Kellim," he choked not fully believing his eyes.

Kellim didn't speak but turned to Aran. Kneeling he placed a hand gently on the young man's chest and cupped his other behind Aran's head. Kellim closed his eyes and began to concentrate. Lewan watched, unable to move as a faint glow began to form around them. Delicate tendrils of light curled out of the darkness and the crash of the waves faded into the distance. Kellim was speaking, but Lewan couldn't understand the words and the more he listened the more he heard other voices, faint, and all around him. He looked about but saw no one. He dropped to his knees wiping his hands across his eyes. At last, Kellim leant forward and whispered in Aran's ear. Almost immediately the young man choked and coughed and then drew in a long aching gasp. He clutched at Kellim, his eyes wide and confused. Kellim held him down and spoke again. Aran struggled less and eventually fell asleep, colour slowly returning to his face.

Kellim sat up wearily, turning to look at Lewan, as he sobbed with relief.

"He's back with us," he reassured, "but needs warmth. We will find what we need in Russon. Quickly, we must hurry."

"What about Cali?" Lewan asked, hope flickering in his eyes.

"I was unable to find her. She is perhaps here now. We should go."

Lewan nodded, helping Kellim carry Aran.

As they trudged over the dark sand, Lewan noticed for the first time the old man's clothes, skin and hair were scorched. For once he looked his age, tired and worn. "What happened to you?"

"I arrived at the coast, north of High Holt, to be met by The Fire of the Sea. She knew where I would appear and when. I transported straight into her range. We fought and eventually, I was able to overcome her."

They struggled along the beach, Russon was still a distance away. Kellim couldn't risk another transport, it would alert Varin to their presence on the island. They took it in turns to carry Aran and paused to rest once. The distance took them longer to cover than Kellim would have liked. He was concerned for Aran and his need to find and stop Varin only grew more urgent as time passed. When they finally reached Russon relief almost outweighed caution. Kellim paused long enough at the harbour wall to assess the area before clambering up the stone steps from the beach. The stone surface made the going easier and Kellim headed directly to the most complete of the buildings. He made use of the remains of a fire he found there, Varin's no doubt, and helped Lewan manoeuvre Aran into a sheltered corner. Taking a dry blanket from Kellim's backpack, Lewan quickly got Aran out of his wet clothes and wrapped him in it. Kellim used the time to search the area with his sense. Varin wasn't in or near the village. That left The Field's Cap and if Cali were here that's where she too would be headed.

"I must go now," Kellim said. "And you, well I would rather you stayed here, but I fear you will follow me, no matter what."

Lewan looked over at Aran and then back to Kellim. "I have to find Cali."

Kellim nodded. "Very well then, the fire will keep Aran company. How much of him will awaken I can not tell." He looked again at Aran. "I've done all I can," he said to himself as much as Lewan.

***

The shout had gone out. Soldiers and Talents rushed to their places lining the full length of the Empress's Hand. Carrick and Merren stood with Chancellor Nirek, Kara, Commander Iresh and two of his aides, looking into the far distance at the ominous cloudbank that approached from the Ildran side of the Ugamas Pass. Behind them, on the Amarian side, the newly formed Amarian air navy held its position with orders only to engage as a last resort.

"It's definitely slowed," Kara concluded, after a final check.

"What are they hiding?" Carrick squinted at the mass.

"Ships. He could have ships hidden in that," Merren replied.

"It would be a way to get close enough and draw ours out. If they've slowed, they may be wondering why our navy hasn't come to investigate," Nirek added.

"Are they out of range?" Merren asked.

Iresh shook his head. "No, but they think they are. We've rushed through a lot of changes." He looked through a mounted navigation lens. "I can't make anything out and I don't want to announce how far our artillery can now reach without a good reason. Is there anything you can do Chancellor to get a look in there or shift some of that cloud?"

"If the wind could be persuaded to help?" Nirek suggested, looking at Carrick and Merren.

"It's worth a try," Carrick shrugged.

"If we draw heat out of the surrounding area and focus it into the ground, we should create enough of a thermal to pull cold air in behind it," Merren explained to the Commander.

"Ma'am, I'm sure you know exactly what that means and with the deepest respect I was lost after - it's worth a try," Iresh straightened, a slight smile on his face.

Merren cleared her throat. "I assume that's polite for get on with it," she said dryly.

"I like this man more every day," Kara said and winked at him.

It was the Commander's turn to clear his throat.

Several Talents were called over and the idea was quickly explained. Focusing their will, each concentrated. At first, nothing happened and Iresh looked expectantly ahead at the closing bank of cloud, and then back to the Talents.

"Patience Commander," Chancellor Nirek said without breaking his focus.

A faint breeze stirred the air and then a rush of wind swept over them. The cloudbank billowed and stirred, before being swept up and back, revealing the prows of at least forty ships. "Let's bloody Segat's nose," the Commander said and then turned, shouting "At the ready!" The call rippled down the line and military ballista and trebuchet crews were poised and ready for action. Iresh signalled again and the air was filled with the grind and whir of mechanisms. Huge levers sprung into motion as the trebuchets flung their loads into the air. At the same time, giant ballistae sent six-foot lances slicing at the enemy hulls. The air was filled with noise as teams of men and women launched wave upon wave of artillery. The Hand struck out with rock, wood and iron.

Shouts went up and reloading began as the first wave hit the ships. Wood shattered; sails ripped and collapsed; their masts severed. Guide and steering fins exploded. Several ships began to plummet and others lost control, swinging sideways into nearby craft. Chaos broke out amongst the Ildran armada. There were explosions as powder weapons went off, hitting their own ships. Some were able to fire ahead sending iron spheres screaming through the air toward the Hand. Out of range, they hammered into the desert floor.

The second wave of artillery hit the ships. Teams and machines worked hard to ready the next. The onslaught was devastating and those ships that could, began to alter course in an attempt to escape. More were hit, their hulls exploding. Field engines failing, they dropped from the sky, erupting in a jagged mess that shook the ground and reverberated off the fortress walls. The desert floor became a mass of fires and shattered carcasses. Several craft pressed desperately forward, trying to reach their original objective, powder weapons firing, their iron projectiles striking ever closer.

"They mustn't reach us, our ships will be forced to engage overhead and we'd take the brunt of the fallout," Iresh was shouting above the noise.

"Then they won't!" Merren answered. She reached out to those Talents able to copy and focused her will. "Wait she muttered," watching the ships advance. They'd stopped firing, saving their ammunition. One of the ships suddenly erupted in a mass of splintered wood, struck by a huge block, from a trebuchet. Falling men and women could be seen, their screams drowned by the noise of artillery.

"Wait," she repeated, sensing the Talents' anxiety. The ships drew closer. Commander Iresh looked to Merren and then back at the closing gap. There was a detonation and a billow of smoke. The sphere arced through the sky. They heard the howl of its path an instant before it struck the nearest fort. High above, men and women ran for cover. They were in range.

"Now!" Merren called. Down the line, others followed. She brought her arms back, artillery roaring overhead, and then swept them forward. The air rippled, racing forward, growing, building into a boiling distortion. The first of it struck the ships like a great wave. Two were swept off course, and the other three rode over it, their prows rising alarmingly and then dipping only to be hit by artillery. The broken Ildran armada fell from the sky, shaking the ground and blinding the air with great clouds of dust.

Commander Iresh gave the call and the artillery gradually ceased in a wave that spread along the Hand. The dust slowly settled, revealing the full extent of the destruction. Before them, black smoke billowed into the sky. Distant and closer explosions cracked the air as fires found powder stores. The cries of Ildran men and women could be heard and some movement could be seen in amongst the wreckage. There was a shout from the wall as an Ildran soldier climbed a jagged prow. He stood defiantly shouting curses at the Amarians and beating his fist on his chest. The tirade continued until an arrow felled him.

"Find out who that was and have them flogged," Commander Iresh snapped at one of his aides. "Caution the archer's Captain. I'll not have insubordination," he added in irritation.

"You ok?" Carrick asked Merren as she wiped her forehead.

"A rest and I'll be fine."

"That was more than a bloody nose," Kara said looking out across the wreckage.

"If only that'd be enough," Merren said. "What do you think Segat has for us next?"

"There were some Talents on those ships," Kara noted. "I noticed some of the blocks being deflected but not many. He'll be saving the Ildran Order for later."

"We haven't seen much of his powder weapons either," Nirek added tensely. "We can be sure he'll deploy those."

"Whatever his plans, he's going to have to get over that," Iresh pointed at the wreckage that started several hundred feet away from them. Yes, they'd dealt Segat's forces a devastating blow and done more damage than he'd dare hope, but he'd played most of his hand to do it. He had one good card left, Segat however, seemed to be holding the deck.

***

Underground, the great iron doors shuddered, disturbing the dust of decades. The second blow sent thunder rolling up the stairway to the surface. The third blow buckled them, opening a gap. The final focus ripped them off their hinges. They crashed to the floor with a resonant boom that echoed into the space beyond.

Varin waited until the silence surrounded him again. He was about to move but then stopped. He looked at his feet as if seeing them for the first time, the floor, his hands and then the walls around him. He was in an underground chamber. Beyond the broken doors, in the next one, was The Field's Cap, the source of the whispering. This was where it had been hidden. Images of Manifland and Russon came back to him. The presence in his head was gone. The whispering had ceased. His will was his own. He turned quickly at the sound of footsteps. A girl descended the steps, eyes fixed on the opening to the next chamber. He was still confused, his mind struggling to piece together events it had witnessed, but not fully comprehended since he'd left Aurt.

The girl stepped past him, brushing against his sleeve. He grabbed her wrist.

"Who are you?" he demanded.

She stopped to look at his hand and then directly at him. Her face was blank. He released his grip, realising she was barely aware of him. She turned and walked into the chamber.

***

Kellim and Lewan reached the gaping hole Varin had made and began a cautious descent down the wide steps. The spiral seemed to go on forever, fading into the feeble light of the wall panels. Lewan tried to keep his nerve and not let his imagination get the better of him. He'd never had to face anything like this before. The fear of the unknown was far greater than any straightforward fight. This was different, no Bryn, no Jai. He felt the weight of the task ahead and a responsibility to protect Kellim and find Cali. He forced aside his concerns, thoughts of how she was and what had compelled her to leave. He knew he needed to remain focused.

Kellim's senses went before him like a tide, sweeping the walls and steps. As he saw the way ahead was clear, he quickened his pace. Far below he could sense Varin and Cali and it puzzled him why The Field's Cap had not communicated with him or one of the other Panids instead. It was possible some part of its construction prevented its manipulation of a Panid. A fail-safe that could give him an advantage.

***

As dusk fell, Commander Iresh set up his final card and ordered the deployment of the Amarian powder weapons. He'd held off their placement, if the Ildran ships, that had tried to attack them earlier, had spotted them an advantage would have been lost. Possibly Iresh's only advantage and therefore not one to waste. The walkway on top of the wall was some eighteen feet in width and these new weapons took careful manoeuvring into position, each was nine feet long and weighed tons. It was hot work, even though the sun had sunk below the horizon. The Commander looked up at the central fortress, if only they'd been able to get some up there, the extra height might have extended their range. Winches creaked and strained as the powder weapons were hoisted onto the walls, the teams worked quietly in the growing gloom and, with The Twins' help, the iron devices were in place before it was fully dark.

Hoists were cleared away and the night watch came onto the walls to take up their posts. The last traces of red faded from the sky, leaving behind the waning heat of the day. The Hunter, Kara and the other Changers now began their patrol of the walls, their keen sense of smell catching every change on the wind, their unmatched eyes keeping watch in the dark. It had taken time for the guards, although pre-warned, to get used to the prowling animals, especially when The Hunter passed, standing six feet at the shoulder she was a disconcerting sight.

Iresh heard Kara approaching long before he saw her. The rhythmic click of her talons on stone carried a long way in the still night air. She transformed while still in the shadows, knowing people found the sight disconcerting.

"You're still up Commander," she greeted.

"I slept earlier. I've always been able to get by on very little."

"It's just as well then. You're not in for a quiet morning."

"You've news?" Iresh asked, turning to look out into the darkness and the few fires still burning on the Ildran's wrecked ships.

"The Hunter can hear movements out beyond the wrecks and the wind's changed direction bringing the scent of many people on the move. I think they're coming."

He folded his arms. "Then they must have a way to clear the wrecks. They can't get over or passed them." He was drumming his fingers on the wall. "I'd like to know what they're up to."

"I could cover the distance and the wreckage in no time," Kara offered.

"I'd rather not risk you on a simple scouting mission," Iresh replied. "The gates have been braced and you can't leap down from here." He paused a moment and turned to look at her. "Can you?"

"No, it's too high. But the danger isn't that great in the dark and I know someone who could help."

"The Journeyman?" Iresh guessed. "If you and he can do this with minimal risk I'll give the go-ahead."

Kara found Lors and between them, they hatched a plan. He transported them from the top of the wall, easily finding safe transport points in the dark amongst the wrecked ships. The Commander waited for their return, distracting himself with the regular reports that came from stations along the entire length of the Hand. The time passed uneventfully and the night watch struck the hour. Kara and The Journeyman had been gone for longer than agreed and the Commander was beginning to worry when they re-appeared, as promised, on the exact spot they'd departed.

"They're out beyond the wreckage," she was out of breath from running and the challenge of negotiating the wreckage. "They're moving in their powder weapons, big ones, twenty feet in length and on huge, wheeled platforms. They're also setting up barrels of what I can only imagine is more powder with long cords coming from them."

The Commander frowned. "I think they're going to try and blast their way through, those lines seem able to carry a spark to the powder. If they place the packs correctly, they might be able to clear a path."

"I could disrupt their progress. If it would help?" Lors offered. "It would be relatively easy to transport myself in, and break the lines. If you need more time that is?"

"Thank you," Iresh replied. "But no. We're as ready as we can be and you've both taken enough of a risk. You should rest. I'll need you before the day is out."

The explosions started several hours before dawn. Distant concussions that reverberated off the pass, lighting up the predawn in tall orange clouds of smoke and fire. Gradually they got closer, the smell of the powder carried along by the prevailing wind. Finally, the last section of wreckage was blown away in a huge ball of heavy sulphurous smoke. The morning light revealed a wide path through hundreds of feet of wreckage and along this pathway came Segat's legions.

The rhythmic thrum of tens of thousands of feet drifted towards the Hand. Beating drums kept time and brazen blasts of horns cut the air announcing the approach. The Hand's own trumpets called out alerting the fortresses and the sections of the wall. The unrelenting Ildran advance continued as battalion upon battalion of soldiers marched out from the pathway, forming deep lines that stretched the full width of the pass. Arrayed behind them were the huge powder weapons Kara had spoken of each pulled along by lines of slaves, who swayed in unison as they heaved the enormous loads.

The Commander registered every aspect of their deployment and weaponry, discussing tactics and possible lines of defence and attack with his captains. Nirek, Carrick and Merren along with every Adept and major Talent on the wall searched the masses for members of the Ildran Order. It soon became evident that they'd arranged themselves similarly into defensive units, each taking on a specified role within the group. Some distance behind the front lines, huge siege towers were being wheeled into place, their unwieldy frames shuddering as they were moved.

The advance stopped several hundred feet from the walls of the Hand. The drums continued to beat and when they finally ceased a great cry went up from Segat's forces.

"Look at them?" Kara said in disbelief.

"And there," Carrick pointed. "Segat's standards. He's actually here."

Nirek grunted. "His Imperial Highness wishes to see our downfall for himself."

"...out of longbow range," Iresh was saying. "But in our powder weapons' range. They don't know we have them. Pass the word to aim for those massive bombardment weapons. If those things hit the wall it'll be turned to rubble."

Activity around one of Segat's huge bombardment weapons drew their attention. It suddenly rolled back with a jolt and a gout of smoke issued from its length. Seconds later a booming detonation echoed around the pass. The projectile struck the ground short of the wall, opening a crater and throwing sand and rock high into the air.

"They're testing for range," Commander Iresh noted.

The great bombardment weapon fired again. They heard the projectile seconds after it hit the wall, some distance north. The impact smashed into the stone with such force it could be felt for hundreds of feet in either direction. The soldiers were alarmed, some touched by the first hints of panic. Group captains had to work to keep them in order and hold their nerve. It was followed by a series of booms and an array of projectiles screamed towards them. The Commander gave the word and the Amarian powder weapons began firing. Shot after shot rang out from the full length of the wall. Segat's forces reacted with their smaller powder fire, the main bombardment weapons continuing at regular intervals. The Talents on the wall also responded with attempts to deflect or shatter the incoming projectiles as they hammered huge chunks out of the massive defences. Noise, smoke and shouts filled the air. The smaller stone spheres did little more than smash on impact, but the huge iron balls of the bombardment weapons were devastating. The walls became cratered with impacts. Upper sections of the battlements crashed to the ground. Soldiers ran for safety and the Hand trembled.

"That bombardment must be stopped!" Iresh shouted, taking cover with Nirek and the others when another projectile hit close by. "They clearly can't fire them often or they'll overheat, but we can't allow them to continue. The Hand will not survive this onslaught. Chancellor what can your people do?"

Nirek thought, willing himself to stop flinching every time the wall was struck. "Our combin…" he ducked as another hit and then had to raise his voice to be heard. "Our combined groups might be able to shatter the carriages they're on, but I've no doubt their Talents are ready for that. Carrick just how much energy can you channel through that staff of yours?"

"Let's see," he replied struggling to make himself heard over the noise and explosions. "Merren, could you distract and give me a shot?"

"I can!" With that the two began to make their way along the wall to a better vantage point.

As the bombardment continued, Kara came up onto the wall. Keeping herself low she worked her way through soldiers, and dust, and smoke to the Commander and Chancellor Nirek.

"What are you doing up here?' Iresh demanded. "You should be below until we need you!"

"Well, it's difficult to rest through all this noise and I'd say you need me now Commander!" she shouted back.

"You have an idea?" Nirek asked.

"Can small packs of powder be made and can those long chords the Ildrans used be cut to burn for only a short time?"

The Commander was momentarily at a loss until he saw Lors working his way towards them. "Yes!" he called, realising her idea. He turned to one of his aides. "Take these two down below and give them any help they need. Be quick!" he shouted to Kara and Lors and ducked as another impact struck.

"Be careful!" Chancellor Nirek called after them.

Using the protection of the battlements, Carrick had positioned himself with a clear view of one of the bombardment weapons. Focusing his will, he drew on the field heavily. Merren focused her mind and began searching out the Talents guarding the weapon they'd agreed to target.

"Ready?" Carrick shouted over the noise.

"I've got them!"

Merren's subtle search turned into a savage attack on the Talents shielding the huge bombardment weapon. Fighting his urge to stay covered, Carrick stood up amidst the deafening chaos. His raised staff flared. Soldiers nearby took cover and shielded their eyes. He brought his staff around, found his target and released. The beam cut through the smoke, slamming into the huge powder weapon, the effect was instant. The super-heated metal was vulnerable and the huge iron tube ruptured.

"Again?" Carrick tried to make himself heard, ducking bits of masonry as he took cover and began to draw on the field.

"One more!" Merren shouted back. She pulled herself together and peered over the battlements as the hail of iron and stone continued to darken the sky. Finding the next mark, she took cover and focused. Another of the huge weapons fired the impact shook the wall and a section of the battlements collapsed taking soldiers with it. Carrick willed himself to stand. Exposed to the deadly storm he released the gathered potential. Yet again the ragged beam lit up the smoke and blew the carriage and bombardment weapon apart.

Carrick dropped to the floor, resting against his sister as the onslaught continued. The noise was becoming unbearable.

"That was hard going!" he shouted

"What did you say!"

"I said, that-was-hard-going!"

Too exhausted to smile Merren waved a hand vaguely at him. Carrick laid his staff across his legs and looked along the wall. Through the chaos he caught sight of Nirek. The Chancellor was shouting, gesturing towards one of the powder weapons and then at them. Then Carrick saw the soldier sprinting towards them. The man almost fell in his haste to grab hold and drag them clear. The air erupted behind them, throwing masonry in all directions.

The repeated fire from the Amarian powder weapons had taken a toll on the Ildran forces and bought the Hand valuable time. Commander Iresh watched through his navigation lens as Segat's legions were being moved, General Immed was correcting his mistake. The General or Segat himself had underestimated the Amarians, the Commander's delayed use of his powder weapons had cost General Immed hundreds of his men and women. But it appeared the General had refused to move the huge bombardment weapons, although slow to reload and needing time to cool, they were having a devastating impact on the Hand. To move them back would lessen their effectiveness, despite the losses. In the smoke and fumes,

Commander Iresh watched as the Ildrans re-deployed, increased the protection on their main weapons and pressed the assault.

Amarian projectile fire continued its defence of the Hand. Carrick and Merren headed for the most damaged part of the walls in an attempt to take out another of the Ildran bombardment weapons before it destroyed the section completely. Several Talents had joined them to support the effort. Nirek organised other groups of Talents that now worked together to damage or disrupt as much of the Ildran artillery as they could. But it was clear, even suffering their losses, that the Ildran bombardment weapons would breach the wall if they weren't stopped completely.

Kara and Lors had their packs. The newly created powder division had listened to their description and worked with all haste. Now, Kara and Lors made their way up onto the walls. The long climb up the steps couldn't prepare the senses for the barrage of sound, light and smells that hit them as they reached the top.

"How accurate do you think you can be!" Kara tried again over the noise as they ducked their way to the protection of the battlements.

"I have a good idea of where the bombardment weapons are. The smoke doesn't block my abilities!" Lors called back.

"Good! Let's make every one count!"

Despite the chaos the Commander could still tell when Lors and Kara had set to work. He'd bought the Hand time and now Kara and Lors were making good use of it. Large detonations started going off at regular points along the Ildran line. The assault on the walls faltered and the break between each impact grew. Fearing a return of tactics, Chancellor Nirek had his Amarian Talents monitoring for any transport points. The Master Speakers and Chanters had heavily warded the wall against this, but Nirek wasn't going to take any risks now.

The Ildran bombardment stopped abruptly and the Commander gave the order to cease-fire. Trumpets sounded and the activity on his section of the wall was redirected. Even before the reports came in, he feared his powder supplies were running low and it wouldn't be long before they were exhausted. Ringing ears gradually adjusted to the relative quiet, and other sounds became audible, falling rubble, coughs and cries, distant commands being barked, all could now be heard. The air was thick with smoke and the smell of powder, soldiers and Talents held cloths over their faces, trying not to breathe in the heavy fumes. The wind was beginning to take the smoke southerly. The Commander hoped for a wind change, one that would blow the sulphurous clouds directly over the enemy. He looked at the reports in his hand and then down the wall. The Hand endured, but the Talents were exhausted, his people shaken, powder supplies were low and his artillery had taken a pounding. He'd played all of his cards.

The uneasy quiet that followed gave his captains chance to take stock and reorganise. Hasty repairs began, reinforcements were brought in, soldiers and equipment were redeployed and Nirek reorganised his Talents as best as he could to anticipate what might come next. Runners with fresh orders were sent to the other sections of wall and the five forts of the Hand.

Carrick and Merren found their way back to the Commander and Nirek, quickly followed by Kara and an exhausted Lors.

"Well done," Iresh praised. "Now get yourselves down below and rest."

"The air's clearing," Carrick noted.

"Still can't see much," Merren said peering out.

"He probably knows we're low on powder and may alter his attack," Iresh speculated.

"He hasn't used his Summoners yet," Chancellor Nirek reminded. "If he's about to alter his tactics it might be sensible to get ours in place."

***

Varin had watched the girl walk through the doorway and into the chamber beyond. He followed.

He'd expected a vast chamber, a testament to the legacy and art of the Panids but walked into a circular space thirty to forty feet across. The walls were smooth and carved with familiar symbols. His eye was caught as one illuminated for an instant. The weak light tracing the symbol and then moving to the next, one after the other endlessly reinforcing the fields the Panids had created to maintain The Field's Cap. Their voices could still be heard in the faint whispering that touched the edge of hearing. The source of the whispering that had plagued him for so long. In the dim light he watched the girl reach the centre of the room. Movement made him look to the wall near her, he almost expected to see a Panid, as something faint stepped out of the symbols. The mass of characters seemed to exude it. He recognised it as a form field, but how it could move without being fully realised he didn't know. It seemed drawn in the air from faint glowing lines that detailed its arms, legs and a body that supported several heads. All different, all set with multiple eyes that glowed with an intensity greater than the rest of its form.

The Field's Cap stepped fully into the chamber, faint tendrils linking it to the symbols it was a part of. Four heads looked in four separate directions, seeing far beyond the walls of the chamber. The fifth head studied Cali, taking no interest in Varin. It began to circle, examining her and then, seeing she was unharmed, the fifth head turned to Varin.

"Do you know us?" the voice entered his head directly.

"I know now that you are the creation of the Panids who sought to bring order to the Talents of this world. We call you The Field's Cap. Beyond that I have little knowledge or understanding of you."

"Yet we know and understand much of you."

The words chilled him. He didn't like the disadvantage, but Varin could only ask "How?"

"You more than any other pushed against us in your need to access more of the field. The Head That Looks South became aware of you. One who stood out amongst thousands."

Varin suspected this was the last of the Elementals, the greatest and most powerful of the Panids' creations. "I became a threat to you, I fought against the restriction you impose on all Talents."

"At first yes and then, hope. As you sought to develop your skills for your own ends, we saw a way for you to aid us. As your ability grew and your connection to the field deepened, we were able to influence you through that connection."

"I've aided you, how?"

"The chamber fails, the words of the Panids fade and are but a whisper. The purpose of our creation is in danger. Harmony must be maintained, the Talents protected against themselves. We needed you to find us and break the wards and barriers that contained us."

"To find you?"

"We can see the world through the eyes of others only. But no one alive today remembers its location."

"There are still Panids alive. They would know your location. You could have used them," Varin snapped.

"This is not allowed. It is immoral that we deceived some of the Children, unfortunate that we were forced to influence you and regretful that The Purpose had to be brought here in this way. To abuse a Panid so, is unthinkable. That we have done, what had to be done, is regrettable."

Varin understood the original function of The Field's Cap, its role to limit the ability of all Talents and so prevent the chance of another Great War. But now it referred to the girl as The Purpose. His role, he now understood, he had been a puppet, a means to an end, but what about this girl?

"Is the girl as powerful as I?"

"The Purpose will be greater by far."

"How did you bring her here?"

"The wandering and then the renegade Children were persuaded to direct her. Bring her closer."

"Persuaded, you mean used, as I was."

"Only persuaded."

"The girl, why do you call her The Purpose?"

"The chamber fails. The Purpose will not be harmed." The head added as if this was explanation enough.

"You have not answered my question."

If the head could register unease, there was a hint of that in the glow of its linear face. "The chamber fails, it is old and will not be able to support us. We are weakening, that which spoke with strength is no more than a whisper." One of the heads turned to the faint glowing symbols on the chamber walls. "Our influence wanes. Our purpose fails." It took a step towards him and all heads turned to look at the girl. "The Purpose will not be harmed." It said this again as if trying to convince itself.

"How will the girl be used?"

"The Purpose will share with us her powerful connection to the field and we will no longer need the chamber. The room will fail, but we will continue as one with The Purpose and the field. Our purpose is everything."

Varin understood fully and knew the girl could not be allowed to 'share' her ability with The Field's Cap. If it became a part of her and thus the field, it would permanently control and limit the abilities of all Talents. He would be constrained anew, his efforts for nothing. His Order would continue as they were. If this could be stopped, an unlimited field would respond to him in a way no other could hope to match. He could force his Order in a new direction and the continent would be compelled to view them with respect. There was an opportunity. Perhaps his wishes could still be made reality, all was not lost. He focused his will and began to draw on the field. The Field's Cap did not react and so he continued.

"You have done much the Panids would frown upon," he played for time. "By your own admittance, it would appear you have lied to your masters and your own kind."

"Our purpose is everything."

"You manipulated the Children and Talents to your own ends."

"That which we were created for must be continued. The Panids willed it above all."

"I could aide you. The chamber could be repaired."

"You are not a Panid. They were many. You are one."

"Others could be persuaded."

The Field's Cap looked at the girl. "Others would not understand."

"Then you realise using her is wrong."

"Our purpose is everything." Its tone had changed. Its answers were becoming defensive.

Varin could see its understanding was limited and focused on one solution. He too had no choice and made his decision.

"Then you will not allow the girl to leave?" Varin asked.

"No," the answer was abrupt.

Varin reached into his pocket and pulled out a small copper sphere intending to throw it at The Field's Cap and the girl.

"Varin!"

Kellim's voice startled him. The sphere skidded along the floor wide of its mark. Without the augmentation of his will, it exploded with less effect, flinging the girl across the room and into the wall. The Field's Cap rippled in the shock waves and faltered, confused by the new sensation.

"You must not harm," it said in bewilderment, its hand reaching out to The Purpose, unsure of what to do.

"You fool!" Kellim shouted, his staff directing the field to disable Varin. The Amarian's staff erupted with light as he retaliated. Kellim shielded himself. The energy hit the wall instead and rippled across its surface. Lewan ran to Cali but was flung to the floor as Varin and Kellim unleashed the power of the field at each other. The air exploded and crackling energy arched like lightning across the chamber. Dazed, Lewan went to move, pain lanced down his leg and he called out. Powerful tendrils of energy flashed about him. The chamber shook and rubble began to fall from the ceiling, Kellim and Varin's struggle threatened to tear the chamber apart. He could only just make out Cali's body lying awkwardly on the floor. Lewan gritted his teeth and dragged himself along. He had to reach her. The chaos about him increased as the two men tore at each other with light. Searing arcs searched for their target. Lewan rolled for cover. Stone exploded about him. Crawling through the chaos he began to panic, Cali wasn't moving. He struggled on.

The endless cycle of the symbols faltered. The Field's Cap looked about it, feeling the change. The form field struggled to cope with the overwhelming flood of new sensations that assailed it. The world closed in as it staggered to The Purpose. Flares of energy cut through it, jarring its form as it drew closer. Lewan saw this and in desperation half scrambled, half fell across the remaining distance in a desperate attempt to block it. The chamber shuddered as The Field's Cap touched her. Too late, Lewan threw himself at the failing form field.

Kellim shouted in horror. The instant Lewan touched The Field's Cap he was overwhelmed. Everything he was ceased, swept away in an instant along with Cali. Varin saw his chance and struck out at Kellim. The Panid was hurled out of the chamber. Varin turned, wielding the writhing potential and unleashed it at The Field's Cap. Raw energy ripped and tore at the walls, the floor and ceiling. The repetition of the symbols ceased and The Field's Cap destabilised and suddenly imploded. Varin was sucked in. He clutched desperately at the floor, but was dragged along. Clutching and scrabbling, his hand finally found a crack. Slabs from the floor began to lift and bounce past him into the vortex. He clung on, legs flailing as the distortion pulled in everything it could. As it collapsed the pull increased and the gale rose to a howling storm. The implosion became a point of brilliant light and for an instant time froze. The point blinked and light flared outwards. Searing the chamber, it expanded upwards, blowing away rock and soil to find release in the open air, a great boiling wave that swept outwards to re-energise the field.

Chapter 26

Segat slammed his hands down on his campaign desk, scattering papers to the floor. General Immed and his commanders stood stiffly to attention, their expressions impassive; any trace of disapproval would earn them a slow death. They all avoided the gaze of the shrouded figures behind the Emperor. They'd began to move, as if floating, coming to a halt behind Immed and his men. Beads of sweat began to form on the men's brows, each resisting the urge to turn, or move away from the figures.

"Why is it you cannot fulfil the simplest of my wishes!" Segat raged, hands still clenched on the desktop. "Why must I suffer this humiliation at the hands of the Amarians? Do you know that they will be laughing at me as we speak? You fail me time and time again." His voice rose even further. "The sky ship attack, a disaster. The powder weapons, futile. You assured me. You promised me!" He bawled.

"I have turned Ildra into a force to be reckoned with," Segat banged his hands on the table again and stood. Almost jumping out of the chair. "From the quivering quaking joke of the continent to the core of an empire. I have built this. My vision, my foresight, my planning and now you, you want to ruin all I have achieved. I have swept the armies of Koa aside. I have been unstoppable. They are terrified of me. But why, why now is my progress faltering?" he jabbed a finger at them. "Two defeats. Two defeats down to your incompetence!"

General Immed looked ahead, jaw clenched, his face burning. His commanders kept their eyes focused on the floor. Segat glared at Immed until the general looked down. He would have continued his tirade, but words failed him. His anger was about to overwhelm him and he could feel his throat constricting. "Kill them!" he managed.

Gloveless hands appeared from beneath the folds of their shrouds, a touch was all it took, a touch delivered before any of the men could react. A touch that blackened, as a parchment curls when caught by a flame. They were consumed in seconds as they screamed and writhed on the floor.

Segat fell into his chair, clutching at the remaining papers in front of him, screwing them up until he had no more strength in his hands. He threw them aside rising again from his chair. It caught his leg and he kicked at it petulantly, sending it crashing to the side as he stormed over to the tent entrance.

"Get me VaCalt!" he bawled.

The Head of the Ildran Order paused momentarily outside the tent, angered by the summons. She was more than his equal, superior in every way, but His Imperial Highness could end her life on a whim. Setting her face she entered, subservience her watchword.

"Sire, you commanded..." VaCalt froze as the shrouded figures moved away from their work and returned to their place behind Segat.

It took seconds for her to recover and Segat watched this with the satisfaction of a child.

"Sire," she cleared her throat and bowed stiffly. "You commanded my attendance."

"What kept you?" Segat snapped.

"I apologise," VaCalt knew excuses, no matter how valid, would not be accepted and so she offered none. Segat had always been volatile at the best of times, but the stress and pressure of this campaign was pushing him even closer to instability.

He was pacing the tent, a hand tightly gripping the dagger he now carried, the other rubbing agitatedly at his forehead. She looked again at the two figures, silent and ever-present, had they covered their hands? The touch that could kill sheathed in gloves of the finest cloth. The figures were a reminder of the knowledge and power denied her and of her mortality. Several of her key Adepts had recently met their end at the touch of those faceless creations and now Immed was gone. She had waited patiently for the day of his demise, but a demise of her choosing, an end she could watch. Now had not been that time, Segat had killed his most experienced commanders. Fool, the words nearly escaped her lips and she looked at the figures.

"Immed has been unable to fulfil his promises," Segat said, still pacing. "I want the Amarian crown VaCalt. I want to sit on that jewelled throne. I want them to pay for the death of Princess DuLek. Yet the Hand remains and my general has failed me."

"My Summoners are ready, Sire. The Amarians will not be able to counter this next assault. Where General Immed has failed you, I shall bring you triumph. The House of Amar will finally acknowledge their role in the death of Princess DuLek. The Empress will grovel at your feet and the throne will be yours."

Segat stopped pacing and stepped closer to her, his face too close to hers. "This promise, you must deliver, VaCalt." He looked meaningfully over at the figures. The Head of the Ildran Order looked away.

***

"Commander! Movement." The aide moved aside so that Iresh could look through the navigation lens. They'd had two days of nothing. The Ildrans had maintained their position. There had been no further attacks and Commander Iresh and Nirek could only guess why. The Amarians had made repairs and then done the only thing they could, and that was to wait.

"What do you make of it, Chancellor?"

Nirek had angled his own lens round. "The Ildran's Summoners!" Not waiting to be told he signalled the order.

The four remaining Amarian Summoners focused their wills and began realising the form fields they had built and prepared earlier. It was now a race against time to complete them before the Ildrans used up the capacity of the field. Create the Elementals too early and the Adepts would not be able to maintain them, start too late and there would be no energy.

On the Amarian side of the fortress Kara and Merren kicked their mounts into a full gallop. Hoping to find the point where the field strength would be strong enough to support a transport to where Tebeb had set up a small camp with the intention of rediscovering his talent.

Soldiers and Talents watched the pass for signs of the Ildran Summoners' work. As time passed and nothing happened, the watchers began to wonder if it had been a false alarm. That they might have more time to recover. Then, someone called out and eyes found the spot where points of light had begun to appear. Several hundred yards from the wall five forms coalesced in the air, signalling the formation of very large form fields. Vapour and sand were sucked into them providing the materials to create living energy. The Commander gave his orders and the remaining powder was loaded. The trebuchet crews set their huge mechanisms to work filling the air with the sounds of their motion as boulders were flung at the emerging figures in an attempt to disrupt them. With blasts of light, Five Fury formed fully, bigger than any previously realised, but still nothing compared to the original Elementals created by the Panids. The harsh noise of their presence almost drowned out the sound of the trebuchets and powder weapons. Rocks and iron struck the Fury, but were either absorbed, or deflected by the sweeping flares that arced from them.

At almost the same time the Amarian Summoners' creations became solid, a fourth form flickered and dwindled, the field unable to support it. Three Blaze erupted into life. Smaller than the Ildran's Fury their molten bodies burnt and roared, a mass of intense heat. Soldiers up on the walls shielded their faces, even at this distance the heat scorched hair. The Blaze walked forward, their Summoners deep in concentration, directing the movement. Soldiers and Talents alike watched anxiously from the wall as the Elementals strode on.

The Twins and The Hunter appeared on the ground beneath the walls of the Hand, Lors only just accomplishing the transport.

"Will he be able to get back here?" Iresh shouted, now having to raise his voice above the noise of the artillery and the Elementals.

"It's a miracle he got them down there!" Carrick replied.

"Can you help him?"

Carrick moved closer to make himself heard. "There isn't enough free energy to light a candle at the minute. The field is strong here, but these things take immense amounts to sustain them!"

"Look!" Nirek pointed as Lors faded. For seconds he appeared in two places, the desert plain below and on the wall near them. Both images wavered and then Lors was with them. He stumbled forward but held up a hand against any help.

"His form's unstable," Carrick called out, rushing over to block further interference.

The Commander turned back to his view of the pass, raising his voice to speak to an aide close enough to hear him. "Wait for them to engage and then concentrate all artillery on the remaining Fury."

Blaze grappled with Fury, their energy fields clashing and coalescing in violent eruptions that swept the ground. Sand and rock were drawn into them, feeding the raging forms, as they struck and tore at each other.

The three Children broke into a run, The Twins' huge trunk-like legs propelling them with considerable speed. Standing nearly as tall as the Fury, they carried huge, curved swords each the size of a full-grown man and great shields the size of doors. The Hunter ran beside them bellowing a roar of defiance at the single Fury they now closed on. The Hunter leapt onto the Fury's back sinking enormous fangs into its neck. Claws latched deep into the body as the creature attempted to shake her off. The Twins delivered and blocked blows, apparently unharmed by the raging energy about them.

The fifth Fury altered its direction in an attempt to head for them amidst a hail of powder weapons' fire and tumbling blocks that slowed its pace almost to a halt.

Merren and Kara had galloped at full pelt until the ambient field was strong enough. Quickly dismounting Merren took hold of Kara's arm and focusing to locate Tebeb's marker, collapsed the distance and brought them to within feet of his small camp.

"Tebeb!" Kara shouted.

He appeared out of his tent and waved.

Kara and Merren ran over. "Whatever you've managed to do here, we need it now," Merren's voice was urgent.

Tebeb's smile thinned when he saw the look of desperation in both women's eyes.

"I'm ready," he said about to walk away from the camp.

"The field is fully committed," Merren warned.

"I can realise them here. They may hold. If not, I hope you have a plan to free some energy when we get there, or my help will count for nothing."

Merren felt him focus and saw the form fields beginning to realise. In seconds six bright orbs appeared in the air, spheres that shed no heat and cast no shadow. These were the Guardians.

"How do we get them there?" Merren asked as she drew on the field and prepared the transport.

"They can take care of themselves. The strength of the field, as we approach the Hand, will be the problem."

The brutal battle raged on as one by one the powder weapons were forced to stop firing. Tension on the wall increased to unbearable levels. Soldiers watched, frustrated at not being able to join the fight. It was becoming clear that as powerful as the Blaze were, they were no match for the Fury. Now unhindered by powder weapon fire, the fifth Fury resumed its ponderous way towards The Twins and The Hunter. Only the trebuchets were firing, their resources dwindling.

Commander Iresh turned to Chancellor Nirek and Carrick in appeal. "Anything?"

Nirek shook his head.

Lors had recovered and was leaning anxiously against the wall, his eyes fixed on the fight, desperate to help.

There was a commotion on the steps behind them as Merren and Tebeb stepped out onto the walkway.

Carrick hugged his sister, "Where's Kara?"

"She transformed to get us here, the mounts were exhausted and couldn't carry us. It took everything she had to maintain the form. She's unconscious but Natesh is with her." Merren slowly released Carrick; her eyes drawn to the battlements. She looked back at him.

"It's not going well."

Everyone's attention was suddenly diverted as a nightmarish scream issued from the plain. Shouts and curses rang out from the wall, aimed at the Ildran Elementals. The fifth Fury had reached The Twins, catching The Hunter off guard, killing her in a blaze of energy. The Twins were now caught between the two Elementals. The captains fought to restore order as archers fired in a vain attempt to help the Children.

"We need something, anything," Commander Iresh looked at Tebeb.

He shook his head. "The Guardians haven't survived. I'll need you to knock out one of the Fury."

"Wait!" Carrick suddenly exclaimed and dashed for the steps.

Merren watched after him.

"What's he going to do?" Nirek asked.

"I don't know," Merren replied.

Lors was anxiously pacing the wall, stopping intermittently to observe the battle, finding it unbearable. One of the Twins was down, struggling desperately in the lethal grasp of a Fury. The other Twin rained sword blows on the second, trying to keep it back from her brother. There was a long terrible cry when she realised, he was dead. The second Fury turned on the lone Twin and the other began to head for the wall. The few Trebuchets still firing were joined by ballistae fire as it came into range, a futile action against such a creature. Set back from this, the three Blaze struggled on with the rest of the Fury. A backdrop of unimaginable ferocity made real. A sight no eye could have ignored but for the desperate efforts of the remaining Twin. The gaze of every man and woman on the walls of the Hand was fixed on her. Willing her to stand, to regain the advantage, or pull free and escape.

Carrick literally threw himself back up the last steps to the top of the wall and fumbled in his pockets, hurriedly dragging out a pouch.

"Hold out your hands!" he urged his sister. "No cup them."

She did as she was told and Carrick poured four medium-sized spheres into them.

"What the..." Commander Iresh started.

"Help indeed," Merren explained.

"Can you use these?"

Tebeb examined them quickly but then shook his head. "Not enough."

Carrick couldn't hide his disappointment and then a second idea occurred to him. "Lors!"

The Journeyman hurried over.

"You can use two of these to transport me close enough to one of the Fury. I can use the rest; it might be enough to disrupt the field, long enough for Tebeb to get to work!"

Carrick looked over at his sister. He felt her staring at him. "There's no other way!" She went to say something but stopped, her face pale.

There was another scream and a ripple of disbelief and dismay ran along the walls. The remaining Twin was dead and a second Fury now headed for the walls, the first was now only fifty feet from them. The roar and din of its energy fields drowned the noise of the few trebuchets and ballistae not out of projectiles.

Lors took the small spheres from Merren's hands, understanding how they worked as he quickly examined them.

"I will do this. They will only work if they are released in the heart of the Elemental."

"What?" she asked, thinking she'd misheard.

He quickly stepped back and focused, releasing energy from the first of the spheres. He was gone before anyone could react. They rushed to the battlements only to be forced to take cover. The Fury was close, its arcs of energy almost reaching the walls. The air prickled. The noise was terrible. Its approach abruptly halted as several explosions deep inside blasted holes in its body, spewing out substances integral to its existence. It lurched forward, its form field rupturing and eating a huge hole in the wall. Blocks fell into the fissure and a section collapsed in a great rumble of stone, dragging soldiers and mechanisms with it. Men and women ran for cover. Others did what they could to rescue those clinging to the edge of the walkway.

Tebeb took the opportunity. The effort was huge and a Guardian sprang back into existence. He sent it directly at the second Fury. The orb flashed through the air swerving to avoid the Fury's arm and then embedded itself in the Elemental's chest. The effect was instant, the energy arcs folded, collapsing back into the Fury as its form field destabilised. Thrashing at the air it fell forward as the Guardian consumed it. A huge cheer went up, but the wall had been breached and Segat's forces now advanced at speed towards it. The desert was eaten up by a dark tide of soldiers that seemed to pour endlessly from the Ildran lines. Behind them, the siege towers began their slow move forward and two huge sky ships appeared over the horizon.

Commands went up along the line and for the first time, the archers and swordsmen and women readied themselves, each prepared for the chance to avenge their fallen comrades.

Tebeb had to work harder to re-energise the Guardian as in the distance the waves of running legions parted as another Fury erupted into being. He sent the Guardian to the nearest of the three Fury still locked in combat with the Blaze.

"I'm not sure I can do that again," Tebeb apologised.

"What if our Summoners stop and dissipate the Blaze?" Nirek asked insistently.

"The Ildrans are working in groups, they can reform the Elementals quicker than I can create the guardians."

"Can any of our Summoners help you?"

"No, they don't understand the form fields. It would be disastrous. I'll keep trying." Tebeb closed his eyes as the Guardian reached its target. The Fury fell as the orb of light consumed it, releasing the Blaze, which immediately started to walk towards the next Fury.

"That's it," Tebeb said. "I can do no more. It's down to Commander Iresh and his people now."

Nirek patted him heavily on the shoulder. "You've bought us precious time." He then headed over to the Commander who was busy issuing orders. The two men talked hurriedly. When they'd finished Nirek came back.

"We're to get the majority of the Talents off the wall. It won't be safe at all up here soon. I'm staying, but I want all of you to go. Commander Iresh knows we're outnumbered twenty to one."

Carrick looked at his sister and Tebeb. They both nodded. "We're staying. You can order your Talents, but we stay. If there's the vaguest chance we can help, we'll be here to do it."

***

Kellim gradually came to, at first aware only of the pain in his back and head. Instinctively he focused his will to repair the damage. The field rushed to respond, nearly overwhelming him. He lessened his efforts, realising it had been restored and with that, memory returned. Sudden grief hit him, images of Lewan and Cali's deaths bursting into his mind. He sat up, a wail of anguish escaped him and echoed around the chamber as his head sunk into his hands.

Weak flickering lights still managed to illuminate the stairway and the settling dust. Eventually, Kellim stood, his initial grief exhausted. Seeing the entrance into The Field Cap's chamber had collapsed he limped towards the rock fall. The doors Varin had ripped aside lay half-buried. Pressing his hands against the rock fall, he sent his mind deep into the chamber beyond. He searched every air pocket time and time again in vain hope but found nothing. The chamber had collapsed. No one, nothing, had survived.

Numb, he headed for the stairs, his staff swept up from the floor into his waiting hand. He stood looking at it for long moments pulling himself together. Others he cared about would be in danger, now was the time to act. He would grieve later. Kellim went to climb the stone steps leading to the surface and then stopped. He focused and his next step crunched on the ground inside the ruin of the cottage. He knelt beside Aran. The boy was warm and unharmed, but still deep inside himself and unreachable. Kellim touched his cheek gently, thinking of the terrible news the boy would have to be given. He raised him into the air, placing a hand on his chest and stepped. From the edge of the quayside, he looked out across the sea. For a second his concentration lapsed and his grief welled. He called out, bending the field to his will and stepping onto the far shore. With an effort, he took control of himself, checked on Aran and with a ragged breath, stepped forward. The warmer air was a new and sudden sensation.

Eth sensed his arrival and looked up, her stomach tightening with anticipation and then anxiety as she sensed the reason for Kellim's grief, her hand went to her mouth and tears welled in her eyes. She threw the basket aside, scattering feed and brood birds across the yard. Shouting frantically for Etefu, she ran to the distant figure. Kellim gently placed Aran on the ground, warning Eth of the field wave now only minutes behind him. He took a long look at the farm and the peace of its surroundings, then turned and took a step.

The breach in the wall had been barricaded and fortified as much as possible. The trebuchets and ballistae were silent and their crews were being evacuated. The first wave of Ildrans reached the wall, falling on top of each other as the arrow-darkened air killed hundreds. The archers had kept the Ildrans at bay, forcing them to shelter under their shields, but now as the overwhelming numbers mounted, the first banks of soldiers had been forced into the breach. Tar and pitch rained down on others along the wall, but now another two Fury had reached it and were ripping into its stone surface. The Blaze that had held them at bay had broken down and dissipated as the Amarian Summoners became exhausted from the labour of maintaining them. Tebeb had fought to bring more Guardians into play, but the concerted effort of the Ildran Summoners had been quicker and more Fury burst forth. The Hand was about to be breached in multiple places.

Near Merren and Carrick's position, the first breach had been overrun and fighting had broken out on the Amarian side. The wall shook as another section was ripped open and this time a Fury stepped through causing utter devastation beyond. The first of the siege towers were almost at the walls and groups of Amarian swordsmen and women waited to meet the first of the attackers. The Hand would be overrun and Commander Iresh was giving orders for key men and women to leave and divisions to fall back to the waiting sky ships.

Iresh came over. "Chancellor, you have to go. The two Ildran sky ships mean business. If they reach our ships, they'll tear them apart. You're of no use here and Amar will need all the help it can get."

His words were blunt but true and reluctantly Carrick, Merren, Tebeb and eventually Nirek accepted them. The Commander ordered two guards to escort them. They were about to leave when word came that the way was blocked. Merren quietly reached for her brother's hand, understanding what this meant. The fighting pressed closer and the Commander drew his sword, shouting orders for a final defence of their position.

"Stay back here," he said finally. "If there's anything you can do, do it." Then Commander Iresh took his leave of them and joined his people.

The small group of four tried endlessly to draw on the overtaxed field but found it unresponsive. There was nothing they could do. Merren tried one last time as the Commander and his people engaged the first of the Ildrans to reach them. She sent her mind out as far as she was able, hoping to reach the edge of the usable field and then a voice spoke. "Shield yourselves. The Field's Cap has failed. A field wave is heading your way!" She faltered and then recognised the voice as Kellim's. "Shield yourselves," he repeated urgently.

"Close your minds. Field wave. Just do it!" she shouted desperately to the three Talents.

The fighting was close, they had no choice but to withdraw deeply into themselves, shutting their minds to the field as completely as they could. Even then, they could sense its approach, rushing, reviving, flooding the ambient field. Then suddenly their heads were overwhelmed with sensation and the presence of the restored field.

When Merren came to, she could see her brother standing staff in hand. Their section of the wall had been cleared. The Commander and his people were still alive, but the battle still raged below and around them. She realised she was on the floor, that Nirek was unconscious and a medic was tending to Tebeb. She managed to get up and the noise from the fighting flooded back. She was confused and then relieved to see the Fury were gone. Unaware and unprotected the Ildran Order had been decimated and few had survived the field wave as it swept passed. With their Summoners dead, or unconscious the Ildran Elementals had collapsed.

Carrick hurried over. "You okay?" he said, making himself heard above the fighting.

She nodded. "I'm fine."

"Most of the Talents are either dead or comatose. I'm staying," Carrick said. "I want you to get Tebeb, Nirek, Kara and Natesh to safety. The Hand is lost; their forces are overwhelming. Even together there's nothing we can do about it."

His sister wasn't listening. Carrick turned fearing the worst but looked straight at Kellim.

Kellim quickly assessed the situation and stepped away, walking some distance down the wall. He stopped and focused his mind on the breach. The torrent of energy that answered his will almost overwhelmed Carrick and Merren. The walkway beneath their feet began to shake and then suddenly Ildran soldiers were scattered as blocks were reformed and crashed back into place. The tide of Ildrans stopped abruptly and the Amarian soldiers fought those trapped with renewed ferocity.

As the walls were secured, Kellim turned his will against all of the siege towers. He raised his staff, incandescent even in the light of the day. The air around the towers hissed and then burst into flames. On the wall, the fighting began to turn as Amarian soldiers fought the startled Ildrans now stranded there.

There was confusion at the base of the walls as thousands of Ildrans found themselves with nowhere to go. Arrows began to rain on them from the bowmen and women still alive on the walkway. Kellim raised his hands and the greatest of the Panids allowed his will to soar. His grief and anger took form and below him, soldiers fled from multiple points amongst their masses. Pools of sand were revealed as panic spread. Form fields began to coalesce in their midst and Blaze burst into life, Elementals created by a Panid towered above the fleeing Ildran soldiers, now falling over each other in their desperation to escape. The tide that had swept towards the Hand now turned in terror.

Tebeb slowly came to. Struggling to his feet he began to take in his surroundings. He saw Kellim, the figure was unmistakable. Seeing him now as an old man was a shock, even with Kara's warnings. He watched as Kellim collapsed his staff and walked back towards Carrick and Merren. But the brother and sister's smiles soon faltered. Kellim began to speak and Merren clutched her brother's arm, before reaching forward to hold Kellim, sobs racking her shoulders. Carrick turned away covering his eyes with a hand as he struggled to contain his grief. The old man stroked Merren's hair, tears rolling down his cheeks as they comforted each other. Eventually, Carrick turned back and gently pulled Merren to him, hugging her tightly. Looking about, Kellim saw Tebeb. The old man walked over to his long-lost friend. Tebeb's emotions sprang out of nowhere as he drew near.

"I searched," Kellim choked. "I looked for years."

"It doesn't matter," Tebeb responded half laughing, half sobbing as they hugged each other fiercely and renewed the bonds of an age-old friendship.

A painfully short time later, Kellim took leave of his friends. He turned away and stepping forward was at the wreckage of the Ildran sky ships. The last of the soldiers ran past him, weapons falling to the ground in a cacophony of noise as they fled for their lives. The Blaze came to a halt behind him, towering giants of heat. He relaxed his will and they dissipated. The pass was empty, only the great Ildran war machines stood deserted and lifeless. Strewn amongst and beyond them, the dead littered the ground.

"Will they never learn," Kellim muttered, his voice thick with regret as he looked back to the Hand. Pausing to collect his thoughts, he took a slow deep breath and turned to walk through the wreckage. Casting his mind ahead, he found who he was looking for and with a fierce wrench, VaCalt appeared, sprawled on the ground before him.

Pure shock registered on her face as she scrambled to her feet and faced him. She went to focus her will but found she was unable. She straightened, quickly turning her look of shock to scorn.

"At last, the fabled Kellim, greatest of the Panids, the Master of the Field graces the scene. Arriving to save the day. Shouldn't you have done that before your kind devastated Koa a hundred years ago?"

"Your knowledge of the past surprises me, you've learnt nothing from the fools who went before you."

She spat at him. "I have learnt all I need from the past. You were betrayed from within by your own kind. The Ildran Order had no such inner weakness. We would have taken our place as rulers of the talentless half-wits that infest this land. It was the Panids' mistakes that have forced this burden on my Order." She stabbed a finger at him.

"You delude yourself," Kellim responded. "You've been witless pawns, manipulated in a game beyond your own understanding. Blinded by ambition."

If Kellim's words confused her, she hid it. "Release me and I will show you ambition."

"I've no hold on you," Kellim stepped forward spreading his hands.

VaCalt started back, attempting to focus her will. There was nothing, she sensed nothing! "What have you done to me!" she demanded.

Kellim continued to walk forward, "You survived the field wave. Be thankful for that."

VaCalt, despite her bravado, stepped aside still trying to access the field.

"Don't turn your back on me," she snarled and went to strike him only to find herself on the floor again.

Kellim turned slowly and as VaCalt registered the look on his face, a chill ran through her.

"You will live for a long time VaCalt," he spoke with no hint of emotion in his voice. "A life long enough to regret everything you've done and every decision that allowed Segat and his armies to ruin the lives of hundreds of thousands. You will be held to account for the actions of your Order. The trial will be public and a humiliation. I've denied you the source of your ambition, the source of your misguided pride." VaCalt's eyes widened as the impact of Kellim's words took hold. "You will never again access the field. Your skills are no more. Your Talent is gone!" Kellim turned. "I will be back for you VaCalt." He took a step and was gone.

VaCalt sat staring at empty space wholly devastated. The full impact and meaning of Kellim's curse stretched out before her.

When Kellim's foot touched the ground again, he stood blocking Segat and a small group of Ildran soldiers. They were attempting to leave the camp amidst the confusion. Men and women ran, grabbing what they could. All sense of order gone, individuals focused on their own escape and survival. Tents and supplies were being ransacked, fights had broken out and feet trampled those unfortunate enough to fall. Overloaded ships fled to the skies, people falling from their sides, riderless mounts bolted, crushing anyone in their way and the machines of war, once the focus of existence, were abandoned.

Segat's guards automatically placed themselves between him and the stranger who had appeared before them. Swords raised as

Kellim reached into his pocket. He looked at the pin-sized object in his hand and with a thought, his staff resized. He spun it around and leaned on it as the guards shuffled in anticipation.

"Allow your men and women to go Segat," Kellim ordered, making it clear he was not about to move.

"Who are you!" Segat demanded, taking a step back, nervously looking behind. "Who are you to demand anything of me? Do you have any idea who I am old fool!"

"Indeed, I'm quite aware of who you were."

"Were? Were!" Segat spat the word, the manner of its use unnerved him. "Is that a threat? Are you daring to threaten me? The Emperor of Ildra?"

One of the guards took a step forward. Kellim looked at the man and shook his head slowly. "Think my friend, is he truly worth the trouble?"

Segat looked at Kellim and then incredulously at his guard. The man stepped back and lowered his sword. The other guards looked nervously at him and then at each other.

"His reign is over," Kellim informed them. "You wouldn't be breaking any oaths if you were to leave now."

"You're insane. My reign, over? You don't know what you're talking about," Segat ranted. "Kill him, hack his treacherous tongue out!" he pushed at the guard's backs. "Do as I say! Obey me. I am your Emperor!"

Kellim brought his staff to hand. The guards shifted uneasily, altering the grip on their swords, clearly undecided, even as

Segat screamed and yelled at them from behind. The guard who had stepped back turned as Segat kicked out at him.

"You coward!" Segat spat at him. "You miserable creature!"

The guard swung his fist and struck Segat across the face, threw down his sword in disgust and with a glare that said all he needed, walked away. Finally, the other guards sheaved their swords and left. Segat stood, clutching at his jaw, somehow unable to comprehend what was happening.

"As I have said, your reign is over. You will come with me to answer for your crimes before the Empress of Amaria, the Revered Essedra of Amar."

Segat flinched as Kellim said her name. "Never," he shrieked and fumbling for his dagger, pointed it shakily towards Kellim. "Never." He threw the blade badly and began running. It hit the ground wide of its mark.

Segat ran back into the camp, desperately pulling over equipment to block his pursuer's path. He fought through the people he had once commanded, whose lives he had controlled, now just another body in their way. Out of breath and near hysteria he burst into his ransacked tent. Segat scrambled over his upturned desk kicking at one of the prone bodies behind. "Protect me!" he demanded desperately. "Get up. I-I command it!" The body flinched and a withered hand fell from beneath the white covering. The field wave had almost killed it, but its touch still had enough power to eat through his boot finding the flesh beneath. Segat screamed, clutching at his ankle and fell. The very thing created to protect him now brought about his demise.

Kellim entered the tent, his eyes adjusting to the dim light. Segat fell back over the desk. The man writhed in agony, kicking and lashing desperately as his form field was consumed. Kellim rushed forward, focused his will and drew on the field, attempting to halt the process. The concentrated field energy stirred a second figure. Drawn to the source it lurched from behind the desk. Pitching forward, a hand caught hold of Kellim's staff, corroding the metal and compromising the structure. Kellim had no time to react and the ensuing explosion flared like a sun, visible in the bright light of the day for miles.

Chapter 27

Ildra fell into chaos and in the coming months, Hallorn and Amaria routed her armies. Perin and Essedra met at the head of their forces, a symbolic gesture of peace, restoring the freedom of the nations who had fallen to the ambitions of Segat. A new King was installed in Ildra and under the watchful eye of Hallorn, Amaria and Akar Immar of the House Havith began the slow process of earning back the trust of his people and the world beyond. Order gradually returned and the two powers withdrew to rebuild their own countries and the lives of their people.

The field wave had affected every Talent on the continent and many Orders found themselves reduced to a few individuals. The Field's Cap had been destroyed, changing the limits of what was possible, clouding the way ahead with uncertainty. Amar kept its word, promising that a year later Chancellor Nirek would welcome, once again, the Heads and representatives of every surviving Order to Amar. The world had indeed changed.

Carrick and Merren stayed in Amaria to help reinstate the Amar Order, reluctantly saying goodbye to Kara before she headed south with Tebeb on a last search for Mia Svara. Knowing the ultimate outcome of the journey did not dampen her determination to fulfil a personal promise.

With mixed feelings and promises to return, Carrick and Merren left Amar and headed for Hallorn and the state memorial services for Kellim, Durnin and all who had been lost. The grand ceremony contrasted with the simple and intimate one Merren and Carrick attended for Cali and Lewan at his parent's farm. The rush of ripening crops stirred by the summer wind added a sense of peace and tranquillity to a quiet day of shared sorrow and memories, preparing them both for the journey north and a reunion with family.

Eth met them at the edge of her valley. She greeted them with widespread arms and felt the terrible ache in both as they embraced. Holding them for long minutes she comforted with words of reassurance and wisdom. Finally feeling the tension in them begin to ebb, she led them through green woodland along the path that eventually wound its way to her farm. Flocks grazed in meadows beneath a blue sky that brought warmth and its own kind of comfort.

Jai saw them first and came running full pelt down the track. He hugged them and for the first time, they all laughed and joked without feeling guilty for doing so.

Bryn shouted from the roof of Eth's barn, as they got closer, welcoming them with a mixture of relief and joy. Sliding down a rope he hugged Carrick before turning to Merren. They looked at each other smiling before Bryn took her hand and pulled her close. Their embrace was heartfelt and lingering.

There was a clatter from the building at the back of the barn as Aran descended its uneven stairs. Appearing from around the corner he paused, hardly believing that they had finally arrived, before dropping his tools and running into Merren's outstretched arms. They both laughed, tears of happiness and grief mingling in the greeting.

"Family reunions," Eth chuckled, putting a hand around Jai's waist. "What could be better?" He put an arm across her shoulder, squeezing it and the two turned and led the others, talking and laughing to the house.

From across the fields, the summer breeze stirred the trees and, in the skies, above, it filled the wings of birds that soared on the higher currents.

https://panids-of-koa-books.co.uk

Printed in Great Britain
by Amazon

31395210R00315